THE POLITICIAN

Maggie Parker

Love from

Maggie Parke

http://www.facebook.com/maggieparkerauthor

The Politician

Maggie Parker

Paperback Edition First Published in the United Kingdom
in 2017 by aSys Publishing

eBook Edition First Published in the United Kingdom
in 2017 by aSys Publishing

Cover Artwork: Christine Moody

ISBN: 978-1-910757-82-6

aSys Publishing
http://www.asys-publishing.co.uk

In Memory of my mother Margaret (Moffat) Miller who gave me my love of reading.

BY THE SAME AUTHOR

CHAPTER

ONE

"So, the Vessel, you tell me he is ready?"

"He is ready. It has taken a great deal of time, but he is finally ready to do as he is asked."

"You are sure? There can be no mistake!"

"I am sure this will be a great victory for Islamic State and for Allah."

A door opened and a manservant appeared in the doorway; he bowed. "Do you wish to observe the ceremony?"

Nodding wearily, Abdulla followed the man and climbed the stairs to watch the proceedings below. The Vessel was there dressed in a white thobe and ghutra. Abdulla looked down as the women disrobed him and dressed him in western clothes. The smell of freshly laundered linen drifted upwards and Abdulla noted the Vessel smiled as the beautiful Rashida buttoned his shirt.

The Vessel looked into Rashida's eyes; he loved her, he was sure. She was the daughter of the man who had recruited him. The Vessel knew there would be pain ahead for them, but they would be together in Janna.

The Vessel smiled at Rashida. He saw her lips move and although he could not hear her voice, he knew she was praying. He said a silent prayer to himself.

"They say praise be to God, who has truly fulfilled His promise to us and has given us land in heritage. We can dwell in the gardens as

we will. How excellent a reward for those who work to honour the blessed."

Rashida took his face in her hands. Her eyes were wet with tears; when she spoke, however, it was with strength and certainty. "I go now, my love, to face Allah and to stand in the Garden. You will join me soon? I will be there to welcome you. There is no greater sacrifice than to enter the Garden having passed as a hero to your people. To have shown the infidels the mighty sword of Allah is praised from the highest power."

The Vessel stared straight ahead. He knew that what he faced was going to be difficult, but he believed in his soul that right was on his side. He had, as Abdulla had said, been born for this moment in time. His whole being had been created by Allah for what he was about to achieve. He was not afraid to die; it would be a moment of pain for an eternity of sitting at the foot of his God.

Abdulla Al Shaman continued to watch the proceedings, unnoticed, from the balcony above them. He looked at his beautiful daughter one last time. He was truly proud of her and knew that what he missed of her in this life, he would gain in the next. He sighed, gestured to his comrade and moved back into the shadows. Preparation was the job of the women. He silently prayed for their success. Their message would resound across the western world if the Vessel succeeded.

CHAPTER

TWO

Scotland August 2015

"**Has anyone seen Mum Auntie Ciara? She appears to have vanished.**" David Black searched the faces in the large room.

"She'll be on the phone or something David. I saw her slip out the back way about ten minutes ago."

David's older brother Dan returned from the bar with a tray of drinks. He looked sternly at David. "She promised for today she'd devote her time to family." Dan Black sighed; he was used to his mother's political commitments interfering with family life.

"She's a very busy lady and in demand babe," his aunt said, standing up and putting on her shoes. "I'll go get her. I am sure she's only outside the door."

Dan watched his aunt take a drink from her wine glass then looked at his brother. He shook his head, "I know Mum's in demand but she said she would switch the phone off for the wedding. I worry about her, all she does is work."

"This is the reception," David said seriously. "She needs to be available bro. It's part of the deal with her being here so close to an election.

"Hope you are not looking for her for work Davie?"

3

"No, Gerry Baker is here. They used to be friends. Dad asked me to find her."

"Is he sober?"

"Who Gerry?" David grinned.

"No, Kenny, Davie. Don't try to be wide."

"Yes, he's been as good as gold. He wants to arrange a meal with Gerry and his wife but he's not sure about Mum's schedule."

"Ask Samira, she's about somewhere. Will your mum want to have a meal with Gerry though? I seem to remember quite a few political disagreements between them years ago." Ciara Clarke smiled, remembering.

"The real question is … will Mum want to have dinner with Kenny? Not whether or not she'll want to have dinner with Gerry and Betty Baker, Davie!" Dan laughed.

"Dan, she has to keep up the semblance of a relationship with Dad or fucking leave him. As she won't leave him, this is her life. Besides I just want to keep him sober, at least until tomorrow."

Ciara Clark put her hand on her nephew's arm, "David you're not your father's keeper honey."

"I know, but I just don't want him starting his pish today. It's Scott and Bhioctoria's big day and there has been a certain amount of interest from the press because she is Mum's niece. I don't think Mum needs a scene either just now with the election coming up." David shook his head. "Only our Toria could book her wedding for three weeks before a general election and, in all honesty, not realise."

Ciara laughed. "Your mother got all the political leanings in our family I'm afraid. I didn't twig either. They just decided to do it before Scott goes to America. Luckily Phil's business partner is the owner of this hotel but we had to take the date that the hotel offered. He gave them the reception as a gift, so we couldn't exactly say it doesn't suit because the bride's aunt is a cabinet minister. Anyway David, from what I hear, your mother's seat is almost guaranteed. The papers say she'd need to go out with an axe to not be re-elected."

"She won't, but Kenny could if he drinks enough!" Dan laughed, relaxing and taking a drink from his pint glass.

"Will you stop calling him Kenny, Dan, it's not funny," David cried, looking annoyed.

Dan looked at him and shook his head. "Did you have a different childhood from me David? Why would I call him Dad? That implies that he has been a father when you fucking well know that he has always been what he is now, a drunk."

"Well he is a drunk who's not drinking at the moment, so let's just attempt to keep it that way," David retorted, pushing his brother.

Dan Black ran his hand through his red curly hair; his blue eyes twinkled in amusement at his younger brother's anger.

"Boys please, it's your mother's choice to stay with him, but she's always there for you. He's trying to stay off the drink just now, so cut him some slack. It must be really difficult. He is an alcoholic."

"Don't defend him Aunt Ciara. You have no idea either why Mum puts up with his nonsense." Dan shook his head and sighed. "It's caused so many fights between us that I don't even broach the subject with her these days."

"They've been married a long time Dan," Ciara replied, shrugging and rolling her eyes.

Dan shook his head and took another drink, some of the white froth sitting on his upper lip. His brother gestured to him with his finger and he wiped it away before speaking. "Anyway, let's hope we can get through some of the reception before he falls off the wagon. Harry is babysitting him. Sorry Davie, but I'm not spending the whole night trying to keep him on water. Harry can't drink anyway when he's on duty. Ravi was doing it, but he said Dad was starting to get on his tits because he is so god damn boring when he is sober. Ravi's keen to do as much partying as he can before he takes off to do his overseas stuff. Harry doesn't mind anyway bud, gives him something to do."

"Great, Mum's security detail is being used to keep her

5

husband drinking fucking water. Do her popularity no end of good, if that gets out."

Dan smiled and put his arm around his younger brother. "Davie, that job in Mum's press office is really helping you on the road to having an ulcer mate. You're twenty-eight, enjoy life. Get yourself a woman, a good fuck might be what you need right now."

"Oh, piss off Dan. I just need to get the next three weeks over with. You're the one with a political science degree. You should know elections are won and lost in the days leading up to it." He smiled at his brother; the closeness between them meant that any difficulties or differences of opinion were usually overcome quickly.

Dan Black laughed. "Her seat is as safe as houses and you know it. You're just looking for something to worry about now." He grabbed his brother's face and kissed him. "That is why I'm just a humble social worker these days little brother, and I'm also a happy family man. Thank God I followed her into social work and not politics mate. Happy to leave Mum's career to you and your pals in the press office. She's done well though Davie, she managed that without any of our help and with an alky husband. We never really suffered as kids either. As Auntie Ciara says, she was always there for us."

"Daddy, Daddy, Katie's touching the cake again, and she's got chocolate all over her dress."

"Where's Mummy, Sasha?" Dan asked looking around.

"She took Kevin to the toilet. Granddad was supposed to be looking after us."

Dan turned and taking another quick gulp from his glass, he put it down and followed his six-year-old daughter.

Outside, in the hotel grounds, Caoimhe Black looked over the bridge at the white water of the River Doon below her, rushing towards the sea five miles away. She was hoping the water would calm her. Her life, in truth, felt like the water, rushing towards something, not quite sure of when or how she would get there but knowing that there was a higher power calling her towards something scary but exciting.

Caoimhe loved her sister and her only niece, but in all honesty, she felt the last thing she needed just now was a family wedding. She'd hoped Kenny would stay at home, but he'd insisted on accompanying her. She just knew this would be embarrassing both professionally and personally for her; Kenny was unable to resist drinking in social situations. Caoimhe was well aware that using her personal protection staff to keep him sober could be considered an abuse of her power by the opposition party. Harry Stevenson, however, was the soul of discretion and only told Jed Livingstone, head of security, what he really needed to.

Caoimhe knew she was a lucky woman. She'd handpicked all her staff four years ago when she had come to office as Scottish Secretary; she had been rewarded with loyalty and support. She stared down at the swirling white foam of the river and wondered, again, how she had got to this stage in her life with Kenny still in it.

"Hope you're not thinking of jumping Caoimhe? Your country needs you!"

The voice from behind her was as familiar now as it had been many years before. Her immediate thought was panic; she turned around slowly, preparing herself. When she did look at him, she was not sure that she would have recognised him had he not spoken first; it was a voice twenty years had done nothing to change. She focused and realised that the good looking young man she had last seen over twenty years ago, was now a very distinguished looking forty-seven year old. He looked like his father, only more handsome than Hector Carter had been. Caoimhe took in the faded, jagged scar on his forehead, a reminder of the last time she had spoken to Tony Carter.

"Tony! You startled me! You look so much like Hector now. How are you? It's been a long time." Caoimhe glanced down at the swirling white foam again. "There's a lot of water under a lot of bridges too." Although aware that she had waited for this moment for a long time, she felt genuinely shocked to her core at how fast her heart was now beating.

Tony Carter smiled. "I'm good Caoimhe. I just thought I'd come over and speak to you before the reception starts, so there'd be no awkwardness later. I saw you from the window. You look great Caoimhe. You haven't aged a bit."

Caoimhe glared at him, her eyes narrowed, and he knew she was angry. "Why would there be any awkwardness? Perhaps it's because you turned your back on me twenty years ago Tony! Why are you walking up to me now and speaking?" she hissed. "Or have you still not remembered?"

Tony looked her in the eye and hesitated for a few seconds, as though composing himself before he spoke. "Oh, I remembered. If you hadn't run off and abandoned me just when I needed you most, then you might have found that out." He appeared calm, a slight smile playing on his lips.

"I abandoned you?" Caoimhe gasped. "You definitely don't have your memory back properly, pal." Anger flashed in her blue eyes.

"Caoimhe, for years I've wanted to speak to you." Tony looked at her and sighed. "You're incredible. You definitely have a politician's selective memory." He shook his head and stared at her. "I have to be sorry for what I did to you? I never walked away from you Caoimhe! I seem to remember you ran from me."

"You forgot about us Tony."

"I had a fucking head injury and amnesia, Caoimhe. You must have realised, that after all we had meant to each other, I genuinely had problems with my memory." He sighed and looked at her, his eyes silently begging. "Caoimhe, please, let's not fight now. It was a long time ago. I just never got the chance to work it out, and by the time I had sorted my head out you were gone. You went back to Kenny big style, worked things out. I suppose I didn't want to interfere."

She raised an eyebrow. "Or you didn't want to look like a bastard." Caoimhe shook her head slowly. "Oh, you're right, it was a long time ago Tony, too long to hold grudges. You and Phil are still mates I assume?"

"Oh yes, Phil and I are still mates, always will be I suppose. We're still business partners. Don't you speak to your sister?" He looked her in the eye. "You've done well too Caoimhe. I've watched your career with a lot of interest."

She nodded and said nothing.

"I do vote for you. I think you're the best thing that's ever happened to Westminster. I hope someday I'll be voting for you as Prime Minister." He smiled, his eyes meeting hers. Caoimhe suddenly felt panic rise as she realised that twenty years had done little to dampen the feelings she had for him; she knew she had to get away.

When Caoimhe spoke again her voice was calm. "Thank you. I'd better go. If you'll excuse me Tony. It was nice to see you. I just came out for some air, I get so little me time these days." Her insides were flipping over and turning inside out; she knew she had to get away from him. Her experience as a senior politician had taught her how to look calm in a crisis. She smiled, but Tony noted that the smile did not reach her eyes; he also thought she looked tired. "I take a few minutes whenever I can."

As she moved away Tony reached out and gripped her arm. "Caoimhe, I really am sorry about what I did. For what it's worth, for years I've wanted to contact you to tell you that." She looked at his hand on her arm then at him. He glanced at her face then took his hand away.

"Tony don't you dare apologise now after twenty years," she hissed. "It was what it was. It obviously meant more to me than you at the time. You made a choice, that's all there is to it." Her eyes flashed angrily at him as she struggled with the urge to grab him and not let go.

"Caoimhe, you're so beautiful when you're angry."

"Oh, fuck off Tony!" Caoimhe turned and walked away. She was shaking and wanted to cry. All the things she had planned to say had gone from her head. The moment to say them had gone too.

Tony watched her go. He took a long drag of his cigarette, and leaning over the bridge he let out the white smoke. He knew that it was still there, all the feelings, all the longing, flooded back. He sighed, watching the white foaming water rush against the large boulders in the river bed.

Caoimhe walked quickly down off the bridge, stumbling in her high heeled shoes on the cobbled path, her heart still beating wildly at his touch. So many times, over the last twenty years, she had imagined this moment. All the things she would say when he told her he missed her and he was sorry. So many nights lying in bed remembering.

"Is that Tony?" Ciara asked, as her sister walked to towards her. "I haven't got my glasses on and can't see. Toria said I couldn't wear them and I've never managed to get used to contact lenses, so I'm struggling."

Caoimhe immediately switched off her angry thoughts about Tony. "Yes, I haven't seen him for years."

Ciara waved; Tony lifted his hand in response. "You and Tony were really good mates at one time were you not? I always thought that he had a thing for you Caoimhe, he used to ask after you."

"I doubt that. We were good friends while I worked with him, we used to have a laugh. Is he still the happy bachelor?"

"God no, he re-married after Claire died. Took him a while, it was about eight or nine years later I think. He went through a lot of women first though. I suppose it's only natural with what happened. It was such a tragedy." Ciara sighed and looked back at the bridge. "We're still friends with him, although he moved to Glasgow for a while. But the wife, Angelina, well that's the difficulty. She doesn't really socialise with us. Phil and Tony, well, you know they always were thick as thieves. More like brothers than mates. Phil put his own business on hold and took over the running of The Deerhunter for a while after Claire died. Of course, that was when you left town. Tony cut him in on a lot of business deals."

"What's the wife like Ciara? I don't think I knew her."

Ciara made a face, "honestly sis, she's a fucking strange fish. I have no idea what he saw in her. She's a bit posh, private school educated, talks with marbles in her mouth. I think she probably married him for the money. She spends all her time with her horses, looks like one too. They have a little girl, Amy. She's nine, poor looking wee thing. Tony has her with him a lot, and of course he has Anjya. She's twenty now, really beautiful. She was the bridesmaid today. She looks like Claire, you must have noticed, it's kind of weird."

"Ciara, I was so lost in my own thoughts I never actually looked much at the bridesmaids. I was concentrating on Sasha and Katie. They've loved being flower girls." Caoimhe grimaced and touched her sister's arm. "Sorry sis, I was kind of thinking about work and about Daimhim. I really am furious with her this time."

"Well, Anjya took over as chief bridesmaid when Daimhim couldn't make it. When they were young Anjya was with us a lot, and her and Toria are still friends, despite the age difference. Tony sent her to boarding school. We think it was because of Angelina, but Anjya seemed to like it."

"Toria was really disappointed Daimhim didn't make it Caoimhe. Such a shame that she couldn't get over from Japan in time."

"She's gutted Ciara. I spoke to her this morning. She was breaking her heart on the phone, she was so looking forward to being a bridesmaid."

Ciara sighed. "Imagine getting stuck in the middle of an airport when there is a hijack going on. Thank God it wasn't her flight, but it could only happen to Daimhim. Why couldn't she get out though? It wasn't her plane?"

"They have to ground all flights when that's happening." Caoimhe shook her head. "It's the usual with my daughter, she's so bloody headstrong. I told her not to go via Japan, but she was trying to sneak in an extra country to her tally. It backfired on her big style. She's fine. The PM offered to bring her out for me, but it's too near the election to be seen to be giving one passenger preferential treatment because her mother is a politician. So, she's getting to stay at the British consulate, though that's because of the security risk. She starts uni next month as well, so hopefully she will settle down and stop all this roving around the world." Caoimhe smiled. "The hijack situation ended peacefully this morning, thank goodness no one was hurt. Anyway Ciara, let's go and see what Toria and Scott are doing. She's such a beautiful bride and I'm so happy for them."

The two sisters walked back to the hotel arm-in-arm. "I really miss you Caoimhe. I know you have to be in London because you are such a big cheese these days, but you're always too busy for us. Let's make sure we do a holiday next year. We're going to the South of France as usual and you need to join us. It's been three years since you came over, Phil's done loads more work on the house."

"I promise I'll try to come this year, but do not tell Kenny about it. The last thing I need is him spoiling it for me like last time."

Ciara nodded at her sister. "Thanks for your help with Scott's career Caoimhe. I'm sure you being Toria's aunt had something to do with him getting that job."

"Oh, I don't know, I just got him the interview. He did the rest himself Ciara. He really is a nice boy, isn't he? You're not angry at me then, sending your only child to live in America?"

"God no Kee, it's an amazing opportunity for them both. Toria has an interview next week with a New York publishing house so if she has a job too it will all be perfect. I'll get loads of shopping trips to New York and a happy daughter, so it's fantastic."

Caoimhe looked around her at the opulent hotel foyer; it was subtly decorated in cream with silver and black trimmings, it looked sophisticated and expensive. "Ciara, this hotel is beautiful, I'm really impressed. I remember it was quite run down when I was last here."

"Tony owns it now, did he not tell you?"

"No, he never mentioned it. He did say something, come to think of it, about seeing me from the office. I never asked, he probably thought I knew."

"After Hector died, he took over The Deerhunter and built up a business. He worked hard. He started buying places, renovating them and turning them into whatever the area needed. Phil did a lot of the renovation work for him. Tony has quite a few really lovely, classy hotels now across the region."

"I didn't know Hector had died. The last I heard he was getting better!" Caoimhe said sadly.

"No? He got about two years then had a heart attack. They said it was the chemotherapy. It left him with a weakness. Hmm, I thought Phil told you. He must have, he said you couldn't make the funeral. I remember because I thought it was strange given how close you and Hector were. I know it was during that time when we didn't see you! He did tell you, didn't he? I told you about Lorraine?"

"Yes, it's so long ago, I forgot," she lied. "I didn't know Lorraine well, because of the age difference, but I really liked Hector, the silver fox, Ciara," Caoimhe sighed. "Tony looks a lot like him now!" She glanced behind her; Tony remained on the bridge, smoking a cigarette and watching her walk away.

Caoimhe struggled through the meal, the speeches and cutting of the cake, sitting opposite Kenny. She found herself searching the room for Tony Carter; this made her angry. Caoimhe looked at the top table; her niece looked beautiful in her designer gown which Phil, her brother-in-law, had joked in his speech cost the same as a small country. Philip Clark could deny his only child nothing. Toria was, although spoiled, clever and had worked hard at university, gaining a first-class honours degree in English Literature. Caoimhe looked at the bridesmaids in their beautiful aqua-coloured dresses. She knew Anjya, Tony and Claire's daughter, straight away and would have even if Ciara had not told her who she was. The resemblance to her late mother was startling. The meal and the speeches ended, and Caoimhe and Kenny moved to be in different rooms. She found she was in demand; many old friends wanted to speak to her. Later, as the evening guests arrived, she noticed Dan trying to get her attention. She walked over, guessing from his expression what it was.

"Mum, sorry, but Dad's really drunk again," Dan said, a rueful smile on his face. "He's making a fool of himself in the bar. David's really upset."

"Okay I'm coming. Dan, he can't help it."

"Mum, when are you going to fucking realise that whatever you had with him went away with an ocean of vodka years ago?" Caoimhe's eyes filled with tears, and her son touched her arm. "Mum I'm sorry, I don't want to fight about him today."

"I'll go and get him into a car," Caoimhe sighed. "Where was Harry?"

"Mum, don't start blaming Harry for this. You know Dad is really resourceful when he's seeking a drink."

Kenny was staggering about the bar; people were looking and nudging each other. He was trying to persuade one of the young bridesmaids to dance with him and the girl was obviously embarrassed and frightened. Anjya Carter was trying to support the other bridesmaid. Harry was attempting to get Kenny to sit down, but before Caoimhe could reach him, she saw Tony Carter appear beside the group.

"Fuck!" Caoimhe thought, "that's all I need!" Tony had his arm around Kenny's shoulder. As she reached them she heard Tony speak to him.

"Kenny mate, haven't seen you for years! How are you?" All the time he was leading Kenny towards the lift at the side of the bar. "Here's your beautiful wife mate."

Tony smiled at her, his eyes daring her to stop him. Caoimhe had no option but to follow the two men into the lift. She leaned against the mirrored wall, her heart beating furiously in her chest, so loud she was afraid the men would hear it. Tony looked at her over Kenny's shoulder; she could see the mirth in his eyes, but when he spoke his voice showed no sign of anything other than friendship. "Just so happens I've a couple of rooms free mate. Why don't you get your head down and sleep for an hour then you can get up and party with me and Phil?"

The lift shuddered to a halt. Tony put a key in the lift panel and the door opened. "This is my private wing. I stay up here when I'm working. There are a couple of rooms I keep for special guests." He took a key from his pocket. "Let's go Kenny. You'll like this room, great view when you wake up mate, and I don't mean just your wife." He tossed the key at Caoimhe. "312!" he mouthed.

Caoimhe opened the door. "This is nice Kenny look; you could have a nice night here."

Kenny looked at her. "Okay, get them off Caoimhe." He turned to Tony. "It's not even my birthday or Christmas. Although mate, you know how it is at our age? If you get a boner you should use it, cos you never quite know when it's gonna be there." Kenny staggered slightly and leaned in closer to Tony. "If your woman is a government servant too, then her fanny being available and willing is another matter. Never was that good in the sack, but she is fucking frigid these days Tony. Doesn't do it for me now anyway," he hissed into the other man's ear."

Caoimhe blushed. "Okay Kenny, let's get you into bed." She pushed him, with Tony's help, onto the bed, took his shoes off then moved towards the waistband of his trousers. Tony looked her in the eye, raised his hand in a small wave and left the room. Caoimhe undressed her husband, who offered very little resistance. She threw the quilt over his sleeping form, tears blinding her. So many times she'd had to do this, she thought to herself. Opening a door, she found the en-suite and tidied herself up. She stared at her reflection in the mirror. Her red curls had faded little over the years. She lifted her handbag and reapplied her makeup. Sitting down on the toilet Caoimhe sighed and dabbed at her eyes. She wanted to cry; seeing Tony Carter had really shaken her. She waited another five minutes, hoping he'd gone back to the reception. Kenny was already snoring loudly. Gingerly, Caoimhe opened the door and locked it behind her.

"You okay Caoimhe?"

Caoimhe looked up; Tony sat in a large antique chair at the end of the corridor, watching her. Walking towards him she threw a packet of cigarettes and a lighter onto the table. "Best if he doesn't burn the place down tonight. Thank you Tony, but for your quick thinking and intervention, that could have got ugly." Caoimhe felt her eyes fill up; she struggled to speak.

Tony stood up. "Caoimhe, come through here. I'll get you a coffee or something stronger." Caoimhe started to protest but he put his hand on her back and gently pushed her through a doorway. He led her along a corridor and unlocked a door, taking them into a beautifully decorated suite.

Closing the door behind them he looked at her and smiled. "You'd better compose yourself before you go back downstairs."

Caoimhe looked around her. "Nice! What's this, the bridal suite?" She took a tissue from her bag and dabbed at her eyes.

"This is my private apartment. Now can I get you something? Do you still drink vodka?"

Caoimhe nodded. "Thanks. I haven't had a drink yet so it would be good, if you're having one. I can't drink when Kenny is about!" She smiled wryly. "Well I can, but it's a recipe for disaster. I can keep things under control if I stay sober."

Tony looked at her and shook his head. "Why are you still with him Caoimhe? He was a fuckwit twenty years ago, he seems even worse now." He poured vodka from a crystal decanter into two glasses, opened a small fridge and took out a can of diet coke. He handed the glass to her.

"Thanks." She took a large gulp, swallowed and placed the glass on the mantelpiece. She looked around. "It's a lovely room Tony. Is your wife here?"

"No, I only stay here if I'm working. Angelina doesn't much like the hotel business. Actually she doesn't like me very much, she prefers her horses." He grinned and Caoimhe was instantly reminded of how handsome he was. "I like that she prefers her horses. Oops I did it again Caoimhe, got involved with someone I shouldn't have. Story of my life it would seem. I never learn." Caoimhe looked at Tony, he moved towards her. "Caoimhe, I've thought about you at least once a day for the last twenty years." She took a step backward as he moved in and kissed her lips. Caoimhe gasped as she realised her back was against a wall.

"Tony no! Don't you dare do this to me now." She put her hands on his chest pushing him away. Tony responded by stretching his arms on either side of her, his palms flat on the wall, gating Caoimhe in. She looked into his brown eyes, twenty years disappeared instantly. He smiled, showing his perfect teeth, and her heart flipped. When he'd kissed her, she'd felt the softness of his lips; she used to joke about him having lips like a girl. "Please let me go, don't do this to me. I can't cope with seeing you again and Kenny's shit tonight."

"Caoimhe, just go with the flow. I'm not stopping you leaving. You know you don't want to go. You could only be this angry with me for being a prick if you still cared." He put one hand on the back of her neck and caressed it. "I'm going crazy here. I've wanted to touch you since I spoke to you on the bridge earlier. Unlike your alky husband I've had a boner since I clapped eyes on you this afternoon. I still can't even begin to contemplate what the fuck you and Kenny are all about, but I don't care right now. All I want to do is this!" He moved in and looking into her eyes he pressed his lips against hers. Tony felt her relax slightly and she responded by moving her own hand to his shoulder. He knew in that instant that he had her. They began to kiss, softly at first and then with mounting excitement, both remembering the passion they had once shared. He pushed her against the wall, pulling off her silk jacket as she removed his shirt. He fumbled with the zip of her skirt then pulled at it; it fell to the ground. He quickly freed her from her knickers. Still with his lips on hers, he loosened his trousers and stepped out of them and his boxer shorts. They kissed passionately, moving apart slightly as he pulled her top over her head. Unhooking her bra, in one swift movement he lifted her up and pushed her back against the wall.

Her mind was screaming out, 'stop this right now! Don't let it go any further!' But she wanted him and couldn't believe what she was doing. She felt out of control and weak but knew she wanted him to touch her, wanted to see if it was still there. For two decades thoughts of this man had controlled her sex life. Caoimhe gasped as he slid inside her, holding her up and using the wall to steady them, one hand under her bottom, the other on the back of her head as he moved against her.

Looking into her eyes, he pulled her face towards him and their lips met again. Caoimhe wrapped her legs around his hips, her hands holding his face to hers. Their kissing became more intense as his tongue brushed against the inside of her mouth then he moved to kiss her throat; she could feel his breath on her, his voice whispering in her ear.

"Caoimhe! Oh dear God, Caoimhe!" he cried out, "It's still there. You and me, it's still there! Fuck sake, you need to let go. I can't hold back much longer, I'm going to fucking explode," Tony gasped.

Caoimhe cried out, her body tensing, as her increasingly intense orgasm overtook every other thought in her head; all that mattered was the release she knew was coming. She couldn't breathe, her body shook and her groin appeared to have a mind of its own, as wave after wave of pleasure surged through her body. When the crest of the wave came, she cried out his name and clung to him. He shuddered and groaned as he too reached the height of passion, his hands gripping her bottom, holding her tightly to him. His legs shook and he wobbled as the intensity of his own orgasm took him back twenty-odd years.

"Fucking hell, it is all still there!" he cried out, still holding her up and against him, kissing her face. He withdrew, shivering. Slowly, he moved on shaking legs, carrying her in his arms as he staggered out of the room and towards the bedroom where together they fell onto the red and gold covered bed.

"Fuck Caoimhe, it's still there darling, still as good. It's still you babe."

Caoimhe put her hands over her face. "What the hell have we just done?" She gasped and tried to breathe but only tears came. She sobbed as she realised what had happened. He gently took her hands away; he kissed her face, tasting the saltiness of her tears.

"I've just taken you to an orgasm, probably for the first time in years, Caoimhe. No one has ever made me feel the way you did babe, not anyone. Look at you, you're still quivering. It was every bit as good as I remembered it being."

"But you still fucking abandoned me," she cried, her eyes filling with tears.

"Caoimhe, it was twenty years ago! I was out of my mind ... literally. I had a serious head injury. I was a fool. I woke up to be told Claire had died and I had a baby daughter who I couldn't even remember being conceived. If I could go back and change what I did, I would."

"But you can't Tony, you can never go back."

"You're the one who left town. I was still here, still in love with you. Let's just start again. You're beautiful Caoimhe. You have hardly aged in twenty years, your body is the same. All my memories are still the same." His lips nuzzled her neck. "I was fucking terrified it wouldn't be as good you know? Like when you have a memory of a food, fine wine or something and you taste it again and the memory is better? You are actually exactly as I remembered, and I was twenty-seven the last time I did that with you."

He kissed her gently and put his hand into her hair, smoothing it back from her face. "Sometimes I thought that I was romanticising how it was with you, but it's real. I used to try to tell myself I had a distorted view of it all, how fucking good we were together. Believe me, I have spent the last twenty years trying to recreate that with every woman I've slept with and there have been a lot. No one ever made me feel the way you did, the way that just was. It's exactly as I remembered, better maybe." He was breathless, his voice husky with emotion as he spoke.

"Well I'm not the same Tony," she gasped. "I'm forty-five, a cabinet minister. I have a reputation to uphold. I've worked fucking hard to be where I am, I can't do stuff like this."

"Well you just did, Mrs Scottish Secretary, you just fucked someone standing up in a hotel room. It was like electricity surging through your body Caoimhe, just like it always was. I've had an orgasm that felt as though it was being drawn from my big toe. If you were with me Caoimhe, and if drink interfered with making love to you, I'd be teetotal. I've been chasing this feeling for twenty years, and I'm willing to put money on you having been looking for it too." He held her down gently as he spoke, she could feel his breath hot against her ear. Her groin was still tingling. She couldn't begin to comprehend what she had just done, the can of worms she was opening. She also couldn't remember the last time she had felt this satisfied sexually. Well she could, but she didn't want to, it was over twenty years ago, with this man.

As though reading her thoughts, he asked, his voice husky with emotion, "when did you last make love Caoimhe?"

"That's none of your business, Tony."

He rolled over and straddled her, holding her down. "Well if you have done it recently, it wasn't with Kenny was it?"

"Kenny is just drunk tonight. He's my husband."

"I know he's an alcoholic Caoimhe, Ciara told me. No one understands why you're with him. I know it's not sex Caoimhe, so what is it? I never got why you went back, why you stayed with him. He's making the newspapers now with his behaviour. That can't be good for your career? Tell me, does he still hit you too?"

Caoimhe pushed him away; she sat up and glared at him. "Tony don't fucking start, you know what it was. I vowed for better or worse. Do I need to spell it out?"

"You were sixteen years old when you did that. You were a fucking child. They forced you to marry him! You ignored your vows twenty years ago Caoimhe, you were about to leave him to be with me."

"Oh yes, and look what happened. You have no fucking idea

what I went through. I just can't do this Tony, you must understand, this is madness. It was twenty years ago, we shouldn't have been doing it then, and we certainly shouldn't be doing it now." Pushing him away and rolling over, she stood up and walked towards the door. "This was a mistake, a great big stupid mistake." To her horror tears began to run down her face again. Tony grabbed her arm and pulled her back towards him, letting her sob on his shoulder.

When she managed to get her emotions under control, he looked at her. "No, it wasn't a mistake Caoimhe. You needed that, every bit as much as I did. My life isn't much better than yours is babe. I have never had anyone who made me feel like you do. You ruined me for other women. God knows I've tried to get over you. I haven't felt like that for twenty years either."

"Stop this nonsense right now." Caoimhe cried, pulling away from him. "This is so not going to happen again. If it's anything, it's a one-night stand and yes it was very pleasant, but it was what it was."

"Pleasant! Fuck off Caoimhe, it was fucking amazing and don't you dare try to say otherwise. There can't be many folks our age who have that kind of electricity between them." He pulled her back onto the bed. "Caoimhe let me help you? Please let me back into your life?"

"No! Tony, no, I can't. It took me years to get over what happened because of what we did. I'm not able to go through it again. I can't even start to tell you what your rejection did to me, what I went through. Look at me, it's been twenty years and it's still fucking killing me. I'm not being a drama queen either. I can't even start to tell you what happened after you turned your back on me. The guilt I felt, everyone saying how tragic it all was and I had to sit there listening, knowing that you and I had been carrying on behind Claire's back for over a year before she died. She looked at him, tears falling freely, "you weren't there to support me. I know you couldn't help being in a coma, but I risked everything for you, my marriage, my kids and my fucking reputation."

"Caoimhe I didn't mean to do it. I didn't know what was going on. I had a fractured skull, I was in a coma for months. My memory was affected. I didn't mean it. By the time I got it all back, you had gone. I loved you. I would have done anything to keep you. You just wouldn't leave Kenny, then when I saw you that day in the hospital pregnant as well! I should have realised then I was too angry to just have been friends with you. Tony shook his head and looked at her, his eyes filling up with tears. "Then later when I did remember, I was so fucking angry. I was in a fucking coma and you were getting pregnant." He looked her in the eye then sighed. "Given time I would have accepted that too, but then you just up and left. Next thing I hear you are playing happy families up north with Kenny."

"Tony I had to go away. I couldn't live with it. What you and I had done, how could we have been happy? Everyone was saying how tragic it all was but I knew that you and I had been doing what we did. I loved you, I went through hell. I had to get away." Caoimhe shook her head; her red curls fell over her face. "You also knew I was still sleeping with Kenny, I never lied to you about that, you knew why. There was no comparison to what I felt for you. We had made all those decisions, then the accident happened. I had to make the best of what I had. I had three children to think about." She looked at him sadly, "even when you did remember, you never came and looked for me. You didn't want me! You walk up to me now and do this? Yet you let me go twenty years ago, and I've never seen you since. If you voted for me, then you must live in my constituency. You never contacted me once in the last ten years since I've been back here."

"I didn't think you would want to see me Caoimhe."

"I didn't Tony, and I don't need this complication now."

"Is that what I am Caoimhe?" he snapped. She knew his temper was rising; twenty years ago he would not have started the argument. "A fucking complication?"

"What do you want to be Tony?"

"I want to be Kenny without the fucked liver Caoimhe, doing what we have just done."

"Oh, piss off and just leave it," she said, looking away.

He grabbed her chin and looked straight into her eyes. "Say you didn't enjoy what we just did. Say it Caoimhe, and I will never bother you again. Say it and fucking mean it."

Pushing him away, she stood up and began to dress. "You know I enjoyed it, but it was an act Tony. You always were a good lover! You knew what buttons to push twenty years ago, and you must have had more experience now."

"Well then, have an affair with me then, I really don't give a fuck now. I've no pride left where you are concerned Caoimhe, as long as I can see you. We managed it before. You know I'll be discreet, but I'll be there for you. Kenny is just a waste of skin. There is no way he does for you what I do, he didn't twenty years ago when he wasn't as much of a drunk, so I doubt that he is doing it now. Does he still hit you?"

Caoimhe turned and stared at him. "Kenny was there for me when you fucking forgot us Tony. He picked up the pieces for me and looked after me. You have just no idea the mess I was in. We might as well have stuck a knife in Claire, because I'm sure that what we did killed her. Kenny helped me to get over it."

"He knew about us?" Tony asked.

"He knows there was someone. He doesn't know it was you, no one else knows. I've never even told Ciara about us."

"Phil and Samira knew," Tony said, looking at her.

"I know, but we don't discuss it. Phil has never told Ciara either! He's closed it off in his mind Tony. He didn't even tell me Hector had died. You're mates, you must know that he blamed me for it all, and that's how everyone would have seen it if we had been together. The scarlet woman, leading the man astray. I couldn't admit to anyone what we'd done."

"What about Samira?"

"She covered for me with Kenny all those years ago. You know she helped us, kept us secret, well she was also there for me after it ended."

"Interesting Mrs Scottish Secretary, you didn't tell your sister, but you told your personal secretary?"

She wasn't my personal secretary then, she was just my friend. Anyway it was years ago. You caught me at a weak moment there." She looked at him; he could see the sadness and regret on her face. "Tony, I can't do this, we can't do this. You have a wife." She sighed and looked him in the eye. "I can't go through it all again. It nearly destroyed me when you rejected me. I just can't do that to Kenny either. He took me back knowing I'd been unfaithful."

"Would he even notice Caoimhe? The only thing Kenny loves, by the look of him, is Smirnoff."

Caoimhe walked through to the lounge and picked up her clothes and bag, walking in to the bathroom. She tidied herself up and dressed, re-doing her hair into the tousled bun that it had been in. She returned to the bedroom he was sitting on the edge of the bed wearing his trousers, putting on his socks. She took a deep breath as she observed how fit he was. He stood up and followed her back through to the lounge.

"Caoimhe can I see you again?"

"Please Tony don't ask." She lifted her glass, gulped down a mouthful and looked into the dark liquid. "I told you, I just can't go through it all again Tony, it almost destroyed me." She took another drink, draining the glass.

"Caoimhe just meet me for dinner, somewhere private where we can have time to talk. I'll even come down to London and meet you there if you want. Let me explain what happened, then if you still want to walk away I'll never contact you again."

"You promise?"

He nodded. "I haven't come near you in twenty years have I?" He looked at her sadly. "When there was never a day I didn't think about you." He lit a cigarette and blew out a stream of white smoke. "I get a fucking charge every time I see you in the papers or worse, on the TV because I hear you speak. I've wanted you so many times Caoimhe, I have fucked women and shut my eyes pretending it's you." He shook his head sadly and his eyes filled up, "but I always know it's not!" He took a long slow draw from his cigarette and looked her in the eye. "I fucking need closure on this too you know. I realise what I did all those years ago, but I was angry at you for years. Please just meet me and talk, hear my side of it all. Like I said, if you can walk away afterwards, I promise I'll never come near you again."

"Okay, but it needs to be after the election. I might need my old job back."

"I doubt that Caoimhe."

She smiled for the first time and her eyes sparkled the way he remembered. "Who knows with these things, I'm a public servant at the mercy of the voters." She sat down on the couch beside him and took his cigarette from him. "I haven't smoked for fifteen years either. You make me indulge in bad stuff Tony."

Tony looked at her, his heart now slowing down. He realised nothing had changed, he felt comfortable in her presence. "What is it like with Kenny? It must be tough?"

Caoimhe nodded, blowing out a long stream of white smoke. "It's hard living with someone who's an addict," she smiled and shook her head. "So, I don't most of the time. He lives up here, I live in London. If I'm in Scotland I normally stay in Edinburgh, as Scottish Secretary I have a residence there."

"When did you last have sex with him?"

"Tony not that, please?"

"When Caoimhe? You owe me that at least. Tell me it was worth it? I lost you to him."

"The last time I had sex with Tony was fifteen years ago. I gave up smoking the same week actually." She shrugged and took his cigarette back from him. "When did you last have sex with your wife?"

"About seven years ago, we've been married for nine. Before we got married we were like rabbits, then she got pregnant and stopped doing it. After Amy, our daughter, was born she didn't want to. I stopped forcing the issue." Tony looked at Caoimhe, a sad look on his face. "I knew I was never going to love her when

I married her, she wasn't you. But as you know, I do that, let the one I love get away and marry the ones I don't."

He put on his shirt; Caoimhe could still see the slightly rippled torso through it. She realised she wanted to sleep with him and knew she had to leave before she threw caution to the wind and did it. Instead she heard herself say. "Is it okay if he stays here tonight?"

"Of course. He'll sleep till morning anyway won't he?"

Caoimhe nodded. "I'll leave Harry, my bodyguard, here. He can sleep in the chair in the hall. Thank you Tony. Can you give the bill to Harry?"

"There'll be no bill Caoimhe, he's my guest."

"Please give Harry a bill Tony. The press has a way of getting to know about things, they snoop. Your staff will know."

"This is my private apartment, the room he's in is a guest room. Caoimhe it's no one's business. If anyone asks we're old friends me and Kenny." Tony stood up and walked towards her. "Caoimhe, please stay. I have to know sweetheart, I need to know if it's like it was."

She shook her head wearily. "Tony, you have just taken me against a wall. The earth moved, feels like the old days to me."

He reached over and pulled her towards him and taking her face in his hands he kissed her. "So, it was every bit as good as it used to be for you too?"

She looked sadly at him and nodded. "Tony, it's all too fucking late now."

"Caoimhe, come back and spend the night with me. Let me just waken up beside you one more time. That was just a desperate fuck, I want to make love all night the way we used to." He looked into her blue eyes and smiled wistfully, remembering. "Even at my age, I reckon with you I could do it."

"Tempting as that is, no Tony, I just can't. My fucking head is spinning. I can't believe what we just did. I don't want to Tony. I lost my head with you all those years ago, I knew it was wrong, you knew it was wrong and I suspect that Claire died because of us."

Tony's eyes clouded over and he stubbed out his cigarette. "I need time with you. I need to tell you all of what happened that night Caoimhe. This is not the time or the place. I fucking carry that guilt every day of my life, but it wasn't as simple as us causing it. Please Caoimhe, before we start dragging up the past, stay with me? Let me love you? Go away from me with the thought of how it can be between us. Let us have one night without sadness and fucking regret."

She looked at him sadly, "I don't think I can do that, I can't open that wound. I think if I do I won't be able to walk away. it didn't work for us twenty years ago." She shook her head sadly. "Why would we think it could work for us now? Tony there is so much water under so many bridges, so many complications, we were young, reckless and stupid, we made a mistake. I'm too fucking scared to do it now. I just can't let myself go through all that again. I'll meet you after the election is over, and I don't have that on my mind too, but I just don't think I can let myself feel like that again. I'm not the same person Tony, probably neither are you." She smiled and touched his face, "I'm a ball-breaker and a nightmare these days."

Tony shook his head and smiled, his face sad. She knew he was close to tears too. "Caoimhe, you were a fucking nightmare twenty years ago!" he sighed.

"Oh, I am much worse now Tony, believe me. I can make grown men cry! Now, how do I get out of here?"

After she left him to go downstairs to speak to Harry and Samira, Tony poured a good measure of malt whisky into a glass. He tipped his still full glass of vodka down the sink in the small kitchen. Truth was, he hadn't drunk vodka for years. In the days after he remembered his relationship with Caoimhe, he'd consumed so much vodka that, even now, he almost vomited at the smell of it. Tony sat down by the window and looked outside; it was raining, the water ran down the windows silently and he could hear the drains gurgling. Below his room the river rushed and splashed against the rocks; the noise, normally so calming, suddenly assaulted his ears. He stared into the glass. He could still feel her presence, her perfume lingered in the room and he could taste her on his lips. He took a drink from the glass and rested his head wearily on the back of the chair. His head was full of questions, the dichotomy that had been with him for twenty years resurfaced. "Why the fuck did I not go after her all those years ago?" he said out loud. "Why did I let her go? Why did I not fight harder?" The years slipped away as he remembered how it had been.

CHAPTER
THREE

March 1994

"Tony, where are you? Can you change a barrel for me please? The Scott's lager is finished and it's on special. Can you do it now?"

Tony looked up from the accounts books on the storeroom table, a half empty bottle of vodka and a two litre bottle of cola in front of him, along with piles of paperwork.

"Sure Caoimhe, if you come down and hold the pipe for me."

Caoimhe walked towards him; he took in her slim figure in the tight black jersey skirt and purple work shirt. Her breasts were high and firm, he noted the slight hint of a safety pin between the buttons of her shirt stopping it from gaping. He liked that he could see her nipples through the shirt. Tony looked her up and down and poked his tongue out. She shook her head and turned away from him.

"Come on Tony just go do it, I've been slaughtered out there while you sit here doing fucking sums! If you would do the accounts when you should, you wouldn't have to work for days and days sorting them."

He watched her go, her long slim legs encased in black opaque tights. He smiled at the white trainers on her feet. Caoimhe was tall; she wouldn't tell him her height. Tony reckoned about five nine, he was six foot two and when she wore heels she was as tall as he was. Her wild red hair was slightly constrained in a purple satin band high on her head and wispy curls spilled out over her face. Her pale skin and bright blue eyes alluded to her Irish descent. Tony fantasised about her; he just knew that she would be amazing in bed. He often wondered what it was like between her and her husband. He wanted her, he had wanted her for years, but flirting was as far as it went with Caoimhe. Tony stood up, walked towards her and nipped her bottom as he passed her.

"Fuck you are such a tease Caoimhe. Let me fuck you," he whispered, "you won't regret it."

"Tony, stop it, that's not funny. What will the customers think?"

"It's only old Sid at the bar, he can't hear us. Everyone else is too far away, the music's too loud."

Tony smiled; he followed her into the corridor. "Come on Caoimhe?"

"No! Tony, what you are suggesting is wrong."

"No, it's not. I'm still a free agent."

"No, you're engaged. I'm a married woman."

He pinned her against the wall. "When are you going to give in, let me make love to you?"

"Never!" she said, laughing and pushing him away.

"Why? You know you want to."

"Tony Carter, you know why not. I have a husband, you and Claire are engaged. She's my friend, I can't do that to her." She grinned and her eyes sparkled. "Besides you wouldn't be able to handle me, and with the amount you drink you probably wouldn't manage it anyway!"

"Why did I not meet you first Caoimhe?"

"Just lucky I guess," Caoimhe laughed, walking away.

Tony grabbed her arm gently and she looked back at him. "You need to get away from Kenny, Caoimhe." He said his face turning serious. "You know you do."

"No I don't!"

"What about the kids?"

"He's their father."

"Caoimhe please, I'm not joking, you know you have to. One of these days he's going to really hurt you. Darling, all joking aside, let me help you get away."

"He's not a bad guy Tony, he just gets frustrated."

"Caoimhe I've seen the bruises on you, he's a fucking wife beater. You're too good for him. It can't be good for your boys to witness that sort of shit. Leave him, come run away with me."

"What? You, me and Claire? Tony this is so not going to happen. Now go change the barrel, give me peace."

Tony laughed, as he went off in the direction of the cellar shaking his head.

Later as they cleared up the empty bar, he poured her a drink; the bottle of vodka was almost empty. "Please Caoimhe, just sit with me? I've fancied you since you were at school, but you were always with Kenny. He's a prick Caoimhe. He isn't even faithful to you."

"I know."

"So why do you stay with him?"

"He's my husband."

"Caoimhe you're twenty-four and you could have any guy you want. You're sexy, beautiful and you're clever. What is it you're doing at college?"

"University, I'm studying social work, a year and a half and I'll have my degree. Then I'll think about going. I need the security of a good job."

"Caoimhe, you could have it all with me. I've good prospects. I've just bought another pub. I'm going to be a tycoon someday."

"So, you reckon you are a better prospect than Kenny? You're engaged to my friend and she trusts you."

"I don't love Claire."

"So you keep saying. Why are you marrying her?"

"I'm not marrying her. I'm going to end it."

31

"Shouldn't you tell Claire that then? You've been saying that for years now Tony. You're really not being fair to her either."

"I will, Caoimhe. It's so hard, I don't want to hurt her, but I really don't love her." He looked into Caoimhe's eyes and breathed deeply. "You're beautiful Caoimhe."

"No, I'm not, I'm ordinary and I suppose passable. Claire's beautiful, and she's the kind of wife someone like you needs. She wants to be a wife and mother Tony. It's all she has ever wanted. Me, I want too many other things to be a good wife, I'm restless and ambitious.

"What did you always want Caoimhe?"

"Not to get pregnant at fifteen anyway."

"Why didn't you have an abortion?"

"I don't believe in them."

"Why did you have another one a year later then, surely that wasn't an accident?"

"I don't know, company for Dan? I didn't want him to be an only child." Caoimhe looked thoughtful, "I also thought that if I'm going to have children, I might as well do it and then get on with my life." She sat back and lifted her cigarettes from the table.

"They're bad for you," he said, taking one from her.

She shook her head and smiled. "So is sex with your boss."

"I'm not your boss, my dad is. And you'd better not be shagging him when you won't let me!"

"Of course, I'm not. Your dad is a very good looking man though, if I was looking for a silver fox it would be him. I'm not even shagging Kenny these days actually. I still don't want any. I've too many other things in my life to think about sex."

"Do you fancy me Caoimhe?"

"No."

"You're telling lies Caoimhe, I think you do. I think you feel the chemistry too. This is not just about me being horny, it's more than that Caoimhe, I'm sure of it. Three weeks ago, I almost had you. You nearly gave in when you got pissed after Johnny Weir's wedding."

She laughed. "I was pissed! So were you. You probably wouldn't have been able to get it up anyway, we drunk a bottle of vodka, then started on the shots. I couldn't lift my head on the Sunday. Maybe I should have just let you have it, then you would stop all this nonsense. You would've been disappointed though, I'm really not that good in bed."

She smiled at him and he took a sharp intake of breath as he registered the sparkle in her blue eyes. "Tony, there's no chemistry, it's all in your fucking head. There's no connection other than an employee, employer relationship and there's no fucking chance I'm going to let you shag me. So, please, stop this nonsense!"

He came around the table towards her; she stood up and moved away, lifting her bag. "You're becoming a sex pest Tony. I mean it, every time you drink now you start this nonsense about chemistry. Just stop it please? We used to have a laugh working together before Hector got ill and you got this notion into your head. I'm going home to my husband and children, to my bed. I have uni tomorrow. I'll see you on Friday. Do you need me to open for you?"

"Only if it's your legs darling!"

"You're disgusting. I bet you're trying it on with all the barmaids."

"No just you, I don't fancy anyone else. Meet me for lunch tomorrow?"

"No, I'm at university."

"Bunk off and meet me?"

"No Tony, please stop this nonsense, I'm not going to give in. I'm married, you're engaged, so just give it a rest. We were drunk Tony, end of." She looked at him and grinned. "You would shit yourself if I said yes anyway. Now, either give me a lift home or call me a taxi!"

"All the customers fancy you. It's your tits and those legs. Can't decide if I am a leg or breast man when I look at your body babe."

She slapped him on the back of his head. "Fuck off Tony. One of these days I'm going to take you up on those offers." Her blue eyes sparkled again as she laughed at him.

"I can wait Caoimhe. I will have you one day." He lifted the phone. "I can't drive you home. I've had too much to drink!"

"You don't say!"

The Deerhunter public bar was becoming busy. It was Friday night and Tony had been surprised when Caoimhe, who normally was reliable, did not turn up to open. "Where the fuck is your sister Ciara?" Tony called across the bar.

"Don't know. She dropped the boys with Mum earlier, her and Dad are taking the caravan to Loch Doon this weekend. Caoimhe said she was opening here."

"She never turned up. Hope she's okay."

"Have you tried calling the house Tony?"

"No answer."

"Oh well, she'll turn up I expect."

"It's not like her Ciara, especially not on a Friday night when there's live music."

"No, it isn't. Phil, how much have you had to drink?"

Ciara's husband looked up from his newspaper spread out on the bar. "Too much to go looking for your sister, it'll be her and Kenny fighting again likely. She needs to get away from that fucking moron Ciara." Phil folded the newspaper and leaning over he put it back on the paper rack. "Fuck sake, she's the feistiest female I know, yet she puts up with Kenny Black. He's just a bastard."

"But he's her bastard Phil," Tony sighed.

"Tony, I'm really worried!" Ciara whispered. "Mum said she had a mark on her face when she dropped the kids off. I think he's hit her again. He's fine until he drinks then he goes for her. Most of the time it's just verbal, she can give as good as she gets. It's that red hair of hers, she has the temper to match. Caoimhe has to have the last word."

Tony looked at Phil who shrugged and put his arm around his wife.

Ciara looked directly at Tony. "She does hit him back and our Caoimhe can pack a punch. I was on the receiving end of it many times. She won't fight in front of the boys though."

Phil shook his head. "He's still bigger and stronger than she is. Most men can really do damage to a woman if they want to. Ciara, we've told her to take the boys and come and stay with us, but she'll not give in. There's not much you can do about it sweetheart."

"She's my little sister Phil."

Tony stood up; he took keys from his jacket pocket. "Hold the fort for twenty minutes mate?" He said, looking at his friend and making a face. "Ok, come on Ciara, we'll go see if she's alright. She's the best barmaid I've got, so I suppose I'd better check."

"I'm the best barmaid you've got."

"No you're not. You're a lazy cow, and your sister does most of the work around here, you have other qualities," Phil said laughing. He stood up, kissed his wife and went behind the bar. "Don't be all night Tony, remember it's my night off. And you Ciara, find your sister and get back. I'm supposed to be on a promise tonight with Bhioctoria away with your folks."

"Phil can you phone Fliss, see if she can come in at short notice?" Tony called, as he and Ciara left the bar. They got in to Tony's car and drove in the direction of Caoimhe and Kenny's home.

In the darkness of the car Ciara sighed, "I wish she would just leave him Tony, but she takes his shit. I know he slept with Aggie Donald last week, everyone does. I'm really worried about Caoimhe. Samira told me yesterday that Caoimhe told her, he pinned her down and head butted her. I didn't get a chance to look, but Sami says that there's a bump and a bruise on her forehead. Where is Claire tonight by the way? I tried to call her earlier, but there was no answer."

"Oh, she's away with her mother at a wedding fayre in Newcastle. Didn't she tell you?"

"I thought it was next week. Are you looking forward to the wedding?"

35

"No, not really Ciara, but Claire is, so I suppose I'll just turn up. Won't be for at least eighteen months though. With Dad being so ill, I have to run the hotel."

"You need a good woman Tony."

"Hmm you're probably right. Do you know any?"

"Yes, Claire!"

They stopped in front of the neat terraced house and Ciara got out and knocked on the door. She tried the door handle, it was locked. Taking a key from her pocket she put it in the key-hole. Tony lit a cigarette and sat back; he looked up as he did and saw the upstairs curtain twitch. Ciara got back into the car. "No answer, and there's a key in the inside of the door. I can't open it. Wonder where she fucking is? This is so not like Caoimhe."

"She's upstairs, I saw her."

"Tony, come help me then? She might answer if you knock. Kenny's out, he is away at a stag weekend in Blackpool."

"Okay, you stay here. I'll climb the fence and go around the back."

Tony tried the back door; to his surprise it opened. He walked through the living room. The house had been trashed. There were pictures hanging from the wall and smashed ornaments. He noticed a bloody handprint on the door. He walked upstairs, his heart beating loudly in his chest. They'd all told her to get away from Kenny. Tony had been in Caoimhe's house a few times; it was always immaculate and this was just not like her. He opened doors looking in. He tried to switch on the hall light; it didn't work so he put the bathroom light on. When he looked up the hall, the lampshade hung at an odd angle and he realised the crunching under his feet was from the lightbulb glass.

"Caoimhe are you there? Caoimhe, where are you?" He saw a light under a door. "Caoimhe are you alright?" He opened it and peeked in. The bedside lamp was on. She sat on the bed with her back to him; she was wearing her work clothes, but her purple shirt was torn and her hair was matted and unkempt. "Caoimhe?" he said softly. She didn't answer. He walked around the bed. She was holding a bloody tissue to her face with one hand, the other held her shirt closed. Her eye was swollen and almost shut; bruising was forming around her eye and cheekbone. "Fuck sake!" Tony gasped, "what has he done to you now? That's not the side with the plate, is it?"

She shook her head.

"What fucking happened?"

"I fell!" Blood ran out of her mouth as she spoke.

"No, you fucking didn't."

"Well don't ask stupid questions Tony. Isn't it obvious?"

"Come on, you're coming back to The Deerhunter with me and Ciara."

"I can't!" Caoimhe cried. "I can't let Ciara see me. If she tells Mum, my dad will start getting involved again. The police nearly charged him the last time. They told him that he was on a warning and will lose his firearms licence next time. He's a fucking gamekeeper Tony, he can't afford to lose his guns."

"Okay put some things in a bag. I'll take Ciara back to the hotel and then come for you. Caoimhe, you can't keep letting him do this to you."

"I know."

Outside in the car Tony looked at Ciara, "the house is in a mess, but she's not there. I must have imagined the curtain moving. She might have gone to Samira's. I'll take you back to The Deerhunter, then go and check. Either way, she isn't going to work tonight. If you and Phil cover, I'll give you next weekend off. I need to get the books cooked by Monday. The accountant is chasing me for them now."

When he knocked on the front door twenty minutes later Caoimhe opened it; she'd cleaned up, changed out of the bloody clothes and was wearing jeans and a t-shirt. Tony noted she was braless, he could see her nipples. "Come on, I'll take you back to The Deerhunter. I'm doing the nightshift, but it's not busy. You can have the staff bedroom."

Caoimhe lifted a small bag. "It's only for tonight Tony, I'll find somewhere in the morning. He was supposed to go to Blackpool, but I don't think he went. He was really drunk." Caoimhe glanced at Tony, safe in the darkness of the car. "Thanks for this and for not telling Ciara."

"We're friends Caoimhe, that's what friends do."

Tony stopped outside the back of the hotel. He rummaged in his pocket and handed her a set of keys. "Right, here are the keys to room nine. Get settled, I'll be up in half an hour. Go up the back stairs, there are hardly any residents tonight anyway. Ciara is on the bar for you. I've called Fliss in to help. She's always looking for shifts."

"Thanks Tony. Can I ask another favour?"

"Depends what it is. I'm not going looking for that fucker to make sure he is alright. Unless it's with a baseball bat."

She looked into his eyes. "Bring me a bottle up, I need a drink Tony. There was nothing in the house, he'd drunk it all."

Tony smiled and shook his head. "One of these days it is going to be a body bag we bring out Caoimhe." He watched her go inside, then parked the car and entered the hotel through the front doors.

"Did you find her?" Ciara asked as Tony lifted the hatch and walked behind the bar. Phil was serving a customer; he raised an eyebrow as Tony passed him.

"Yeah, she was at Samira's, she said she'll call you in the morning. She's okay. You were right, she'd had a row with Kenny and walked out."

"Where you going?" Phil asked, as Tony lifted a bottle of vodka and a pack of diet coke cans from the store.

"To do some creative accounting, Gavin is chasing me for the books. I told you! I need them done for Monday. Gonna have to work tonight and probably tomorrow on them." He looked at his friend, "I'm going upstairs to work."

Caoimhe got out of the bath and pulling a towel around her she unlocked the door. Tony stood outside, leaning on the door frame, a litre bottle of vodka under his arm, a six pack of diet coke in his hands. He looked her up and down. "All ready for me then?"

"Not tonight Tony please? I'm feeling quite vulnerable. I need a friend not a chat up line, even if it is a joke! Come in and let's get pished the way we used to."

Tony put the bottle of vodka on the table and pulled a packet of half eaten crisps from his pocket. "My fucking dinner thanks to you! Charlie has gone home and I'm not cooking. Want some? I can get you something cold from the kitchen if you're hungry Caoimhe."

She shook her head then winced as pain shot across it. "Don't want anything to eat. My mouth's cut inside too, so the salt in the crisps would sting." Caoimhe went through to the bathroom and returned with a glass then lifted a cup from the tea accoutrements on the dresser, took the bottle and poured a generous measure of vodka into each; she opened a can of coke. "I suppose I should take painkillers, but I'd rather drink."

Tony moved over to the window and shut the blinds, he could see her reflection in the glass. She sat down, still only wearing the towel and took a gulp of the drink. The towel slipped back over her thigh. He took a sharp intake of breath. "Caoimhe, fuck sake! Cover yourself sweetheart, I'm seeing Nirvana from here." He moved over and sat down beside her.

She shook her head smiled, then pulled the towel around her. "Sorry Tony, I forgot what a sensitive little soul you are. Does my ginger minge upset you?"

"No, it excites me actually, I want to taste it!" He shook his head and sighed. Leaning back on the couch he closed one eye and looked at her. "Right, enough, we need to stop flirting like this. If you're not going to let me make love to you, can I just be your friend again?" Tony took a sip of her drink and made a face. "Christ Caoimhe, you really do want to get pissed." He drew his eyes away from her legs and looked her up and down, noting several different ages of bruising on her arms and chest. "Fuck sake you're covered in bruises."

"I just want to get drunk Tony, then I can forget and sleep." He moved towards her, noting the tears forming in her eyes.

"Oh, Caoimhe, you need to leave him sweetheart. He can't keep using you as a punch bag."

"It doesn't happen as often as you all think Tony, he's having some problems just now. Honestly, he doesn't. Please stop looking at me like that."

"What happened?" Tony asked quietly.

She shrugged and looked away, "I took the boys to Mum's. When I got back he was already pissed. He asked if I was working, I said I was. He just went on about me being a whore and sleeping with other guys. Then he started throwing up stuff that happened years ago. We had a fight. You should see him."

"I'm sure you came out worse. He's a fucking coward and a bully Caoimhe. Your Ciara is worried sick about you, and she is the most self-centred person I have ever met. Caoimhe, has there been anyone except Kenny? No one would blame you if you did."

"Tony, you know I don't do other guys. I know I'm mouthy and I flirt a bit, but I've only ever had sex with him. I was fourteen and a virgin when I started going out with Kenny." Tony could see the regret in her blue eyes as she spoke, but as quickly as Caoimhe let her guard down, she raised it again. Changing the subject, she sighed, "I have a fucking essay to write this weekend. I already had to get an extension on it." She grinned and nudged him. "My tutor is trying to get into my knickers just now, so I can get away with some stuff. Fuck it all, let's get pished Tony, like we used to. I better get dressed though."

"Must you?"

She looked at him. "Where's Claire?"

Tony took a long drink from his glass, before looking at Caoimhe and wincing. "Newcastle, with her mum. Wedding fayre."

"Fuck Tony, you really need to talk to her."

"I know."

"Look at us Tony. Both with people we don't love and not able to leave." Caoimhe took another gulp from her glass, shivered, and her teeth began to chatter. Tony stood up and moving over to the bed pulled the top cover off; he wrapped it around her. He too gulped down the vodka and poured them both another.

He stood looking at her. "Caoimhe! I could never treat you like this. I could never harm a hair on a woman's head. You don't deserve it." He moved over and sat beside her again and gently touched her bruised face. She winced and pulled away from him. Tony jumped to his feet, "I'll be back in a moment, don't lock this door," Tony said, walking towards it.

Downstairs in the bar, Ciara was serving. Phil followed him through to the storeroom. "What are you up to?" Phil hissed. "You better not have my sister-in-law up there Tony." He looked at Tony, who nodded slowly. "Fuck sake, you prick. Are you mad?"

"Shoosh Phil, Ciara will hear you!"

"I fucking knew it Tony. The moment you went back out again after bringing Ciara back, I knew."

"She's in a mess Phil and she doesn't want Ciara to know. I just need ice for her face."

"Tony mate, don't go there, please don't get involved. We've all told her to get herself away from him. Ciara's dad and I warned him off the last time. I've got to the stage where I just think Caoimhe has a screw loose."

"Phil she's bruised and battered, I'm not going to take advantage of her. She is a friend in trouble. I'm going to clean her up and let her sleep here tonight. That's all bud, I swear."

Phil raised an eyebrow, "Tony please don't do it mate, you could be opening Pandora's Box pumping Caoimhe, exciting but fucking deadly! Stick with Claire mate, she's uncomplicated ... and fucking sane," he hissed, as Tony made his way back down the corridor.

Five minutes later Tony was back in room nine, carrying an ice bucket and a tea towel. She'd finished her drink and poured another; she still sat on the sofa wrapped in the blanket, still not dressed.

"Here, you'd better get some ice on those bruises, you are going to look like a losing boxer in the morning. Ice might take some of the swelling down."

"I'll cover it with makeup as usual," she sighed.

"You'll need a lot of fucking makeup Caoimhe." He took the ice, wrapped it in the tea towel and handed it to her. Tony finished his own drink, looked at his watch and sat back down beside her. "We've just polished off half of a litre bottle in forty minutes, Phil and Ciara are going to work on tonight if I give them next weekend off. Said I had the books to do. Phil guessed you're here but I didn't tell Ciara. He won't say anything to her. He won't want the hassle and earache it would cause him. I told Ciara I found you at Samira's, then I called Sami and let her know, just in case. She says she'll come over in the morning. She's taking Ravi to his swimming lesson, so she'll be in town."

"Thanks, I love my sister but ... "

Tony smiled, his eyes sparkled. "You two are so different for sisters, aren't you? You want to save the world and she lives in her own wee bubble where she is the princess. You don't even look like each other, with her being so dark and you with all that red hair. Is one of you adopted?"

"I look like my dad's side, she favours Mum, that's all. If you look closely, you can see the resemblance. Her personality? Who fucking knows? She was always a princess, my dad spoiled her rotten. I think it's because she looks so like Mum. My mum's a bit of a diva too though, Dad plays into that. You know Phil indulges Ciara, so that's probably it." Caoimhe smiled and nudged Tony. "I was the son Dad never had. Even now we're really close. I can hunt, shoot and fish as good as any man, not to mention drink and smoke."

Afterwards neither of them were sure what happened; the alcohol took away some of their inhibitions. She remembered him as being gentle; she was vulnerable, needed comfort. She'd never taken the next step to their flirting and let him touch her before. As she poured another drink, he moved towards her. "Let me see your face now?" Taking the icy bundle from her, he looked at her, moved in closer and gently kissed the swollen, purple bruise on her cheek. Pushing her hair away from her face he kissed her eye lid then her lips. She stared at him, tears building up in her eyes.

"Please Tony, don't do this, I'm drunk. I don't have the strength to say no tonight, I just want to be held. I'd better get dressed." Caoimhe lifted her glass and taking a large gulp, she stood up; the blanket fell away. She wobbled and the towel joined it on the floor leaving her naked.

Tony stood up, took the glass from her, put it on the table and moved towards her. He began to kiss her. She didn't resist; her eyes wide like saucers as his hands wandered over her naked body. She shivered. "Tony, we shouldn't be doing this. Claire? Kenny? I can't Tony."

"You can darling. I promise I'll stop if you tell me you don't want to. Please let me kiss you better?" he whispered. "I've wanted to do this for years." To his amazement, she began to kiss him back; her fingers fumbled with the buttons on his shirt. They sank to the floor.

They didn't make it to the bed and made love on the floor of room nine, her straddled on top of him. Caoimhe gasped, she felt as though she was on some sort of auto-pilot and instinctively knew how she wanted it to be. Alcohol took away any inhibitions she might have had. Tony, so close, so good looking. He was gentle, but she could see the amazement on his face as she moved against him.

Caoimhe had never experienced passion of this magnitude; she cried out, clinging to him. Her body shook as she climaxed, she gasped and struggled to catch her breath. He pulled away slightly, as his groin told him he was close to orgasm; he knew she was ready for more.

Caoimhe was still shaking and gasping; Tony lifted her and carried her over to the bed. "God you're beautiful, that prick doesn't know how lucky he is. Caoimhe, I don't want to spoil the moment but do we need a rubber?"

She shook her head and began kissing him again. "I have a coil!" she whispered as she held on to him, her arms around his neck, looking into his eyes. "Please do that to me again. God you're good at this Tony."

He laid her on the bed and moved on top of her. Stretching his neck to reach her breast, his lips closed over her nipple. She cried out and arched her back. Pulling his face upwards she began to kiss him, his tongue slid into her mouth. His hands gripping her breasts, he entered her again, passion mounting quickly as he felt her body tighten. Tony gasped as Caoimhe ground her hips against him, meeting each thrust. Her legs moved upwards and tightened around his hips, holding him against her.

She clung to him. He felt her body become rigid again, crying out as she climaxed, seconds before he let go, shuddered and gasped as his own orgasm began. The intensity of it took his breath away. He whispered her name repeatedly; she held on to him, her body convulsing and when the feelings subsided she looked him in the eye and burst in to tears.

"Whoa darling, it wasn't that bad surely?" He kissed her bruised face, his fingers gently wiping away the tears now pouring down onto her cheeks, still flushed from their recent lovemaking.

"I've never felt it like that before! I never knew it could be like this," she sobbed, gasping for breath. Her body shook and she could still feel the tingling in her groin.

"You've never come? What? Caoimhe, you have been shagging Kenny since you were 15! He's never made you come?"

She shook her head, "I do sometimes. But fuck, Tony, it's never been like that. I'm still tingling. I couldn't breathe and I thought I was going to die. Then it just ... sort of exploded. Fuck Tony ... maybe it's the vodka?"

"Fuck sake Caoimhe, what are you doing with him? I was sure he must be great in bed for you to put up with his shite." He kissed her and held her bruised face in his hands. "Caoimhe it was good for me too. In fact, the best I've ever had. We must find a way to be together. I knew it would be like this, I felt the chemistry between us."

"I'm an adulterer. They still stone women to death in some countries for doing what we just did Tony."

"They're fucking jailing men for beating their wives in this country Caoimhe."

"He didn't beat me, we were fighting. How many times do I have to tell you?"

"He should be fucking punished for what he does to you."

She looked at him sadly. "It doesn't work like that, trust me! I called the police once Tony, when he hit me hard. They just told us to behave. It was because I had hit him back. They said it was a fight not domestic violence." She sighed. "When I don't fight back, it's over quicker, a few slaps the occasional punch. It only happens when he is really drunk and I have no way of knowing when he is going to turn on me. I just can't keep my fucking mouth shut Tony, most of the time I think I cause it to escalate."

"For fuck sake Caoimhe, listen to yourself. No man should hit a woman, no fucking way. You should be able to say what you like without being a fucking punch bag. He's a big man Caoimhe. What is he, about six four? He is at least two inches taller than me, and I'm six foot two. He must weigh what, eighteen stone now? He has turned into a right fat bastard since he stopped playing rugby." She shrugged and wrapped the white cotton sheet from the bed around herself as though seeking protection from it. Reaching for her cigarettes she offered him one, he shook his head watching her intently. She balanced the ashtray on her chest. Tony reached over, lifting his trousers he pulled a cannabis joint out of the pocket and lit it; inhaling deeply he offered it to her.

"No thanks!" she grinned. "Not when I've drunk as much Tony, I'm crazy enough." Caoimhe jumped up and ran over to the couch. Lifting Tony's discarded shirt from the floor she put it on. She lifted the glass and bottle, scooping up some ice into the glass and the rest onto the tea towel she held it to her cheek. "Fuck my face hurts." She looked at him. "I can't believe what we've just done! Think we've taken our friendship to a whole different level Tony!"

"It was good though sweetheart. I can't believe how fucking intense it was Caoimhe, it was unbelievable. I don't even want to go again yet, I'm so satisfied. Give me half an hour though!"

"Tony, we can't. It was fantastic, but it's so wrong, too many people could get hurt. Claire, my kids, even Kenny."

"The people who are going to be the most hurt, are you and I Caoimhe. If we don't take this chance, we're going to really regret it."

"I can't Tony, I'm married!"

"You owe that fucker nothing. He's left you in some mess this time Caoimhe. I want to go and kick his fucking head in. I'm many things darling, but I have never hit a woman." She sat down on the bed beside him then lay back with her head on his chest, amazed at how comfortable she felt with him. Tony put his free arm around her and kissed her forehead. "Sex has really sobered me up. Are you going to tell me the truth about why he hit you this time?"

Caoimhe sighed. "He wants me to give up university Tony. He never mentions it when he's sober, but the minute he gets drunk it's a threat."

"What? You can't. You would have gone if you hadn't had kids so young, and everyone knows how intelligent you are Caoimhe. I know you love Dan, he is a great wee guy, so is David, but you should have had an abortion."

Caoimhe sighed and a puff of white smoke rose into the air. "I wasn't going to tell you what started it Tony. I was so fucking angry at him. He told me tonight he used dodgy durex when we first had sex. He meant to get me pregnant. I was only fifteen, so stupid, naïve. It burst a couple of times, I just accepted it. He put a pin prick in them. He told me Tony, he trapped me."

"What? The dirty bastard!"

"He told me he owned me and I was his property. I was scared this time, it was different." She began to cry and Tony looked at her.

"What else did he do Caoimhe?"

"He tried to rape me, he's never done that before. He has slapped me, punched me, he even kicked me once, but tonight, he tried to force me to have sex. When I refused, he tried to hold me down, but I kicked and punched back.

She began to sob, burying her face in Tony's chest. "He doesn't know I have the coil in. I just couldn't take a chance with him, so I went to a clinic in Glasgow and got it fitted. He said a baby to look after would put paid to my ambitions, so he was trying to get me pregnant." She sighed, "I really should just have let him. It's one of two things with Kenny. Either he can't or it's over pretty quickly." She looked up at Tony, "I was just so angry, I fought him, I don't even know why. It was just, well ... I was so angry I was determined he wasn't getting it. Then he couldn't stay hard ... and well, he ... " Caoimhe looked up at the ceiling, "he really lost the plot and kept hitting me. I was scared."

"I'll be there for you Caoimhe. You need to leave him."

"I know. I just want to finish Uni first. I can't afford to stay on the course if I'm not with him. It'll be okay for a while now, he always feels sorry after he does it."

"Let me help you financially?"

"Fuck off Tony, I'm not taking money from you." She grinned despite her tears. "Especially not now, that's called prostitution."

"You take it from Kenny."

"He fucking owes me Tony. He owes my boys, his boys." Caoimhe looked up at Tony as she spoke. "You also need to think about this. Maybe we should just put it down to experience and leave it? You really need to consider what this could do to Claire if she finds out."

"I know, I know, I don't want to hurt her, but what can I do? It's nothing to do with you or what we have just done. I don't love her Caoimhe. I told you I got involved because of her looks, I'm fucking ashamed of myself for being so shallow, but there's no chemistry there." He looked her in the eye, she could see genuine sadness written across his face. "She's lovely but not very bright Caoimhe, you know that."

47

"Tony, that's not fair, her and Ciara just always lived on their looks. Ciara met Phil, he loves her despite her empty-headed nonsense, and well you and Claire, two best friends, with two best mates. "You're all so good looking, you look like you've stepped out of the pages of a magazine." Caoimhe sighed and touched his face. "Maybe you just need to be grateful for what you have Tony, I've told you that. Other men are jealous of you being with Claire, she's beautiful. Her and Ciara, they both are. Me and you? We'd kill each other Tony. We fight enough without being involved. Yes ... the sex was good pal, but I've no one but Kenny to compare it to. You've been with Claire since you were sixteen."

"I've slept with other woman too Caoimhe, but I think given a chance I could love you." Tony looked her in the eye and gently smoothed her red hair back from her face. "The arguments with me would never lead to violence, I reckon that they would lead to the kind of sex we just had. I quite often bring women up here Caoimhe. There's just not enough with me and Claire. I know it's wrong but ... "

"That makes you a great fucking prospect Tony. You're really talking me into a relationship with you."

"Caoimhe, I swear on my dad's life, if I was with you, I'd never need another woman. You and I sweetheart, there is so much fucking chemistry between us, but it's good stuff, not the ugly kind you and Kenny have. Caoimhe after what it was like with us, can you walk away from me now?" He looked into her eyes, tears gathering at the corners of his own.

Caoimhe shook her head. She knew she wanted him. She wanted to feel the intensity of their lovemaking again, and she also knew in that instant that she would never have that with Kenny. "Let's just play this by ear. There is so much at stake, to be honest Tony I'm not a good prospect either." She looked at him and sighed. "I don't think I'm cut out to be in a relationship. I love my kids but I don't know, maybe I've got some kind of mental disorder. I just don't think I am capable to being a wife. I try to be, but I just get so fucking angry at Kenny sometimes. I do want it to be like Ciara and Phil, but it's just not there." Caoimhe closed her eyes. "I really do need to sleep Tony, I'm absolutely shattered."

Tony pulled the bedclothes over her and tucked her in. "Sleep babe, you're safe here." He lay watching her sleep; he couldn't believe she had allowed him to make love to her and he also couldn't believe it had been as good. He lay remembering the first time he had met Caoimhe. Phil had met Ciara and suggested he come on a double date with her friend Claire. Tony had been struck by how beautiful Claire was and they had become an item. Tony knew from the beginning the relationship didn't fulfil him, however he got involved.

That first New Year, sixteen-year-old Tony had gone with Phil to Claire's house. He had been struck by Ciara's younger sister straight away. Different from Claire and Ciara; gregarious, intelligent, funny and beautiful; not in the obvious way her older sister was. Fourteen-year-old Caoimhe appeared all legs and arms, and he was reminded initially of a character from books he used to read to his little sister, 'Pippy Longstocking.' Tony vaguely knew Caoimhe's boyfriend, Kenny Black, from the rugby club. He didn't much like him, but Tony and Caoimhe had got on well from the start.

Tony was instrumental in getting Caoimhe a job in the hotel his father owned, and over the years they became friends. When she'd become pregnant at fifteen and married Kenny a week after she turned sixteen, Caoimhe had continued to work in the hotel. Tony had always felt attracted to her, but nothing ever happened. They were friends. However, as Tony had alluded to earlier, after working at a wedding a few weeks before, they'd continued to drink after everyone else had gone home. Hector, Tony's father, had been diagnosed with cancer and was undergoing gruelling treatment; Tony had taken over the running of the Deerhunter.

For Tony, the sexual attraction had been sudden. They had both been very drunk, which was something they did occasionally. They decided to jump around on a bouncy castle, which had been there for the children. Caoimhe had grabbed his hands to bounce higher and they had fallen, she landed on top of him. Tony tried to kiss her and she slapped him, laughing. The feeling had been overwhelming, he wanted her. Since that night, he had continually tried to talk her into sleeping with him. He looked at the sleeping figure in the bed. Now he had her, he had no idea what he was going to do with her, but knew he didn't want to let her go.

Tony reluctantly tore himself away from the bed, looked at his watch, dressed and went downstairs. His head was full of thoughts when he entered the bar. He looked around, Ciara wasn't there. Phil was locking up. "I sent my wife home, she was falling asleep. It wasn't too busy after the band left." He looked at Tony. "How is Caoimhe?"

"Sleeping, we got drunk together."

"Tony, please tell me you haven't slept with her mate?"

Tony shrugged. Turning his back to Phil he took a glass and put it under the vodka optic and pressed it twice. "I haven't slept with her!" he said without looking up.

"You fucking have, you fanny," Phil cried. "Mate, please do not do this. You have Claire, and you have a life. Caoimhe, she is fucking wired to the moon at times. She's Ciara's sister and Claire is Ciara's best friend for Christ sake. Tony, please don't do this to me. Fuck Tony, don't do this to yourself." Phil put his own glass under the optic and pressed. He looked at his friend and shook his head. "Have you any idea how much trouble this could cause? Think with your head, not your balls please!"

Tony looked at him and sighed. "I have to see where this goes mate. There's a spark with her, I just need to see what happens. I've always liked her, you know that, Phil. Please do not under any circumstances tell Ciara."

Phil nodded. "What was it like?"

"Unfortunately, it was fucking incredible."

Phil looked puzzled. "Unfortunately? What does that mean? Is it worth starting World War Three?"

"I wanted to be wrong Phil, scratch the itch, get her out of my system, but I think I might have opened a whole new can of worms." Tony looked at Phil, sighed then rolled his eyes to the ceiling. He lifted a can of coke and opened it, pouring it first into the glass Phil held out and then into his own, before taking a long gulp.

Phil sighed and shook his head sadly. "Told you mate, exciting, but fucking deadly. She is too fucking fiery and too intelligent. Women should be like Ciara and Claire. She won't leave him you know? Caoimhe won't admit when she's wrong, so she'll stay with Kenny. She'll chew you up Tony and spit you out. Bert and Morag are worried sick about her, that prick is going to murder her one of these days. Bert got drunk last weekend, he spoke about shooting Kenny and burying him up on the moor."

"Well it would be a solution, wouldn't it?"

"Tony be careful mate, listen to reason, don't be led by your balls!"

Tony walked slowly back upstairs after Phil left. Caoimhe was fast asleep, her red curls spread out on the pillow. He was reminded of Julia Roberts in 'Pretty Woman.' He had only gone to see the film with Claire, to please her, but had been struck by the actress's resemblance to Caoimhe. He got undressed and got back into bed; she stirred and opened her eyes. He looked at her and they began to kiss again.

When she awoke the next morning, he was watching her. "Good morning beautiful!" he whispered. "You were amazing last night." Tony brushed her hair from her face. "I've got to have you babe. I haven't been able to sleep Caoimhe, don't think that I'll ever be able to be with another woman. I've never felt like that with anyone else."

Caoimhe rolled over and looked at him. "Don't be a fucking sap Tony, it really doesn't suit you. I'm sure it was just the vodka and the fact that I gave in. I bet it was just because it was new." She stood up, picked up Tony's discarded shirt, went into the bathroom, and turned on the bath taps. She came back through buttoning the shirt, walked over to the mirror and studied her bruised and swollen face. She rummaged in her bag and brought out a satin hair band and used it to tie up her hair. "I'm really sore this morning and having sex with you four times, has added another sore bit. I'm going to soak in a bath. When is Claire back?" she asked, looking at him in the mirror.

"Not till tomorrow, we can have another night together. You cannot go back to Kenny, Caoimhe. Not after what he's done to you. I'll find somewhere for you and the boys. There's a flat above the new pub I bought with Phil. He's going to do the renovations." He looked in to her eyes. "It's not great, but it would do to start with."

"Tony, let's just take this slowly, I need time to think." She stood up walked through to the bathroom and turned the taps off. "Come on, come in with me Tony?" Tony did as he was asked and Caoimhe stepped into the bath and sat between his legs, resting her head on his chest. His arms circled her and he kissed her neck and shoulders.

He tightened his arms around her, "Caoimhe please don't go back to him, I'll find somewhere for you to go. I'll pay Phil's workers double to get the flat finished."

"Tony, don't be ridiculous. Can you imagine the scandal this would cause? You and me, it just can't happen." She looked around at him. "Besides, we have had one night together. We could hate each other next week. You're as fucking mental as me, we would probably tear each other to pieces."

"Ah, maybe's aye maybe's no, but just think of the fun we'd have making up. Caoimhe we did it four times last night and each time it was the same, like a fucking earthquake. My cock feels as though it's been through a shredder now, but by tonight I'll want you again.

Caoimhe smiled, remembering. "Let's just see where this goes before we start making promises." She looked up at him and grinned. "You'd better go and do the breakfasts, it's gone seven. I'm going to have to stay up here all day in case Kenny comes looking for me! I'll need to finish my essay too." She watched as he got out the bath and moved over to the sink, lifting a razor from the shelf above it. "Tony, I'm going to go to Samira's when she comes over. I think it will be for the best, don't you?"

"No babe, I don't, I think you and I need to see where this is going. Besides, you can go to Samira's tomorrow can you not?" He watched her in the mirror as he shaved; he felt confused, he'd kind of hoped last night that he would feel different when he was sober. He knew he didn't and he wanted her more now. He wasn't sure what he was going to do. He had not thought further than the part where he had sex with Caoimhe. If he was honest with himself, Tony had never despite his chasing her for the last few weeks, thought there was any way she would sleep with him anyway.

***

Their affair carried on through into the following year. Caoimhe went back to Kenny of course, as she always did. He swore he was sorry and Caoimhe did not react to his behaviour any more. He also did not object to her being at university and to her amazement began to go for counselling about his alcohol use. In truth, what he had done to his wife had scared Kenny Black. Caoimhe knew, however, she didn't love him. She could not however imagine how she was going to get out of her marriage. In some ways having Tony there, made it easier for her to remain with Kenny.

Tony initially continued to see Claire, too afraid of the consequences of finishing with her. However, after a row over setting a wedding date, the relationship ended. Tony remained resolute it was over. He tried hard not to pressure Caoimhe. Like her, his Catholic upbringing meant there was a great deal of guilt about their illicit relationship. They fought often, and as Tony had forecast, their making up was as passionate as their arguments. Tony hated the idea of Caoimhe going home to Kenny, but felt he was not in a position to stop her. Tony knew he was in love with her, but he was not entirely sure she felt the same way.

CHAPTER

FOUR

"Claire's pregnant, Caoimhe!"

"What? I thought it was over?"

"It is, but she's nearly six months gone."

"How?"

Tony shrugged, his face miserable and worried. "I don't know. She has just found out. She says she didn't know!"

"It's possible Tony, it happens."

"Fuck Caoimhe, what am I going to do? I can't leave her with a baby. She's too far on for an abortion, even if she would have one. I offered to pay for her to go private, but it's too late. She wants me to marry her."

"Are you going to?"

"I don't want to Caoimhe, I want to be with you. Our parents and Father Iain are involved now. You know what that's like?"

"Oh yes, been there, it ended up with us down the aisle. We were only sixteen and eighteen though. You and Claire are twenty-six and twenty-seven!" Caoimhe looked Tony in the eye. "That's old enough to make your own mind up. Fucking Catholic parents Tony, they never stop owning you."

They were upstairs in the hotel. Room nine had become their haven. Caoimhe had known since she entered the bar an hour before that there was something wrong, something bothering Tony. They'd managed to slip away when the bar wasn't busy.

54

Phil, who'd come in for a drink after work, reluctantly covered for them. Tony's father had stepped away from the running of the hotel while he underwent treatment for cancer for a second time. Tony had asked Caoimhe to take on some extra duties related to the hotel. This allowed her to work some night shifts and therefore meant that they could spend time together. Kenny did not appear to mind; when he wasn't drinking he didn't mind much about anything. Kenny, accepted the pay rise Tony made sure Caoimhe had. Like most people in the town, Kenny assumed that Tony Carter would be no threat to him, given his relationship with the beautiful Claire. Kenny was also struggling to get his accountancy business up and running, and the extra money was useful.

Caoimhe knew what she and Tony were doing was wrong. She didn't know if she could end the relationship now. Somehow, they managed to work on and finish their shift. Caoimhe called Kenny and told him she had to do a nightshift.

Back in room nine at the end of the evening, Tony looked miserably at Caoimhe. Everyone else had gone home and there were only three guests in residence, all of whom were on the other side of the building. "I don't want to marry her Caoimhe."

"You have to. It's not Claire's fault we're doing this."

"No! But I don't love her, and it's over. I couldn't believe it when she called me. I thought she was looking for something she'd left at mine." He sighed. "Caoimhe I don't love her, I'm never going to. I know that now, because of how I feel about you darling."

"I don't love Kenny and I manage it. Maybe it's easier if you don't love them?"

"I don't even know how I fucking managed to bairn her Caoimhe. After you and I got together I only slept with her occasionally, when I had to. She was on the pill too. Luckily she's not that into sex." He looked down at Caoimhe who was lying in his arms looking up at him. "God, I just heard myself say that. I'm a bastard Caoimhe, aren't I?"

She nodded. "Yip we're both going straight to Hell. Do you think she could have done it deliberately Tony?"

"What do you know?"

"Nothing!" she lied.

The truth was, several months before, Ciara not guessing about the relationship between her and Tony, had told her Claire was thinking of trying to get pregnant to force Tony into marriage. Caoimhe had suggested she told Phil, but Ciara knew he would go straight to Tony and refused to do this. Caoimhe had been going to warn Tony, but then he and Claire had parted. Caoimhe just assumed she had not managed it. She really did not want Tony to have bad memories of Claire either. Caoimhe's other difficulty was Ciara told her in confidence, and she could not break her sister's trust.

"Caoimhe, the truth? What did you hear? Why would she wait months to tell me?"

"Maybe so she was too late for a termination? It doesn't mean she did it deliberately."

"What have you heard Caoimhe? Tell me!"

"Honestly, nothing, I would have told you if I had. She was probably just fed up with you putting off marrying her Tony. You were running out of excuses. You need to do it. We can just carry on doing this."

"No! No, Caoimhe we can't, I hate this sneaking about. You don't like it either. I want to be able to kiss you in public, have days out, go out for a meal, lie on the beach together in summer. You know, normal everyday things couples do. I'm fucking sick of hiding away and fucking sick of us being a guilty secret." He looked into her eyes and kissed her on the lips. "You're my soulmate babe, and I don't give two fucks what people think. We know the truth."

"Tony, we need to be careful, you don't want to hurt Claire any more than I do. I love you Tony, but I'm not free. It's not right and this is our punishment. Maybe this is all we get, but it's good, we have so much." She kissed him. "I get to spend time like this, you make my eyes water, and the earth moves. How can Claire not want some of that?"

Tony shook his head sadly and kissed her, "Caoimhe we have a chemistry you and me. It's just you and me sweetheart. It's like that with you, but not her. I've been with other women, what we have is unique. I need to have you, you're like a fucking drug. Let's just run away."

Caoimhe laughed bitterly, she shook her head. "You couldn't leave your family, any more than I can. I'm almost finished with my degree and once I get it, I can get a job and support my kids. You're a good guy Tony, you'll do what's right. I love you, but I think I'm too selfish to be in a relationship anyway."

"Caoimhe, will you still work for me?"

"Of course, just not as often, weekends only. We'll have to work around our partners." She shook her head and looked at him, "I should feel guilty getting Kenny to babysit so I can screw you." She said quietly.

"Are you still sleeping with him?"

"Tony don't ask, you promised you wouldn't ask."

"Are you Caoimhe? I've no right to ask you not to, given I've managed to bairn Claire. Are you still fucking Kenny? I need to know."

"Tony he's my husband. I do it when I have to."

"Don't you get confused?"

Caoimhe smiled sadly and shook her head. "No, there's no comparison. With Kenny it's like a chore, doing the dishes or making the tea. With you, well it's ... " She rolled over on top of him. "With you it's like this ... "

Afterwards she lay in his arms feeling safe and protected.

"What's it like with Kenny? Is he good to you? How can you do it, not slip up? When I did it with Claire I tried not to think about you, I was so scared I would call out your name or something." He sighed, "but I know what you mean, what you and I have is just so different."

"Tony, sometimes I dream about you and me making love. I wake up coming. He thinks it's him and gets on then it's like a little tremble. "With you it's a fucking earthquake." She sighed and her eyes filled with tears. "I've even tried keeping my eyes shut and pretending it's you, but that doesn't work either." She looked up at him, tears now rolling down her cheeks. "Luckily he's more into pleasing himself than bothering whether I get anything out of it and it doesn't actually last long." Her voice cracked and she buried her face in his chest. "I could be a blow-up doll. He doesn't make love to me Tony, not like you do. I'm just a ride, nothing more. I make a few noises and moan a bit so he thinks he is giving me pleasure, and he never questions it." Caoimhe sighed and gulped back tears, looking up into his eyes. "Sometimes I just give him a blow job and then he doesn't actually have to do anything."

Tony looked at her and kissed her wet face, "I'm so sorry I asked Caoimhe, I never meant to upset you. I try not to feel jealous of Kenny, but I hate the idea of him touching you when I know you are meant to be with me." He pulled her closer, "when this is all over and everyone knows, I hope he comes looking for me! Because I'm going to kick his fucking head in for all the times he's hurt you."

She leaned back against him and sighed. "That makes you the same as him. You and me Tony, it's about chemistry, not just familiarity, isn't it? You're such a good lover and you are better endowed than him too. I don't want anyone else, but I just need to get through every day. If I have to be a spunk bucket for him sometimes that's just part of it all." She put her hands to her face and covered it. "Oh God, I'm a terrible person, wanton hussy. Tony what we are doing, it goes against everything I believe in, but I just don't want to stop. You've taught me what real love is all about. I do love you. I know you don't believe me, but I really do. You're what gets me through everything else."

Tony's heart soared; he couldn't hide his euphoria at her admission. He kissed the top of her head. "Babe we need to come clean, just face the music, you know that, don't you? I want to be with you all the time. I'm so fucking proud of you Caoimhe. The way you have followed your dream, worked so hard to get your degree, but you've juggled a job, a house, a family, and me."

She nodded. "Tony I'm sorry, I'm just so scared you'll give up the chance of happiness with Claire and I won't make you happy. She really loves you and she'll be a much better wife than I could ever be." She paused, struggling to speak, overcome with emotion, her eyes filling up again. "Sometimes, I think I drove Kenny to drink because I'm such a cow."

"Is that what he tells you?"

She nodded, unable to speak, tears now running down her face. He wrapped his arms around her and held her close, letting her sob, crying himself. "Honey, how can someone so fucking intelligent be so stupid? It's not you, it's him. He needs to justify his behaviour. Kenny's family, they're all drinkers and wife beaters." He stroked her hair and looked into her eyes. "Let's just wait a month or two, tell them both when we have a plan. I'm going to tell her I can't marry her and look for somewhere for you, me and the kids to live."

The following evening, she walked into the bar to start her shift. Phil sat reading a newspaper. "Where's Tony?" Phil looked up and motioned with his head. Caoimhe lifted the counter and walked through behind the bar into the store room.

"He's in crisis talks with Claire and their families. They're pressuring him to marry her. All of them, even Hector. Caoimhe, I think he really does love you, but this cannot go on. Much as I think Kenny's a prick, how long do you think you can keep this up? Caoimhe, Tony is a good guy, better than you deserve. You need to leave Kenny!"

Caoimhe nodded. "I know, I just wanted to wait until I finished my degree. Everyone will think I left because Tony has money. I will support myself and my children."

"I do not get your logic Caoimhe. I think you're soft in the head! You're using Kenny to do it, isn't that the same thing?"

"Kenny fucking owes me Phil. I work bloody hard in the house, he does nothing. I run after him hand and foot to keep

59

him sweet. I work here and do twice the work rest of you do."

"Stop being so fucking pig-headed and selfish Caoimhe! There are others involved here, not just you. Tony stayed with Claire to cover for you, now there's a baby on the way. She's a lovely, sweet girl and she loves him. I struggle with the whole thing. My wife is your fucking sister and Claire's best friend." Phil sighed and Caoimhe knew he was caught firmly in the middle of the mess she and Tony had caused. "Claire may have worked it out anyway. She told Ciara that she thought Tony was seeing someone else. Tony reckons she suspects it's you."

"You're kidding?"

"He doesn't care Caoimhe. It's only because of you and your bloody-mindedness that he hasn't told her. I would have said move in with us until the dust settles, but Ciara is going to be forced to take sides on this and she doesn't suspect it's you. Your mother will go mad as well, you know that don't you? Tony says Claire kept asking him about you, yesterday?"

"He didn't tell her, did he?"

"No, but he says he went to see her and she could smell your perfume on him."

"Christ, if she tells Kenny it could start him drinking again. I just need some time."

"Caoimhe, you're off your fucking head. Tony Carter is a good guy, Kenny is a prick and you can't seem to let go. Please Caoimhe, either leave him this time, or end it with Tony and walk away."

***

Caoimhe waited all night, the bar wasn't busy and after Phil left, she busied herself cleaning the gantry, continually watching the clock above the bar. Just before closing, Tony appeared from the back of the hotel. She looked up at him as she served up last orders to the three regulars left in the bar. Her first thought was how tired and drained he looked. "Okay boys, this is it. Drink up quickly because it's a school night, I need to get to bed, and

Caoimhe needs to get home," Tony shouted, lifting glasses from tables.

As Tony locked up, Caoimhe went through to the hotel kitchen and put on the kettle. She was sitting at a table in the dining room with a mug of milky coffee when he came through. He bolted the kitchen door then sat down across from her. She pushed a cup of hot chocolate towards him; he lifted the mug and took a sip. "Caoimhe I'm so fucked up. Claire's mother has booked the wedding. It's three weeks tomorrow. She wants us to do it before the baby comes. Now Dad's in remission, I don't have that excuse either. I nearly told him about you tonight when he was giving me the, *you have made your bed, you must lie in it,* talk. I don't fucking want to marry her, I'm such a fucking wimp." He put his hand on top of hers and looked into Caoimhe's eyes. "She could smell your perfume on me yesterday, I almost told her, babe, she kept asking."

"I told you to have a shower and change before you went to meet her Tony. I knew she would notice, women do! That's how I know when Kenny has been with someone. What are we going to do?"

"I'm going to have to tell her. She has me going to a meeting with her priest tomorrow, I'll tell her then. Caoimhe, you need to tell Kenny too. I'll come with you when you do. We can't wait till you finish uni. It's only a couple of months now anyway. If the fucking money means so much to you, I'll lend it to you and you can pay me back. I'll do a proper loan agreement, make everything legit. I need to tell Claire about us Caoimhe. I can't keep this up, it's fucking destroying me."

She looked at him and nodded, tears in her eyes at the look of relief on his face. "Tony, can we just tell Kenny first though. Once you tell Claire, she'll go straight to him, he might start drinking. I need to make sure that my boys are not caught up in the firing line."

Tony looked at Caoimhe and sighed. "Okay I'll end it and tell her that it's just because I don't love her. I don't know what is worse anyway." He shook his head sadly. "Saying *'I don't love you Claire'* or saying, *'I love someone else.'* Either way, she's going to be hurt, isn't she? When it comes out about us, I'm going to lie and say we got together after she and I split up. There have been so many fucking lies, Caoimhe. You need to tell him Caoimhe, you need to tell Kenny. Just tell him you're leaving. You can move in with Ciara and Phil until I can find us somewhere. Phil rented out the flat above the new pub on a year's lease last month, so it's not an option now."

"Okay Tony, I'll tell Kenny. I won't need you there, he's not drinking. Hopefully he'll leave me, and I can keep the house. I can't go to my parents, I'd get dragged to Mass to confess my sins and I would get lectured every day."

"Fucking families Caoimhe, sometimes I wish I was a fucking orphan," he smiled and shook his head, "or a Protestant."

Caoimhe smiled back, "I think morals are the same for any religion babe. Although, if we were Mormons it would be okay to have two wives."

"You know what I mean. We're both going to have Father Ralph at the door when we do it."

"Ciara is going to go mad as well Tony. I mean, her and Claire, they are fucking twins." Caoimhe sighed again and looked at Tony sadly. "Phil had a right go at me tonight. He said I'm a selfish cow and he's right Tony. Claire is going to get really hurt now and there's the baby too. If I had just not been so pig-headed and determined to stay with Kenny, you might have ended it before she got pregnant. I actually don't deserve you do I?"

"Caoimhe, don't blame yourself babe. I'm not a kid, I made choices. It suited me to carry on and stay with Claire. I should have ended it with her long before you and I started this. Caoimhe, if I had loved her, I would never have cheated. It suited me to carry on, so I kind of deserve all I get now. I do love you Caoimhe, and I don't want anyone else."

"I know." Caoimhe smiled thorough tear filled eyes. "Sometimes I wish you didn't Tony, I don't deserve you."

He moved around and came to stand behind her, massaging her neck and shoulders. "I want to make love to you right now darling." He kissed the top of her head and moved away.

"Really, Tony? That's what got us in to this mess!"

"No, to be honest with you, what I really want is to take you outside into the car and just run away with you. Pick up your kids and just keep going. When we were on Arran, I didn't want to come home." He sat down on the chair beside her and leaned back, looking at the ceiling.

"We'll need to run away once this gets out!" Caoimhe said miserably. I'll be the town whore. You'll be the bastard who walked out on his pregnant fiancée. They'll read our names out in the Mass." She looked up at him, like her his face was wet with tears. "We wouldn't be in this mess if I'd just left him when we started this Tony." She stood up and looked down at him. He pulled her towards him and put his lips against hers.

"Caoimhe don't beat yourself about sweetheart, it takes two to tango. I'm as bad as you, worse maybe." He whispered in her ear. "I love you so much Caoimhe, I can't help how I feel."

Looking directly into Tony's eyes, Caoimhe straddled him on the chair; she could feel his erection growing, pushing against her through her clothes. He began to undress her. Unbuttoning her purple work shirt, he pushed her bra up as his mouth found her nipple. Shivers floated through her body. Breaking away from him and jumping to her feet, she pushed her skirt up over her hips and removed her knickers. He slid his trousers over his hips and pulled her back down onto his lap; straddling him again, she put her hand down and guided his erect penis.

"Fuck me babe!" he whispered in her ear. "Make me forget it all with your fucking incredible body."

The chair tapped loudly against the stone floor as she cried out. "I love you Tony." In the misery that surrounded them, the intensity of their simultaneous orgasm was an oasis in a desert of pain.

Afterwards, he was solemn. "I'm glad we've made the decision.

We couldn't go on like this sweetheart, we need to come clean. "We're not exactly kids Caoimhe. I need to grow a set and just tell her. You need to walk away from Kenny. Once we do that and it's all out, then we can just brass neck it out. My dad will be fine once he gets over the shock. He likes you Caoimhe, he'll accept us." Tony smiled and looked at her. "To be honest, I think he had a thing about you before he was ill. He's had a few women since Mum died, but they never last long. I suppose you and the kids could move in with me and him just now?"

"No, it wouldn't be fair on the kids with him having been ill. He's a grumpy git at the best of times. Besides Tony, it would really put a knife into Claire, wouldn't it? We should just wait and get together later, after the dust dies down. It won't lessen the hurt for Claire, but it would allow her to save face."

Tony sighed. "I just never wanted to hurt Claire, and this is not just about me and you. But you're right, I'm going to end up hurting her more now and I'm always going to have to have a connection now because of the baby. You know what babe? I actually wish I could love her. Does that make sense?"

Caoimhe nodded, knowing there was nothing left to say.

Tony leaned back, still holding Caoimhe on his lap and grabbed his cigarettes from the table. He lit two and handed one to her. "A hundred years from now Caoimhe, who is going to care? What have you got on tomorrow?"

"I have a party meeting."

"You're really into this politics thing, aren't you?"

"Yes, and it's important Tony. The Labour Party is the best way forward for people like me. I'm secretary of the local branch. Someday I'm going to be your M.P. Tony, so I need to have no scandal."

"You'll be a great member of parliament Caoimhe, you're so intelligent and you really care about people. But, your real strength lies in that great big gob of yours, afraid of nothing, except leaving your fucking man. Yeah, I can see you as a Member of Parliament."

"Someday I will do it, I swear." She laughed for the first time and kissed him.

"What leave your man?"

"No, be an MP. I might even go further than MP. As you just alluded to, I am a rent-a-gob, but I do know what I'm talking about."

"Oh, I could be the prime minister's husband could I? The next Dennis Thatcher."

"You would need to marry me Tony, to be that."

"You think I'm not going to?"

"Don't know? I would have to be divorced, wouldn't I? We couldn't get married in church because I would be divorced. With our backgrounds, would you really feel married if you did it in the register office?" She looked him in the eye and smiled. "Tony, you might be making a big mistake wanting to go the whole way with me? I'm wayward, stubborn, ambitious and generally nuts."

"I love you, crazy woman, but I'll never try to possess you. I love that you are your own woman. I don't care whether you marry me or not. You could be the first prime minister to live in sin. We could set precedence and get rid of the stigma of being in a loving relationship and not married. It's this small-town mentality Caoimhe, and the bloody Church's antiquated hold on us all." He kissed her, and looked her in the eye. "But we're getting married Caoimhe, just to show the world we can. Where we do it doesn't matter. I'll tell Claire tomorrow, but you need to tell Kenny. Hard as it is to drag myself away from you, it's getting late and you better get home babe. Come on I'll give you a lift."

CHAPTER

FIVE

"Hi Claire, how are you?"

"I'm getting bigger by the day Caoimhe. Was it like this when you were pregnant? All I seem to do is run to the toilet to pee. It's murder. Oh and the heartburn!"

Caoimhe felt awkward. As she tidied up the dining room, she avoided looking at Claire and kept working. She had come away from the bar to avoid seeing her; however, Claire had sought her out.

"Caoimhe, it's been ages. Hope you are going to come to my hen night? Make sure my man gives you the night off. It's a week on Friday, the week before the wedding. We're having it here."

Caoimhe tried to look normal but her heart was beating loudly in her chest and she was scared Claire would notice her discomfort. "Ciara told me, but I need to work Claire, Fliss is going to be away at a study weekend. But I'll be here, serving you all, because the groom can't."

"Can't do what?" Tony said, coming through from the bar. He was wearing a grey suit with a crisp white shirt underneath. She recognised the hand-painted silk tie as being her Christmas present to him. Caoimhe took a deep breath. He looked so good, she wanted to rip the shirt from his back and make love. She glanced up at him; she knew he felt the same. She could see the desire in his eyes, but there was sadness too.

Claire stood up. "Look at your tie Tony, is that the right kind for a meeting with the priest?" Caoimhe noticed he put his hand to the tie and touched it before glancing over at her. Claire appeared not to notice. "Fasten your top button." She opened her bag and handed him a pile of papers. "This is the Order of Service and the invites. Mum needs your guest list. I got the ones with the pink flowers on it." She put one on the table. "Have a look Caoimhe, let me know what you think? Oh, silly me, that's the one I have been using to practice my new signature!"

Caoimhe looked at the Order of Service, Claire Louise Carter was written several times on it. Tony looked over her head at Caoimhe; they made eye contact. His appearance showed he was tired and emotional. "Love you!" he mouthed. Caoimhe wondered if Claire noticed. She was inclined to think that she wasn't aware of anything other than the plans for the wedding. Caoimhe wanted to go over and hold him and tell him it would be okay. In that second, she realised how much she loved him, and she wanted to shout it out. Instead she heard herself say. "Are you coming back to lock up?"

Tony nodded. "Yes, we'll be a couple of hours. Claire has booked the church out at Dryburgh, where she was christened."

"Father Iain is marrying us though. Father Ralph was a bit stuffy because I'm so far on," Claire added, looking straight at Caoimhe. "I just love the Dryburgh chapel, it's so beautiful and romantic." She looked straight at Caoimhe as she spoke.

Caoimhe knew in that instant that Claire knew there was something between her and Tony; she played the game though and replied. Caoimhe knew Claire did not have a vindictive bone in her body, that's what made what she and Tony were about to do so awful. "It's nice there Claire. I was at a christening a few months ago. Bad road though, be careful folks." Caoimhe hoped she sounded normal; her heart was beating so fast, she was sure she sounded breathless. She couldn't look Claire in the eye.

After they left Caoimhe threw the Order of Service on the fire and watched it burn, then went through to the bar. Felicity was pulling a pint of lager for one of their regulars. "There's a live band on tonight, it'll be busy. Is he coming back in? Or is Phil helping out?"

Caoimhe sighed. "Phil and Ciara are away this week; Loch Lomond, Cameron House, I think. It's their anniversary."

"So, it's you and me until the blushing groom gets back."

"Seems so."

"Caoimhe, are you alright? You look upset!"

"Oh, minor row with Kenny."

"He's really good looking, your Kenny."

"Yeah, well, looks aren't everything, Felicity."

"What about Tony, Caoimhe? Don't you think that he is doable?"

"Tony?"

"Yes! He's really good looking, don't you fancy him?"

"No not really, but we're friends. I suppose I don't think of him like that."

"No? Not ever?"

"No Fliss, not ever."

"I'd do him in a heartbeat Caoimhe. Those eyes, gives me the shivers just thinking about him. I don't think I've ever seen anyone with more come to bed eyes! I've tried everything to get him to notice me, but he doesn't. I suppose he must love his fiancée. Claire is nice, isn't she? Really beautiful. Glamorous, like one of those models."

"Hmm, I was at school with her Fliss."

"Really? She speaks so nicely, I thought she would have gone to private school. Her family are loaded, aren't they?"

"Yes, her dad has money, but he is really down to earth. He wanted Claire to go to the local schools. Claire's mother is a real snob though, really snooty. She was fur coat and no knickers before she met Claire's dad, according to my gran. Because of my dad working for Lord Dalmarnock though, she didn't mind Claire being friends with Ciara. Our mum's the same. Ciara and Claire were in the same year, Samira and I were in the year below

68

them, but we all went around together." Caoimhe felt herself near to tears, "I need to pee."

"Okay, but be quick, it's getting busy!"

Caoimhe shut the staff toilet door and locked it. She sat on the toilet and wept. All she could think of was the lies she had told. She realised it was all falling down around her and people would be shocked. It was a small town, everyone knew everyone and everything about them. Having affairs of the heart and living together in sin were still things that happened in the city. They had been so careful, only Phil and her best friend Samira knew about her and Tony. Phil was her brother-in-law, but she knew he would never tell her sister he had known, even when it all came out. Ciara and Claire had been best friends since primary school and Ciara, would never understand what Caoimhe felt for Tony.

Caoimhe was not sure she understood herself why the chemistry with Tony was so strong. She knew however that it was bigger than either of them. She loved Tony. She knew if there was such a thing as a soulmate he was it, but she felt an enormous sense of guilt. She even felt guilty about Kenny. Caoimhe was sure if she had not gotten pregnant when she did, she would not still have been with Kenny now. A fact she suspected that Kenny had always known. Which was possibly why he had made sure she did get pregnant.

Her life with Kenny had carried on. Caoimhe made meals, cleaned the house, studied when she could, usually late into the night. She loved her boys; she took them to scouts, karate and watched them play football. Caoimhe recognised they were growing fast; even sober, Kenny did not really take any interest in them.

Caoimhe's father Bert taught the boys to fish and to love the countryside. After having two daughters Dan and David became the sons he never had. Caoimhe knew they did not lack a positive male role model. The boys, despite her efforts, were developing an unhealthy opinion of Kenny. It was Kenny's own fault Caoimhe knew, but she also knew he was still their father. Both boys were tall, good looking, intelligent and despite Kenny's behaviour and drinking, well-adjusted and happy. They did well in school, especially David her younger son. Dan was sporty, and aged eight he was already running competitively.

Caoimhe, despite her misery, smiled when she thought of her boys. They were very similar to her and Ciara; David, with his father's dark hair and her pale freckled skin and Dan, with her red curls and blue eyes. She wondered what they would think about her and Tony. The boys already liked him. When they visited the hotel with her, Tony always made a fuss of them and had done before he and Caoimhe were an item. Tony liked children, unlike Kenny.

CHAPTER

SIX

Tony started the car and drove out in to the street. His mind was in turmoil. He felt that he did not know what to do for the best, but he knew he could not picture his life without Caoimhe in it. Claire, excited about her upcoming nuptials finally being within her grasp, continued to talk. "This car must go Tony. It's a single man's car an MR2, no room for a car seat." She happily read from the Order of Service using a small torch, chatting about the wedding and the bridesmaids. She did not appear to notice Tony's silence, taking it for agreement, he assumed. They turned off the main road towards Dryburgh village and suddenly Tony knew he could go no further. He drew off the road and into a large lay-by; Claire looked up.

"Tony, is there something wrong with the car?"

"Claire, I have to tell you something."

"What is it?" she said, smiling.

"Claire, I can't marry you."

She stared at him, her eyes wide, her mouth opened. "What! Don't be ridiculous Tony, of course we are getting married. It's just wedding nerves."

"Claire, please listen to me. I can't marry you because I don't love you. I'm sorry, but I can't do this. I'm never going to be able to love you and you deserve more. Claire I'm sorry, I have tried hard over the years, but it's just not there for me.

She looked at him. "I can't believe you are saying this. Is this some kind of joke?"

"I wish it was Claire. You needed to know, I've been trying to tell you for years. I just don't love you, think about it have I ever said it to you?"

"Who is it?"

"What!!"

"There's someone else Tony. I've known for months that there's someone, and I think I know who she is." Tears ran down Claire's face. Tony felt his eyes filling up as he looked at her, in the darkness of the car.

"It doesn't matter Claire, it doesn't change anything. You're beautiful and a lovely person, you'll meet someone else, Claire. Someone who'll love you the way you should be loved. I don't love you, I've known for years and that's why I kept putting off marrying you. I kept hoping it would come for us, I really did. I never wanted to hurt you, I swear. I've been a fucking cowardly selfish prick."

"Have you taken leave of your senses? I'm seven months pregnant with your child."

"I thought I could marry you Claire, I really did. I don't want to hurt you but I can't live a lie anymore."

Claire began to weep. Sobbing, she cried, "Is it Caoimhe? Are you having an affair with Caoimhe Black?"

"Claire, It's not about someone else! I wanted to love you, I don't want to feel like this either and I never wanted to hurt you. Claire it's not your fault, it's mine."

"No Tony, you're not doing this. I've waited long enough for you. We're going to that church and you are going to speak to the priest as we planned. If you don't, you'll never see this child."

"Claire I'm sorry, but I'm going to take you home. I can't do this. I'll support you and the baby, but I cannot do it. I can't live a lie. It's not fair to either of us or the baby." He started up the engine and turned out onto the main road.

"Is it Caoimhe you are sleeping with Tony, tell me? I know I could smell her perfume on you the other night. End it Tony, I'll forgive you."

"I can't do it Claire. I just can't marry you."

"I'll tell Kenny, Tony, I swear I will. He'll fucking murder her if he knows, and that will be it. You bastard Tony, she's my friend. You are shagging my friend." Claire's sobbing became louder, she struggled to speak her voice coming out in short gasps. Tony hated to see her so distressed but he knew he had to do this. Claire punched him on the side of the head. "And her, how could she stand there tonight and talk about the wedding? Fucking whore! She always was ... pregnant at fifteen! Now she's going after you. How fucking low can you go?"

Tears began to build up in his eyes again. "Claire please? This is nothing to do with Caoimhe! I can't do it, I just can't. I told you, I'll look after you and the baby, but there's no future for us as a couple." He started to drive down the road.

"Are you sleeping with *CAOIMHE? FUCKING TELL ME TONY. TONY TELL ME! YOU FUCKING OWE ME THAT MUCH.*" She began to hit and punch him. "*FUCKING TELL ME YOU BASTARD. ARE YOU SHAGGING HER?*"

"YES!" he cried. "Yes, Yes. I'm sorry, I really am. I'm in love with her Claire. I tried, we both tried not to be. She's going to tell Kenny. I'm going to be with her Claire." Tears ran down his face and he wiped them away with the back of his hand. "You have to believe me Claire. I never meant to hurt you. I wanted to love you Claire. I don't want to do this to you, but I don't love you."

"I fucking hate you," she screamed at him.

"I fucking hate me too Claire, and believe me, you can't hate me more than I hate myself, but I'm taking you home!" He put his foot down and the car sped up. Suddenly she grabbed the steering wheel as they turned a corner.

"I swear, I'll fucking kill us both Tony. Tony, I fucking hate you," she screamed in his ear. "I'll hate you forever!" were the last words he heard.

The lorry never saw them; it was too late by the time Tony

realised it was there. He heard the smash, then the crash, as the car was thrown in the air and rolled over and over then there was blackness. The little silver MR2 lay upside down in the ditch, the visible wheel still spinning; the lights shone down to the river below.

In the hotel, the night was long and when Tony did not return to the bar Caoimhe was mildly angry with him. She and Felicity coped, however, with the deluge of customers and most people were good natured. Somehow, they managed to get to the end of the night. Some of the regulars helped with the glass collecting and washing. "No sign of Tony yet?" Felicity sighed as Caoimhe drew the bolt on the door. Caoimhe shook her head.

"You go, I'll hang on and wait for him. Kenny is at home with the boys anyway." Much later Caoimhe woke suddenly, her head resting on the big table in the back room. She'd tried to stay awake; however, she must have dozed off. She looked up it was five am and he still was not back. Caoimhe knew something was wrong. Frantic, she paced the floor, her stomach in knots, fear growing in her heart. This was not like Tony. He was reliable to a fault. He took his hotel duties seriously and had big plans for the development of the best hotel in town. Caoimhe also knew he would not have willingly let her down.

It was breakfast time when Lorraine Carter came to the door. Caoimhe gasped when she saw Tony's teenage sister. Sobbing, she told Caoimhe about the crash. Both Claire and Tony in critical condition, the baby girl delivered after the crash appeared to be okay, just small. Lorraine, unaware of the relationship between Caoimhe and Tony, asked if she could keep the hotel opened, organise staff cover. Caoimhe agreed; it was half term, she didn't have university. Besides it was the quickest way she could think of to get news of Tony. Caoimhe hugged Lorraine and agreed that she and Phil, when he came back from his weekend away, would work the hotel between them, at least until they knew what was likely to happen.

After Lorraine left, Caoimhe had sat weeping at the big table in the dining room. She knew that she had to compose herself and keep going. Caoimhe stood up and began to ring around the staff, knowing she needed arrange cover for the next few weeks. She called Kenny and explained why she had not come home. Shocked at the news and sober he had asked if there was anything he could do to help.

Felicity, also a student, agreed to come in and this allowed Caoimhe a few hours rest. Caoimhe made the breakfasts, served them, handed over to Fliss and then lay down in room nine, sobbing quietly so as not to be heard. Holding one of Tony's shirts so she could smell him, she was not sure whether the scent of him in the bed made things better, but she felt it brought her comfort.

The news spread around the town like wildfire. Over the next few days Caoimhe barely lived. She couldn't eat, and sleep was impossible. She and Phil agreed that he, as Tony's best friend, would bring her news. As Phil said, there was no point in alerting everyone to the situation between her and Tony. It was Phil who told Caoimhe, four days later, they had switched off Claire's life support machine. Phil who held her and let her cry into his chest. Tony was in a coma, only his father and sister were allowed to see him. Caoimhe tried hard not to let Ciara see how upset she was.

Caoimhe locked herself in room nine for a few hours, telling them she needed to sleep having just worked thirty-four hours in the hotel. Caoimhe had hidden the shirt from the cleaners. She pulled it out and held it close, smelling him on it. It brought her some comfort. She knew, however, she had to go home, face her husband and family.

Phil tapped on the room door. Caoimhe let him in and then sat down on the bed. "Are you okay?" he asked.

Caoimhe shook her head. "Oh Phil, this is all my fault isn't it?" Her brother-in-law sat down and took her in his arms.

"It was an accident Caoimhe, these things happen. Let's just hope and pray he comes out of it. We don't know what happened yet." He looked sadly at her. "We might never know." Phil sighed and tightened his arms around her. "The police told Hector Tony just swerved right across the road. He was just coming off that bad bend at Craigend farm. Maybe he was going too fast, you know what he's like driving." He paused and looked at her, his eyes sad and struggling with his own emotions. "Caoimhe they never went to see the priest either and were heading back into town."

Caoimhe stood up, tears running down her cheeks unchecked. "Phil, do you think he had told her? He said he was going to end it with Claire. Why would he head towards the church to do it? Surely he wouldn't have still gone to the rehearsal?"

"Caoimhe, I think he'd told her and they were arguing. From what the police are saying, there's no real explanation. Other than he made a mistake because he was distracted or was driving too fast."

"Phil, I asked him not to do it. I suggested he should marry her, but we were going to tell Kenny and Claire it was over and just sit it out. This is probably my fault. He would have told her a year ago, it was over, if I had not kept on about staying with Tony."

"Oh Caoimhe, you're your own worst enemy, do you know that? I've agreed with Hector I'll take over running of the hotel until we know a bit more. Hector's not fully back to health yet. Nigel can run my business for me and I've found a manager for the other pub. I can concentrate on The Deerhunter."

Caoimhe returned to university after half term; she had to, she needed to finish her degree. She knew Tony would understand. She knew she had to study and pass her final exams.

On the day of Claire's funeral Caoimhe worked serving the meal. She comforted the weeping relatives, listened to the story of the new baby, who Claire's mother had called Anjya, saying that this is the name her daughter and Tony had chosen. Caoimhe knew this was untrue, but said nothing. Tony had told her he hated the names Claire liked. She listened to the story of her being buried in her wedding dress with the ring she was going to wear on her finger. Caoimhe felt her heart would break.

The national press picked up the story, sensationalising it.

The bride who had died going to her wedding rehearsal, the poor motherless baby and the fiancé lying in a coma.

Caoimhe had gone to see him in the hospital after the funeral. Hector hoped that hearing some of his friends voices might rouse him from his coma. She was with Phil and Ciara so she couldn't touch him. She looked at him, lying in the bed so still, so pale, a jagged stitched wound snaked from above his right eyebrow into his hairline. She wanted to reach out and touch him, hold him, tell him to wake up. Instead she spoke to him about the hotel, told him to get back and let her get a break. She tried a few times over the next few days to see him, but each time either Hector or Lorraine were there.

Caoimhe felt as though her heart would break. The pain of knowing he was lying there so ill was almost physical. She wondered whether she should tell Hector the truth, but she was not sure how he would react. A week later she returned to the hospital on her own, waiting outside until she saw Hector and Lorraine leave before making her way up to the ward.

Caoimhe sat at his bed and held his hand, whispering her love for him. She watched the numbers on the machine monitoring him raise as she spoke and she knew on some level, he could hear her. He looked so pale and vulnerable lying in the bed. His face calm and serene, the stitches had been removed from his face and head, but the scar was red and angry looking. His plaster covered leg was raised on a pulley at the end of the bed.

"Hi Caoimhe!"

Caoimhe quickly let go Tony's hand and looked up. Debbie Kerr stood in the doorway in her nurse's uniform. They had been school friends; both played in the hockey team.

"He's doing well Caoimhe and healing. I forgot you worked for him. It's tragic, isn't it? He's so good looking and the nurses are all falling in love with him." Debbie smiled wryly. "I keep telling them, 'wait until he wakes up and you see his eyes. You could swim in them.' Are you okay Caoimhe? You're very pale! Are you and him close? I know Claire was Ciara's best friend."

Caoimhe nodded. "Yeah, Tony and I are good mates. We have a laugh working together. It's really awful about Claire. I don't know how he is going to be when he wakes up." She looked at Debbie. "He will wake up? Won't he?"

The other girl shrugged. "He should Caoimhe, but you just never can tell with these head injuries. He had a blood clot on his brain and they had to operate. It was touch and go for a few days. They won't know until he comes around, if there's any damage."

"You mean brain damage?" Caoimhe began to panic. "What could happen to him Debs?"

"He could just have a bit of memory loss, or at the other end of the scale he could come out with a different personality. I'm going off shift, do you fancy a coffee? We haven't met up for ages."

"I can't Debbie, I have to go and get the boys from school. We can catch up soon. Come around some night."

"How's Kenny?"

"Still breathing unfortunately!"

CHAPTER
SEVEN

June 1995

"Can you possibly do Saturday night?" Phil raised an eyebrow as Ciara spoke to her sister.

"No I bloody can't Ciara, I've got to study for my final exam. It's on Thursday, and I feel fucking awful. I've had that bug that's going around. You work here too Ciara, and Phil's mother is only too happy to look after Toria. You don't do anything else. Why is it me doing all the late shifts? It's been ten weeks now, I've done every Saturday late shift." She picked up a pile of ashtrays and stepped out from the bar. Caoimhe looked up and saw Hector Carter coming in through the door. She knew immediately from his face, it was good news. Unable to contain herself she moved over, still holding the tower of glass ashtrays. "Hector?"

"He wakened this morning Caoimhe. He's really confused. He doesn't remember anything of the accident. It is early days, but he recognised me. They think he'll sleep most of the time now. His other injuries are healing, but he's been in a coma. We just need to wait and see." Hector looked around. "Thank God for you three!" Hector said, nodding at Ciara, who was sitting at the bar with the rota in front of her. "The only reason the hotel has kept going is because of you. I'm feeling a lot better by the way. I'll be able to help out here again now Tony is recovering."

Caoimhe put the tower of ashtrays back on the bar and went to make coffee. Hector sat with them for their coffee break, chatting and making plans with them. When he finished, he thanked them again and then stood up to leave. Caoimhe and Ciara resumed the work they had been doing when he arrived. Phil walked over to the door with Hector and shook hands with him. "Phil, let's leave it a couple of days and I'll let you know when you can see him." They heard Ciara cry out and the loud smashing of glass on the stone floor ...

"Christ Phil, Caoimhe is on the ground," Hector gasped. Phil ran over to where his wife was holding her sister. She opened her eyes, her face deathly pale and looked up at them.

"Did you fall?" Phil asked.

"I don't know!" Caoimhe groaned. "I think I fainted."

Phil picked her up, carried her through to the residents lounge and laid her on the big sofa. "Caoimhe are you alright?" Ciara cried. "Fuck, you gave us a fright there."

"I fainted I think. I'm not sure why, but it's probably because of all the extra shifts, uni and the kids. I'm exhausted," she whispered. "I need to go to the toilet. I feel really sick too." Ciara put her arm around her sister and walked her through to the staff toilet.

The two sisters sat on the tiled toilet floor after Caoimhe had been sick and Ciara held her hair. "Well that's a first," Ciara joked. "Never done that when you're sober before have I? You need to stop eating at the hotel too Caoimhe. You're getting fat; I noticed when Phil carried you through to the lounge."

Caoimhe looked at her sister as the reality dawned on her. "Fuck Ciara, I haven't had a period in I don't know how many months." She put her hands to her breasts. "Shit, my boobs, they are spilling out of my bra and sore. I think I'm pregnant."

Ciara breathed in deeply and stared at her sister. "Fuck sake Kee, how did that happen?"

Caoimhe shook her head, her face pale. "The usual way I expect. I was fucking careful Ciara, I went to Dr McRae and he sent me to the birth control clinic at the Royal in Glasgow. They put in a coil and didn't put it on my records, so no one knew. I didn't want my name read out in the Mass."

"The coil?" her sister asked, making a face. "What was wrong with Kenny getting off at Paisley?"

Caoimhe looked at her sister and grimaced. "Well, the old withdrawal only works if the man withdrawing is sober enough to do it. He won't use condoms. After he told me what he did when he got me pregnant with Dan, I wouldn't trust him with them anyway."

Ciara shook her head. "Well I'd better nip around to Boots and get you a test. Trust you! I've been trying for three years and you do it with no problem. Mum will go ape-shit if you are Caoimhe. She and Dad are hoping you'll leave Kenny when you get your degree. Just shows how much they hate Kenny that they're willing to face the priest. I think Mum got really scared when Dad started talking about bumping Kenny off and burying him up on the moor."

"Well that's that then," Caoimhe said two hours later, as she stared at the pregnancy test. It was undeniable proof that there was indeed a baby on the way. Whose baby was it though? She struggled to think, she couldn't remember when she had last slept with Kenny, it had to have been months ago. She realised that the funny feeling in her tummy recently had been quickening which meant if she was following the same pattern as she had with her two boys then she was around four months pregnant. She couldn't believe, after having had two children, that she hadn't realised she was pregnant.

Caoimhe sat down on the floor of the toilet, her back against the wall. She looked at the cubicle; she and Tony had had sex in there once when he had followed her into the toilet. They had taken risks many times, too many times to even contemplate when she could have got pregnant. The feeling between them had been bigger than both of them. The longing for each other, meant that they sometimes just gave in to temptation. Although their relationship had been a very sexual one, they talked a lot too and enjoyed a lot of the same films and books. Tony said they were soul mates. Caoimhe wasn't sure; she had been mainly terrified that she would hurt him.

The way she felt about Tony was all new to Caoimhe. She loved people, her children, Ciara and her parents, but when she thought about Tony she got a feeling of longing in her gut. Ciara's voice snapped her out of her thoughts.

"Have an abortion sis. Don't tell him and just do it. It's a bag of fucking cells, not a baby. David's nearly eight. You don't want to start again, do you? If you go to Doctor McCrae, he's a Protestant, he'll get you sorted. The whole town knows what Kenny is like when he's drinking."

"He hasn't drunk for fourteen months Ciara. Not since I went back to him. He's been seeing a counsellor." Caoimhe sat down on the floor of the hotel toilet and put her head in her hands. "He got a fright that last time as well."

"He fucking kicked the shit out of you and tried to rape you, Caoimhe! It was lucky Samira looked after you. I can't believe you're contemplating having his baby after all that! What about all your studying, your career?" Ciara looked at her sister and seeing the determined look on her face sighed. "Oh, let's change the record Caoimhe, you won't be fucking listening anyway. I'm so glad Tony is out of the coma. I hope that he is not left with ... you know ... brain damage." She looked sadly at her sister. "I miss Claire so much."

"Have you seen the baby again?" Caoimhe asked her. Guilt overwhelmed her every time she thought of the motherless little girl, currently living with Claire's parents.

"Yes, she's beautiful. I went around to see her now she's home. She's so tiny. They're hoping it will help Tony to get over losing Claire."

Caoimhe took a deep breath and asked the question she had

wanted to ask for months. "Did you know Claire was pregnant, before she told Tony, Ciara?"

Ciara nodded slowly, then shrugged. "She did it deliberately to get him to marry her. Doesn't much matter now, does it? I think I was the only one who knew, she stopped taking the pill. I didn't think it was right, but she really loved him Caoimhe, and he kept stalling. I think he is a bit of a commitment phobic. Phil reckons he didn't love her enough to marry her, but they were together for years. Claire thought he was seeing someone else, that's the other reason she decided to get pregnant."

"Was he? Seeing someone else?" Caoimhe asked holding her breath, hoping her sister would ask.

Ciara shrugged. "Phil said he didn't think so, and Tony would have told him, wouldn't he? What decent woman would get involved with Tony Carter? Everyone knew he and Claire were together. If he was, it was probably some fucking little tramp who drank in the bar. Did you know anything about him with anyone else?"

That was her cue, her chance to share her problem with her sister. She knew in her heart though that Ciara was still too upset about Claire to deal with it. So Caoimhe simply shook her head and changed the subject.

"Do they know how the accident happened yet sis?" Caoimhe said quickly, looking at the floor, not daring to look her sister in the eye.

Ciara shook her head. "No, the cops who come in here say that Tony swerved right across the road and into the path of the lorry. They'll be hoping that Tony can tell them what happened now he's come around. The car was really mangled, Phil went with Hector to see it. It's a miracle that he survived." Ciara took her sister's hand and pulled her off of the floor the toilet. "You better get to the doctor Caoimhe and then do some thinking. I need to go and do my shopping."

When Caoimhe walked back through to the bar Phil was alone, filling up the gantry. She could see his face, dark as thunder, in the mirror. He glared at her and turned around. "I can't believe you Caoimhe! You're fucking bairned? He's been in a coma probably because of you and you let Kenny get you pregnant? That's going to help Tony recover. Are there no fucking limits for you, you selfish fucking cow? That guy loves you. He was willing to put up with your fucking selfish fucking ways because he loved you! Claire most likely fucking died because of you and you were getting fucking pregnant!" Caoimhe had never seen her brother-in-law so angry.

"Phil I ... I need to explain!" she whispered.

"Did Kenny rape you?"

"No!"

"Caoimhe, the truth is written all over your fucking face. Fucking bitch, you let him end it with Claire! Put us all through this and then you get fucking pregnant! Don't even think you can ask him to forgive you for this. Stay out of his fucking life Caoimhe! Or I swear, I'll tell the whole town what you are! You make me sick! You and Kenny Black, you deserve each other." he hissed, as Ciara came back through the door from the street, carrying shopping bags.

CHAPTER

EIGHT

"Pregnant?" Kenny Black looked at his wife. "How the fuck can you be bairned? You barely look at me these days Caoimhe and I can't remember when I last pumped you. How far on are you?"

Caoimhe looked at him. "The scan reckons I'm four and a half months."

"It's not mine Caoimhe! I know it's not!" Kenny looked sadly at his wife, "and so do you!"

Caoimhe gasped and began to protest.

Kenny put his hand on her arm and shook his head sadly. "Don't lie to me Caoimhe, I need you to tell me the truth. We haven't had sex often enough in the last year to make a baby. You've been with someone else haven't you? There are weeks, maybe months, between us having sex."

"Kenny! It only takes once." She shook her head sadly, suddenly she felt too weary to lie. "You're right, I actually don't know if it's yours or not."

"It's not mine, much as I wish it was. Between your course, extra shifts at the hotel and my work, it has been a while since we did it Caoimhe."

Caoimhe looked at Kenny; she couldn't believe he was as calm. Tears pricked at the corner of her eyes and her heart was beating much too fast in her chest. She shook her head. "I'm so sorry Kenny. I don't know what to say now."

"Caoimhe, I don't know what happened, but you're my wife, and I love you. I know I've not been the best husband but I want you back. What's another kid Caoimhe, it's just another tattie in the pot, isn't it? Who was it? Caoimhe? Who was it? I'm trying to be reasonable, but I need to know!"

Caoimhe began to panic. She had been about to tell him the truth and then she stopped. She wasn't sure why. "It was someone at the hotel, a guest, he was here for a stag weekend from Ireland," she heard herself say. "I got drunk after work and arguing with you and it was a one-night thing."

"Was he better than me?"

"I don't know! I was pissed! It wasn't something I'd ever done before or since, but it just happened."

"We'll bring this baby up as mine Caoimhe. It'll have my name and we'll never speak about this again. You need to leave the hotel though. I don't want you working there. We don't need the money now that I have the business up and running. You've finished your degree too. Have the baby and then look for work. I've been offered a big oil company contract in Aberdeen. I wasn't going to accept, but if I do, it would mean that we can move away and make a new start. The boys are young enough to adapt. I've been a prick Caoimhe. Now that I'm sober, I can see that. Let's try again?"

"Kenny, I don't know? I need to think about this. I probably should try to find the father and tell him."

"Caoimhe, if it was a one-night thing surely you don't want to let this guy know? Or do you want me to tell people about it? That will do your career a lot of good, especially your political aspirations. Who wants a whore as their MP?

The hospital ward was quiet. It was mid-morning; Caoimhe had been for a scan. She had to see him, it was her last hope. Nearly five months had passed since the accident. Caoimhe hadn't been able to visit Tony. He'd not wanted to see anyone apparently, other than Lorraine, his father and Phil. Caoimhe missed Tony, she felt as though her arm had been ripped off. Phil was still not speaking to her but Caoimhe had been keeping updated on Tony's progress through Ciara and Samira. He'd apparently come out of the coma with months missing. Phil told Samira he'd asked Tony about Caoimhe, but Tony did not appear to know what he was talking about. Caoimhe had wondered if it suited Phil not to remind Tony, realising that he would have a great deal of explaining to do to his wife. Caoimhe knew Phil had never been comfortable with the relationship and suspected it was more loyalty to Tony than her or Ciara that had bought his silence.

Caoimhe looked around the door of the room. He was sitting up in a chair. His leg was out of plaster now, but a set of crutches sat beside the bed. Tony raised his hand in greeting. "Hi, Caoimhe. See, I knew that I'd get you into my bedroom one of these days. I was wondering when you would say 'Fuck it, I'm going to see him even if he doesn't want visitors.' I've missed you Mrs Black."

"How are you?" she asked. She tried to sound casual; she wanted to touch him, wanted to hold him and tell him about the baby.

He sighed. "I was in traction for four months Caoimhe and in quite a dark place mentally, but I'm getting there. I should be able to go home soon."

She sat down. He was pale; he had a large jagged scar on his forehead and a smaller one under his right eye. She again resisted the urge to reach out and touch him. He looked at her, smiling. She realised immediately he looked at her that he didn't remember they'd been in a relationship. Her jacket opened as she moved. He stared at her.

"Caoimhe, fuck sake! Are you bairned?" he said, looking at her swollen stomach."

She nodded.

"Well, so much for you going to finish your degree and leave Kenny, Caoimhe. You fucking deserve all you get. He's a prick."

"Tony!"

"Caoimhe just fucking go, I don't have the energy for this. We were good friends you and me. Fuck, I even thought at one point before that you and I well ... I was about to get married though wasn't I. Now I have to bring up a baby." He looked at her sadly. "So, do you. Caoimhe, I'm sorry." His gaze softened, "It's none of my business I know. I've all these fucking strange thoughts going through my head just now. Caoimhe I don't know what's real and what I've dreamt."

He looked at her again and shook his head. "I've months missing. How the fuck did I get to the stage where I was about to get married? There's a little girl too. I can't remember Claire being pregnant. The last thing I remember clearly was Johnny Weir's wedding. You and I getting pished, jumping about on that bouncy castle. It feels like it was yesterday."

"Tony, that was nearly eighteen months ago!" She remembered because that had been when she first realised she was attracted to him, he had tried to kiss her that night. The night of the beating from Kenny, which had started their affair had been a few weeks later.

"Look Caoimhe, please go. I don't want to be rude but I can't think straight." He lay back on his pillow and turned his face to the wall. She stood up and walked away, tears blinding her but feeling she needed to keep her dignity intact. She went home, told Kenny that she would go to Aberdeen with him.

Baby Daimhim was born in Aberdeen Maternity Hospital on a cold November night; born on the stroke of midnight. Caoimhe realised that her daughter shared a birthday with Hector Carter. The baby was 7lb 3oz and perfect, with wispy red curls and Tony's eyes. Caoimhe had followed the tradition of Gaelic names in the family as set by her Irish great grandmother. She chose carefully, Daimhim pronounced 'Dawveen' was an old Gaelic name. Kenny was not there when Caoimhe's daughter came into the world. Caoimhe had gone into labour suddenly, two weeks early and Kenny had sent her to hospital in an ambulance, saying that he would need to get a baby sitter to collect the boys from school. He never appeared. Caoimhe struggled through a twelve-hour labour with only the midwife holding her hand. She looked at the beautiful baby girl lying in her arms in the delivery room and saw Tony's eyes looking back at her.

Caoimhe had wept all night and wanted to call Tony, tell him; her pride would not let her. Instead she called Samira and wept over the phone. Samira talked her out of calling him, pointing out that to tell Tony about the baby would cause more problems for them both at the moment. Instead, Samira drove the six hours to be with Caoimhe. Kenny did not visit her in hospital and paid no attention when Caoimhe brought her daughter home. Her mother and Ciara came to help but didn't think there was anything untoward, as he paid very little attention to the boys either these days.

Initially Kenny's business did well. Caoimhe found a childminder and after-school clubs for her boys, took up a part-time social work post and got on with her life. She became heavily involved in local politics. Kenny, however, could not remain alcohol free for any length of time and although his business thrived and grew, he was not capable of working a lot of the time. Caoimhe managed to keep it going and eventually found a good manager and kept an eye on it herself when Kenny was drinking.

Daimhim grew into a beautiful child with Caoimhe's flaming red curls and pale skin. To the ordinary observer, she was like a miniature version of her mother. Caoimhe, however, could see the resemblance to Tony as she grew up. If anyone noticed the fact that she had brown eyes when both her parents had blue eyes, they never commented. Her relationship with Kenny continued for a time and then just fizzled out. They had a row on Daimhim's fifth birthday when he tried to make love to her and couldn't manage it. He slapped her, she walked away. They never slept together again. The threat of domestic violence was still there but Caoimhe never fought back. Most of the time Kenny drunk himself into a stupor, incapable of doing much.

Kenny continued in the pattern of binge drinking for a few weeks and then months of sobriety. He never bothered much with his wife or children, sober or drunk. Caoimhe kept herself busy with her children, politics and social work, at times, running Kenny's business when he was incapable or in rehab. Eventually they got a good offer for the firm and sold up. This coincided with her youngest son David going to university in England and Caoimhe being asked if she would consider standing for election as an MP back in their home region. Being a local girl and in a safe labour seat, she romped home with a good majority and the family initially moved back to their home town. She took ten-year-old Daimhim to London with her and got her settled in a good school there, coming back to Scotland when she needed to. With Samira as her private secretary, and a part-time nanny, Caoimhe juggled the duties of a Member of Parliament with parenting.

Kenny remained in Scotland; they stayed married and from time to time lived as a family for appearances sake. There was no real reason for this decision, Caoimhe just did not see the point in upsetting everyone with divorce. Neither of them spoke about resuming a physical relationship. She knew that he did still manage to have sex with other women and it didn't bother her. She had the occasional dalliance herself, but they never lived up to the comparison with Tony Carter she always made.

The days turned to weeks, the months into years and Daimhim grew up. Dan initially studied politics but then decided against a career in politics and completed a graduate programme in social work. He married and he and his wife Elaine gave his parents three grandchildren in four years. He and Elaine were happy; his experience of life with his own parents had taught him what he wanted. David, studied at Oxford and graduated with a first-class masters in journalism. Initially he worked for a local and then national newspaper, before taking a job in the government press office.

Daimhim grew up in to a beautiful gregarious young woman,

who was even more outspoken and outgoing than her mother. Like her eldest brother, she decided to study political science, but she had no intention of becoming a social worker. Daimhim had her mind set, she would follow her mother into politics at a senior level. Headstrong and even more determined than Caoimhe, Daimhim Black was thought of within the labour party as being on course to be the youngest cabinet minister ever. Ed Wilson, the labour party leader and Linda his wife, having no children from their relationship had become adoptive grandparents to her and thought of her as their own. Daimhim loved Ed and Linda, and they loved her. Ed especially could deny her nothing.

Caoimhe's outspoken nature and quick wit made her a favourite in the party. When Edward Wilson had come to power as labour prime minister, the beautiful, gregarious, patriotic, Caoimhe Black had been the natural choice as secretary of state for Scotland. Ed loved Caoimhe in a fatherly way, but he was not blind to her potential. He also trusted her and knew that she was loyal to him. Caoimhe and Ed's wife Linda, had struck up a close friendship. She, Samira and of course Daimhim, became part of the Wilson's inner circle. Caoimhe's popularity with the public and with the party grew. She was strongly tipped to be a leading contender for another major position in the new cabinet after the forthcoming election.

When Edward Wilson had announced that the general election would be September 2015 there had been a lot of speculation as to why. He had however decided that he wanted to do it earlier and Ed always got what he wanted.

CHAPTER
NINE

19th September 2015

"Congratulations, Mum. And with a thirty percent increase in your majority! Well done you," David said, grinning at Caoimhe.

"Where's your father?" Caoimhe asked, looking anxiously around her.

"It's okay Mum, he's sober, he promised me he'd play fair, he's stuck to it. He's attending his AA and behaving. We'll wheel him out for the obligatory family photograph later." Samira walked over, she wrapped her arms around Caoimhe. "I'm so pleased for you, not that I had any doubt that you would do it with a big majority. You've been the most popular politician in Westminster for the last four years. You can't do any wrong here either, it would seem."

Dan rushed in and kissed her cheek, smiling broadly. "Well done you, sorry I'm late. I've a surprise for you! Look who I found outside Mum?" Caoimhe smiled as she saw her daughter come out from behind Dan. "Daimhim you made it up? Darling, I'm so pleased you're here. Ravi, you too? It's great to see you. I thought you were off yesterday?"

Ravi smiled and hugged Caoimhe. "Tomorrow, Aunt

Caoimhe! I just wanted to make sure you were re-elected first then I could leave knowing that the country is in safe hands." Ravi Samira's brother, was the same age as Dan. He and Dan had been best friends since nursery school. Samira and Ravi's parents were both dead. Their mother had died in childbirth and their father, having never got over the death of his wife, died after a heart attack when Ravi was seven. Samira shared all Caoimhe's political views and the two women had been at school, then university, together. Samira at seventeen had become mother and then at twenty-three, a single parent to her brother. She had looked to Caoimhe to help her in the early years. The friendship between them had continued to strengthen and the three boys had been close since childhood. David and Ravi had shared a flat whilst at university in Oxford.

"I can't believe that you're going off to Pakistan. Why now? Daimhim asked."

Ravi smiled. "I just want to do some good Daimhim. My law degree and experience should mean I can get involved with some interesting stuff. I've been keeping well for the last couple of years so I need a new challenge. What about you gorgeous, did you enjoy your travels?" Caoimhe listening, smiled; she realised Ravi was attracted to Daimhim who appeared oblivious to it. Ravi had spent so much time with them whilst growing up that he was part of the family. Caoimhe's parents regarded him as their fifth grandchild.

Daimhim kissed his cheek. "I'll tell you about it later. First, tell me, why Pakistan? Why now Ravi? I thought you weren't interested in travelling?"

"Oh, I wasn't really, but it's time now for me to knuckle down and do something other than shuffle papers about an office. I need something I can get my teeth into. I also want to know more about my culture Daimhim. After growing up in Scotland and only knowing my mother's white Scottish family and not my dad's side, I really want to explore that part of me. If I can do that and work in human rights, which is always what I intended to do then it's got to be a good thing. What about you, I don't suppose Pakistan will be on your travel list?

Daimhim smiled. "I'm scaling down the travel for a while now. I've been most places. I loved India though, so I'm thinking that Pakistan would be similar. Maybe I'll come out and see you next holidays. For now though you know I have got a place at Glasgow to study political science and social policy Ravi? I matriculate next week, so that's it for a while!" Daimhim smiled and glanced over at Caoimhe. "I'm going to be just like my mother if I can."

Caoimhe's phone rang. "It's the PM!" Samira hissed, nudging David, seeing Edward Wilson's name on screen.

Caoimhe moved off into the corner. David watched her with a curious look on his face. His mother's face gave nothing away as she spoke. He saw her pull over a chair and sit down, he realised she looked tired.

"It's a big one!" he whispered to Samira. "It's got to be either depute or chancellor. She only got re-elected an hour ago. Usually it would be a couple of days; it was when they offered her Scottish secretary."

"Ed, how are you"?

"I'm good Caoimhe thanks, congratulations on your victory. I'm glad you got your result as quickly."

"Yes, I'm glad too and with an even better majority. You're through too, I take it?"

"I'm fine Caoimhe, much the same as you, increase of ten percent, not as much as you, but still good." Ed paused and took a deep breath. "Caoimhe. It's no secret I want you at my side this time. I would like you to be depute, but I'm going to give you the choice of depute or chancellor."

"Oh Ed, I could be the first female chancellor. That is tempting. Who do you have in mind for it if I accept depute?"

"Well if you accept chancellor, I'll make Alex depute. I know you and him haven't got on as well as I would like you to, but you could work well together and be a good team if you gave him a chance Caoimhe. You're the more experienced, I'm not sure he would be right for chancellor if you're depute. I'd rather you were depute but I realise chancellor would be more of a challenge for you. Alex's balls are in your court! You could do either. Hell, you could do my job too!"

Caoimhe laughed. "Maybe one day Ed, but I'll never be a threat to you."

Ed Wilson smiled to himself. "I know Caoimhe. There are not many senior politicians who could say that and have me know, without a doubt, they're genuine. Well, can you decide now? Do you want a few days to think it over?"

"No Ed, I'm egotistical enough to want to go down in the history books. You've got yourself the first female chancellor."

"Good girl, don't tell anyone outside your office yet, I'll announce it as soon as all the results are in. Will you be back in London tomorrow?"

"Yes, I have a Violence Against Women strategy meeting tomorrow afternoon. So, I'll be leaving tonight. Harry has gone to bed so he can drive me back down south through the night. I'll sleep in the car." When Caoimhe returned, she looked thoughtful. Kenny had joined the group; he smiled at her, putting on what he called his politician's wife look.

"Well?" David mouthed.

"Chancellor!" she whispered to him. "Don't say anything yet though. With Graham retiring this time, there is a gap. Ed offered me the choice between that or depute leader."

"Oh Mum, that's fantastic. Who's depute?"

Caoimhe wrinkled her nose. "Alex Stanley. We have to get back in, though. It will be shadow cabinet otherwise."

"It's looking good Mum, there's a major swing just like the polls predicted." Samira, Ravi and Dan were watching a monitor.

"Mum, it's going to be a landslide by the look of it," Dan said, smiling. "People are happy with the progress that's been made in the last four years."

Kenny appeared at his wife's side. "Caoimhe, the Scottish Television crew want to interview you. They're talking to Daimhim."

Caoimhe looked at her daughter; she was furious with Daimhim, and Daimhim knew it. She smiled slyly as the presenter walked away from her, towards Caoimhe. Caoimhe had worked hard to keep her children out of the limelight, especially Daimhim, and had kept a court order in place until she turned eighteen. Caoimhe did not want her daughter's face to be known, to ensure she was safe and could move around unnoticed. Caoimhe knew Daimhim was deliberately thumbing her nose at her.

Samira looked at Caoimhe and sighed, "she's young and ambitious Kee, just like you were once. Give her some slack, don't have a go at her here. Come on they're waiting to talk to you. With a bit of luck, they'll edit Veenie out of it."

***

Tony Carter sat, glass of malt whisky in his hand, watching the election results. He wasn't particularly interested in politics, but he did follow Caoimhe's career. He had not spoken to her since the night of the wedding, but he had thought about her almost constantly. He smiled as the news anchor began to speak to Caoimhe, and he noticed she was wearing the top and skirt she had worn to the wedding. The memory of removing them came in to his mind. Tony laughed when he realised he had an erection. He looked at the people standing around her; Kenny looking sober and two young men who he knew, from the wedding, were her sons. The camera zoomed in on Samira and a young male who he recognised as Ravi, Samira's brother. Standing next to him was a young female with the same titian hair as Caoimhe.

Tony realised instantly that this young beautiful woman was Caoimhe's daughter. The presenter put a microphone in front of her. He sat bolt upright when she spoke; he could see and hear his eldest daughter Anjya. "Fucking hell!" he gasped, as realisation hit him between the eyes. He gulped down the remainder of the whisky, stood up and poured another drink with shaking hands.

He didn't know what to think. He needed to speak to her, see her. If Amy had not been asleep upstairs, he would have gotten in his car and confronted her there and then. He looked at the clock on the wall; it was four in the morning. He couldn't call a babysitter now. Tony rewound the sequence several times; he could not believe Caoimhe had not told him.

After a sleepless night, Tony finally managed to get mobile numbers from a friend and after a few attempts trying to speak to Caoimhe, he called Samira. "Sami, it's Tony Carter. Can you arrange for me to speak to Caoimhe, there's something I need to discuss with her?"

"She's gone back to London Tony, driving through the night. She has an important meeting this afternoon." Samira said, hesitating, "can I help?"

"Sami, it's urgent. I need to see her, speak to her as soon as possible!"

"Tony I'm afraid it won't be possible for a couple of weeks. Maybe even a month. She's just so busy Tony, tell you what. She is up in Scotland on the fifteenth of October. She has an engagement to open the new hospital on Arran. She'll be at her parents for their golden wedding that weekend. You know it's in The Deerhunter? Why don't I arrange something then?"

"Samira, that's weeks away."

"Tony, she's really busy! I promise I'll try to get her to speak to you, but I'll need time to arrange it. Tony ... she might not want to see you."

"Sami, she'll see me. What's her daughter's name by the way?" There was a silence; he heard Samira take a deep breath and then exhale.

"Samira, what's she called?"

"Daimhim!"

"Beautiful name, she stuck with the Gaelic then, family tradition? Dawveen? How do you spell it?"

"D-A-I-M-H-I-M. Tony please, leave this alone. No good can come from opening old wounds." Tony could hear the panic in

Samira's voice, "let sleeping dogs lie, please Tony?"

"No chance Sami, I want to speak to her ... you know why, don't you?"

Samira took a deep breath before she spoke, "I can hazard a guess! Look this line may not be secure, I'll meet you in town tomorrow. I'm in Scotland anyway. You know where her constituency office is? Is two-thirty okay for you?"

Samira opened the door of the town centre office and let Tony enter. She had sent the staff away early; most of them were hungover from the night before when Caoimhe had organised a party to celebrate her victory. Tony kissed her cheek then sat down.

"You look shattered Tony!"

"I haven't slept. Samira, please? I need to speak to her, and I want to see her to do it. I promise Samira, I won't do anything to embarrass her, no matter what happens. I would imagine she gets enough of a red neck with Kenny, but I need to see her. That girl is my daughter, and one of you should have told me. Does Phil know?"

Samira sighed and shook her head, remembering sharing the pain with Caoimhe when she discovered she was pregnant and when Daimhim was born. "Tony, I think I'm the only one who actually knows Daimhim is yours. How did you find out?"

"I saw her being interviewed after the election. She looks like Caoimhe, but when she speaks on camera, she sounds like Anjya. Why didn't you tell me Samira? Fuck, why didn't Caoimhe?"

Samira looked him in the eye and shook her head sadly. "What was Caoimhe supposed to do? You abandoned her. She had to make the best of it. Kenny offered her a way out and she took it. She had the baby to think about. She had been to hell and back, worrying about you and not being able to tell anyone. She plucked up the courage to come to you in the hospital, knowing it was obvious she was expecting, hoping you would ask her."

"I told her to fuck off instead," he said quietly. He closed his eyes and shook his head.

Samira nodded. "Please Tony, just let this go. It's been over twenty years! Daimhim will be twenty on the fifth of November."

"That's Hector's birthday!"

Samira nodded.

"Sami please, just arrange something, otherwise I'm going to come looking for her. As I said Sami, I won't embarrass her, but I'm not leaving this either." He stood up. "I Googled her name Sami. You do know what the English translation of Daimhim is, don't you?"

Samira sighed and nodded. "Little deer. It was the only clue, other than the fact she has your eyes. Kenny and Caoimhe both have blue eyes. Two blue eyed parents can't have a brown eyed child."

"Sami, I loved Caoimhe, you know I did. Please Sami, get her to see me? I'll wait until she comes up. After all, I've waited twenty years. Are you going back to London tonight?"

Samira sighed and nodded.

"Well, please make sure you tell her."

It was the following evening before Samira could talk privately to Caoimhe. Her new office had been announced and Caoimhe's day had been taken up with interviews and meetings.

"He said what?" The panic showed on Caoimhe's face. Samira knew this was never a good thing with her friend. Caoimhe, when in panic mode, acted on impulse and often this backfired on her. "Fuck sake Sami, how could he know? Only you and I knew she was Tony's baby! God, he must have worked it out. What am I going to do? Samira, I never told you this because I wanted it to be a secret ... I wanted to forget ... " She looked at the floor then took a deep breath. "I had sex with him the day of the wedding."

"What? How did you manage that? Shit Kee, you need to be careful."

Caoimhe blushed to the roots of her red hair, her face scarlet. "I know Sami, it was a knee trembler really, standing up against a wall."

"What! Outside? You dirty bitch." Samira giggled, her dark brown eyes sparkling.

"No, in his apartment. I can't believe it happened. Don't look at me like that, it's not funny Sami. I lost control, reckon now I've opened a fucking can of worms."

"Caoimhe Black, you're unbelievable! You've called him every name under the sun for twenty years for what he did. You see him once and have sex with him? Fuck sake woman, are you mad? You fucking cried for two years over him."

"Sami, it was bizarre." Caoimhe groaned remembering. "He kissed me. I said no, I can't do this, and then about two minutes later … I'm naked with my legs around his waist, being fucked against a wall. It was over in a few minutes, but I felt as though I was going to stop breathing because of the intensity of the orgasm he gave me. I've been thinking about it ever since. He wants to see me, to talk about what happened. He said he'll not give me any hassle or cause me grief, but if he has worked out Daimhim's his child, then he might." Caoimhe looked at Samira, who could see the pain in her friend's eyes. "Sami, you of all people know what I went through after his accident. I just can't let myself feel all that again. I loved him so much. I thought I was going to die from the pain of missing him. Remember the state I was in? The feelings are all still there Sami, but we're both married now and how can I do anything in my position. Worst of all though, I've lied to Daimhim her whole life. I always wanted to tell her, but I knew if I did she would go looking for him. Sami, I'm terrified of how I feel about him. He … He … obviously still has feelings for me too. Was he very angry?"

Samira pursed her lips then shook her head. "No, I actually think he was still in shock. He was kind of quiet and sad. It must have been fucking awful when he worked it out. Maybe you should just go with the flow, give yourself time to think then go speak to him. What's the big issue really? Daimhim knows Kenny isn't her dad. Tony's a decent guy Caoimhe, he'll not do anything to damage you. Was it the way it always was with you and him?"

"Oh, Sami, it was just ... " Caoimhe rolled her eyes.

"Kee this is so not the right time for you to do this." Samira shook her head sadly. "Anyway, put that somewhere else, because Ed wants to see you. He asked if you could go over."

"Did he say why?"

"No, he just phoned and asked if I could get you to drop by. Hope Linda is alright."

"If it was Linda he would've told you Sami, you're as close to her as I am. Probably work."

***

Caoimhe took the glass from the prime minister and smiled. "Ed, thank you for this chance, I won't let you down."

"I know that Caoimhe!" Ed looked her in the eye and motioned for her to sit down. "Once again, we need to talk about Kenny. The papers are claiming that he was violent towards you! Caoimhe, the opposition are making statements about whether you should be leading domestic violence campaigns when you're a victim yourself! Why didn't you tell me he battered you? Why keep it a secret? Why fucking stay with him? You need to make me understand this!"

"Ed, it was years ago. You know he's an alcoholic? I've never hidden it. We used to really fight and there were a couple of times where it went too far and he hurt me. I've a plate in my cheek caused by him when I was seventeen. Well to be fair to him, we were arguing at the top of a flight of stairs, I pushed him, he pushed me back, and I fell down stairs. I was pregnant with David at the time. I hit my face on the banister and shattered my cheekbone. There'll be medical records. Most of the time it was superficial, but yes, he has been violent towards me. Not so much now, I make sure I'm never alone with him. Like all bullies he is a coward, he won't do it in front of anyone." She took a drink from her glass and sighed. "It was bad years ago, he was quite violent, but I probably was too, in those days."

"There's also a story doing the rounds about you doing the

dirty deed with Jimmy Barnwell." He looked kindly at Caoimhe. "I wouldn't blame you if you did Caoimhe, in fact I would encourage you to do it and lose the fucking parasite." He raised an eyebrow and shook his head. "Jimmy's a prick though Caoimhe. Be careful with you and your staff's mobiles, they may be being hacked. We think that's where the rumour came from."

"It was a one-night stand with Jimmy, Ed. It was just one of these things, too much vodka. He'll deny it of course. If he doesn't, I'll spoil any illusions the public have about him."

"Really! I thought he was a stud?"

"Oh no!" Caoimhe grimaced, "well not with me anyway."

Ed put an arm around her. "I'm speaking as your friend here Caoimhe, not your boss, but do I need to replace you heading up the DV thing?"

"No fucking way Ed. I want to tell people about what I went through with Kenny, but I can't. I can, however, make sure that the system in this country is set up to help people understand what domestic violence is and what it does to people. Strange as it might seem, I don't want to expose Kenny either. It's really complicated and he mostly plays the game."

"Caoimhe, you need to be careful now and Kenny needs to not embarrass you either. What about rehab if you won't divorce him?"

Caoimhe shook her head. "He has been mostly off the sauce. We're looking at one abroad whilst he's sober and motivated. There's a place in Italy where you go for a year, it's a kind of kibbutz set up and it has a high success rate with addiction. We kind of think that it would kill two birds with one stone the kids and I."

"Caoimhe, I don't get you and Kenny. He doesn't make you happy, you have no relationship. You don't sleep with him ... do you?"

Caoimhe shook her head, "no, not for a long time. Ed, it's complicated, I can't really explain!"

"We're elected officials Caoimhe and public morality will also come into it. I'll only be able to protect you so far if things go wrong. On a personal level, Linda and I just want you to be happy."

Caoimhe smiled. "My work makes me happy and my kids and grandkids."

Ed shook his head. "Caoimhe, you're a beautiful, intelligent woman, you deserve more. I'm not going to lecture you my friend, but if you need to talk, my door is always open. Now, what are you up to after the State Opening of Parliament? I'm having a reception. You and your family will be there?"

Caoimhe smiled, glad of the change of subject matter. "Dan and Daimhim can't get down, but David, my parents and Ciara will be here. In two weeks, I'm off to do some stuff in Scotland. I'm opening the new hospital on Arran. They asked me because of my local connection. I have my parents golden wedding that weekend anyway, so I discussed it with the First Minister and agreed that because it's NHS, I would do it."

"You do realise that you'll be spending less time in Scotland now?"

She nodded. "I'm up for it Ed, we Scots in Westminster must stick together. Anyway, how's Linda this week? I planned to go and see her tomorrow. She was sleeping when I went on Tuesday, then I had to rush off to Scotland."

Ed smiled. "She's doing well thanks Caoimhe. We're going to make the announcement this week. Thanks for all your visits to her. She really values your friendship, so do I Caoimhe. It's been hard, especially having to bring the election forward, in case she didn't make it to May, but we won with a bigger majority anyway. Hopefully once we announce it, folks will realise why I needed to do it."

Caoimhe touched his arm and looked at him sadly. "You know I'll be there for you both. Maybe once the public know Linda has a terminal illness, the rest of the country will be too. The treatment will buy you some more time?"

"Yeah maybe even till Easter, but we should at least make it through Christmas now.

"Oh Ed!"

"Hey, when the time comes you and Alex will be able to take over and hold the fort for me with no problem. I also know that with you, there will be no takeover bid. With Alex alone, well, I would not be so sure."

"No, he is probably as loyal to you as I am, I don't think you have any worries on that score. Anyway, I'm tired and need my bed. So, I'll catch you later."

***

Caoimhe walked into the hospital room. Linda Wilson was sitting up in bed reading a magazine. Caoimhe tried not to notice the drastic weight loss and the pale, drawn look on her friend's face. They hugged; Linda smiled at her. "I know what you're thinking Caoimhe. I now have the body I slimmed all those years to get. Don't you dare cry Caoimhe Black! You're supposed to be the woman with balls of steel. I won't have tears in this room. This has to be my happy place just now."

"How are you really, Linda?"

"Caoimhe, I'm fine. The pain's not so bad now that the operation sorted that and the chemo is finished. I should be able to go home in the next couple of days. I'll use the hospice for respite, once Eddie has made the announcement, and we can be honest about it all. Caoimhe, I'm a bit worried about you though, you look tired. Is Kenny behaving?"

Caoimhe nodded. "We're trying to pack him off to Italy, he's more optimistic about this place. It's only going to cost the flight over, which is good and it's a therapeutic community, like a Kibbutz."

"You should send him to a proper Kibbutz, right on the Israeli fucking border and use him as cannon fodder."

"Linda!" Caoimhe gasped, looking at her friend. "I could never wish him dead. He is the father of my children."

"Caoimhe you need to get him out of your life, he's a fucking parasite! You could be happy, with someone who really loves you."

104

"I'm going to divorce him Linda. I've made the decision and spoken to a lawyer. I just want to try to do it quietly."

"Just do it Caoimhe. I wish you and Eddie fancied each other, because I know you'd look after him after I'm gone."

"I'll look after him without a sexual relationship, you know I will." She gently kissed her friend's cheek. "Besides, after the op and the radiotherapy, you'll have loads of time."

"No I don't, it's running out and let's not waste precious time Caoimhe, pretending otherwise. I'm going to be lucky to see Christmas, never mind Easter." Linda took Caoimhe's hand and looked into her eyes. "I need you to promise me you'll make sure that my Eddie is alright afterwards. I need you to look after him. I always hoped that you and he would get together after I'm gone, but that won't happen will it?"

"Afraid not Linda, I love him in a fatherly sort of way, he's the same."

"Pity, he's a good lover Caoimhe, very attentive and well, just lovely," Linda giggled. "Really well hung too and knows how to use it to maximum effect." She looked at Caoimhe and smiled slyly. "Probably just like your hotel guy, from all those years ago." She tightened her grip on Caoimhe's hand. "You will make sure he's happy? I can't bear to think of him unhappy. When the time comes, introduce him to someone, he shouldn't be alone. You're the only person I trust to do this Caoimhe. If you don't, I'll come back and haunt you, I swear."

"Linda, you know I'll look after him and I promise you, when the time is right, I'll make sure he meets someone. I'll also make sure it's someone who will cherish him." Tears built up in her eyes. "I promise!" she whispered.

"Caoimhe, you and Samira are my closest friends. I trust you with my life and with my husband's." Linda let go Caoimhe's hand and smiled. "Right enough melancholy, you still haven't told me about the wedding. The pictures were great. I knew that suit would work. I noticed that you wore the skirt and top on election night."

"Yes, you have good taste Mrs Prime Minister. You were right, it was worth the money I paid."

"Okay Caoimhe. What happened at the wedding?"

"What?"

Linda raised an eyebrow and looked straight at Caoimhe. "I know you like the back of my hand Caoimhe Black! When I mentioned the wedding, you blushed and looked away. Remember I'm an expert on neurolinguistic programming. Something happened! You didn't sleep with Kenny did you? That would be suicidal."

Caoimhe shook her head and her cheeks flushed a deeper shade of red, remembering what had happened with Tony. "No chance, I'd prefer a vibrator. Kenny can't anyway."

"If he asked? Would you?"

"Would I fuck! Hell would need to freeze over first."

"Well, what then?"

"My … as you call him … hotel guy, Tony. I ran into him again and well … "

"You didn't?"

Caoimhe, still blushing furiously, nodded. "I did. It was a one-night stand, literally. Standing up against a wall Linda, but oh God, he made the earth move and my eyes water. Linda please, you can't tell Ed! I don't need the complication that him knowing would bring just now. I only told you about Tony and I all those years ago because I trust you."

Linda nodded. "I couldn't tell Eddie, he would just worry about you Caoimhe and from the look on your face he should. Are you going to see him again?"

Caoimhe shook her head; Linda noted the regret and sadness on her friend's face. "No, amazing as it was, I'm going to try not to open that particular can of worms Linda. Not just now anyway. I need to focus on my work, get bedded down, before I think about anything else. Now please, can we change the subject?"

Linda shrugged. "If we must, but Caoimhe, life is short, and I know you love this guy. You've never stopped loving him. It's

106

written all over your face, and it's also probably why you have never been able to be with anyone else. Caoimhe go for it, chemistry like that doesn't happen every day."

"It's just too complicated Linda. There's a lot at stake, and things I never told anyone about!"

Linda looked into her friend's eyes again. "Caoimhe this is something I always wondered about. The story about the one-night stand and you getting pregnant. It's not true? This Tony, he's Daimhim's father, isn't he?"

Caoimhe nodded. "I never told anyone Linda, I just wanted to believe it wasn't. I'm so scared now, because he's worked it out and I'm going to have to tell Veenie the truth. You know what she's like Linda, she's going to go nuts at me. Anyway, I'll sort it out. Can we change the subject?"

"You know Caoimhe, you can't keep changing the subject. You're going to have to deal with all of this before it bites you on the bum! My Ed will understand Caoimhe, he really will. He'll support you in this, give him a chance! As for Daimhim, don't use her as the excuse for not facing it. She'll be fine once she has a strop. Okay, I'll let it drop, but please Caoimhe, deal with this? Tell this Tony how you feel. You know you love him!" The two women spent an hour talking about Caoimhe's children and grandchildren, before Caoimhe called Harry to come and get her.

CHAPTER

TEN

"Fuck Samira, the sea is choppy today, hope this boat gets in. I love Arran normally, but I prefer using the helicopter, can't believe it broke down. It looks good though I suppose, me going the same way as the public.

Samira smiled. "Your sister is on Arran by the way. She rang to ask if you could have dinner. I said I thought that would be okay as the chopper should be fixed or replaced. She's staying at a new spa hotel Phil has shares in. She's arranged a table for dinner. It's a golf break with her ladies who lunch and their men apparently. She says you've to answer your bloody phone."

Caoimhe made a face then looked at her friend. "I knew she was looking for me. I thought it was about the party for Mum and Dad though, so I decided I would get this trip over with and then speak to her."

"You also need to speak to Tony Caoimhe, he's not going to wait forever."

"I know, I know, I'll do it this weekend, the party is in The Deerhunter. I'll try to grab ten minutes then."

"Caoimhe, you're not going to sort this mess in ten minutes."

"I know, but I agreed to have dinner with him after the election. I'll arrange that, stall for more time."

Samira looked at her. "Why?"

Caoimhe shrugged and raised her palms. "So I can work out what I'm going to fucking do."

"You know what Caoimhe, this is one instance where you should just go with your gut feelings. Tony and you, well you had something special. You never have got over him. This is a second bite of the cherry for you. Don't run away from it this time."

The day was a success. Caoimhe opened the new hospital then had lunch with the local dignitaries, smiled a lot and made conversation. She'd always found it easy to separate her work and personal life. The moment Caoimhe switched into politician mode, she could focus on her work. Caoimhe loved Arran and had spent a lot of time there when she was younger. The only time she and Tony had managed to get away on a break had been on the island. She remembered it with bittersweet emotion. They had spent a long weekend on the island, a few weeks before the accident and the end of their relationship. Samira had covered for her with a story about a visit to relatives in England. Samira had gone down south alone, whilst Caoimhe and Tony had spent four days on Arran.

Being back on Arran Caoimhe could not help thinking about that weekend. They'd arrived on separate ferries, her getting the later one. She'd run into an old school friend on the boat. Tony had picked her up from the ferry terminal in Brodick and taken her to the house he had borrowed from a friend for their stay. It had been an old converted church, on the quieter, east side of the island; they'd made love with the lights from the stained glass shining through onto them. Caoimhe had lovely memories of walking hand in hand along the beach, wrapped up against the cold wind, hill walking in the snow and making love in the open air, high up in the hills on a picnic blanket. It was a beautiful memory which, over the years, she had thought of many times. Caoimhe often wondered if Daimhim had been conceived that weekend.

As she faced the Scottish press after the opening of the hospital, Caoimhe fielded the questions about her political aspirations, given the news that Linda Wilson only had a few months to live. Choking back tears, she told the gathered national press representatives that she was devastated and would be there to help the prime minister personally and professionally, when and where he needed her. No one watching could fail to see that Caoimhe was genuinely upset about Linda Wilson's illness. Afterwards, she and Samira had driven around the island with Harry and she had stopped at the converted church where she had stayed with Tony. As they stood looking up at the stained glass windows, Samira smiled at her friend. "You have it bad, don't you?"

"Sami, I just don't know what to do! On one hand, I long to see him again, nothing has changed, he still makes me go weak at the knees and I'm dreaming about him. On the other-hand Sami, there is never a right time for Tony and me, is there? He's married now and I still have Kenny around my neck like a fucking millstone dragging me down. I asked him to divorce me and he said no. The lawyer Ed got me says that we can get it because of all the evidence of his behaviour and the fact we don't live together. I was kind of hoping for an annulment but that's unlikely to happen quickly. The lawyer reckons we could get a divorce in less than six months. Maybe then, I can start to think about me and Tony." Tears built up in Caoimhe's eyes and she sniffed loudly.

Samira rummaged in her pocket and handed Caoimhe a packet of tissues. "Tony still loves you Kee, you can see it in his eyes. He looked so sad when I spoke to him. I never got why you didn't just tell him, you knew he loved you. In fact, all of us felt at the time that he was the one with the stronger feelings. Phil and I used to talk about it a lot in the early days. He thought you would hurt Tony, I'm afraid I agreed."

"I don't know what it was at the time. I loved him Samira you know that. I didn't know how much, at the beginning, it was just the sexual feelings. I couldn't get enough of him. I was afraid I would hurt him too, that's why I held back initially. As time passed I realised how much I needed him."

"You know the state I was in when Claire died. I didn't know if I could be with him! Then when I found out I was pregnant, and he forgot about us, I think I took it as a sign that we were not meant to be together. It was the shock and the guilt about Claire's death and him having the baby. I don't know Samira, I just make personal decisions badly on impulse and then I regret it all. With Tony and me though, I think it was the Catholic thing. You know, the guilt? We both felt it. He could have found me if he had really wanted to Sami and he never did try."

"He actually did, but Phil and I stopped him. You had Daimhim when he remembered, it was New Year. We thought it was for the best and talked him out of it. He was okay at first when he came out of hospital, just sad and confused, as though he knew something special was missing. The problems came when he eventually remembered your relationship. He was angry, drinking a lot and was going to come and tell Kenny about you two. Oh fuck, Kee, I wish you had both just gone to fucking confession and got it over with. You should have been together."

Caoimhe smiled sadly and nodded. "I know! The thing is Sami, if I see him, I'll end up sleeping with him. I'm not sure what it is with me and men Samira! I'm a strong, independent woman, but when it comes to men I'm in a relationship with, I'm a walkover. I'm also a fucking cow to them." She sighed and put her arm around her friend, "come on, let's go and see my sister, before I have you crying along with me."

They walked arm in arm back to the car, where Harry sat behind the wheel. Caoimhe smiled through her tears as she got in the car. Harry looked at her in the rear-view mirror; his eyes met Samira's, she shook her head and rolled her eyes.

Caoimhe, wrapped up in her thoughts, failed to notice and sighed. "Fuck, I hope I don't have to eat with Ciara's friends, ladies who lunch give me the fucking dry-boak! That lot were never interested in me before I was a Member of Parliament. They were downright racist about you. Fuck, I hope Ciara has booked a table for just us."

Harry winked at her in the mirror and smiled. "Sami and I

have a pressing engagement to see to when you have dinner, just in case. The last time, that fucking old cougar Marta, the red haired woman with the younger husband, kept putting her hand on my crotch. Then that other fucking cow, the blonde one with the face like a melted wellie, she referred to Samira as 'the little brown dyke'. To be fair, Ciara was horrified and did tell her how racist and sexist she was though.

"That's the thing with folk like them, they don't get that they are privileged, the way they live. It's a bit like being a big fish in a small pond." Caoimhe shook her head, "they really don't live in the same world as us. They are mostly women with rich husbands. Or rich widows like Marta Reynolds, her husband died having sex with another woman, but he left her loaded."

Caoimhe looked around the new hotel. It was beautifully decorated and the dining room was spacious, with a wall of glass looking out over the sea towards the mainland; Caoimhe knew that on a summer day the view would be stunning. Today the trees were billowing over to the side, as the wind blew the rust-coloured autumn leaves around the grounds. White sand from the beach was swooshing around and hitting the glass wall. The mainland could not be seen, which told Ayrshire-born Caoimhe that a storm was closing in.

"Caoimhe, you look great. How long have you got?" Ciara asked, as Caoimhe was shown to the table. To Caoimhe's great relief, there was no sign of Ciara's friends and the table which was in a corner away from other diners was set for five. However, both Samira and Harry still pleaded work and disappeared. Caoimhe hugged her sister and kissed Phil on the cheek.

"I have a couple of hours. To be honest I would have booked a room if I'd known you were here and just stayed."

"Well if you would return your bloody calls you would have. Can't believe they let you run the country Caoimhe! What do you do when the president of America calls?" Ciara shook her head and nudged her sister as she spoke.

Caoimhe smiled. "He's a nice guy, but a wee bit of a letch

really, he has got it into his head I would be interested." She giggled. "He's not used to women not dropping their knickers at the sight of him, so I try to miss his calls. He calls me pretty woman! I heard Julia Roberts was most annoyed when she heard. He's like that with every female though. I get Samira to answer sometimes. He hasn't worked out she's gay yet."

"Hank Butterfield fancies you? Fuck sake Caoimhe, you should grab some of that! He's really good looking, and powerful men like him are usually great lovers," Ciara said, her eyes sparkling with mirth. "You could be the first lady!"

Phil looked at his wife. "What do you know about powerful men? You have only ever been with me, and you and Toria walk all over me!"

"I read the gossip magazines dear, and they are full of gossip about him. Bachelor American president! You could do a lot worse Caoimhe."

Caoimhe giggled. "He wants into my knickers, not my heart sis." She looked around her. "This hotel is amazing Phillip, so much light and space."

Phil smiled proudly. "I wasn't just involved in the building, I helped in the design of it. I worked with the architect, and we knew because of the setting, we could get the light into every bit of it, even in winter. The summer will be something else, you'll need to come back when you have time and see it then. The glass on the coast wall cost a fortune. It is reactalight which means it darkens itself when the sun shines on it, so you can always see out but the light still gets in. It's full this week Caoimhe, it's doing well. An exclusive boutique spa hotel was just what the island needed. Anyway, can I get you a drink before dinner?"

"Oh, yes, thank you, vodka please. I'm not hungry though, the meal at lunch time was heavy going. It was traditional Scottish fayre, so it was stodgy. I've kind of got out of the habit of eating at lunch time. I'll just have a snack if that's okay?" She looked at the menu. "Pate please," she said to the young waiter, "and any type of chocolate cake."

113

"Yeah well, that's a little light bite and not at all stodgy sis," Ciara laughed. "How do you manage to stay so slim eating stuff like that? It's just fat, fat, fat."

Caoimhe turned to her sister and grinned. "The alcohol soaks it all up. I'll have a couple of drinks. The chopper will take me straight into Westminster."

"You're going back to London? Thought you were going to stay up here for the rest of the week? You'd better be going to make the party at the weekend Caoimhe. Mum and Dad will be really disappointed if you don't."

"Chill out sis, I'll be there. I had planned to just stay in Scotland after today, but I have an important meeting the day after tomorrow. I'm driving back up with Samira and Harry Thursday night. Do you need me to do anything?"

"No sis, just be there please. You have missed so many family occasions over the years. What about Kenny?"

"He's off to Italy. Dan is with him to make sure he goes, but he'll be back for the party. Dan, I mean, not Kenny." She crossed her fingers. "Hope he stays there. It's for a year minimum, maybe he'll meet a nice woman and run off. I'm divorcing him folks. I should have done it a long time ago."

"Thank God Caoimhe! I don't even want to ask why now? I'm just so pleased you are doing it. Does he know?" Ciara looked relieved and Phil nodded.

"Not yet, I asked him but he refused, so I've started the ball rolling. I'll tell him once he is settled in rehab." She looked at her sister and brother-in-law. "To be honest, I should have done it years ago, but I just never got around to it. His behaviour recently though, has meant that it's just time cut loose." She made eye contact with Phil and knew immediately Tony had told him about the wedding night." Caoimhe blushed, as Phil raised an eyebrow and shook his head. Ciara, oblivious to the situation, continued to speak and Phil said nothing. They chatted about their respective children and Caoimhe spoke about her grandchildren, who she was looking forward to spending some time with whilst she was in Scotland. Caoimhe had just finished a piece of chocolate cheesecake when Samira slid into the seat beside her.

"How many of them have you had?" Sami said, smiling and pointing at the drink. "You look relaxed though, you've needed it Caoimhe. We will need to go soon Mrs."

Caoimhe smiled at her friend. "Just the one, Sami. It's good to chill though." Samira's phone rang. She moved away to answer it then left the dining room, returning a few minutes later. She looked worried.

"What's up?" Caoimhe asked.

"Caoimhe, I'm afraid the helicopter can't get off the mainland because of the weather. The storm has got up. I've just spoken to the manager and the hotel is full, he can only give us two singles."

"Well you and Harry take them then." Caoimhe giggled, nudged Phil and then looked over at her sister. "Ciara, Phil, hope you weren't hoping for a night of passion, I may need to bunk in with you two."

Ciara stood up and smoothed down her dress. "I need to go to the loo! Phil, please can you go and see if they can find her a bed for the night?"

"What? You don't want me in with you?" Caoimhe said, her eyes sparkling with mirth.

"No I don't. Phil and I have some heavy loving planned Caoimhe, and it doesn't involve voyeurism," her sister whispered, blushing as her husband grinned back. "I don't just play golf and lunch sis, there's Anne Summer's parties too. We can't all be high flying working ladies, some of us need to be the woman behind the men and do the fundraising."

Phil stood up and moved towards the door. "Wait a minute Sami, I'll see if I can do anything." He returned smiling. "One of the partners is going to give you his suite. You're the fucking chancellor of the exchequer after all. It looks good for our business." Ciara returned to the table and Phil raised his eyebrow and repeated, "the boss is going to give up his room Ciara." Caoimhe took in her sister's confused look and looked at Phil.

"Where will he sleep?" Ciara asked.

"Oh, there's staff quarters, might do him some good to slum it for once. It is only for one night after all." Phil tossed a key card at Caoimhe. "I'm not giving up my night of passion with my wife, not even for you Caoimhe. He's on his own anyway." She saw the look pass between her sister and her husband.

"I hope you have extra clothes Ciara? I'll need to borrow some."

Phil smiled. "She has enough to last her a week and we are only here for three days." He nudged his wife. "Just don't give her the French maid outfit, she won't need it!"

"Hey, I could do French maid. Not much point when there's no man and I don't do housework though. Hey sis, you didn't buy anything else from the Anne Summers parties did you? Some do-it-yourself stuff?" She nudged Phil, both of them laughing at her sister's scarlet face. Even as a child Caoimhe could make Ciara blush. They sat for another half hour talking. Caoimhe knew there was something that Ciara was desperate to tell her.

"Well, when you two are ready to stop being secretive you can let me know. I could really do with a bath to be honest. I'm going to take my drink and go up. Is the owner of the suite around? Can you ask him to come and see me so I can thank him properly? Give me an hour. I really want to soak in a bath if there's one."

"Oh, there's a bath." Phil stood up and inclined his head. "Come on, I'll take you up. It should be ready now, and he was getting his stuff out of it when I came back down."

Ciara moved away from the table. "I'll go and get you some clothes and a nightie from the gift shop."

"Don't worry about the nightie, I never wear them anyway." Phil raised an eyebrow and nudged his sister-in-law. "You want to educate your sister, Caoimhe. It's like going to bed with Nanook of the North sometimes."

Caoimhe giggled. "She was always the same. When we were young we shared a double bed and she used to wear socks and knickers, as well as her nightie and housecoat. It was like sleeping next to a fucking radiator some nights."

Phil laughed. "Aye then she starts kicking all the bedclothes off because she is too warm and you end up freezing while she lays starfish across the bed."

"I feel the cold!" Ciara laughed, blushing. "And what if there is a fire during the night?"

"Well the firemen won't get as much of a thrill rescuing you as they will with your sister, will they?" Phil gasped, nudging Caoimhe again.

Caoimhe was astounded when she followed Phil into the hotel room. She had stayed in a lot of nice suites, all over the world, but for a small Scottish island the room was exquisite. It was spacious with a four-poster bed and a sunken spa bath behind a screen in front of a large window wall, which looked out over the bay. Scented candles burned around the tub. The room was richly but subtly decorated in deep crimson and gold. She walked over to the bath and turned the gold-plated tap on.

"Fuck, this is beautiful Phil. It reminds me of somewhere else though … " Her heart jumped; it reminded her of Tony's suite in the River Doon Hotel. She realised Phil had probably been involved in the refurbishment of that too.

Phil smiled and put his arm around her shoulder. "The boss keeps it just for himself. He's a fucking twat, but he's impressed by the fact that you and I are related. Still, he is the major shareholder, so we kowtow to him."

Ciara re-appeared with some clothes. "Underwear too, although my bras won't fit you, your boobs are much bigger than mine."

"It's only for one night Ciara, I can manage with the bra I have on." Caoimhe smiled at the box of complimentary toiletries and the basket of confectionery on the dressing table. She lifted the vodka bottle from the dresser. "Grey goose! Nice touch Phil, thanks." A bottle of Cristal champagne peeped out of a silver ice bucket. She took a strawberry from a plate beside it and popped it in her mouth.

"Enjoy!" Phil said as he hugged her, kissed her cheek and left, pushing his wife in front of him.

Caoimhe took off her clothes and wrapped herself in the luxurious white towelling robe lying folded on the bed. She turned off the main lights and put a handful of scented bath salts into the bath which was now nearly full and then tied up her hair. Ignoring the champagne, she poured vodka into the glass and scooped up some ice from around the champagne, before pouring coke. Easing in to the tub, she pressed the button to start the jets. Caoimhe sat for a moment, enjoying the sensation. She began to play around with the controls. Pressing deep massage, the powerful jets pounded her back and she moved down, letting it hit her between her shoulder blades. This was where Shelagh, her massage therapist, told her she held all her own and the country's tension. "Oh, that's so good," she said out loud."

"I'm so glad!" a familiar voice said behind her. Caoimhe looked up; Tony Carter was standing looking down at her. The candlelight flickered, showing only half his face. His shadow loomed over her.

"What the fuck are you doing here? How did you get in? Oh, I get it! That's what Ciara was so confused about? Nice Tony. Well played."

He waved a card. "Spare keys my dear. I'm the co-owner of this hotel. I asked Phil not to tell you because I knew you wouldn't want to speak to me. For the record, I might be a God in between the sheets, but arranging the breakdown of a helicopter and a storm is way beyond even my capabilities. It was my idea to give you my room, not Phil's, but we're now going to have to tell your sister something."

"Tony, no!" Caoimhe groaned. "Tony, I want you to leave. I just don't need this tonight. I need time to think."

"If you had just answered my calls Caoimhe, all I wanted was to talk to you. You ignored me!"

"I couldn't speak to you, my phone's being hacked. MI5 think it's the gutter press, so I can't talk to anyone. I intended to come see you at the weekend. Tony, please will you just leave?"

"Why should I?"

"Because I don't want you here. I don't want to see you. I am so not ready to face this. Please Tony, just go. I need time."

He sat down on the edge of the tub and looked into her eyes. "You've had twenty years to think about this Caoimhe! We need to talk! Today, tomorrow, next week, next year? There is not really any difference is there? I need answers Caoimhe!"

"About what?" Caoimhe asked, looking at him.

"You know what, the small matter of my daughter! You know, Daimhim Caoimhe, and the even smaller matter of you not fucking telling me about her. Why did you do it? Why did you let me think the baby was his Caoimhe?"

"How did you find out?"

"I saw her the night of the election on TV and when she speaks, looks and sounds too much like my eldest daughter Anjya to not be mine. Fuck sake Caoimhe, you should have told me. I've lost twenty years of her life because, as always, you make decisions and don't consider anyone but yourself."

Caoimhe stood up. She reached for the robe and got out the bath. "Tony, don't go there. I came to the hospital to see you. You knew I was pregnant! I understand that day, your memory had gone. But later, you didn't work it out then?" She paused, tears welling up in her eyes, the memory still painful even after all the years that had passed. "Oh Tony, I wasn't a hundred percent sure which of you was her father to be honest. I thought she was yours but as soon as she was born I saw you in her. Kenny guessed she wasn't his right from the moment I told him I was pregnant. I told him it was a one night stand, a guest at the hotel." She looked at him and sighed. "You were in hospital. I was going to tell him the truth. Then I panicked and I just said the first thing that came into my head. I found out I was pregnant the day you wakened from the coma Tony. I was all over the place."

"Does she know Kenny's not her father?"

Caoimhe nodded. "He told her a few years ago, she was about fourteen. She was having a normal teenage tantrum and she shouted at him something about him never being a father to her.

He was pissed and roared back at her. '*That's because I'm not your fucking father. Your mother's a whore. She doesn't even know who fucked her.*' To be fair, he was never bad to her, but he mostly ignored her. He was much the same with the boys, and he definitely is their father." She smiled ruefully. "In fact, it's so bad that Dan asked if there was any chance Kenny wasn't his dad either."

Tony looked at her and sighed. "Can I meet her Caoimhe? I won't tell her who I am, but I'd like to get to know her."

"Tony, please? Leave well alone. No good can come of this. What about your wife and your other kids?"

He took the champagne from the bucket, lifted a glass and raised it to her.

Caoimhe shook her head. "No, pour the vodka. This isn't a champagne night Tony! When you're around I need vodka. I've already had two, so I need to be careful. Make it a long one please." She sat down on the couch. He walked over, handed her a full glass and sat beside her. "You're not having one?"

"I'll have the champagne if you don't mind. I also need to drink when you are around and I am celebrating the birth of my second child after all. I can't drink vodka these days, I went off it years ago. I'm really a whisky drinker now."

"Fuck sake, lah-de-dah! Too common for you, is it? You used to do vodka intravenously Tony, that's where I got the taste for it."

Tony looked at her and shook his head. "After I remembered about us, I drank myself into oblivion with vodka and actually sickened myself off it."

"Oh!"

"Fuck Caoimhe, what a fucking mess we made of it all." He reached over and touched her hair, pulling the elastic band from it and watching her titian curls fall down around her shoulders.

"Christ, you're even more beautiful than I remember. I don't know what to think just now. I kind of expected you to deny I was her father."

She shrugged. "There have been too many lies already Tony, it doesn't change anything. You're a married man, I'm still handcuffed to Kenny and I can't afford a scandal just now. It would be better to just go our separate ways."

He smiled. "You don't want that Caoimhe. I know you want me, you've wanted me from the minute I walked in here."

"You're very sure of that," Caoimhe whispered, looking into his eyes. She knew there was no point in denying it.

He put his hand on her throat then pulled back her robe to expose her breast. "Your nipples are standing out, sign of desire my dear. I can also see it in your eyes Caoimhe. Your pupils are dilated. I want you too sweetheart. I've had a hardon since I walked in here. Since the wedding, I've thought about you constantly. The electricity between us, it's still there after all this time. We've wasted twenty years. I need you Caoimhe, I always did. I'm not Kenny you know, I'll never embarrass you."

"I've not been able to get you out of my head either," she admitted, looking him in the eye and shivering. "I don't know what we're going to do about this?"

"Let's not think past tonight darling." He pushed her back onto the couch and untied her robe. "Oh Caoimhe, I want you so much." Still fully clothed he opened the robe and moved towards her; one hand began to rub her left nipple. His other hand ran through her hair then gripped her chin. He kissed her mouth, gently at first and then forcefully. Hovering over her, his mouth sought out her nipple and began to nibble on it.

Caoimhe's back arched and her fingers trembled as she fumbled with the buttons of his crisp linen shirt. Pulling away from her, Tony shrugged the shirt off. Caoimhe felt him move as he kicked off his shoes. Kissing his way down her body until his mouth was level with her groin, he moved swiftly, pulling her to the edge of the couch and kneeling in front of her. She gasped as his tongue probed. Caoimhe cried out as her pleasure grew. She grabbed his head, pulling him to her as an avalanche of sensation invaded her body. Holding his head against her until the orgasm ended, she lay trying to catch her breath. Tony got up from his knees. Caoimhe sat up, unzipped his trousers and pulled them over his hips. Pulling him towards her she took his penis in her mouth.

"Fuck no Caoimhe, don't do that please. I'll be like a wee boy and just come. I want to make love babe." He pulled away and sat down beside her. "Give me a second to calm down a bit!"

Caoimhe stood up and dropping the robe on the floor she straddled him. Never taking his eyes from her face he reached down and gently guided his penis inside her. Caoimhe moved against him, kissing his face, his mouth. Tony held her tightly, his mouth seeking out hers and then moving slowly down to her neck to her throat.

"This was always your favourite position Caoimhe," he whispered in her ear, "always have to be in control don't you?" Moving his hands down to hold her bottom, he pushed her back so he could see her face. Looking straight into his eyes, she tightened her legs around his back and held on to him as they moved together. Tony's breathing became laboured, he gasped as he felt the stirrings of what he knew was going to be an explosive climax. She held on to him, crying out with him as she reached a crest of her own.

"Fuck sake Caoimhe, just let it go!" he gasped. "I need to come babe, I can't stop!"

She clung to him; her body shook as he held her. Together they fell back onto the couch, her still on top of him. His manhood throbbed; his strong arms holding her firmly against his body as he milked the last remnants of his own orgasm before feeling her body go limp. Tears were now running freely down Caoimhe's face as she gasped and tried to get her emotions under control. When she looked at him, his face was wet with tears too.

Saying nothing, Tony led her over to the big tub. They got in, she lay back against his chest and he wrapped his arms around her kissing her head and neck. His hand moved to cup her breast as his fingers played with her nipple. Outside, the storm raged but they were oblivious to anything but each other. The power went out as the storm grew, but they continued their bath by candle light.

"Caoimhe, I need to be with you darling. I know it won't be

easy. I will be discreet babe, your political career is important. The country needs you, I know I'll have to share you. We need to talk about what happened to us Caoimhe. There are things I need to know." He nuzzled her neck. "Then there are things that I need to tell you."

They talked for hours, only stopping to run more hot water into the bath when the power was restored for a few minutes before going out again; the years slipped away. He told her about the accident, about Claire's reaction to his admission of the affair with her. He told her the circumstances of how he came to be on the wrong side of the road in front of the lorry. "I just continued to say to everyone that I didn't know what happened. I have never even told Phil that bit, but I need you to know Caoimhe."

Tony spoke about the ten months where he had no memory of their relationship. His shock when he remembered and realised he had lost her.

Caoimhe cried as she recalled what had happened to her, how she had struggled; her emotional wounds still raw after twenty years. "I came up to the hospital that day Tony. I was seven months gone. I was hoping you would ask me if the baby was yours but ... you didn't remember. I panicked and to be fair to Kenny, he accepted that he was as much to blame as me."

"Well he would Caoimhe, he did everything he could to get you in the first place and then to keep you. I can't believe that you are still with him. You must have been married thirty years now?"

She nodded. "It's been in name only for a long time, Tony. We haven't really lived together for the last ten years, and since I became an MP I've lived in London. He's up here."

"Why Caoimhe? Why are you still with him? Does he still hit you?"

"Not really. Believe it or not, the last time he really hurt me physically was that night you and I got together! I think he got such a fright, he went for counselling. It didn't work for the drinking but had some impact on anger management although I make sure I'm never alone with him. He probably would, if he thought he could get away with it. He's quite pathetic now Tony. He stopped being interested in me, and I suppose if you have no passion then you don't really fight do you?"

"He's a bully and a coward Caoimhe. I doubt it's got anything to do with passion. It's violence, that's all it is. He can't win, so he hits. He's a fucking waste of space!"

Caoimhe shrugged. "He was actually quite good to me when I was pregnant with Daimhim. I think he kind of realised that I could get another man. Oh Tony, I have tried so many times to analyse what happened with Kenny and me, but I have to give him some credit for taking on another man's child. The relationship just became a habit really, and I suppose it suited me too. I could concentrate on my political career, without guilt. My kids and grandchildren are the light of my life though. We moved to Aberdeen before Daimhim was born. As I said, he was okay until I went into labour, and then I think it became a reality. I gave birth alone, Tony. I wanted you so much that night. I kept looking at her and thinking that you should be there." Her eyes clouded over as she remembered. Watching her face, reflected in the mirror beside the bath, he could see the pain; still there, even after two decades.

"I almost called you the night she was born and told you Tony," she admitted, looking up at him. "I had been awake all night because of the birth and was really tired. The pain and longing for you was so bad it was almost physical. I realised then how much I loved you and what I had lost. I called Sami instead and she talked me out of it." She began to sob and he wrapped his arms around her and held her, kissing her head and face.

"Kenny wasn't there? Couldn't he just have done that, been there for you?"

"Well he tried, but he just couldn't do it. He was never bad to Daimhim, but he just couldn't love her. For a while he managed to throw himself into work. He built a successful business, but eventually the alcohol became a feature again and we got a good offer for the business."

"I fucking hate him Caoimhe, for having what was mine and not appreciating what he could have had with you."

"He can't help it Tony, it's an illness. He can go for long periods not drinking. We've had him sober a year, then he goes on a bender and that's it for a few months until he stops again. I haven't had a physical relationship with him for fifteen years now. He couldn't make love and to be honest it suited me." She shook her head. "I will rephrase that, he couldn't get an erection with me. Yet he appears to manage with others. It was okay until the last couple of years when he started openly being seen with other women."

Tony looked at her and raised an eyebrow.

"Oh, the other women are not a problem for me. It keeps him busy, gives him a hobby. Best of all, it keeps him away from me and my kids." She smiled wryly. "It's the fact that he was doing it openly, when we agreed to be discreet."

"So, you've had other men? You were such a sexual being Caoimhe, and although it pains me to think of anyone touching you, I didn't want you to be alone either."

Caoimhe nodded and smiled. "I bought a vibrator and that was it." She blushed. "When I used it I always had you in my head. After the way sex was with you Tony, I couldn't be satisfied. I did try. I have been with other men but one night things mainly, it just wasn't you. You said once that there was chemistry between us and I think you were right. That kind of connection only happens once in a lifetime. I think you ruined me for other men."

Tony kissed her neck and pulled Caoimhe back so her head was resting on his shoulder; he tightened his grip on her. "When I remembered we had been together Caoimhe, I came looking for you, but then I wimped out again. I thought that if you and Kenny had three kids and were trying to sort it out then I should maybe just leave well alone. I never considered the baby could've been mine. I suppose I was so angry that last day I saw you, it never occurred to me to think it wasn't Kenny's." He looked around at her, meeting her eyes. "Now it just seems so fucking obvious. I don't know Caoimhe, maybe I was more brain damaged than I thought."

He sighed and Caoimhe, watching in the mirror, saw his eyes cloud over as he remembered what had been a very painful time. "You know, I think subconsciously perhaps, it was the Catholic self-flagellation thing going on." He began to cry again. "Darling, I felt so guilty about Claire and what her last conscious moments were like, I perhaps punished myself. I used to be able to speak to Phil about you, but it was difficult for him with Ciara not knowing. He got really upset with me one night when we were both pished. Said he couldn't cope with me keeping asking about you, so in the end I just got on with it. I did have other women. I slept with a lot when I was trying to get over you. It was okay, nice even, but nothing like what you and I had. Angelina was a friend of a friend. I was a bit taken with her, her being so posh I suppose, and when I first met her she seemed keen. She got pregnant with Amy and I thought ... why not? It was just when you got elected to parliament and I thought I could never get you back. I gave up and just married her. She married me for my money. I have a lot now Caoimhe. I worked bloody hard and built the business up after Dad died. I think the longing I had for you drove me and made me work harder than I would have. Anyway, I'm worth a lot these days."

"I made a big mistake with Angelina though," he sighed. "At least Claire was a nice person. Angelina doesn't have many redeeming qualities. I haven't really had sex with her since she had Amy. She only rides horses! I don't care, neither does she. I get a shag here and there, and it's fine, a release of tension." He pulled her around to face him. "I don't know whether it's psychological, but it just never feels right. There was always something missing. The moment I was with you the night of the wedding, I knew what it was."

He sighed and again looked around at her. "You know, much as I wanted you, there was a bit of me hoping that it wouldn't be as good now, and then I could have some closure." He moved away from her. "Fuck Caoimhe! Why is it still so fucking powerful between us?" He reached over and handed her the glass of vodka, then took a sip of his own drink; he put it down. "When I masturbate, I think of you, but it's more than that isn't it? It's smells, feelings." He laughed out loud. "I have such a thing about that Kenzo perfume you wore, I keep a bottle in the bathroom here. I've fucked women I didn't even like because they were wearing it."

"She smiled. "I noticed, but I changed years ago."

"What do you wear now?"

"Izzey Miyake, d'issey.

He smiled. "I'd better see if there is a bottle in the gift shop then. I have a feeling loving you is going to mean long periods with only my head and my hands for company. All those years we've been apart, I'd go to bed with a woman, and it would be okay. Then I'd wake up in the morning and realise that it wasn't just the sex, Kee, it was everything. We talked, we laughed, we liked each other's company."

"We were friends Tony, best friends I suppose. It wasn't all about the sex although it is amazing, isn't it?"

He nodded and sighed. "The night of the wedding Caoimhe, I knew. As soon as I started making love to you, it was still there with you. It was exactly as it was twenty years ago, better even. Do you know what I regret most though?"

"What?"

"That first night we did it, all those years ago, when we were both drunk and Kenny had battered you?"

She nodded, casting her mind back, as he continued.

"I should never have let you go back to him. I should have been braver and just said 'you're not going back,' because I knew then that no one else would ever be able to do it for me."

Caoimhe sighed. "Tony, you did try to stop me, everyone did. I don't know why, it's just me, and there's times I know I should give in, but I cannot admit I'm wrong. My head is telling me to stop, shut up and to ask for help. I'm a fucking nightmare, so determined to do it my way. I just kind of get blinkered to everything and I keep going. I've mellowed quite a bit over the years though. I think with you, I felt so guilty about Claire and what we had done, it was easier to run away than to say to you I was pregnant with your child. I think I was punishing myself and you."

Tony tightened his grip around her and sighed. "I live every day Caoimhe, with the knowledge Claire died because I was a fucking bastard. If I had just grown a set and admitted it all. I could have supported you Caoimhe. I could have looked after you. Claire would never have got pregnant and I could have been there for you when you did. When I think about you all alone giving birth to our daughter, I want to cry. I love my girls Caoimhe. I'll love Daimhim too. I just wish I had been there for you. Was it awful?"

"Oh, it was okay. My mum, Samira and Ciara got there a few hours later. It was alright, I didn't want him there anyway Tony, I wanted you." Caoimhe looked up into his eyes. "Look there's no point in regrets, it can't change anything, and the worst part of all of this for me too was Claire. She didn't deserve what we did. Even when she suspected, she didn't challenge me, and from what you are saying about the crash, it was because of us that it happened."

"No, it was where I told her Caoimhe. I should have just done it and got it over with. I drove with a hysterical, pregnant woman in my car. I should have done it before we went or taken her home first. I wanted to get back to you though. Fuck Caoimhe, I had just ruined her life, and all I could think about was being with you without having to hide it all. It was after that weekend here, I knew I would only ever want you. Remember the church? Pity you're not staying longer, I keep the keys for Archie. I've another hotel on the island. The guests pick them up there."

"I went there today Tony, drove around the island and stood outside it."

He smiled ruefully and kissed her neck. "I'm a sad bastard too. Sometimes when the longing for you is strong and it's not in use, I go and sit there, remembering."

"What we did was so wrong Tony. We should have stopped

before we had feelings for each other. We should have had some self-control." She shook her head. "I just couldn't stop. I loved you from that first night Tony. I was so scared of hurting you though, I kept denying it to you and to myself. I thought if I stayed with Kenny, then I could tell myself it never happened. I think it was the need to punish you and myself that drove it."

"The last twenty years have been my punishment Caoimhe. I thank God every day that Anjya survived. She's been the light of my life. She's just so lovely, beautiful with a sweet nature. I told her everything I could years ago. Claire's mother was filling her head with nonsense. She asked me one day for the truth about her mother. I didn't tell her it was you. Just that I had loved another woman and lost her. Thing is I've never wished I hadn't been with you. I just wish I'd made you leave him."

Caoimhe looked at him. "If wishes were horses. You did what you did. I did what I thought I had to. There is no point in going over it Tony. We can't change anything. What are your daughters like?"

"Anjya is beautiful like Claire was. You saw her at the wedding didn't you? Nature wise she is also kind like her mother but clever too. It's funny, I always thought she looked like Claire until I saw Daimhim on TV that night." He reached over and pulled his wallet from his trouser pocket and took out a photograph, two girls, faces looked back at her.

"This is Amy, my youngest girl, she's really timid and shy. Angelina is not fond of children. I think she had her to trap me and it worked." A solemn, sad looking little girl stared back at her."

"Oh Tony, she is so pretty but serious and sad looking."

Tony nodded, "I try really hard to be mother and father to her, but it's not the same is it? Anjya is great with her, really looks after her. They're very close. This is Anjya. You can see the resemblance to Daimhim can't you?"

Caoimhe smiled then nodded. "Yes, although she's dark. It's a look, isn't it? What are we going to do about it, they're sisters? I can't afford any scandal right now. I need to talk to the PM and tell him. He knows about Kenny's problems. He doesn't understand why I won't leave him either."

"What's he like?"

"Ed?"

"Yeah. I wondered if you were sleeping with him. I just don't understand why anyone can resist you Caoimhe. You're not, are you? Shagging him?"

"Good God no! He's not like that, he's really loved up with Linda. She's been very ill for a while, as everyone is now aware." Caoimhe looked sad momentarily and Tony, watching her face in the mirror, caught this.

"Why did they announce it after the election? Surely public sympathy would have been there if it had been known how ill she was?"

"Our think tank felt that if people knew before the election how ill the PM's wife was, it would affect how they voted. You know? Like they would not see the strength in a man who loves his wife, only the weakness of him losing her! He is such a great guy. Linda is his second wife, they've both been through divorce. Linda and I are close friends Tony. Her first husband was an alcoholic, she's been supportive. I was also one of the few people outside her family who knew about her cancer. She's had it for about three years and known for most of the time it was terminal." Caoimhe sighed, "She's a very brave lady. I love her very much, so does Daimhim. Linda and Ed have been like surrogate grandparents to my ... our ... daughter. I think she filled a gap for them, having no kids."

"Thought he had a daughter?"

Caoimhe nodded. "Ed has one daughter from his first marriage, Caroline. She lives in Australia and has no children." Linda wasn't able to have children. Daimhim came into their lives as a precocious ten-year-old, and they sort of adopted her."

"Don't you mean precious?"

Caoimhe laughed and shook her head, her eyes bright with mirth, "believe me Tony, when you meet our daughter, precious is the last thing you'll think. Linda calls her mini-me. To be honest, she and Daimhim were hoping Ed and I would get together after she dies, but there is no attraction on either side. But, I do love him in a fatherly sort of way. He took so much abuse and criticism when he changed the election date. He didn't want people to know the truth, so he just rode it out. I think that's what he will tell me to do." She looked at Tony. "He reminds me of your dad, he's quite similar actually. I nearly told Hector about us when you were in the coma. I often wondered what he would have thought."

"I told him about you and me Caoimhe, not long before he died. He was having a go at me at the state I was in. He of course, like everyone else, thought it was all because of Claire dying. It all came out about you and me, the guilt I felt." Tony sighed and gripped her hand, looked into her eyes. "He said I was a fool for letting you go, and you would be the only woman I would ever need. His death was so sudden. He was fine, in remission, and none of us knew there was a problem. I found him in the bar on the floor. He locked up and then must have just dropped dead. He was only 54. You heard about Lolly?"

Caoimhe nodded. "I didn't really know Lorraine. Because of the age difference, I suppose. It was sad though. Why did she do it? Suicide is a permanent solution to a temporary problem Tony."

"Oh, it was a lot of things Caoimhe. Dad being ill, my accident, not being able to have children, Dad dying so suddenly. The final straw was when her husband Brian, left her to be with his pregnant girlfriend."

"Tony! That's just like us isn't it? It must have been awful for you."

"No, to be honest I knew what Brian was going through. It helped me to deal with it all. My only regret and my Anjya's too, is we didn't realise how depressed she was. Anjya had become her child really, it had a big impact on her. However, the depression was just too big for Lolly."

Caoimhe sighed. "For a long time, I was worried that Kenny

would die. I would feel responsible, because sometimes I wished he would just disappear. It wasn't logical because he is actually too selfish to do that. Everyone was wishing him dead and I had all the guilt about Claire to deal with. That's, I think, why I never told him about you and why I stayed with him."

"Are you really going to divorce him Caoimhe? Why now? It's not all about you and me is it?"

"Seeing you again and what we did the night of the wedding, how it felt. I knew that I couldn't live a lie any longer. I've carried him, like a fucking hump on my back, for years. It's time to shake him loose and hopefully he can find happiness too, without me to blame for his drinking."

"Will you commit to me Caoimhe?

"Yes Tony, but my political career is important. I can make a real difference. I don't want to deny you, but I just don't think that this is the time to divulge it. I need to sort out my life, and so do you. Let's just lie low for a while, see each other when we can. I've already started divorce proceedings. I'm going to speak to Kenny about the divorce again, try to get him to consent so there's no unpleasantness. There's no physical relationship, we lead separate lives. I just need to wait it out. He's out of the country in rehab. If he doesn't consent, it'll just take longer. My lawyer reckons that there's enough evidence to prove that he is being unreasonable withholding consent, but it's not guaranteed that a judge will grant it. Tony, if he finds out about you and me, he may be able to stall it all for longer. When he's in rehab and sober, he's more reasonable."

"How many times has he been in rehab?"

Caoimhe shrugged. "Hard to say. He doesn't ever stay long enough for it to make a difference. Each time, he promises he's ready. It's cost us thousands over the years."

"Why did you go back to him? It would have been over years ago if you had left when you found out you were pregnant with my baby or, if you had told him the truth. I'm not having a go babe. I just want to understand."

"He offered me a lifeline Tony. I was pregnant and scared. I was always such a disappointment to my parents, I just couldn't tell them. I wanted to tell Ciara, but she was so upset about Claire. I felt like the town bike. You had rejected me and I was too fucking proud to tell you. I hoped that Phil would work it out, he didn't ever ask. He of course, thought I'd got pregnant whilst you were in hospital. I guess he was so worried about the way he thought I'd treated you, and Ciara finding out he knew about us, it never occurred to him. He didn't speak to me for three years. If it did cross his mind after Daimhim was born just seven months after your accident, he never asked. He thought it was all for the best. He really was trying to protect you Tony. He probably just blanked it and accepted the baby was Kenny's. Ciara just assumed it was. I let her think that. When you told me to get out of the hospital that day, it was one of the lowest points in my life. I didn't think I could recover. I couldn't talk about it because no one knew. That's why I told Sami about the baby. She was struggling with the death of her father and her sexuality at the time, and she and I supported each other." Caoimhe began to cry, and he pulled her close.

"Oh fuck Caoimhe, I had a head injury darling. I ... I must have been aware of something though. I remember being angry at you. I couldn't work out why I was so fucking mad.

"When did you remember Tony?

"It was about ten months after the accident. I can't believe now, I never twigged about the baby. It was weird, I went back to work and it was okay. I obviously had Anjya, and I used to take her to the hotel with me in those days cos Lolly was still at school. I still thought Claire and I had made the decision to have the baby. That's what everyone was telling me." He shook his head. "I thought it was the head injury that was causing me not feel anything for Claire."

Tony sighed and looked at her again. "I remembered talking to you after Johnny and Sandra Weir's wedding. I'd told you that night, I didn't love Claire. I was, at that point, also beginning to realise I wanted to be more than friends with you and felt the chemistry between us. I remembered us getting pissed and jumping about on the bouncy castle and trying it on with you. You kicked me into touch?"

Caoimhe nodded smiling, remembering. "I nearly gave in that night. I fell on top of you, you tried to kiss me then I slapped you." She shook her head. "I felt it too. I got a charge and wanted sex. I was really pissed. I went home and almost raped Kenny." She smiled. "Never told you that, did I?"

Tony looked up at her and sighed. "What a fucking mess we made. Anyway, when I remembered it all, I was at The Deerhunter. Anjya was teething and I had been up all night. I was really knackered so when she got sleepy I took her upstairs. I went in to room nine, laid her on the bed. I went to lie down beside her. Suddenly I had a flashback, you and me on the floor of that room. I went downstairs and asked Phil. He told me at first I was imagining it. Then, when I pressed him, he told me that you and I had been together. He reminded me about not wanting to marry Claire and then it all just came back, just like that! I remembered the accident, but also what I felt for you. I went looking for you but Phil would not tell me where you were. He was angry with you, I was too Caoimhe. I just wanted to ask you why. I found out from your dad that you were in Aberdeen and I came through at once. Honestly, I drove all night. I don't know what I was going to say to you if I had found you." Tony sighed. "I should have worked it out Caoimhe!"

"Oh, Tony how could you have, I covered it all up, I didn't even tell my own family. Ciara still doesn't know Kenny isn't Daimhim's dad."

"I think I always felt you didn't love me as much as I loved you Caoimhe. There had been so much heartache and suffering. I suppose I just tried to get over you. The pain was always there though. I do have a confession, I didn't vote for you until this election. I did vote labour, but I lived just outside Glasgow and only moved back here last year. I'm kind of separated from Angelina, so I mostly move around my hotels now. I keep meaning to buy somewhere, mainly because of Amy, but I never get around to it, and living in the hotels suits me."

"Do you know what Tony? I had worked out that you didn't live in my constituency before Ciara told me. As an MP, you get to know all the local worthies and everyone with money who is in your constituency. I never came across you in nine years. So, it figured that you didn't live in my constituency."

"I deliberately avoided seeing you babe, but I never stopped wanting you Caoimhe." He chuckled. "Other people masturbate to porn. I did it to Question Time." He kissed the top of her head and spoke into her hair, breathing in the scent from it. "When all the rumours started in the press last year, about your marriage, I knew I had to try one last time. I had to see you. I think it was about closure though. I gave Scott and Toria the wedding reception as a present because I knew you wouldn't miss it, you being Toria's godmother. I was like a fucking stalker that day. Like a lion watching a herd of wildebeest, waiting to separate one from the herd so he can attack. As soon as I saw you take that call, I followed you on to the bridge then casually strolled over. I was fucking shitting myself Caoimhe, you're a scary lady." He tightened his grip around her. "I thought I'd blown it. So, I was over the moon when Kenny started his pish. I just had to get you alone. Then when you didn't stop me when I kissed you, and went the whole way with me, fuck, I was blown away. I just couldn't believe that you gave in so quickly, because I would have pursued you to the ends of the earth by that point."

"I found that so weird Tony! I'd been mad at you for twenty years. In fact, I think that anger drove me sometimes to be successful when everyone thought I would fail. I'd rehearsed so many times what I would do, what I would say. In my head, it never went you bastard. I hate you. Strip me naked and fuck me." Caoimhe smiled and looked up at Tony. "In my head, there was pain and suffering for you first." She sighed and kissed his cheek. "Tony I don't think I ever stopped loving you, but I'm just so fucking stupid, headstrong and determined. I cut my nose off to spite my face all the time. Ed calls me Maggie Thatcher, with a red rosette. Only she '*wouldn't* turn,' I actually can't when I'm in full flow. It's like my brain's telling me to stop and my mouth doesn't listen. I'm also a selfish cow Tony. I did want you to suffer though because I suffered. Funny, I never really considered how much you might be suffering too."

"Caoimhe, I had pain and suffering every day for twenty years. I love Anjya more than life itself, but every time I look at her I see Claire looking back at me. I never stopped missing what you and I had. I think for a long time, I just thought it was my punishment." He kissed her gently. "We had better get out this bath. We've been in it for two hours and I'm shrivelling up here."

Caoimhe laughed and looked at her wet, wrinkled hands. "My granddaughter Sasha calls it stripes. She won't get out of the bath until she has stripes."

Tony stood up; Caoimhe reached over and pulled out the plug. She threw him a towel and lifted one herself. "The wedding ... fuck!" She shook her head. "Truth is Tony, if I was thinking anything, I was thinking, if I just had sex with you again I would get you out of my system. I was so shocked when I came like that again. What is it with us Tony? I've never been able to capture that with anyone." She grinned. "Or anything. I've bought about twenty different vibrators over the years. I could open a fucking sex shop. I have every type, shape and size!"

"Was Johnny Plastic better than me?" Tony asked, grinning at her; drying himself vigorously with the fluffy white towel.

"Would I be here, with all the complications that this is going to bring, if he were?" She looked into his eyes as they sat down on top of the bed together. She rested her head on his shoulder. "I even had one-night stands with people because they reminded me of you. One of them was Jimmy Barnwell."

"The actor?"

"No, the fucking dustman! Of course, the actor. He's a labour activist. He made it clear he was interested. I suppose I was flattered. I found him quite handsome, and there was something about him that reminded me of you Tony."

Tony frowned. "He's supposed to be a really well hung stud. Didn't he do it for you?"

Caoimhe took a drink from her glass and giggled. "For the record, he's normal size. He's not even good with what he has got. He didn't manage it. Blamed the drink, but I think he was intimidated by me."

"You? Intimidating? Not you Caoimhe. How could anyone think that?"

Caoimhe giggled. "Ed says that all the men's balls jump up inside them when I'm in full flow."

They made love again and slept in each other's arms. She woke feeling comfortable and warm. Caoimhe lay for a few moments watching Tony sleeping; his long dark lashes curling onto his cheek. Looking at the clock on the wall, she kissed his cheek then shook him awake. He rolled over, smiled. "So, it wasn't a dream then?"

"Tony it's six a.m. You'd better get up and get out of here before someone see's you. Let's just keep this between us for now?"

He pulled her into his arms and kissed her. "If that's what you want I can be your guilty secret babe." They made love again, with the same passion as the night before.

"Are you getting the first ferry?" Tony asked as they both dressed.

"No, the second one. We're waiting to see if the chopper makes it over. When are you going back to the mainland?"

"Tomorrow. I'm going to have to spend today avoiding your fucking sister now. You'll need to tell her Kee, because Phil wont.

"Did you tell him about the wedding?"

"Our little shag? No! I just said we had talked and I kissed you. I did say I was going to try to see you again. You need to tell Ciara babe, she knows there's something now!"

Caoimhe nodded. "I'll tell her after the party. I need to get that out of the way, play the dutiful daughter and all that. Are you invited to my parents party, seeing as it's in The Deerhunter?"

"Yip."

"With your wife?"

"Oh yes. She won't come though, she hates your sister. You know what Princess Ciara is like? Angelina is very similar to Ciara but not in an endearing way. Oh, and I once called her Caoimhe by mistake when we were making love. I told her I fantasised about you, which is partly true. I think that she was quite pleased. It gave her an excuse to stop sleeping with me. She doesn't like sex and she certainly doesn't like me or poor wee Amy. I'm going to do nightshift at the hotel that night just in case you can get away. So, if you fancy a trip down memory lane, in room nine?"

"Tony I'm supposed to stay at Ciara's, but I'll see what I can do. I might be able to sneak out once they've all gone to bed." She grinned. "Room nine, that'll be a real headfuck. We shagged our way around that room didn't we?"

"It's the only room in the hotel I haven't refurbished. It's exactly as it was twenty years ago." He smiled sadly. "I never rent it out and it's only used for staff. I'm quite a sad bastard Caoimhe, with all my memories and stuff. I never got over you."

Caoimhe giggled. "Tony, the hotel would be like a nineties shrine if you did that everywhere we had sex." She shook her head. "We did it everywhere. The toilets, male and female, public and staff, the bar, the kitchen. Remember the night in the storeroom?"

Tony laughed, remembering. "God where did we get the energy? I used to be doing it with you all night and then get up and do a full day's shift."

"We did do it in some really memorable places. There can't be many areas of the hotel we didn't have sex in Tony."

He began to laugh. "The bridal suite, remember we did it during the reception and the bridal couple arrived, and we didn't get to change the sheets before the wedding night!"

Caoimhe looked at him. "All I could think of the next morning when they were checking out, was that they had spent their first night as man and wife in our soiled sheets. I was, at least, mortified when they commented on the perfume on the sheets being a lovely touch. You were through the back, pissing yourself laughing."

"Fuck Caoimhe, we did do it everywhere, didn't we?

"The cellar, with Phil just feet away and not knowing," Caoimhe smiled, remembering.

"Oh, he knew Caoimhe. He heard us. Poor Phil, he was mortified."

"I think room nine would be a turn on for me now. I'll try to get away Tony." She looked him in the eye. "Did you give my parents the venue as a present too?"

"Oh yes, just in case Scott and Toria's wedding didn't work." He smiled. "When I knew that all was not well with you and Kenny I did start plotting. I had to give it one last try as I said. I told myself that it was about closure. I never told anyone by the way, not even Phil. I came to realise that over the years Phil worked quite hard keeping us apart Caoimhe. To be honest, when I told him about the encounter at the wedding, he never said much. He did come and get me when you needed a hotel room last night. I knew you were here, of course, but because of the time factor, I was going to wait until the weekend to speak to you. Not that I didn't want to, but I didn't want to rush things. Fate has been on our side recently, hasn't it?"

CHAPTER

ELEVEN

"It was a good party, wasn't it?" Ciara and Caoimhe were relaxing post-party in Ciara's lounge. Everyone else had gone to bed. They were both reasonably sober as their parents did not think women should drink, and they had to try to do it in secret. Ciara handed her sister a glass. "Okay sis, spill the beans! What the fuck is the story with you and Tony Carter?"

"What?"

"Kee come on, I'm not daft. What happened on Arran? I won't say anything, you're my sister. Blood is thicker than water." Caoimhe looked at her and made a face. Before she could speak though, Ciara nudged her. "I know Phil knows something! He said I needed to ask you. Why did Tony not want you to know he co-owned the hotel? I also know he was in your room sis, I saw him go in, I came back to bring you some jewellery. Then there was tonight, he was watching you. Your eyes were continually searching for him." Ciara looked at her. "I never thought you kept anything from me Caoimhe, but I'm getting the impression that there's a big secret here."

Caoimhe closed her eyes and took a deep breath. "Oh Ciara, I've wanted to tell you for years. Poor Phil got dragged into it all, and we made him not tell you."

"Caoimhe! You were sleeping with Tony all those years ago?" Ciara's eyes were huge, her mouth opened and then closed as the truth dawned. "When he was with Claire You!" You were the other woman. Oh my God Kee, why on earth didn't one of you tell me? I always suspected he had a thing for you, but I never imagined that it was reciprocal. I thought you and him were just pals. Why on earth did you fucking stay with Kenny if you could have been with Tony? Fuck sake! Tony has always been such a great guy!"

Caoimhe nodded. "I couldn't tell you Ciara. You were so close to Claire then you were so upset when she died. It happened after Kenny beat me up one time. I stayed at The Deerhunter and Tony and I got pissed and slept together. We tried to stay away from each other, end it, but there was just too much there."

"Oh Caoimhe, it must have been awful for both of you!"

"It had been going on for about a year when Claire died. We'd decided to be together. He was going to tell her the night of the crash."

Ciara looked at her. "Caoimhe, I would never have judged you. I loved Claire, but you're my sister! I'd have been angry, but I would have been on your side."

Caoimhe looked at her sister, tears welling up in her eyes. "I tried, I just couldn't Ciara. There's things I didn't tell you. Stuff I should have told you about."

"Fuck sake Kee! He's Daimhim's father?"

"You know?" Caoimhe gasped. "How?"

"Daimhim told me a couple of years ago. We were talking about Kenny and why you stay with him. The wee soul had to talk to someone. She wanted to know if I knew who her father was. She begged me not to tell anyone. I kept my promise. I never even told Phil. Of course, I just believed the story about the drunken one-night stand. Was it him?"

Caoimhe looked at Ciara and nodded. "Yes," she whispered.

"Well that would explain why she always reminds me of Anjya! Oh Caoimhe, why on earth didn't you tell me? Does Kenny know it was Tony?"

"No, the only person who knew was Samira."

"I'm going to fucking kill my husband Caoimhe. He should have told me. Twenty fucking years, you two have kept this from me."

"Don't blame Phil, he and Samira are the only people who knew about us, but Phil didn't know about Daimhim. He thought she was Kenny's."

Ciara looked at Caoimhe and gasped. "That's why he was so angry when you were pregnant! That's what you fell out over. I thought it was a bit of an overreaction."

"I never told Tony either. Oh Ciara, he forgot about our relationship because of his head injury and I panicked. Phil has been a good and loyal friend to Tony."

"What are you going to do now?" Ciara asked.

"I'm not sure. Ciara, sex with Tony, it's unbelievable. Right from the first time we did it all those years ago, it was like electricity. There is such a connection between us. The earth doesn't move! It fucking swallows us both. Ciara, I just never told you at the time because of you and Claire, and then I didn't know how to. You were so devastated when she died. How could I tell you that I was the other woman? That day I realised I was pregnant, remember we were in The Deerhunter? I almost told you then, but you made a remark about Tony sleeping with some little tart and I couldn't risk telling you. I was feeling so fucking guilty about it all Ciara. What we had done didn't rest easily with either of us. He felt as guilty as I did, we'd agonised over it for months, but it was all falling down around us and we decided to tell Claire and Kenny. Then the accident happened, and it all went out the window. Ciara please don't have a go at Phil! He was never comfortable with it all. I think he just buried it, and him and Tony, well, they never discussed it much after. I also need to tell you, he never told me Hector had died. I think he just did not want me to see Tony. He also could have told Tony about me, when he couldn't remember and he didn't until after I left, and Tony remembered something and asked him. Ciara I'm almost certain it was about what it would do to you."

Ciara put her arms around her sister. "I'm not sure how I would have reacted all those years ago to be honest Caoimhe, but I hope I would have been there for you. Promise me you'll never do that again, keep something from me? Fuck, you and Tony! You'll need to be careful. Kenny is such a prick Caoimhe. He's a loose cannon."

Caoimhe's phone buzzed as a text popped up. She picked it up and read out loud. "I'm in bed in room nine, please come to me?" She smiled at Ciara, "room nine is where it all used to happen. Remember he used that as a staff bedroom?"

"Fuck! That's why he won't let that room be refurbished. I once suggested it and he went nuts at me for touching it." Ciara smiled. "I'll call you a taxi. What about Harry?"

"Would be a shame to wake him."

"Do you love Tony, Caoimhe?" Ciara asked, as they stood at the door waiting for the taxi.

"Yes, I think I always have Ciara, sad bastard that I am, I just never got over him."

The taxi driver smiled. "No room at the inn?"

Caoimhe nodded. "Something like that. It's my parents golden wedding and it's easier for me to stay in a hotel than make the journey home. We're going to do the family breakfast thing in the morning."

"You used to work there Caoimhe. I remember you serving me years ago before you were our MP! Okay, let's get you there then.

The back door of The Deerhunter was open. Tony stood in the doorway. The taxi driver waved, and Tony shook hands with Caoimhe for appearances sake as the taxi drove away. Giggling, Caoimhe followed Tony up the back stairs. He shut the door to room nine and immediately began taking off her clothes and his own. He pushed her back against the wall. "Oh God Caoimhe," he whispered, "I've been hard since I saw you at seven o'clock tonight. I need to have you, I'm in fucking pain now." Tony looked into her eyes before continuing speaking, his voice breaking and the sound, coming out in short bursts. "I come too quickly. I need to do this first and then we can have a bath together. It's ready for us to go into, like old times. Then we can start again, I want to make it last and last."

Caoimhe was, however, lost in her own orgasm and not caring. "Let it go Tony, we have all night." Grabbing his head, she pulled it down till their lips met; he gasped as their individual orgasms came together and became one. Afterwards they collapsed on the bed panting and still shaking.

"God, I love you Caoimhe. Fuck, I said it first. I never told you I loved you, did I?"

She shook her head. "Well, not for years anyway, Tony. You need to be sure this is what you want. It won't be easy."

"Caoimhe, I'm in love with you. I've never wanted anyone the way I want you. We've wasted too much fucking time. I'm not prepared to lose any more, Caoimhe! I'm not a confused frightened boy, I'm a man who knows what he wants."

In response Caoimhe rolled over onto her stomach and rested her chin on his chest, looking up at him. "I loved you twenty years ago, I still love you now. You know what? You make me feel like a teenager, Tony Carter."

"I can't believe I'm fucking a cabinet minister."

"I can't believe you are either. Now! Let's soak in that bath before it's too cold.

They eventually got out of the bath, made love again slowly then like old times, slept in each other's arms.

Her phone buzzed and wakened them. Caoimhe picked it up, smiled and handed it to him. "Harry," she whispered. Tony's eyes twinkled as he read the text.

"Where the fuck is you, boss? Let me know if you have been kidnapped by aliens? Otherwise get your arse back here before I have to call in an alert."

She texted him back. "I'm fine Harry, gone to see a friend. I'm back at The Deerhunter, be home later." Caoimhe took the cup of coffee from Tony, "I need to tell him, otherwise they'll start digging. I don't know why they don't just electronically tag us. You don't have any big secrets do you Tony? MI5 will investigate you. Ed's my friend but he's a politician first. Jed, the head of security, will de-brief Harry when we get back. He'll want to know who I came into contact with. Poor Harry will be shitting buttons just now, worrying about where I am."

"Fuck! They'll find out I am a spy for Mr Kipling! I go around bakeries and get their secret recipes."

"Is there much to know Tony?" Caoimhe asked.

Tony shook his head. "Other than my being in love with a fiery redhead cabinet minister who isn't my wife? No. I'm quite boring now Caoimhe. I've thrown myself into work and building up an empire. I'm a rich man now. I pay my tax on time. There has been the occasional female, but no married ones, not after what happened with you!"

Tony drove Caoimhe to her mother's house, kissed her and smiled. "Breakfast and then a couple of hours sleep. I won't be able to do the all-night sex and then work all day without sleep, the way we used to." He looked at her intently, "Kee, I need to see you. We need to sort something out so that we can meet up as often as possible!"

Caoimhe, comfortable in the darkness of the car, reached over and touched his lips with her finger. "Just try and not worry. We will, it might take a bit of planning but we'll manage it. You've got all my numbers now. I'll speak with you tomorrow."

CHAPTER

TWELVE

"Okay Caoimhe, let's have it? You didn't ask to see me for nothing!"

Caoimhe sat down in the lounge at 10 Downing Street. "This is difficult Ed. I need to tell you something personal and I don't know how you are going to react."

"Try me? I hope it's something to do with you divorcing that wanker."

Caoimhe nodded. "It's partly that Ed. I'm seeing someone, and I don't want to stop. I also want to keep my job."

Ed raised an eyebrow. "Who is he? It is a him I take it? You're not going to tell me you're a lesbian, are you?"

Caoimhe shook her head. "He used to be my boss. Twenty years ago we had an affair and it ended badly. He's Daimhim's father Ed. I ran into him at my niece's wedding, and well, it's on again."

Ed shrugged. "What do you want me to say Caoimhe? If the press gets wind of it, the opposition will use it, you know that. The public are mostly tolerant, there are leaks about Kenny's behaviour, and perhaps we just let them tell of the domestic violence! The times he left you in such a mess, people thought you had been in a car crash!" Ed sighed and looked at her over the top of his glasses, his eyes sad. "You told me it wasn't serious Caoimhe. He was kicking the shit out of you regularly."

Caoimhe raised an eyebrow. "How did you find out about that?"

"Your mother told Linda about the beatings that he used to give you. Oh, don't look at me like that, it was the day of the State Opening." He looked her in the eye. "So, I had Jed investigate."

"Ed!! You'd no call to do that. If you had asked, I would have told you. It wasn't always his fault. I was as bad."

"Caoimhe, you are my priority here, not your husband. He doesn't hit you now, does he?"

Caoimhe shot him a withering look. "He wouldn't dare! Oh, if I'm honest, he probably would if he got the chance. I don't take any chances. I'm never alone with him when he is drinking and I don't argue. The last time he seriously hit me was years ago. That's how the thing with Tony started, he cleaned me up. We got pissed and that was it." She smiled remembering.

"Caoimhe, do you love him?"

"Kenny?"

"No, this Tony?"

"Yes!"

"Is that love worth your career?"

She nodded, "Ed I think it might be. I hope I'm not forced to choose."

"Let's pray it doesn't come to that Caoimhe. I'm going to really need you with all that's going to happen when Linda's health deteriorates. I need to be able to focus on her, knowing my position is safe. You're one of the few people I know, without question, will be loyal to me." Ed grinned. "I would have made you depute you know, but Alex can't count."

"Ed there are loads of loyal people in your government. Alex, he's ruthless, but actually I think he is more a threat to me than you."

"Do you want a drink?"

She nodded. "Thanks Ed."

He handed her the glass. "Thank you for being so honest with me Caoimhe. I'll try to protect you and support you, but it will all depend on whether there is a public outcry. Are you going to go public?"

She shook her head. "I kind of think that I'll be able to keep it a secret for now anyway. At least until we are both free from our respective spouses."

"I take it there is a real story in all this?"

"How did you know?"

"You're not a good liar when it's about yourself Caoimhe. I suspect that's why the public like you so much. You are transparent, which is not usually a good quality for a senior politician, but it works with you."

"I'm actually a really good liar, Ed. I've got some awful secrets in my past. How long have you got?"

"All night, Linda is at the hospice."

Caoimhe took a sip of her drink and began to tell him her story, leaving only the mechanics and intensity of the act out. She realised there were limits to what she was willing to share with this kind man, who was more like a father at times than her boss. When Caoimhe finished, he was staring at her open mouthed.

"Jesus Caoimhe! What a fucking story. I can't believe that you two have been through all that and we never knew. You're a very brave resilient woman. He's a lucky man. I hope he realises that? Who knows about it all Caoimhe?"

"The full story? Just Samira, Phil and Ciara. Harry knows we're involved now. I had to tell him because I was sneaking off to see Tony and he got upset. Jed will have been giving him a hard time."

Edward Wilson smiled. "You know how it is Caoimhe. Actually, we didn't find out about this Tony, so that's good, means it really is a secret. We did unfortunately find out about Kenny! You realise there is another woman?"

Caoimhe nodded. "Makes it a bit easier to do what I am doing."

"Her name is Elizabeth Baker!"

"He's sleeping with Betty?"

"You know her?"

"Her husband is an old friend of his." Caoimhe chuckled. "Well, well, I always thought she was a bit of a prude. She's a nurse and quite a poker up your arse type. I never could abide her, she was always kind of funny towards me." Caoimhe began to laugh loudly and Ed looked at her, as she tried to speak. "She was at Toria and Scott's wedding. She was telling me how she's a manager in addictions. Reckons she's quite an expert in it. Fuck she'll need to be, if she's sleeping with Kenny. He's more like a fucking project than a lover!"

Ed waited until Caoimhe got her laughter under control. "You don't tell Kenny anything do you? You know pillow-talk?"

"Hell no, I wouldn't tell him where Tesco's is. It's kind of hard anyway when the pillows are in different countries! I don't see him often enough to have any conversation with him if I can help it. He reads it in the papers like everyone else. You know I only see him now a couple of times a year when I need to. I don't know why I didn't end it years ago. What I've done has not been fair to anyone, least of all him. Oh Ed, I'm so sorry about doing this now. It could get worse, I'm going to have to tell Kenny I've petitioned for divorce. I don't know why he has hung on in there either, to be honest. He gets nothing from the relationship."

"You've kept him for at least the last ten years Caoimhe. He has been falling on and off the wagon ever since I've known you. You never know Caoimhe, without you to blame for his situation, he might just make it this time."

Caoimhe shrugged. "I've always just felt guilty about what I did to him, but I suppose when I think about it, he stopped being a husband and father years ago."

"Okay, well, you need to have legal advice and the press office involved Caoimhe. Will David cope?"

"He'll be fine. Both he and Dan have thought for years that I should just cut Kenny out of my life. Daimhim, of course, agrees. Ever since he told her he was not her dad, she's wanted me to leave him."

"Do you think he'll use that? The fact he is not her father?"

"Probably, he does act as though he is the injured party, which I suppose he is. I was never promiscuous Ed. Tony was the only man I slept with back then, I never put it around."

Ed put his hand on her arm. "I know Caoimhe. I can't even start to understand how you must have felt, but it does help to understand why you stayed married. I'll arrange a meeting for tomorrow to discuss it all. Caoimhe, I have to tell Alex. As DPM, he'll need to be in the know."

Caoimhe made a face.

"Come on, he's okay. You need to cut him some slack. You and he could work really well together if you just give him a chance, get to know him."

"I don't want him to know about my sex life Ed. I prefer it that he thinks I'm frigid!" She looked Ed in the eye and grimaced.

"He didn't?" Ed gasped. "When?"

Caoimhe smiled, she nodded. "Oh, he did! It was a while ago, not long after you made me SOS."

"Did you?"

"No of course not! That really would be shitting on my own doorstep. I was a bit brutal with him though. I didn't mean to be, it was a wee bit of a shock. He had just married Jill and I suppose, I just did what I always do when I'm taken by surprise."

"Take no prisoners?" Ed laughed. "Well, well, that also explains a few things, and here was me thinking I had a handle on my team."

Caoimhe took another sip of her drink. "I did think about it, when I calmed down, he's a good looking man. There would have been no strings, but it would have been too complicated."

"Ed, Kenny and I, well we don't ... you know ... not for the last fifteen years."

"I'd guessed that. So, there have been men?"

"A few, not a lot, I've been very discreet. I am only forty-five, not dead from the waist down yet."

"So, did you do the deed with Jimmy Barnwell?"

She stood up shook her head and smiled at him. "No I didn't lie to you. Jimmy couldn't manage it. So, I'll be safe enough, he won't want anyone to know that. Anyway Ed, I better go."

"What're you going to do about Daimhim?" Ed asked, taking her empty glass from her.

"That, I don't know! She knows Kenny isn't her dad, he told her years ago. She just doesn't know who is. I'm so sorry about this Ed. I know you just don't need this complication now."

Ed smiled and shook his head. "Know what Caoimhe? You are like a fucking thunderstorm, but it's what makes you special. You're as crazy as your fucking name, and Daimhim is just the same. What a future she has!"

"You're one of the few people who can pronounce our Gaelic names."

"Hey, it took me five years to say your name properly."

Caoimhe laughed. "My Irish granny used to pronounce it Keeva, that's the correct pronunciation. The family say it like that. Everyone else, says Keevy. It actually means magnificent."

"Oh, I know Caoimhe! I think you are pretty magnificent. Can I tell Linda all this?" He looked at Caoimhe and smiled. "She already knows, doesn't she?"

"Most of it Ed. She's a good loyal friend. Anyway, thanks for the drink."

Caoimhe moved towards the door. Edward Wilson stood up; he walked towards her and pulled her into a hug. Holding her close, he kissed her forehead.

"I don't do that with Alex by the way. This Tony, I hope he realises what a lucky man he is?"

She nodded, kissed his cheek, her eyes misting over and then opened the door.

"Ed."

"Hmm."

"Thanks for listening and understanding."

After Caoimhe left, Ed sat for a few minutes then he lifted the phone. Jed, can you come in now please?"

CHAPTER

THIRTEEN

"Hi Tony, glad you could make it, thanks for waiting." Caoimhe grinned at him, "are you ready for your tour of the House of Commons?"

He smiled at her and nodded, "wish I could just pull you into a corner and do things to you though. I'm still getting a rush, thinking about last night."

"I'll ignore that statement and show you around. Afterwards, if we have time, I'll show you around me. This is where I work, where I do my business. You're a curious constituent today, by the way. Only Harry knows who you are, and because I'm in here, he has made himself scarce. He's my friend, but given his position he needs to step back from any potential scandal. If he doesn't, then they'll replace him. He's younger than you think. Actually, he's the same age as my sons, but he is so worldly wise, I forget."

"What's his story? You know, the scars on his face and hands? He looks as though he was burned?" Tony asked.

"He was, in an explosion in Afghanistan. Harry was a Marine. He was in a land cruiser when a rocket came through the middle of it. Everyone on the left side died, including his best friend. Harry and the men sitting on the right side lived but were badly burnt. He managed to get through the emotional stuff with Help For Heroes assistance. He got the job with us when he recovered. Most of the men he was with have alcohol or drug problems now.

He, however, made it. There is survivor guilt, and he needs to take time off when that happens. Mostly, he is A1 fit, both mentally and physically. He has treatment for the emotional scars every now and then, but considering what he went through, they're not too bad."

"God, I want to touch you!" Tony hissed in her ear as she took him around the building, doing the guided tour, acknowledging other members and introducing Tony where appropriate. They finished the tour in the restaurant where they were served dinner. Caoimhe kicked off her shoes and put her foot on his crotch, under the tablecloth, her face poker straight as she continued to look at him and talk. She could feel the hardness in his trousers under her foot and she smiled as she watched him struggle with the urge to touch her.

"You're a fucking witch, Caoimhe Black. I want to throw you on the table and do it, right here right now."

Caoimhe smiled. She looked around her at the other diners. "Well that would certainly cause a bit of a stir and let them all know who you are."

Tony looked around him. Most people were eating and drinking and paying no attention to them. There were, however, he recognised, some very important people in the dining room. "Why do they think I'm here Caoimhe?"

"Oh, rich businessman wanting to donate to party funds probably. That's all they'll see." She giggled. "A lot of them think I'm gay because of Samira and me. The rest think I'm frigid because of Kenny. If only they knew about what you do to me. Ed is okay about it all, you and me I mean." She smiled again and sighed. "Well as okay as he can be. You see, if there's a scandal, he'll only be able to protect me so far."

Tony looked into her eyes. "I enjoyed watching you in action today. When you were arguing with the Leader of the Opposition, you were tremendous. There I was in the minstrels gallery! I wanted to stand up and shout, *I'm sleeping with this woman and she is amazing!* I couldn't stand up though because I had a fucking boner.

Caoimhe laughed. "Well that's something different. They call me the ball-breaker in the House actually. It's that bike or dyke thing! To be a woman in a powerful position, you don't have to be as good as the men, you have to be better. If you sleep with a man you are a bike, if you don't you are a dyke." She sighed and looked back at him, a hint of sadness in her blue eyes. "What happened with us Tony, it drove me at times. It made me hard, well tough, really. It taught me how to carry on and hide my feelings. They all think I'm some sort of Iron Lady you know? Ed thinks David Summerville is scared of me."

"He looked scared today Caoimhe, you were amazing. He's usually so pompous, the Tory leader. Appears to go with the job, doesn't it?"

"He's actually alright in private. I don't agree with his politics Tony, but we get on in social situations. To be honest, the House is all about theatrics. I could probably be an actor if I wasn't in politics." Caoimhe wriggled her toes and pressed on his groin. Smiling at his discomfort, she carried on speaking. "The real political struggle takes place away from the public eye, and it's much more civilised than you think." She smiled. "The real danger comes from within your own party. There are so many ambitious, ruthless people." Tony put his hand down and moved Caoimhe's foot. She immediately put it back.

"Caoimhe, please take your foot away from my balls, or I will take you over the table! Seriously babe, I'll need to sit here until my hardon goes." They finished their meal and sat talking, enjoying each other's company. They had spent a few days together, going to the theatre, taking long walks around Wimbledon Common, doing all the things they couldn't do twenty years before. Tony had to fly home that night though. Caoimhe had been unable to get away, so she'd arranged to see him at Westminster. Caoimhe smiled and stood up.

"Come on and I'll show you my office, the view is amazing. There'll be no one here now. It's late and everyone will have gone." She led him through a maze of corridors, before stopping outside a room. She led him inside and pulling around a Do Not Disturb sign, she locked the door after her.

"God Caoimhe, this is amazing. You can see right across the river from here." Tony sat on the edge of the large, dark brown antique desk. She walked towards him. His arms reached out and he pulled her closer. Their lips met and he began to kiss her. She returned his kisses. He looked into her eyes as her fingers fumbled with his trousers. Opening the fly she slid her hand inside, loosened the button and pulled the trousers down over his hips. Caoimhe continued to look into his eyes as she dropped to her knees in front of him. Her mouth closed around his manhood, he held onto her head and sighed as pleasure mounted. "Caoimhe I'm really close, please darling," he gasped, his voice coming out in short gasps, "I want to be inside you."

She moved, stood up and began kissing him as he unbuttoned her blouse. His hands moved to her breasts, pushing her bra upwards, "now that is my favourite view ever!" Tony's mouth followed and he took her left nipple between his teeth, as his other hand dispensed with her trousers and knickers. Pulling her around, he entered her on the desk. Within minutes, she clung to him shivering, meeting each thrust until her body gave in to the mounting pleasure. Realising he'd held back to allow her to reach a climax, Caoimhe pushed away from him and dropped back to her knees. Taking his manhood into her mouth, she allowed him to complete his own orgasm. She felt his penis stiffen as she worked her way around it. He cried out, grabbed her head and held it steady. As she felt the rush of semen filling her mouth, she quickly swallowed. He gasped, and she held on to him as his legs wobbled.

Caoimhe stood up and wiped her mouth with the back of her hand. She stood in front of him. "Think about that when you are sitting on that flight home tonight, Tony. When you go home to your wife, think of what is waiting for you here. Keep that in mind when you ask her to give you a divorce."

He pulled her towards him and looked deep into her eyes. "I love it when you're assertive."

"Yeah, it's a strange concept for me!" she laughed.

CHAPTER

FOURTEEN

Caoimhe smiled as she lifted the telephone in her office. "Thanks Jan!" she said, waiting a few seconds until she heard the click of her secretary putting the call through. "Tony, how are you? What did Angelina say?"

"She was fine as soon as I said she could keep the house in Glasgow and the horses. She just said okay." "We saw a lawyer yesterday and it's all in hand. Really, easy actually. I would have done it years ago, if I had known."

Caoimhe, smiling at the sound of his voice, gasped. "I'm not surprised! The financial settlement is significant and the house. What about Amy?"

"She was devastated because she thought I was going to leave her. I don't think Angelina likes her very much. She won't let me have her full time. I suspect because she would lose her bargaining tool, but I'll need to spend a great deal of time with her Caoimhe." Tony sighed and Caoimhe knew that part of his life was painful for him. "Anjya was happy for me. I didn't tell her about you. I'll need to tell the girls but not yet. Anjya has a flat in Glasgow. She's in the second year of her law degree so she'll be fine."

"Tony! I want you so much. I really miss you. Will you be alright financially with the settlement being as much?"

"Caoimhe, I'm a very rich man now, it doesn't matter. I can be with you without looking over my shoulder. I didn't tell Angelina about you either. Just that I wanted to go it alone. She was happy, I think she was relieved. What about Kenny sweetheart? How was Italy?"

There was a long pause before she answered his question, choosing her words carefully. "Well, that wasn't easy. He refused to accept it. I told him that it is happening, it's over. He threatened to go to the press with the story about Daimhim, but I just told him to do it. He doesn't know about you anyway. The government think tank is very ruthless when it is protecting its own Tony. They'll start the rumour mongering and stories about him hitting me if he does. Ed thinks that the fact that David is my press officer will add validity because if his own son is willing to leak information then it must be true. He also says that they'll just address the domestic violence issue as they are doing anyway, with me as the poster girl. In any scenario, Kenny becomes the bad guy which I don't think I really want Tony."

"He deserves all he gets for the beatings he gave you Caoimhe, and he's a parasite. He's fucking lived off you for most of his life. You forget I was there. I cleaned you up more than once! Don't you dare feel sorry for him!"

"Tony that's what my kids say too!" Caoimhe sighed, "it's sad when someone says something like that about their father. I have great kids Tony, I want you to meet them properly, but I don't want to tell them about our past yet."

"When Caoimhe? When can I meet them?"

"Soon, probably in between Christmas and New Year, they're all going to be here, the grandchildren too. I'm thinking of having a dinner, inviting Samira, Ed and Linda if she is well enough. I'd normally have Christmas with the kids in Scotland, but with Linda so ill, we just don't know how it'll go. I also have the Chancellor's country residence in Buckinghamshire, Dorneywood, but again, with the situation with Linda, I'd rather be in London, although I can get back quickly from Buckinghamshire."

Tony smiled to himself, knowing that his patience with Caoimhe was now being rewarded. "Anyway, I better get off and let you get home Kee. I love you, and I'm really desperate to get back down on Friday. What're you doing tonight?"

"I'm having dinner with Linda. Ed is out of the country at a summit in France. He won't be back until the day after tomorrow. Anyway, I'd better go Tony. I'm getting a bit emotional at the sound of your voice and I just want to jump on a plane and come to you. Harry will pick you up on Friday by the way; he's dropping someone else off at the airport, so meet him in the VIP area."

***

Linda Wilson was lying on the couch in her sitting room. She looked well and the fact that she was terminally ill was not visible in her appearance.

"You look great Lin, you have even put some weight back on."

Linda smiled at her friend. "Steroids and a concoction of drugs, I'm afraid Kee. I'm taking a cupful of tablets at a time. I should be glowing in the dark, the number of chemicals inside me. Anyway, enough about me, that's getting repetitive and boring Caoimhe Black. Tell me some juicy gossip or tell me about your love life, or both, whatever is more titillating."

Caoimhe smiled. "You'll meet Tony soon Linda, on the twenty-eighth for dinner with us all. I'm really looking forward to hearing what you think, after you've actually met him."

Linda giggled and nudged Caoimhe as she reached for her coffee mug. "I am going to really struggle to talk to him without imagining you and him doing it Kee. I can't believe how sexually active you are. I mean Ed and I, well, we always thought we were so into each other, but you two are just unbelievable!" Linda sighed and looked wistful. "That's what I'm reduced to these days, hearing about your love life."

Caoimhe looked sadly at her friend. This was a conversation they had had many times in the last six months. "Is he still struggling with it all Linda? I thought he was getting there,

159

accepting it? Poor Ed, this is so hard for him. He loves you so much Linda, and he still fancies the pants off you."

"He's scared he hurts me or something I think. He just can't do it. I've tried talking to him and reasoning. He just keeps saying, *'wait till you're a bit stronger.'* It's driving me mad. We have so little time left. That's where being prime minister and his ego take over Caoimhe. He can't talk to anyone about weakness. You're going to have to watch him after I die! He'll not show any weakness! You will look after him? Won't you?"

Caoimhe, unable to speak, nodded, tears building up in her eyes.

CHAPTER

FIFTEEN

December 22nd December 2015

"You look like the cat that's got the cream!" Caoimhe said as she closed the door to Linda Wilson's sitting room. Linda, sitting at the table, was wrapping gifts with colourful paper and humming softly to herself. Linda's gift wrapping skills were legendary amongst her friends. She loved Christmas and planned it in advance. Her gifts looked almost too good to open most of the time.

She handed Caoimhe a Santa Sack, "that one's for the children. Can you give them to Dan to take back? The other bag has yours, David's and my beautiful girl's in it. When does she get here? I can't wait to see her!"

Caoimhe smiled. "Daimhim will be here tonight. She'll no doubt come right here to see you, probably before she comes to see me. You spoil her Linda."

"I'm about to spoil her even more Caoimhe! I've left her everything in my will. Ed agrees. She's the child we never had and the nearest to a grandchild we're going to get. I spoke to Caroline, she's fine with it. She loves Daimhim as much as we do. Look after them all when I'm gone Caoimhe?"

"Linda, why do you keep asking me that? You know I will. Why do you need to keep saying it?"

Linda's faced clouded over and she sighed. "Because you're the only one around me who's dealing with the fact I'm dying Kee. The only person I can talk to about it, other than the Marie Curie nurses. Hey on a lighter note, Ed finally gave in last night, we made love. I was knackered after, but oh Kee, it was just ... he was crying Caoimhe. I tried not to get upset, but it was very emotional." Tears ran down her face as she spoke. Caoimhe wiped her friend's eyes with a tissue then embraced her, her own tears falling, unchecked, onto the other woman's shoulder.

"I don't want to leave him and you all Caoimhe," Linda sobbed, "sometimes I get selfish and think it's just not fucking fair. We were supposed to have a life, we had a fucking plan. Ed was going to steer you, guide you towards party leadership and you were going to take over. We were going to retire to Norfolk and live for years by the sea. I'm fifty-seven Caoimhe, I was supposed to live to be a hundred. I wanted to see Daimhim settled, getting married, having kids." She looked at Caoimhe and smiled through tears. "I wanted to see you divorced from that fucker, too!"

"Oh, you'll see that. The lawyers reckon I could be divorced by early summer."

Linda Wilson put her hand on her friend's shoulder and smiled sadly, "I won't Caoimhe. I only look okay because of the drugs. Inside, the cancer is eating away at me and making me weaker every day. They say you know when you are going to die? I think it'll be soon."

Caoimhe looked into Linda's eyes. "I don't want you to leave me ... I don't know what I'm going to do without you either Linda," she sobbed.

"You are going to be just fine Caoimhe Black. You have Tony now. Thank goodness I'm finally going to meet him this week. I have this picture of him in my head and I want to see if it's correct. For now though, I need to get these presents wrapped and you need to get to the Dorchester because you have a hot date."

Caoimhe took out her phone and flicked through the photographs in it. She handed the phone to Linda.

"Oh my God, he is even more handsome than I thought, Caoimhe. Those eyes, you could swim in them." Linda giggled and after another look at the picture, handed the phone back to Caoimhe. "God, how do you manage to keep your hands off him? I'd be pulling him into the bushes."

"Oh, there's quite a bit of touchy feely stuff Lin. I do find it difficult not to keep touching him. Sometimes we don't make it to bed and do it standing up against walls and stuff. I just can't get enough of him! Speaking of which, I need to go. I've got a financial reform committee meeting this afternoon, which won't start until I get there. Then I'm meeting Tony for dinner before he catches his flight home. I so need to leave time for some hot loving, because when he comes back down next week all the family will be here, so there may not be opportunity."

"Oh, you make me so jealous. I miss that kind of thing, but at least I've got something to think about, after Ed and me." Linda laughed and hugged her friend, "now go! I want to hear all about it tomorrow."

***

"I hate the last night with you Tony, that goodbye, then the wait to see you again. Yet this'll be our life from now on. My work is here, and you have your girls to think about."

"When can I meet your kids Caoimhe? I want to meet them. Then I need you to meet my girls."

Caoimhe smiled and looked at Tony. "Mine will all be here for New Year. We'll be together on the twenty-eighth. If you can stay for New Year, great, but if not I'll make dinner on the twenty-ninth. Dan is down here this weekend. He's worried about Ravi. Samira has had some contact with him and they are concerned he's becoming ill in Pakistan. They're going to do some sort of video link to one of Samira's uncles. He has managed to get Ravi to visit. Ravi's psychiatrist will sit in, out of camera."

163

"Is Dan staying for Christmas then?"

"No, he'll go back home Christmas Eve and come back after Christmas. It's too much hassle to bring the kids down for Christmas Day, so they have it at home. Usually I go there."

Tony looked thoughtful. "What's the story with Ravi, what is wrong with him? I take it he's ill? He was a pretty normal wee boy. I remember him coming into the hotel when he was about eighteen, before he went to university."

"Ravi has diagnosed mental health problems Tony. Not a lot of people know but Samira's dad had it too. There was a traumatic incident when Ravi and David were students at Oxford and it set it off in him. I'll tell you about it some other time. Ravi copes well with it normally and is sensible about what he can and can't do. It's well-controlled by medication though he can go into episodes and can self-harm. He also hallucinates. He's been keeping well for the last couple of years, and when he's well he's a sweet boy. When he gets ill, he normally knows to do something about it, but he was apparently a bit strange on the telephone to Dan the other day. They just want to check. Dan will go home right after he's met with Samira."

"Daimhim is flying down tomorrow night for the holiday, and so we can do some shopping in the Boxing Day sales. Obviously, David's my press secretary, so he'll be with us for Christmas. We're planning to have Christmas lunch with Ed and Linda."

Tony looked at her and smiled. "I can't believe I'm in the Dorchester, about to do unspeakable, sexual things to the Chancellor of the Exchequer."

Caoimhe giggled. "I love it when you talk dirty."

Tony pulled her towards him. "Come here and I'll give you a preview." He moved in and began to kiss her. He led her over to the bed and sat down taking her with him. He buried his face in her breasts; opening her shirt slowly and pushing her bra aside, he closed his mouth around her nipple.

Caoimhe shivered as she ran her hands through his hair. He unclasped her bra with his free hand and her breasts sprung free.

She pulled his tie from his neck and began to loosen the buttons on his shirt.

Tony gasped and held her at arm's length. "Caoimhe, it's not that I don't want to, but they will be arriving with our room service order at any moment."

"Well you started it!" Caoimhe whispered in his ear, she pulled away and slowly sank to her knees in front of him. She unzipped his trousers and pulled them over his hips. She began to touch him and play with his penis before taking it in her mouth. Tony gasped as she moved her mouth up and down, using her tongue to tease into every part of it.

"God, Caoimhe, stop!" he cried out, "I'm going to fucking explode!"

She ignored him and putting both her hands under his scrotum, held his balls, playing with them. She heard her phone buzz, alerting her to a text, but she ignored it and carried on. She felt his penis grow harder and pulsate, his breath was coming in short bursts. He grabbed her head, holding it steady with both his hands. She heard him cry out as he ejaculated into her mouth. She swallowed quickly and grinned as she stood up. "There, there, there!" she whispered, kissing her way back up his body. Tony jumped as there was a loud knock at the door. "Just in time for dinner!" she whispered, rushing to hide in the bathroom as he adjusted his clothing before opening the door.

They had just sat down to eat when Caoimhe's mobile rang. She put her finger to her lips as Tony protested. "It's Alex Stanley!" she mouthed. "Alex what's up? I'm in the Dorchester meeting an old friend for dinner. Harry's in the bar, he probably didn't hear his phone. What?" Tony knew from Caoimhe's face something was wrong. He saw her eyes fill with tears. "Oh God, no. Not yet, not this quickly! I saw her earlier; she was wrapping presents Alex. Okay I'll come straight over; I should be there in about twenty minutes. Thanks Alex, I appreciate you calling. I didn't notice Ed's text; just tell him I'll be right there."

Caoimhe stood up, tears welling up in her eyes. "It's Linda; she has taken a sudden turn for the worse. Tony, she's not expected to last the night. I won't be able to see you again before you go home. I'm going to have to be here and you have to be back in Scotland for Amy and Anjya. I may have to cancel the dinner on the 29th too, I'll call you." She kissed him, texted Harry and he called her. "I'll meet you outside, Harry. Go and get the car."

"Are you alright sweetheart?" Tony's brown eyes looked sadly at her.

"I'll be fine Tony. You just keep hoping; she knew, we all did, that this day would come, but she was well right up till lunch time. I saw her this morning. Linda is such a good friend, almost like a mother to Samira and me. I need to reach Sami too and tell her, but I'll do it in the car." She kissed him. "Hope you have a lovely Christmas darling; I'll call you soon."

Tony kissed Caoimhe and held her for a few seconds. "I wish I could stay, but I have to go because of Amy. She'll have a miserable Christmas if I'm not there, but I'll see you soon. I'm still going to come down on the 28th . Even if we can just snatch a few hours it'll be enough, but if not, don't worry." He kissed her again. "I'm a big boy Caoimhe; I realised what I was getting into, and I don't care. Call me later; let me know you're okay. I'll be there for you darling."

Caoimhe, Daimhim and Samira were with Ed when Linda passed away in the early hours of Christmas Eve morning. Alex, who had a young family, had gone home to his constituency the evening before, at Ed's insistence. Caroline and her partner flying from their home in Australia but could not get on a flight till boxing day. Ed clung to Daimhim who was sobbing. "Thank you for being here with me girls. It has made it easier. It was so peaceful in the end, wasn't it?"

"Ed, Daimhim, can I get you two a drink? Samira asked, wiping away her own tears. "I really need one.

"Samira, it's five in the morning!" Caoimhe whispered.

So, this is not an ordinary day, is it?" Samira said, dabbing at her eyes with a tissue.

Ed smiled sadly. "I think I could use one actually. Caoimhe? What about you?"

"Not for me thanks, I'll just have a coffee. Sami, you get the drink for Ed and you two, I'll do the coffee."

"You should go to Scotland to your family Caoimhe. It's Christmas; I could get a chopper to take you and Daimhim."

"No I don't Ed, my parents, Dan and Elaine, they all understand; besides, I really don't feel like celebrating Christmas either. I can make us a Christmas dinner if I have to. Ed, I promised Linda I would look after you."

"Caoimhe! The staff are still here; they'll make dinner for us. Samira, you better get home; Karen will be expecting you. What's the latest on Ravi?"

"He's actually a lot better than we thought Ed, but I wish he would come home. I'd feel better if he did, but as you all keep reminding me, he's an adult and needs to feel in charge of his own life."

Ed decided not to make the announcement of Linda's death until after Christmas. His staff rallied around him and Caoimhe supported him, as a friend. They spent the Christmas period discussing Linda and holding each other together.

When Ed's daughter arrived two days after Christmas Ed thanked Caoimhe and told her, "I'm going to go to Chequers with Caroline and Sharon after the funeral; when I come home, I'm coming back to work." He looked at her sadly, "trust Linda to die with the least amount of fuss and during a break anyway. I'm really going to miss her."

Caoimhe hugged him and kissed his cheek. "You and her, you had a wonderful marriage. Linda was so in love with you Ed. I've lost a mother figure and a wonderful friend. Daimhim has lost a grandmother, I'm sorry about her Ed! I had to send her to Dan's; you know what it's like? She's young and it's her tragedy. She loved Linda so much Ed, and she loves you. Linda always made such a fuss of her. I loved her too Ed, she was such a special lady!"

Ed smiled. "I know; she was one of a kind. She thought of you as the daughter she never had Caoimhe, she loved you too. As for Daimhim, Linda was so proud of her. When you came in to our lives with that little girl it was a godsend. Not being able to have children was hard on Linda. It's not easy being a politician's wife either. So much focus goes on the man, but Linda was the driving force behind me. Caoimhe, thank you for everything you have done this last week, but you need to go see to your family now. I'd love you to deliver the eulogy at the funeral; it's what Linda wanted too. Now, what about this man of yours?

Caoimhe's eyes sparkled, despite her tears. "Which one?"

"The one who makes your baby blues sparkle, and I think, the one who's going to look after you in your old age Caoimhe."

"I saw him for a quick lunch today. Jed has vetted him and found nothing; he's been cleared to stay at No 11, as my guest."

"Just lunch?"

"Okay, he's still there, but no one except Harry knows. I gave the rest of the staff the week off. I'd really like you to meet him soon, Ed."

Ed smiled and hugged her, "I'd like that Caoimhe, I need to see for myself, this man who you've loved for most of your life. I'd want to make sure that he's good enough for you. Your choice of men so far hasn't been good."

"Only because no one ever measured up to Tony, I'm afraid! We won't make it public until we really have to, because it's our business isn't it?"

Ed Wilson frowned. "What about Kenny?"

"He appears to be doing fine, still phoning me and the boys and making threats, but so far nothing. The divorce petition is ongoing, so hopefully it'll be over soon."

"Is it going to cost you financially, Caoimhe?

"No, not really, when we sold the business, I invested the money so he'll be a wealthy man. I've been looking after him, financially, for the last 10 years and not touching it. So, he gets the house in Scotland and enough to live well. The lawyers have made him sign a declaration that he'll not embarrass me if I give him the money.

"He's a lucky man Caoimhe, I hope he realises it? He would have nothing if it wasn't for you."

Caoimhe shrugged, "at the time we sold the business he was so unstable, I felt he would just piss it against a wall. I just gave him everything he needed, and we kind of got in to that habit. He was an accountant Ed; he knows the score." She looked at Ed and grimaced. "The agreement will only work if he is sober. If he gets drunk; well it's like firewater to the Indians. With Kenny, it's anyone's guess what he'll do."

"Well, for now, stop talking. Go and entertain your man" he grinned, "whatever way you see fit. Just don't fuse the lights with all that electricity!"

Caoimhe looked at him and her face reddened, "Ed!" she gasped.

Ed chuckled, "Linda was my wife. When I found out about Tony, I was really worried about you and your choice in men. She told me what you told her. Fucking earthquakes and typhoons I hear!"

"I couldn't possibly comment Ed" Caoimhe whispered, looking at the ground. "It would be like telling my Dad."

CHAPTER
SIXTEEN

"Daimhim is on her way. Dan and Elaine are already at the church Mum. Dad has been on the phone again."

"David, I don't want to speak to him. I told you it's over, I don't care what he threatens."

"Mum I'm glad you have finally seen sense but it's a pity he can't do it amicably. How could he possibly think that there's anything left between you?"

"I have tried David; he just will not accept it is over. I can't do it anymore."

"Mum, I'm not having a go!" David put his arm around his mother and kissed her cheek. "There's someone else isn't there?" David looked into his mother's eyes before speaking again. "You have a boyfriend, don't you?"

"Why are you asking?"

"There was a man here last week, when I was in Scotland. I know Harry wasn't here either, so it wasn't him."

"Who told you there was someone here?"

"There was some talk, and Harry didn't deny it. There were men's toiletries in your bathroom."

"What are you? A fucking detective, David?"

"I heard the maids talking Mum. They were looking for signs, because you gave them the week off and paid them double for it."

"It was their Christmas bonus."

"Mum!"

"Okay, there is someone."

"Is it a fling?"

"No, I'm in love with him, but I'm not going to show there is anything serious until I'm divorced, and I have to."

"Who is he mum? It's not Jimmy fucking Barnwell is it? Dan thinks it is. Daimhim said she read about you and him in some magazine!"

"I think you all need to mind your own business. I don't interfere with your love lives. So, tell your siblings, and take note David!"

"Mum, it's not Jimmy, is it?"

Caoimhe shook her head and smiled. "David, I'll introduce you at some point. It's going to be permanent. I want your brother and sister to be here too; we're friends more than anything else at the moment." She grinned. "Well, friends with benefits, actually."

"No Mum, I'm your press secretary, I need to know, in case the maids talk outside. I might need to answer." He smiled, pulling her into a hug. He kissed the top of her head, "as your son, I need to know you are with someone who will cherish you! Whose stuff is it? It's someone with money and taste!"

"Just say it was your stuff."

"Mum, please, difficult as this is, I need to know!"

Caoimhe smiled slyly. "Okay, come through to the sitting room."

David sat down on the couch and put his coffee mug on the table. "Okay mother, explain, spill the beans? Who is this mystery man?"

"David, the man I am involved with is called Tony Carter. He used to be my boss years ago when I was a student."

"I know who he is, he's Uncle Phil's mate isn't he? I remember him from the hotel when I was a kid. He was always nice to us when you took Dan and I in. He bought me a game, that time when I got my appendix out. He's also the one who got Dad out of the bar at the wedding, isn't he?"

"He's Phil's business partner, David."

"When did you start seeing him?"

"Toria and Scott's wedding I suppose. I hadn't seen him in years and there was just a connection."

"How come we're only finding out now? That was more than four months ago! Mum, you never said a thing."

"I was going to introduce you at Christmas, but with Linda dying so suddenly, I had to focus on supporting Ed. David, I'm entitled to a private life."

"Not from us you're not. Why didn't you say anything? That's why you are suddenly so keen to divorce Kenny. Why didn't you tell us? Don't you trust your own children?"

"Oh David, you're not a kid. Work it out. He's married too son, and he's just separated from his wife so the fewer people who know now, the better."

"Does the PM know?"

"Yes! He met Tony a couple of days ago, they got on. He likes him."

"What's he saying about Dad?"

"Who, Tony?"

"No, Ed Mum!"

"He'll support me as much as he can. He doesn't like your dad, David, so he's happy for me."

"No one likes my dad Mum, not even Dan and I, and we're his flesh and blood. Mum I don't remember a time when he was ever a nice guy. Was there a time?"

Caoimhe sighed and looked sad. "David, I married him because I was 16 and pregnant. I wanted to love him and for a while I really thought I did. In those days, you just accepted your lot, but as I grew up I realised there was a big world out there. I went back to university and in our world women didn't do things like that. They were not supposed to be ambitious. I grew away from him; I think I caused a lot of his problems because he probably loved me in a weird way. This situation is not all his doing David. I've done things I'm not proud of too. He took me back, carrying another man's child. He might not have been the best father, but he provided for her and you two."

"Mum for fuck sake! You worked every hour there was, and you held his business together most of the time. You still got up and took us to football training and were there for us. I can, in some ways, understand his indifference to Daimhim, but there were times when I needed a father. Luckily Grandad did a lot of the male bonding stuff with us. My father never really did anything but drink. Mum, you were the one who was there for us. You must have been like some kind of superwoman, the way you held it all together for us."

Caoimhe smiled. "I was a hyperactive child who grew into a hyperactive adult. So work was never much of a hardship for me, I thrive on it. Even now I have the energy of someone half my age and a low boredom threshold."

David sighed, shook his head and looked seriously at Caoimhe. "Mum we need to do a press release about you and Dad splitting and we need to do it now. The divorce is filed. It's common knowledge that he's a drunk. So, it shouldn't be too hard. This is the right time to do it, when everyone is focussing on Linda's funeral. As Ed, would say, a good day to bury news."

"David, your dad has an illness."

"Mum, I remember him hitting you, and according to Gran he used to beat you up regularly. She has photos."

"What?"

"Dan and I remember seeing him kick you one Christmas day and other stuff. My gran, she kept photos of you with black eyes and split lips and things."

"No she didn't."

"Oh, she did Mum, and I've seen them. There is one of you with a fractured cheek bone and the medical records will be there too. So, if Dad starts his pish, I will personally see that it gets into the papers, and before you start defending Kenny, I've told him that." Mum I do remember you with bruises and hearing Gran and Auntie Ciara talking."

173

"David, we used to fight. I gave as good as I got most of the time. I've always been, as your granddad would say, a handful. Sometimes It wasn't always as cut and dried as he hit me, other times, yes, he beat me up badly, I found it hard at times to know the difference, that it was wrong and no one should hit each other in a relationship." Caoimhe shook her head and looked at her son. "I've gone over it in my head so many times, why it happened why I didn't leave him. When I was younger, I could pack a mean punch son." She sighed. "Granted, I usually came out worse; probably at that time I still thought I loved him. I mean if you feel angry enough to fight, there must be passion in there too."

"What changed it Mum?"

"I'll tell you sometime David, just not now. You ask too many questions."

David stood up and hugged her. "Mum you're popular and the first woman chancellor, so you can ride any storm Kenny brings."

"David, don't you start Dan's nonsense about calling him by his first name, he's your father."

"More's the pity. Why couldn't you have slept with the stranger to have me? I have his fucking genes Mum, so does Dan."

"I was 15 years old David, I thought he was God. I was a kid in love. I can never regret having you and your brother."

David looked thoughtful and nudged his mother. "How do you know this Tony is a good guy? Your taste in men is a bit fucking warped. Jimmy Barnwell, Mum?" he said, smiling and raising an eyebrow.

"That was a one-night stand."

"He's a prick Mum. What if he does a kiss and tell?"

"He won't."

"How do you know?"

Caoimhe sighed and looked at her son. "David it's a long, long, story and not one I care to share with my son. I don't have the energy for it. Let's just say Jimmy won't want people to know what I know."

"Did you?"

"No, he couldn't manage it. My balls are too big for most men David."

"Mum, maybe I shouldn't be your press officer if you're going to have a sex life." He grinned. "A boy can only take so much scandal about his mother's going's on." David's eyes, so like Caoimhe's, sparkled. "Christ you're having more fun than me, and I'm 28."

The phone rang, David answered it. "Okay, right, okay yes, that's fine." He put the phone down. "The car's here. Mum, I've prepared a press release about you splitting from Dad. If you get a chance can you let Ed know?"

"David, it's his wife's funeral, have a heart."

"He's a politician too Mum. Like I said, he knows this is a good day to bury news."

"Today, he is a grieving husband."

David was right however; the announcement that Caoimhe Black had separated from her husband was relegated to a small column in the newspapers which were full of the story of the funeral. Caoimhe's emotive eulogy was reprinted on the front page of every tabloid the next morning. The press mentioned that she had given this speech whilst grieving over the loss of her thirty-year marriage.

CHAPTER

SEVENTEEN

19th April

"Honestly your mum, she was the best barmaid I ever had, your Auntie Ciara was really awful. I had to employ her of course. Ciara that is, because Phil was my partner and my best friend, but I was glad when she stopped working and started being a lady who lunched."

Caoimhe smiled, remembering. "Ciara was so lazy! Do you know she used to talk people into taking shots because she hated pulling pints? It was too much like hard work for her!"

Tony laughed, remembering his frustration about his best friend's wife. "She couldn't pull pints; they had heads that went through half the glass. Her breakfasts were burnt. We used to find her asleep when she was supposed to be changing the bed linen."

Caoimhe laughed. "It was just as well Phil's business did so well and he could afford for her to not work. She has always just been a lady who lunches. She has a whole group of friends who are the same. She does play golf though, mainly because that's what the ladies in her circle do."

Three months had passed since David and the press office had announced the split between Kenny and Caoimhe. They had told the country the split was amicable and that they would remain friends. Caoimhe had received the decree nisi and knew in five weeks the decree absolute would come through and she would be divorced and a free woman. Tony had been divorced for several weeks. She and Tony saw each other discreetly a few times a month. They were seen in public but always in mixed company, never alone. David had met Tony several times prior to this night, because he lived and worked in London. The two men had got on well. Tonight, Caoimhe had finally introduced him to Daimhim, Elaine, Dan and her grandchildren who had come down for the Easter weekend. The evening appeared to be going well.

Dan had spent the day with Samira. Ravi had come home for three weeks, two months before and had his medication altered. Both Dan and Samira reported that he was responding well to the altered medication but they had not been able to speak to him since he had returned to Pakistan. Ravi was working with children orphaned by the unrest. Today, they'd spoken to Samira's uncle who assured them that as far as he could ascertain, Ravi was doing well, and his health was not causing concern. He was, however, working in a mountain region where it was difficult to remain in contact.

Caoimhe had decided to cook a meal for her family and have Tony as a guest. The meal was successful; all three of her children were polite and respectful to Tony. Initially wary, as the evening had progressed they had all relaxed and appeared to like him. Dan cornered her in the kitchen as she took a tray of sticky toffee pudding out of the oven. "Elaine, can you take the pudding through?" he said to his wife, who was helping Caoimhe.

Caoimhe made eye contact with her daughter-in-law who smiled. "Dan, you look so serious! Is it so hard to know that your mummy has a lover? I like him a lot Caoimhe. I can't believe that you have ended up with someone from your home town though. He's lovely, ooh so sexy; in fact, he's a really fit, silver fox." Elaine laughed at her husband who was glaring at her. She lifted the pudding and disappeared out of the door.

Dan looked at Caoimhe, a serious expression on his face.

"Mum, he's a nice guy, I like him too, but you need to be careful. If Dad finds out, he might dig his heels in. You want to be divorced before you take up with Tony publicly. Dad's doing okay, but you still have six weeks to wait for the degree absolute. He could stall, if he takes it into his head to do so."

"Dan, we are publicly 'just friends'; we have known each other for years. I used to work with him as you know, well for him really. He's a successful business man now, I like him a lot."

"Mum cut the crap, you're so loved up it would be hard to hide it if you're together. You're lighting up like a candle when he speaks. You can hardly keep your eyes off him. He's the same; he watches your every move." He put his arm around her and kissed her cheek. "I'm so glad that you are with him though Mum. I've never seen you so happy." There was a pause before Dan continued. "Mum can I ask you something personal?"

"Hmm," she said, distracted, loading dishes into the dishwasher.

"Tony, he's Veenies father isn't he?"

"What! How did you know?" she spluttered.

"I'm a social worker Mum, trained to observe behaviour and people. I can see the resemblance. It's not apparent right away, but it's there, it's mannerisms, ways of speaking, his smile. She also has his eyes! It's definitely an argument for nature over nurture. Mum, I don't want to know the gritty details. Does Tony know?"

"Yes, he does now. He has known since just after the election. I never told him at the time; there were a lot of reasons why I couldn't. He saw Daimhim on TV with you and David after the election and guessed. He has another two daughters, one of whom is only a few months older than Daimhim. He saw the resemblance to her. No one knew, except Samira at the time." Caoimhe blushed. "I actually wasn't sure until she was born Dan. I'm ashamed to say I was sleeping with both him and your dad."

Dan looked at her and raised an eyebrow. "Wow Mum, really!"

"It's a long and tragic story honey. It was a very painful time for both Tony and I for different reasons. I was still only twenty-five at the time she was born remember, but I had been married for nine years. If David and Daimhim haven't noticed Dan, please don't say anything. I just want her to get to know him first before I tell her."

Dan sighed and nodded. "Okay Mum, but I don't think you're being fair to Daimhim or to Tony. These things have a habit of biting you on the bum. Mum, please do it soon, before anyone else notices." He smiled, his normal happy-go-lucky nature coming through, "because I would not like to be in your shoes, if my little sister finds out some other way."

She nodded. "Thanks for not being shocked. It's a lot for a son to take in, his mother having a covert sex life."

Dan put his arm around her kissing her cheek. "Mum I just want you to be happy, and despite Dad's behaviour over the years, I actually want the same for him. I think he might sort out his life this time without you. I mean he's not had a drink now for almost a year, and this must have been stressful for him too."

After dinner, David took his brother and sister to the airport for their flight home and then went out for the evening. Caoimhe and Tony settled down in front of the TV. She lay back against him, her head on his chest and his arms around her. She told him what Dan had said.

"Daimhim is coming back down next month, after I get back from Prague Tony. I'll speak to her then. I'm so glad you can come with me, it will be good to get away."

"She's so beautiful and so clever and funny," Tony said, smiling down at Caoimhe. "I'm just a little in love with her already. I also need to speak to Anjya about the situation but I'll wait till after you've told Daimhim. There's only seven months between them. If the situation was different, if you had stayed in Ayrshire, they would have been in the same class at school likely. I hope they'll be friends Caoimhe."

Caoimhe rolled around and put her arms around his neck. "Tony, make love to me, let's just forget about the world for now."

Tony nuzzled her neck and smiled. "Is that your answer to everything?"

"When you're lying there looking so god damn handsome then yes, it's the answer to my need for sheer unadulterated passion."

Tony kissed her neck and smiled as she shivered and pulled him closer. "I can't believe I'm about to make love to the Chancellor of the Exchequer, in 11 Downing Street."

"You're not; you're talking about doing it. Now shut up and get on with it," Caoimhe whispered, nibbling his ear lobe. He shivered and smiled.

"God Caoimhe, I have a permanent erection when you're around, that's not good for a man my age." He began to kiss her, gently at first then with more and more force. She felt his manhood pressing against her through her clothes. Suddenly, he jumped to his feet, lifted her into his arms and ran with her, squealing loudly, through the house to her bedroom. He laid her on the bed, removing her clothes as he kissed the length of her body. He rolled over. Taking her nipple between his teeth, he gently nibbled and she moaned as he slid his hand between her legs, his fingers rubbing and probing. She arched her back and pushed against his hand. "Tony, I need to feel you inside me, not just your fingers."

She began to kiss his neck as her fingers fumbled with his shirt and she eventually pulled it over his head. She unbuttoned his trousers, pulled them down over his hips and straddled him. He reached down and guided his penis inside her. She gasped as he pulled her down hard on top of him. She leaned forward and he began to kiss and caress her breasts as she moved against him. Moaning and pushing against her, his excitement mounting, he cried out. "Oh God, each time we do this, it just gets better and better. I never thought it could improve, but it has gone from fantastic to unbelievable." He pulled her face down to his, kissing her neck, her throat and then her mouth met his. Their orgasms when they came were simultaneous. They clung to each other as the full intensity of their love making washed over them.

"Some people just have chemistry Tony!" she gasped. Afterwards, spent, she lay in his arms, her body still quivering from their lovemaking, drifting towards sleep. Caoimhe jumped as her phone rang. "Who is it? Who's calling at this time of night?" she looked at her watch, "ten past one in the morning. Never good news, a call at this time is it?" Samira's name came up on the screen. Caoimhe lifted the phone. "Sami what is it? Calm down hon, breathe, tell me what's happened?" Tony watched Caoimhe's face as she listened. Eventually she spoke. "Right Samira, just get in a taxi and come over here. I'll let the gate know." She put the phone down. "That was Sami; she's in a right state, something about Ravi. God, I hope he's not ill again! He was doing so well. I was worried about him going back abroad, but all reports are that he's doing a fantastic job."

When Samira came in twenty minutes later she was still distraught. Tony stood up and hugged her. "I'll go up to bed Caoimhe." He said letting go of Samira.

"No, it's alright Tony, you are part of Caoimhe's life now and I trust you." Samira sobbed.

"Sami what is it? Caoimhe asked gently, looking from Samira to Tony.

"It's Ravi! He appeared at the flat tonight, he's ill Kee. I didn't even know he was in the country. I'm so frightened; he was raving about a government conspiracy, he's really not well. He's gone off to ... I don't know where. He appears to have been going to some kind of radical, Islamic meetings! He was raving about Jihad and having to be a martyr to the cause."

Caoimhe could not believe what she was hearing. "Samira, he's never been interested in religion or politics," she gasped. "Let's go and see if we can find him. He might have gone to his own flat."

"We need to let Harry know!" Samira said, quickly.

"It's not Harry, it's Colin. He's gone with David," Caoimhe told her friend. "I'll call Jed on route. This is a personal family matter Samira."

Tony looked at them. "Is that wise?"

181

"Tony, it's Ravi, I've known him since he was born!" Caoimhe said quietly. "He's not dangerous, he's schizophrenic. His medication needs altering probably. He'll be frightened. It's better that Samira and I, who he knows and trusts, take him in to hospital. Tony, remember I was a mental health social worker?"

"Caoimhe, I don't want to sound like a prophet of doom! That was over ten years ago, sweetheart. You really should leave this to the professionals."

"Tony, please just go back to bed. Come on, Sami."

"No, I'm coming with you, in fact I'll drive," Tony said quickly.

There was no answer at Ravi's flat; Samira let them in with her key. The house looked as though there'd been a hurricane through it. Clothes hanging out of drawers, broken crockery in the kitchen, the television was lying smashed on the floor. "Shit there is not an inch of floor we could walk on," Samira sobbed. They left it as is it was and returned to Samira's flat. To their amazement, Ravi was there, he had fallen asleep on the sofa. Samira called the local hospital and arranged for Ravi to be admitted. As Samira made them coffee, Ravi wakened and came through to the kitchen.

"You drugged me!" he shouted at Samira. "You're with them. They're all trying to stop the will of Allah. They're trying to kill me."

"Ravi calm down. Please stop shouting? We're your friends," Caoimhe said quietly. "Please sit down and let us get you some help."

"You're the fallen woman. You're the face of the establishment. You're a harlot! You're with her." He pointed at his sister, stabbing his finger into Samira's chest. Ravi turned and walked away, when he reached the door he swung around and addressed the room. "She lies with woman, she who comes from the same womb as me."

They followed him through to the lounge, Caoimhe tried to corner him. "Look at me, Ravi, focus, we're the people who love you," she cried.

Ravi looked from Caoimhe to Tony and then at his sister.

Suddenly he pushed Caoimhe, knocking her over and ran towards the door, passing Samira, who put her hand out and grabbed her brother. He broke free and jumped over the sofa.

Tony stepped forward. "I'm a friend, please listen, you're not at all well son. You need to calm down."

Ravi moved towards Caoimhe, ignoring Tony. "I am the Master of the Day of Judgement. You will have painful punishment Caoimhe Black, because of the sickness of the infidels. You have denial in your heart." He ran for the door and opened it, running out into the street.

"Well that worked well!" Tony said. "Fuck sake Samira, he's in a really bad way."

Samira began to cry again, "he's quoting from the Quran, it's all messed up though, it's his illness I think."

"You better call the police Sami!" Tony sighed, putting his arm around Samira. "He's not safe, he could be a danger." Samira looked at Caoimhe and then back up at Tony.

Caoimhe shook her head vigorously. "No, he's not Tony, he's a danger to himself! But you're right, we need to alert the police so they can detain him under mental health legislation, not criminal. Oh Samira, I'm so sorry, I really thought he was well."

Samira stood staring at the open door as though expecting her brother to walk back through it. "I knew he was unwell, even though the signs were different this time." She looked from Caoimhe to Tony. "My dad used to get like that. I don't know what to do Caoimhe. I'm so scared for him. This is not the time in history to become a radical Islamist is it?"

Caoimhe shrugged and looked from Samira to Tony. "Let's go back to Downing Street, we need to let Ed know. Samira, you're my Private Secretary, we have to tell him. We can do all the calling from there."

Tony tightened his arm around Samira's shoulder. "I thought he was okay with you being a lesbian?"

"He is normally, Tony." She rested her head on his shoulder. "That's just his illness again. I don't know what happened in

Pakistan. He's not normally political either. I should never have let him go."

Caoimhe sighed, "Samira he's nearly 30, he's an adult and at the time he appeared to be really well." Caoimhe reached over and touched Samira's arm. "It'll be okay Sami. We'll get people out looking for him and hopefully get him into treatment and our old Ravi back."

CHAPTER

EIGHTEEN

"Fuck sake Caoimhe, listen to yourself! This is a full-scale terrorist alert. Samira understands and accepts it, why can't you? Alex Stanley shook his head and sighed. "Her brother is missing. He's been online with anti-government and anti-British propaganda. He's been supporting the murder of hostages; he must be found. Samira needs to lie low. We can't be seen to be making allowances because she's a party member and your PPS!"

Caoimhe glared at him, "Alex I understand what you are saying, but that's racist. There are millions of law abiding, good people who are Muslim. They might not agree with this government but they also don't agree with terrorism either. Samira has been a good and loyal party member, you're not going to ostracise her because of Ravi. Who, may I remind you, is ill. This government, our party, stands for breaking down the walls of diversity and we cannot do this to her because she is the brother of someone who might, whilst in a psychotic episode, have these leanings."

Caoimhe looked over at Edward Wilson who was sitting behind his desk, looking serious. "Ed, you know Ravi, we don't know what has happened in Pakistan. He's gravely ill, not a terrorist. If he had been linking to extreme groups, then surely the CIA would have picked it up given the connection to us. We need to find him, get him treatment, not arrest him and make an example of him." Caoimhe felt frustrated, she knew how Ravi would be portrayed and she knew it was not him. "Ravi doesn't think like that. If you get him into hospital he will, once he is treated, go back to being the same lovable boy he was. He doesn't even follow any religion, he never has; you know that. Alex, Ed, I'll not deny my friend. She'll remain with me, or so help me I will fucking resign." Her words hung in the air as the door to the Prime Minister's office was knocked on loudly.

"Ed, Caoimhe, it's getting worse." Jed Livingstone, head of security cried, coming through from the outer office. "He's now putting notices about you online, saying that you're the reason he has been ill. There are images of the beheading of hostages in numerous countries, he says that you and Ed are the behind it. There is a particularly graphic one of a woman being brutally raped by Arab men. He's superimposed your face on her Caoimhe. He's moving around, so we can't get a trace on him. Saying he's planning to teach you a lesson Ed. There is also some really nasty stuff about Linda. We need to be on high alert now; we cannot take a chance. After seven-seven, very clear guidelines were put in place for potentially dangerous extremists."

Caoimhe stood up and glared at Jed. "He's ill, Jed. Yes, he has for some reason got himself caught up in something, but he's ill! Not dangerous, he's not a terrorist either; you have no evidence for that statement."

"Fuck sake Caoimhe, stop and think about this!" Ed banged his fist on the desk in front of him. "We cannot avoid this becoming public now! Ravi is dangerous to you, personally and professionally. The public will see this as you condoning his behaviour." Ed looked sternly at Caoimhe as he spoke. "I agree with her about Samira, Alex, but I do think she should lie low. More for her own good Caoimhe, than for ours."

The door was knocked again; David entered, accompanied by his brother.

"What are you doing here?"

Dan looked at Caoimhe. "David called me. I just

about-turned, got back on the flight. We need to try to find him Mum."

"No Dan, this isn't one where you should get involved," Jed said quickly. Caoimhe nodded in agreement.

"Boys leave it to the professionals for now," Caoimhe said quietly, "they'll treat him with respect, and once he is safe you can get involved."

"Mum, Ravi might just respond to us," David cried.

Dan nodded and sighed. "Mum, Samira and I were afraid of this. He seemed normal last time he was here, but he had been finding out about so many atrocities when he was in Pakistan and he is a caring person. It doesn't really matter whether they were real or not! He believed the British and American governments were conspiring. He appeared well though and entitled to his opinion. There's no way Ravi in his right mind would be an extremist. He's been radicalised. He did tell me he had met a woman he wanted to marry; he never told me her full name. He said she was the sister of someone he met while he was at Oxford. Her name was Rashida; her brother was Achmad. They were mates I think."

"Jesus! It could Achmad Al Shaman!" Jed gasped. "How could we have missed that connection?"

"It is Achmad Al Shaman. He was at Oxford the same time as us, but they were never friends," David said, shaking his head, "in fact Ravi didn't like him, because he was a bit extreme in his views, he avoided him. There was an Asian Students society. Ravi left it because of Achmad and his mates. I remember he said they were all hypocrites because they were down on the western world yet were taking an education from Britain."

"Is this significant?" Ed asked. Caoimhe and Alex looked at each other then at Ed. Jed gestured to Caoimhe and nodded his head at Dan and David.

"Boys, would you mind going next door please?" Ed sighed. "If it's a matter of international security the less you know the better."

"We'd better get Iain here too!" Caoimhe said quietly. "Ed, we didn't tell you because of how ill Linda was, and then it appeared to quieten down, so it got lost in everything else that was going on. There was some stuff at New Year. Iain and I dealt with it, but we didn't think that it was significant then, there has been nothing linking Ravi to it until now. You always told me Ed, don't ask permission in an emergency, ask for forgiveness."

Ed shook his head and lifted the telephone. "Janet get me Iain here please, tonight. I don't care where he fucking is Janet. I need the foreign secretary and I want him here, get him out of the wedding. Tell them to sober him up and have him here." He put the phone down and turned back to Caoimhe and Alex. "Okay, now you two tell me what you know. We'll deal with you keeping me in the dark later. I need a fucking drink!"

Caoimhe looked at Ed and then at Alex. "Abdulla El Shaman is an up and coming agitator in the style of bin-laden. He is dangerous, ruthless and a real threat to security. He's believed to be responsible for the beheading of the aid workers in Rajasthan. Caoimhe said, "he's also been linked to the unrest in Syria and Isis. She took a deep breath, "and, for the kidnap, rape and murder of the British ambassador's daughter in Qatar, last year."

"Christ, she was only seventeen," Ed gasped. "I understood intelligence was that it wasn't political?"

"We only found out recently Ed." Alex sighed. "You had so much going on. Caoimhe, Iain and I were handling it. It's not gone public yet anyway."

Ed looked directly at Caoimhe as he spoke. "Caoimhe I know you love Ravi like a son, but he's not your son. He has the potential to be really dangerous, because of his mental health."

Caoimhe sighed. "I know that Ed. The security of the country must come first and I accept that. However, we need to try to end this peacefully and quietly."

"What's the story with Ravi?" Alex asked. Caoimhe lifted her glass and took a sip before replying.

"It's a congenital thing we think. The mental health, it runs through their family. Samira's dad and an uncle had the same

188

condition. The thing is, Ravi's mental health problem was not apparent until he was in his last year at university. He got drunk and went out with a young lady. They slept together, only she already had a boyfriend she had neglected to tell him about. The boyfriend found out she'd been with someone else. She panicked and said Ravi raped her. He was arrested and you can imagine the scenario? Young beautiful white woman, accusing an Asian Man. He was treated harshly, almost interrogated, held for days charged, then initially remanded in custody. He was suspended from university, held in custody for three months. Then the girl admitted she'd lied. They were only too willing to believe her over him. It was overtly racist. We were fighting to get him out, we knew he wasn't capable of rape."

"How could that happen?" Alex asked.

Caoimhe sighed and shook her head. "The boyfriend beat her up and the police were called. At that point, she told them he'd realised she'd been with someone else. She said she'd been raped because she was scared of him. The young woman was terrified of her boyfriend and had already been a victim of domestic violence, but no one checked this out. He was allowed to be present when she was interviewed. So, she lied."

"During the time, Ravi was in prison, the first episode of mental health difficulties occurred. We all hoped that it was just because of the circumstances and was reactive! You know post-traumatic stress, but, it took a year for him to be well enough to continue with his course and finish. Then any time of stress it reappeared, he was never violent. Just scared, he would retreat into himself. He was later awarded a six figure, compensation."

Caoimhe shook her head and wiped away a tear. "He was never the same again, he was only 22 when it happened. He eventually graduated a year late with a first in law, but has never been able to practice because of the illness. He's been well for the last couple of years. He wanted to explore his heritage. There's no way, Ravi had these leanings before he went to Pakistan. He may have known the Al Shaman's whilst he was at Oxford, but you heard what David said, they were certainly not major friends. David would know, he was there at the same time but on a different course, they shared a flat. Ravi had really no interest then in his Asian heritage. He considered himself British, he didn't follow any religion."

"Jed, you had better start looking in to the connections at Oxford." Caoimhe sat down looking up at Jed, "David will be able to help. I'm struggling to see him as an extremist, but whilst he is as ill … I don't know. Sami will be able to tell you who his psychiatrist here is. Perhaps it's worth speaking to them to find out. Dan has spoken to him recently. He might have picked up something."

Jed put his hand on Caoimhe's shoulder. She shook her head and looked up at him. "Caoimhe I don't want to compound your misery, there's another problem. Kenny has been talking to a magazine, and the nationals are about to pick up on some quite personal matters."

"What now?" she groaned. "Is it the stuff about Daimhim?"

"Caoimhe, it's not true, is it?" Jed gasped, looking at Caoimhe. "He's claiming that you slept around and he put you through university only for you to reward him by getting pregnant and not knowing who the father was."

"Jed, Tony Carter is Daimhim's father. It's a long complicated, very painful story and she doesn't know. She knows it's not Kenny, but I told him I slept with a stranger and I have never told anyone the truth. Get David to speak to Kenny. He had a big story prepared, if Kenny tried this."

Ed moved over and put his arms around Caoimhe. Alex and Jed stared at them. The prime minister kissed the top of her head. "We need to let them leak the story Caoimhe. He isn't worried about you when he's doing this. He's not drinking again either, is he? Could he have found out about Tony being Daimhim's father?"

"Don't think so, only myself, Samira, Ciara and Tony know. Dan guessed, but none of them would talk about it." Caoimhe looked around the room. "Thing is, as I said, Daimhim doesn't know!" I'm working up to telling her."

The door was tapped lightly and Harry put his head around the door. "Iain Milton-Daws is on his way. He's been drinking but they're feeding him coffee. Hopefully he should be sensible but it's Iain! Caoimhe I'm going to go back to number eleven with the boys. Sami's there too."

"Thanks for coming over Harry," Caoimhe said, smiling wryly at her bodyguard. "I really appreciate it. Hope I didn't interfere too much with your love life?"

Harry shrugged and winked at Caoimhe. "The evening had already reached a suitable conclusion."

Ed looked at Caoimhe. "Will you be alright?"

Caoimhe sighed and glanced at her colleagues. "Look I'll be fine, there are more important things. I think we should just ignore the story. I'm more worried about Samira. She needs to be protected because if Ravi really is that ill, he may target her. I suggest that she stays with me and we agree that she keeps a low profile. I'll not turn my back on her. Karen, her partner is a pilot and is in Australia so she would be on her own. She'll be safer here than anywhere else with our security. Harry, you can take her to her flat to pack anything she needs. Take Colin with you and be vigilant, because Ravi went back there before."

Ed and Alex looked at Caoimhe. "You need to be careful here!" Ed said quietly. "You're emotionally involved. If he contacts any of you, you cannot handle this yourself."

"Ed, for Christ sake, do you think I would put everyone, including Ravi in danger? Of course, I wouldn't handle it myself."

"You need to make sure your family know that too." He shook his head. "Especially Daimhim, make sure she follows instruction, Samira too. If he contacts her we need to know?"

Caoimhe nodded. "Ed the security of the country is at stake here. You know there's no way I would jeopardise that. Harry or Colin will look after Samira just now."

Ed stood up. "Does anyone want another drink?" Alex nodded

and Caoimhe shook her head. "Not for me," she said quietly. "If there is nothing else for me to do, I'm going next door to try to get some sleep. I think you two should do the same. If Ian has been drinking and is in Yorkshire, you are talking a few hours before he gets here. Jed can brief my family."

"What about Daimhim? Her and Ravi are really friendly?" Alex said.

Caoimhe nodded. "All three of my kids are close to him. I don't want to call her in the middle of the night. Jed, could you alert Annie?"

Alex looked at Jed. "Who's Annie?"

"Annie is head of Daimhim's small security team. After her escapade in Japan I decided to hire someone Alex." Caoimhe sighed. "Jed's team received intelligence the hijack was meant to be Daimhim's flight and that she was the target because of me. With her going to uni and her bolshie nature I felt she might be a sitting duck. She's my daughter. I pay Annie myself, I don't use tax-payers money for it, but she links directly to Harry and Jed."

"David and Dan are both very low key. The police protect them. Daimhim well, she is just so like me, gobby, opinionated and likely to get into scrapes."

Alex smiled. "She may have a future in politics then?"

"Undoubtedly!" Ed said laughing. "I remember her being about fourteen, and her getting into a very adult argument with that ambassador to America what was his name? Sonny something or other. She would have put many politicians to shame, the way she put her views across. I thought, *someday this little lady is going to be a formidable figure in politics*. Ah, the passion of youth, socialist idealism, and that feisty temperament. She is, just as Linda always said, a mini me Caoimhe."

Caoimhe smiled and put down her Glass. "Okay I'm going next door."

"Is your man still there?" Jed asked.

Caoimhe nodded. "He's going home tomorrow. Jed, you will let me know if there is any news? The police can call too if they need to speak to any of us." She smiled ruefully and left the room.

Jed followed her out.

Alex looked at Ed. "Tony Carter? She's still seeing him then?" He chuckled and grinned at Ed. "Lucky bastard, can you imagine what she must be like in the sack?"

Ed whistled and shook his head. "I try not to picture that Alex, but after some of the things she told Linda about her and Tony. Well it's hard not to."

The house was quiet; everyone had gone to bed. Caoimhe suddenly felt exhausted. She crept into her bedroom, assuming that as the house was quiet, everyone was asleep, but Tony was sitting up in bed reading from a kindle. "I couldn't sleep Caoimhe, poor Sami, she was distraught, but your boys are fantastic they were looking after her." He watched as she took off her clothes dropping them on the floor, he put his arm around her as she got into bed beside him. "You look shattered honey you need to get some rest, or you will be no use to anyone.

Caoimhe looked up at Tony and sighed, "Kenny has given an interview saying he's not Daimhim's father. Implying that I slept around and don't know who her father is."

"What are you going to do?"

"Ignore it for now, I think, hold me Tony. I just need to feel your arms around me tonight. I need to feel safe." She looked at him. "I'm not good at being vulnerable, but, I need you to know that with you. I do feel that I'm protected and safe."

Tony smiled, tightened his arms around her and kissed her gently. "Do you want me to cancel my flight tomorrow?"

"No, it's best that you go home and carry on as normal. No one really knows about us, so you should not be bothered by the press or anything. It's better you're not here. I just hope that they can find Ravi before he hurts himself." She looked up at the ceiling and then at him. "Or someone else ... it's really hard for me to think of Ravi as being dangerous. Must be worse for poor Samira. Fuck Tony what next? It never rains but it pours."

"Try to sleep!" He whispered in her ear, holding her close he kissed her forehead, "sleep it will be clearer in the morning babe.

CHAPTER

NINETEEN

Three months passed without any sign of Ravi; he continued to stay online, making threats but always staying one step ahead of the security forces trying to find him. There was talk that he was out of the country. That the Al shamans had managed to get him to Syria via Turkey. Parliament broke up for the summer recess; Caoimhe remained in London whilst Ed planned to go to Australia to visit Caroline for a month. Alex and Caoimhe had developed to her amazement, a strong friendship, and she realised that she had mistaken ambition for ruthlessness. Alex took over the helm of the government in Ed's absence but both he and Caoimhe remained fiercely loyal to Edward Wilson.

Daimhim moved into 11 Downing Street during her summer break. Caoimhe had banned her from travelling due to the security risk. Daimhim was still unaware Tony was her father. Caoimhe was still worried about Daimhim reacting badly if she told her daughter the truth. Caoimhe felt she needed some time. Tony had tried to be supportive but he was growing worried that Caoimhe was never going to tell her. Caoimhe travelled up to Scotland for a few days for meetings. Tony had moved into the River Doon Hotel. He had bought a new home in the area, but it was not ready for him to occupy as he was having renovations done. On Caoimhe's last day she managed to get to Ayrshire to see him. She was due to fly home early the following morning. After a dinner in the hotel restaurant, they had a few drinks.

Caoimhe felt stressed because, once again, Tony brought up the subject of telling Daimhim she was his daughter. Back in Tony's apartment, she poured herself another drink. Ed had flown to Australia that afternoon, leaving her and Alex in charge of the country. Caroline, his daughter, was undergoing treatment for cancer, and after losing Linda he was understandably distressed and worried.

The friendship between Caoimhe and Ed was strong. Daimhim, who had over the years become close to Caroline, had stayed with her when she was in Australia on her travels. She had wanted to accompany him, however Caoimhe had forbid it. She knew Ed did not need the worry of Daimhim, and, Caroline needed to feel she had her father's undivided attention. Caoimhe had also realised that if Daimhim went away it may look to Tony as though she was stalling telling her again. However, Daimhim and Caoimhe had argued and currently were not speaking.

"Don't you think you have had enough?" Tony asked. "Caoimhe, we need to talk about Daimhim. I understand why you didn't want to speak in the restaurant. I've tried hard to be patient with you Caoimhe, but, this has gone on far too long. How is she going to feel when you do tell her? From what I can see, she's going to take it badly now that you have let her get to know me, and still not told her."

"Tony please? Just let me have a little more time; Daimhim, she is so headstrong, I just need to do this my way. I keep trying to broach it, but, there is never a good time with her just now. She's down for the summer, so I'll do it soon I promise."

Tony sighed and looked at Caoimhe. "Let me be there when you tell her then? I can help, support you, explain to her what happened from my point of view."

"No, Tony, that would just make her angry. I know my daughter Tony, you don't. She'll go mad at me, I don't want it to cloud her future relationship with you."

"Can I just point out she's my daughter too, and it's because of you, I don't know her!" Tony's face showed how angry he was.

Caoimhe knew she should stop drinking and try to calm down. As usual, she ignored her gut instinct, instead she finished her drink and poured another. She knew she'd drunk too much and she also realised that she was getting angry at Tony. Her head was telling her to stop, but true to form she couldn't.

"I'm trying to understand Caoimhe and I don't want to put pressure on you but I need that commitment from you."

"You promised me you would not put pressure on me for anything." Caoimhe took a long gulp of her vodka then put the glass down. She moved over and began to kiss him; he pushed her away and stared at her. In response, she dropped to her knees in front of him, and began to unzip his trousers.

He grabbed her arm and pulled her to her roughly feet. "Don't you fucking, dare, Caoimhe! You can't sort everything with a fucking blow job. How dare you insult my intelligence, this is not just about me and you." "What the fuck is wrong with you tonight Caoimhe, talk to me?"

Tony was, Caoimhe realised, angrier than she had ever seen him, again she heard the cue in her head to stop but ignored it. "Don't nag Tony, I don't want to talk! Not everything can be talked about. I'm a fucking adulterous woman and the whole world is going to know. I just don't know how to tell her. When I do, what do I say? Oh by the way, Tony and I are your parents! You have a big sister whose mother we killed because of our relationship. Oh, and you have a little sister who is seeing a psychologist because we have fucked up her life too. Nice one Tony." She screamed in his face. "Let's tell the world that the woman in charge of the coffers of this country, is just a tart like her ex-husband says."

Tony shook his head he was Caoimhe realised furious, but, when he spoke, he sounded calm. "You haven't learned anything from what happened before to us. Am I ever going to come first with you Caoimhe? I love you, and I understand your position, your job. I will never put that in jeopardy. I need your kids to know about what we were to each other! I want to be able to have Daimhim call me Dad. Even if it is in private. I want to be able to tell at least Anjya about us."

"I need more time Tony, stop making it sound as though this is all my fault."

Tony shook his head. "Your divorce is final now; there is nothing to stop us being a couple." He looked at her, "I need commitment from you. It's the same as it was all those years ago, isn't it? All about me meeting your needs and you only giving enough to keep me sweet. I've lost twenty years of my daughter's life, because of your pig headedness. I will not lose another moment. If you do not tell Daimhim about us, as soon as you go back to London. I'll tell her my fucking self. I will never betray you, but I'll not be your fucking puppet either. I've loved you for twenty two years and I'll still love you God Help Me for the next twenty two, but, she is my daughter and she doesn't know."

True to form Caoimhe's anger rose, she looked him in the eye and pulled herself away from his grip. "Don't you fucking, dare speak to my daughter Tony. I'll not be held to ransom, not by you or anyone else. I fucking decide when I do things, not even you will tell me, and love does not make the fucking world go around Tony. It causes heartache and fucking pain!"

"Do you know what? I can't do this Caoimhe?" The anger flashed in his eyes as he spoke. "I'm going out and hopefully you'll sober up and come to your fucking senses."

"If you walk out that door Tony Carter I'll not be here when you come back. You can just fuck off Tony; I don't need this right now. I swear Tony, go and I'll not take you back."

"Well at least I'll fucking know where you are this time, and that you are not in danger of becoming a domestic violence statistic." He shouted, as he left, slamming the door behind him.

***

Sitting on the private flight back to London Caoimhe stared

197

ahead. Sobering up now, she couldn't believe what she had said to Tony. She wanted to cry. She glanced at Harry, he put his hand in his pocket and handed her a clean white cotton handkerchief.

"You heard us?" She asked looking at him over the top of the hankie.

Harry nodded. "I wasn't eavesdropping Caoimhe. I couldn't help hearing you yelling at each other. I'm not going to ask you about you and him years ago, but I heard enough to know he's Daimhim's dad. I don't get it Caoimhe, surely that will cause her less anguish than thinking you slept with a stranger?"

"I don't know Harry, I've lied to her all these years. I struggle to say the words, "*I'm wrong!* I also struggle with sorry! And I love you!"

You're your own worst enemy Caoimhe, you know that, don't you? Why do you do that, push people who care about you away?"

"I shouldn't drink Harry. I'm as bad as Kenny when I do. Every mistake I have made. I have been drunk when I did it."

"Was Tony a mistake, Caoimhe?"

"I don't know just now. I was scared all those years ago, he was giving up chances of happiness with his fiancé to be with me. I told you about her dying in the crash! What I didn't tell you, was we had been in a relationship for a year. Tony was in a coma for a couple of months after the crash. When he came out of it he had amnesia, I'd found out I was pregnant and panicked. Kenny offered me a way out and I took it, but when Kenny told Daimhim he wasn't her dad, I should have told her the truth then. That was my moment and I didn't. I was still angry at Tony and scared of how I felt Harry. I'm not good at being scared and vulnerable, I've backed myself into a corner and I don't know the best way to get out now."

Caoimhe looked at her friend and sighed, tears running freely down her cheeks. "Now, I think, what if I make a fuck up of this and he has given up his life for nothing? I'm a bad risk Harry; I can't seem to get it right with men."

Harry put his arm around her and pulled her close. "You know what Boss? They're right about you; you are a fucking nutter. The guy loves you, he wants to take care of you. Yet you can't give in and just let him love you. Do you think you're not good enough for him or something? You keep your life in little compartments and you don't like them mixing do you? You're a control freak Caoimhe." Caoimhe looked Harry in the eye sighed and nodded.

***

In Ayr Tony wakened in his hotel room. When he returned to the apartment, she'd gone. He'd not intended to put pressure on Caoimhe, but her stubbornness, drove him mad. He couldn't believe they had fought when they only had one day together. He knew he loved her, but felt that he had fallen at the first hurdle. Could he really cope with Caoimhe and her public life? Was he being unreasonable? Did she love him enough? Did he love her enough? He sat down at the small dining table. Tears began to fall and he let it go, head in hands he leaned on the table in front of him and wept.

"Dad what's wrong? Dad?"

Tony looked up, Anjya stood in front of him her face showing the shock at seeing her father crying.

"Sorry, darling, I forgot you were going to be here this morning. I'm okay, really, just some stuff going on."

"Dad, talk to me. You've been seeing someone, haven't you?"

"How did you know?"

"Oh, little things, red hair in the plug hole, lipstick on your shirt. Your sudden all too frequent business trips. "She must be special for you to cry. I have never seen you do that, not even when Auntie Lolly, died."

"Oh, I cry darling all the time, just not in public." He smiled through his tears. "Not very manly, is it?"

"To cry Dad? My generation would say that's very manly." She put her arms around his neck and kissed his cheek. "Do you want to talk about it?"

"It's very complicated Anjya and really hard to explain."

"Try, Dad, I might be able to help?"

"Anjya, I can't darling, it involves other people, and it's really confidential. Can we just leave it for now, I'll tell you in time."

"Dad, no matter what it is. I won't say anything; you surely trust me?"

"Of, course I do Anjya, it's well, just complicated and if I tell you then it's out there and I actually don't know how you are going to react."

"I am not getting another brother or sister, am I? That's what you said when you were trying to tell me about Angelina being pregnant. Tell me you haven't got this woman pregnant?" She giggled. "Dad you have! You dirty bugger. We really need to have a talk about contraception."

"I haven't got anyone pregnant Anjya, not recently anyway."

"No Dad, I was close to the mark, I know you. I know when you are lying, when I mentioned pregnancy you reddened up. Daddy you've never lied to me, we agreed, if we ask each other a direct question, we must answer truthfully."

"Who's the parent here Anjya? You're much too fucking sensible. Can't you go and take drugs, go to raves or mug old ladies or something?" He kissed her cheek. "How long are you staying anyway?"

Anjya, looked at her father and smiled. "As long as it takes for you to tell me your secret?" Anjya kissed his cheek and looked at Tony. "I'm going back Monday night. Jimmy is back from America on Wednesday, I need to get the flat tidied up." She smiled. "That gives me four days to beat it out of you. Now I'm going to get changed and then you can buy me lunch. There is a new restaurant opened in Ayr I want to try."

"I own 13 Hotels! I'm not paying competitors Anjya. We can eat here. What are you doing tonight?"

"I'm going out with Georgina and Carol. Tomorrow, I'm taking Amy to get her nails done. I had to phone to arrange it, Cruella sends her venom. She says can you just keep Amy here until Monday? One of her horses is in foal. Maybe she's going to skin it and wear it."

"Stop calling Angelina, that." Tony laughed wiping away his tears. "She's not that bad."

"She is Dad, she's the fucking wicked witch of the west and you know it. Maybe I should vet potential girlfriends, the way I used to."

Tony smiled and stood up. "What's the story with you and Jimmy?"

"Don't change the subject Dad! This is about your love-life not mine."

"Come on, I'm curious? You've been living with him for a year now, and I haven't asked?"

"Dad he's my flatmate, and my best friend, my best gay Friend!"

"Oh!"

CHAPTER
TWENTY

"Dad you keep checking your phone, just phone this woman! She is probably doing the same. You've been doing that for three days now. She's probably waiting for you to call her!"

Tony put his phone on the table face down. "I doubt that."

Anjya looked from him to the television. "Why are you watching question time? I thought you hated politics?" Anjya stared at the television then suddenly she looked around at him and gasped. "It's her isn't it, Caoimhe Black? You used to know her years ago. She has red hair, the ginger hair in the plughole! Fuck Dad, she's married; I know her daughter."

"You know Daimhim? How?" he gasped.

"Well I first met her through Toria Clark obviously, they're cousins. Then I got to know her through the university debating club. She joined a couple of months ago. We're not exactly best friends, but she is okay, I like her. Is she going to be my new stepsister?" Anjya said laughing. "Dad what is it? You have gone white. Dad I'm just having fun. Fuck Dad!" Anjya gasped, looking at him. "You're not sleeping with Daimhim are you? Now that would really shock me."

Tony put his hands over his face, suddenly he felt too weary to lie anymore. "Anjya, she's my daughter and therefore your half-sister!"

"What? You're kidding?" She looked straight at him, the shock registering on her face. "You're not kidding, are you?"

He shook his head. "I'm afraid not. Anjya I didn't know sweetheart. I only found out a few months ago."

"She's the same age as I am Dad!" Anjya frowned and then looked at her father. Her mouth opened and she gasped, "Caoimhe Black is the woman you were in love with? Uncle Phil's sister-in-law? My mum was Aunt Ciara's best friend, dad!"

"Anjya, I'm so sorry, but the truth is I never stopped loving her. We got together again when Toria got married."

"When you took Daimhim's dad upstairs? Fuck, not Daimhim's dad, you're Daimhim's dad not Caoimhe's husband! Dad, she went up with you! **You didn't did you? With her husband in the next room? Jesus Dad!** Does Daimhim, know?"

Tony looked at his daughter and sighed. "That we're in a relationship, yes."

Anjya looked at him, tears gathering in her eyes. "That you're her father?"

"No, and you can't tell her. Caoimhe has never told her and she needs to do it. That's the reason we fell out. I wanted her to tell Daimhim before I told you and Amy. There's only seven months between you two. Is Amy asleep?"

Anjya nodded. "I need to hear the whole story Dad. Difficult as it is to think of what you and her did to my mum, I need to understand." She smiled through her tears. "At least it's not a shock. I wasn't a wanted child Dad and it would appear that neither was Daimhim. Was there no contraception twenty years ago? Or were you just careless?"

"Anjya, you know you are my golden child and nothing will ever change that."

Anjya nodded and smiled through tear filled eyes. "Three girls to three mothers! You're a tart Dad, do you know that?" She moved over to the sideboard and lifted a glass. "Do you want one? I'll pour, you start talking."

Half an hour later Anjya moved over and put her arms around

Tony who had tears running down his face. "That is the whole story Anjya."

"Oh, Dad, I'm so sorry; it must have been awful for you both."

"It was what it was. I was such a bastard Anjya, but the one thing I will tell you, is that from the moment I set eyes on you, I loved you darling and that will never change."

Anjya nodded. "Dad you need to go and see her, Caoimhe I mean, and sort this out. You and her, you both kind of need to grow up and get your act together. I mean the pair of you have left all these casualties in your wake, and you're fighting like children."

He smiled sadly. "She drives me mad Anjya. She takes no prisoners when she's on a roll."

Anjya smiled. "From what I have seen, Daimhim is the same. You are not exactly even tempered either Dad, when you blow you blow. I must have got my temperament from my mother."

"Claire was a lovely person Anjya, with a sweet nature. I really wanted to love her, but I just couldn't." Tony's eyes clouded as he remembered the painful time surrounding his daughter's birth. "Thing was darling, it was never there. I think I really wanted it to be love, but it just didn't have the spark. Once Caoimhe and I got together then there was no way that it would have worked with Claire. My life would have been so less complicated if I could have just loved her." Tony looked sadly at his eldest daughter. "I never meant to hurt Claire. Caoimhe and I have it on our conscience. That's what drove us apart and it's probably why she never told me about Daimhim."

"What are you going to do Dad?"

"I'm not running after her any more Anjya, she knows where I am," he said wearily.

"Dad it sounds as though you ended it, not her."

"Oh, it was just a fight; we used to argue when we were together. Caoimhe is feisty and determined as I said. I used to always be the one to run back when we fought. Then we would make up with sex, which was phenomenal." He blushed. "I can't believe I'm telling my daughter about my sex life. I'm not backing

204

down this time, she needs to tell Daimhim. She already knows Kenny Black isn't her father. I don't get why she can't just tell her I am. I met her Anjya, and we got on. I've told Caoimhe that if she doesn't tell our daughter the truth, I will. I don't want a big public announcement; I just want her to know who I am."

"Who does she think is her dad?"

Tony sighed. "Some random stranger her mother had a one-night stand with, a hotel guest."

"I saw that in a newspaper in an interview with her ex-husband but I thought it was just because she was divorcing him. Poor Daimhim, imagine having you two for parents."

"Well, she gets you for a sister, so that should even it up a bit."

"Dad, just call her. Caoimhe, not Daimhim. You know you're going to eventually. We're going down to London next week anyway, for the concert. You can meet her then."

Tony shook his head and his face darkened. "I will not, not this time Anjya. This is too important."

"How will you know if she has told Daimhim then?"

Tony put his arm around his daughter and kissed the top of her head. He looked into Anjya's eyes. "Daimhim will come looking for me.

CHAPTER

TWENTY-ONE

Jed Livingstone came into the room. Caoimhe looked up. Iain Milton-Dows came through from the kitchen with a cup of tea in his hand. "Caoimhe, Iain, you wanted a briefing about Ravi? We are almost sure he's out of the UK. MI5 have intelligence that put him in Turkey two days ago, but it's unconfirmed. If he is, it's likely he is trying to cross into Syria. However, it has been several weeks now and no sightings of him in the UK. The internet stuff is coming mainly from abroad now."

Caoimhe sighed and looked at the two men. "Oh dear Jed, I was really hoping against hope that he was still in the UK. He really needs help with his illness. If he's had no medication for months, then he'll be absolutely mental now. Hearing voices and hallucinating. He could be dead Jed; he was always at risk of suicide when the depressive part of his illness kicked in."

Iain looked at Jed. "What else do you know Jed? I know there's more."

Jed sighed. "Yes, there's more! I've only just got this from MI5, the lover Rashida, she's dead. She blew herself up inside the National Assembly in Islamabad a few hours ago. She went in with a small group of women, saying they had information about a threat to security. They spread out once inside and blew themselves up. There were several explosions around Pakistan today. We are now on high alert. We think Rashida Al Shaman's death is significant. It's martyr stuff Caoimhe; we'll need to be careful of copycat activity."

Iain sighed and looked at Caoimhe. "It's not the best time for this to happen, with Ed and Alex away, but you'll need to be the one to make decisions. Ed left you in charge. We'll brief him as soon as it's morning in Australia, and we'll call the security group together tomorrow. Best wait to see what Ed and Alex think."

Caoimhe looked at her colleague. "The death of his girlfriend could drive Ravi over the edge. Christ, he's out there and ill, now this, no one is safe. We need to find him, he'll need treatment. This is all I need right now. Thank God I stopped Daimhim from travelling this year. She's mightily pissed off with me just now, but it would appear it was the right decision. I'll step up her security and not allow her out without someone."

Jed Livingston shook his head. "Caoimhe, Daimhim will be in no real danger just now. We'll know if Ravi comes back in. We generally get intelligence quickly on any cells so there's nothing about just now. Ravi is out of the country, we're sure of it."

Iain stood up, "I'm going to head home now Jed, if there is anything call me and Caoimhe straight away. Caoimhe, I'll call you in the morning."

"Okay Iain I'll speak to you then. Jed, I'm not convinced that they got him out the country. I don't think he would harm Daimhim, but I suppose I never thought he would target me. I'm going to bed now and we can talk in the morning. Good night Jed."

***

Caoimhe stretched as walked through to the dining room carrying her breakfast. Daimhim sat at the table already dressed and eating a slice of toast. "Are you going out today darling?" Caoimhe asked, as she and Daimhim sat drinking coffee.

"Yes, I'm going to meet a friend Mum; Annie's coming with me." She smiled. "What about you?"

"Oh, nothing much. I need to be around with everyone else being away. Alex was supposed to be here but with his dad being so ill, he has had to go to the Isle of Wight."

"Is that where he grew up?"

"No, he's from Bristol, his parents retired to the Isle of Wight. It's not good with his dad, he's not expected to live. He only retired last year too. What a year it's been for us! Linda dying, all the stuff with Ravi, Kenny's fucking kiss and tell, now this with Caroline being ill and Alex's dad."

"Mum you really need to make sure you get a break. You didn't get away last year either. You are entitled to have a holiday, you know."

Caoimhe sighed and nodded. "I was hoping to get away with Ciara and Phil to their villa in France Veenie, but that's not going to happen. I do need to get up to Scotland though to see your Gran and Gramps before they go. I've been putting it off." Caoimhe looked momentarily sad. "They are going to ask for an explanation about you, after Kenny's kiss and tell."

"You're putting off going to Scotland because of the situation between you and Tony. Mum, what's the story with you and him? Will you please tell me what is going on? We all really liked him and he made you smile. You were great together and you're obviously missing him, what happened?"

"Daimhim, it's a long story and one where you and I need to be sitting down calmly while I tell you. I'm a bit stressed out about that and other things just now. I do miss him, but Tony and I, well it's just complicated and I think it's probably for the best that I keep out of his life. Tell you what Daimhim, if you are not doing anything at the weekend, let's go to Dorneywood."

"Mum I'd rather you just call Tony and get him to go with you, you know you want to."

Caoimhe smiled and Daimhim knew her mother was fighting tears. "I think I might have burned my bridges Daimhim. Sometimes my mouth just runs away with me, and when you say things without thinking, once it's out its out. Look I'll tell you everything, just come to Dorneywood with me and we can talk. I need your help with something anyway."

"Promise you'll tell me what happened?

"I promise. Now, will you be in for dinner?"

Daimhim shrugged. "Can I call later? I'm not sure yet. I was supposed to meet my brothers for lunch, so we might just go out and get drunk; it's not often we're all together now ... "

"Daimhim be careful, you know we're still not sure that Ravi is abroad. Some of the on-line stuff was being done in the UK. But the woman he was in love with, blew herself up yesterday in Pakistan. So, if he is in the UK, he'll be in a terrible state. You need to be alert at all times darling."

"Mum, that's awful. Were many people hurt?"

"Quite a few by the sound of it and there were a series of explosions by suicide bombers all over the area yesterday. So, we are back on high alert. Jed reckons that they have intelligence saying Ravi is in Turkey, but you can never be sure about it, as it's mainly unconfirmed sightings. If it is Turkey, then he's got himself involved in some dangerous deadly stuff Daimhim. I just struggle to get my head around it all. If this girlfriend is dead and he was in love with her it could be dangerous because of his illness. I'm more worried about him being a danger to himself. I need you all to be careful Daimhim. This is really serious stuff, and he may not be the boy you knew."

"Ravi would never harm me Mum! He and I, well there was a bit of a spark between us. I'm a wee bit shallow I suppose, and I didn't know if I could cope with his illness. I didn't act on it. He'd never hurt me, even when he's been ill he's responded to me."

"Daimhim, have you heard from him? You know you need to tell me if you have?" Caoimhe looked sternly at her daughter.

"No Mum I haven't!" Daimhim said sadly. "I keep hoping he'll call me. I've tried his mobile loads of times; it's always switched off. I'm really frightened they'll shoot him if he shows himself."

"Daimhim you must tell me if you hear from him, so that they don't shoot him on sight. If we can find him we can get him into hospital and get him help." She looked her daughter in the eye. "Daimhim he was really bad this time and it looks as though he has been exploited by extremists. He was not the Ravi I knew when I saw him. I'm not sure how much of the stuff being posted is from him. I mean they know some of it is coming from abroad and some from the UK. He can't be two places at once can he?"

Daimhim nodded. "Mum I really think Jed is right and he's abroad. They'd have found him by now if he was here. Or, he would have made contact. He has always come out of episodes fairly quickly in the past."

"Yes Daimhim, because he has had the right medication. The people who're exploiting him will be making sure he doesn't have treatment, because if he was in his right mind he would not agree with their methods. There's a lot of information about radicalisation around just now, sometimes they target vulnerable people like Ravi. They break them down and fill them full of propaganda." Caoimhe wiped away a tear. "It's so hard to think of Ravi that way. I just keep thinking if we can get him, talk to him, we could bring him around. I hate the way the press is portraying him. The stuff they are saying about him is so untrue. Yet from what I saw Daimhim, he really was lost in the radicalisation process. It just wasn't our Ravi." Caoimhe sighed and then smiled. "Anyway darling, have a good time with your friend. If you are out with your brothers, all of you behave yourselves and get home at a reasonable hour. Another thing Daimhim!"

"What now?"

"Stop wearing my bloody shoes, those ones you have on were expensive. Take care of them. They better come back on your feet and undamaged."

***

The coffee shop was crowded. Anjya waved and smiled when she saw Daimhim come in. "Hi Daimhim, glad you could make it. I suppose you are curious about why I called you."

"It's good to see you Anjya. Actually most of the friends I had down here are no longer living in the capital, so it's good to see a friend. Mum has got some sort of security buzz just now so I'm feeling stir crazy. I was a bit surprised when you messaged me, but I'm intrigued now."

Anjya looked at Daimhim. "Could we go somewhere a bit more private?"

Daimhim looked around her, "what about that Green Park across the road. Annie, we're going across to sit outside," Daimhim called to Annie, who nodded and sat down at a window table with her coffee. "I have to have security all the time just now, there is a high alert and we are kind of caught up on it."

"Oh, Annie is your security? That explains why she is always with you."

"Why, what did people think?"

"They thought you were an item, her and that other girl."

"Chloe is Annie's relief," Daimhim laughed. "I can assure you that I'm not gay, I like men too much. Oops, that's not why you are meeting me, for coffee?"

"What? No, I'm 100% hetro too. Why I called you is much more complicated than being attracted to you. Although when I tell you what it is, you might wish I was here to ask you for a date."

They sat down under a large tree. Anjya looked at Daimhim. "God I'm really nervous now. This seemed like a good idea, but I don't know where to start now." She took a deep breath and gulped down a mouthful of coffee.

"Thing is Daimhim, my dad is Tony Carter."

"Mum's friend Tony? Wow, I didn't know that. Of course, Anjya Carter. You don't look like him. Do you know what happened, why they aren't talking? I really liked him, thought they were perfect together, and now she won't even discuss him. She's like a bear with a sore head, has been for the last few weeks. Has he told you what happened?"

Anjya nodded. "Daimhim I don't know how to put this so I'm just going to come right out and say it." Anjya took a deep breath

211

and looked straight into Daimhim's brown eyes. "He's your father too; which means you and I are ... "

"Sisters," Daimhim gasped. "Fuck! I never saw that one coming Anjya. Why would they keep it a secret? Mum and Kenny are divorced; he's already disowned me to the world in the press anyway. I'm going to fucking murder her for this." She picked up her phone.

Anjya put her hand on Daimhim's arm. "Please don't call her yet Daimhim, listen to what I have to tell you first. It is really complicated. They fell out because your mum kept promising to tell you and then didn't. He doesn't know I'm telling you. I kind of forced it out of him because he has been miserable since they split up. At least you knew your mum had a boyfriend. I didn't even know about her. Sorry, I babble a bit when I'm nervous. Daimhim, please say something!"

Daimhim stared at Anjya, her mouth opened and closed. "I don't know what to say, why on earth would she keep hiding it? She knew we all really liked Tony. You are sure?"

Anjya nodded. "Apparently one of your brothers knows too. My dad just wanted to tell you all, and your mum wouldn't do it. He thinks she was scared of how you would react."

"But, you and I are the same age Anjya!"

"It's a long story. They had an affair when they worked together. She was married and he was engaged to my mother."

Daimhim raised an eyebrow. "He cheated on your mother and you're okay with that?"

Anjya shrugged, "I never knew her Daimhim. She died in a car smash. She was pregnant with me when she and Dad were in the crash. I was born that day. They switched off her life support machine a couple of days later."

"Oh Anjya, how awful. This must be terrible for you too?"

Anjya nodded, "thing is my mum and dad had split up, then she told him she was pregnant. He had stalled on marrying her, probably because he was with your mum too. Anyway, according to your Aunt Ciara, who was my mum's best friend, she got herself pregnant with me deliberately. Then she didn't tell him until she was six months gone. Which is quite good, or I might not have been here because he wanted her to terminate the pregnancy." Anjya smiled ruefully. "Well, pregnancy outside marriage, it was a bit of a problem in those days in their circle. Their families were pressuring him to marry her."

"My Aunt Ciara, knew he and Mum were having an affair?" Daimhim gasped, "she told me she didn't know who my father was. In fact she said she didn't even know it wasn't Kenny."

Anjya shook her head. "No Uncle Phil did, but apparently, they never told Aunt Ciara because she was my mum's best friend and your mum was afraid she would react badly. She never told anyone about him being your dad Daimhim. She ran off and they didn't see each other till Toria and Scott's wedding. They'd not seen each other for over twenty years, but, when they saw each other, well! It's some mess, isn't it?"

"Fuck sake, Mum's always lecturing me about morals how could she do this, lie to me I mean. She said I was the result of a one night stand and she didn't even know his name."

Anjya looked at Daimhim and shrugged. "Apparently, they'd been seeing each other in secret for a long time and she wouldn't leave her husband. My mum got pregnant with me to trap him; because she loved him and was fed up with him stalling. They'd been engaged for years. Then the accident happened, he won't talk about how it happened says he can't remember. I think they were probably arguing and he lost control of the car. Anyway, they delivered me then had to switch off her life support machine. Dad was in a coma for a couple of months and when he wakened his memory had gone and he forgot about Caoimhe and him. She meanwhile had found out she was pregnant with you. When he remembered about their relationship, he thought you were her husband's and he didn't want to rock the boat so he didn't see her for twenty years. He brought me up though Daimhim, he's really is a great dad and my best friend."

Daimhim said nothing and stared at her new sister.

"Tragic tale, isn't it? I'm sorry Daimhim, but you and I are sisters and I wanted you to know. We also have a younger sister Amy, who's nearly 10, and the worst fucking ex stepmother you could imagine. And they think the young are fucked up?"

Daimhim shook her head in disbelief and finally found her voice again. "Why would Mum keep it a secret? She knew we all liked Tony." She repeated. "Why would she tell my brother and not me? Which brother?

"The older one," Anjya said quietly, "Dad said he guessed, so technically she never told him. Apparently, you have certain mannerisms that are his, and your brother noticed. Your eyes are his Daimhim, I'm looking at you and I can see him. That's how Dad found out about you. He saw you being interviewed the night of the last election and noticed the resemblance to me. He's not normally slow to pick up on things, but after twenty years, the penny dropped?"

"Why, if she cared about him and had an affair with him would she run off and stay with Kenny? Why would she deny me my father, my whole life? Why didn't she tell him about me? They obviously loved each other then and now, so why?"

Anjya could see that Daimhim was now becoming angry, she laid a calming hand on Daimhim's arm, and said gently. "He told me that she came to see him when he came out the coma. She was pregnant and he assumed that the baby was her husband's. He got angry at her, apparently, your dad ... sorry I mean her husband, beat her up badly a few times and they all wanted her to leave him. Dad said that before they started the affair they had been good friends, him and Caoimhe and he remembered that, but, not that they had been together. When he remembered about the relationship he still never realised that the baby could be his. Don't be too hard on your brother. It really wasn't his place to tell you?"

"Dan's here in London for the next couple of days Anjya. I'll murder him for not telling me. I won't call my mother yet. I'm too shocked and angry at her." Daimhim paused and looked at Anjya.

214

"I'm going to speak to Dan though. I really have to take this out on someone." Daimhim picked up her phone. Anjya watched as she called her brother. "Dan, why didn't you tell me about Tony?" She hissed. "Exactly how long have you known?" There was, a few seconds, silence before he spoke.

"Oh, she has finally told you, I told her three months ago, you needed to know. Please stay calm, I didn't know what to do Veenie. I think that might have been why her and Tony fell out. Sorry Sis, what could I do? It just wasn't my tale to tell, she promised she would talk to you. I'm meeting David for lunch do you still want to come? If you do, will you stay calm? I knew something like this would happen. I told her to tell you before someone else noticed the resemblance.

"Can I bring someone to lunch?"

"As long as it's not that scary bodyguard Mum got you. Our Davie is terrified of her, he thinks she fancies him."

"Annie will sit discreetly in the bar as always Daniel. I don't want her to hear what we have to say to each other. I don't want witnesses to what I'm going to do to you." Daimhim said menacingly. "Does Davie know?"

"Nah, he would be shitting himself Veenie he'd have told me. The resemblance is so subtle that only detective like folk would notice it." Dan laughed nervously, knowing his sister was still angry. "I just happened to be sitting across from you that first night we all had dinner. At first, I thought that Tony kept looking at you because you look so much like Mum. Then I noticed mannerisms and the final thing, you have his eyes. Who're you with anyway is it a guy?"

Daimhim looked at Anjya and smiled. "No Anjya Carter, Tony's daughter Dan. My sister, she came and told me who I really am. Which is a bummer, when neither you or our mother did."

There was a sharp intake of breath and then a silence. "Veenie I'm so sorry babe, that must have been a shock. Look come and meet us for lunch. We'll discuss it then. Do you want me to tell David?

215

Daimhim sighed. "Not yet, he'll only overreact."

"Cuckoo we love you, you know we love you, don't you?"

Daimhim smiled despite herself. "At least I have two sisters to share my nest now. Okay you fucking treacherous bastard, I'll see you in an hour, I love you too."

"Nest?" Anjya said raising her eyebrow, as Daimhim put her phone back in her pocket.

Daimhim laughed for the first time since Anjya had broken the news to her. "My brothers have called me cuckoo, since they found out Kenny wasn't my father. Cuckoo in the nest. I think, to be honest, they're jealous that Kenny is not my dad. You know it's strange, my brothers remember them fighting and him hitting her. I've never seen that side of him." Daimhim, shook her head and sighed. "Mum never says a word against Kenny. They never argued, they just went about their lives. He didn't treat me any different from the boys and they are his natural sons. He ignored us all most of the time when we were younger. The boys are eight and nine years older than me, so by the time I was ten they were both at university. It was really just me and Mum most of the time."

"That's I suppose like me and Dad, I had my Mum's parents too, my Papa is great, but my Nana well she never really got over my mum's death." Anjya sighed and Daimhim knew this was painful for the other girl. "Dad was good about it all, but Nana well she made my mum and dad sound, like it was love story. I kind of knew it wasn't before he told me. Dad never wanted to hurt my Nana, but he did tell me the truth when I was younger. Not that he was with your mum, just that he had loved someone else and lost her. So, it was me and him against the world. I never liked Angelina from the moment I met her, luckily, she wasn't around for long. What was it like for you growing up with someone who wasn't your Dad?

"Once Mum became an MP, I never really saw much of Kenny either." Daimhim looked at Anjya and smiled. "She was mother and father to me, her and Samira, her friend and private secretary.

I had Nannies and babysitters, but I wanted to have a dad because all my friends did. Even when I took it out on Mum, she never said a thing against Kenny. Ed and Linda Wilson, became like my grandparents. I also had mums' parents who are brilliant. When I found out Kenny wasn't my father, I was fourteen, for some reason we were all together, we had a fight he told me. I think I was relieved to be honest, after that, I stopped worrying about it. I'm angry at her, and confused as to why she didn't tell me about Tony, but, my mother is a pretty, amazing woman! I suppose she thought I would react badly to the news but she should have told me." Daimhim took a tissue from Anjya. "I suppose I'll need to try to be adult about all this. I need to speak to Dan about what she told him, so I can think about how I'm going to broach this with Mum. My brothers, well they tease me, but we're all really close." Daimhim looked at Anjya and smiled. "Anjya would you like to meet Dan and Davie? They're having lunch near Westminster."

"I don't want to intrude. I've not told Dad where I am, he is back at the hotel, he thinks I've gone shopping. I really want us to get to know each other Daimhim." Anjya reached out and touched Daimhim's arm, her eyes filled with tears. "My dad's a great father and he is desperate to be yours too. I know this is a shock though, it was for me too. He really does love your mum, but they just seem to keep getting it wrong."

An hour later the two girls joined Dan and David, for lunch, after a few drinks they began to discuss the situation. "You'd better speak to Mum, Daimhim, there must have been reasons." Dan said quietly. "Hopefully when she realises you know, she'll spill the beans."

Daimhim snorted and looked at her siblings. "I bet there were, how could she lie to me for all these years? A one-night stand! they were having an affair. Tony told Anjya, they were together for 18 months, she would not leave Kenny."

"Well we never understood that either did we?" David said shaking his head in disbelief. "Now we find out she did this to Tony too. You know sometimes, I think our Mother is fucking mad, folks. For someone who is running the country she has made some really dodgy decisions in her time."

"David that's an awful thing to say." Daimhim gasped. "She's a really good mother; she has always been there for us, she's a great leader too."

David grinned. "You were ready to put her in front of a firing squad when you got here Veenie. So, don't act it. But we can say it because we love her." He nudged Anjya and laughed. "Honestly Anjya, be happy it's Tony's blood you and her share. She's as nuts, as our mum."

Dan looked thoughtful. "I suspect the reason she struggled to tell you was it was painful. She said it was a long and very tragic tale. Now we know most of the story, it just must have been the most awful time for them both. Mum has strong morals, you two know that, this is not something she would have done without feeling bad. I knew when I saw them together they were very much in love; you could see and feel it." He looked around the table. "Know what I think Anjya? I think it's guilt at your mother's death! I think the good Chancellor thinks it was her fault she died. That catholic upbringing kicking in. Maybe she should just go to confession and get it all off her chest?"

"I can't believe that you deal with these things with humour, it's so like my dad and me. What are we going to do about Dad and your mum?" Anjya smiled at Dan and David, then looked over at Daimhim. "You're very lucky to have two big brothers. I grew up with just me and Dad. He was an absolute tart when I was young, he was a great dad, but there was a succession of females. Then he hit the jackpot and married Cruella D'evil, AKA Angelina, my wicked stepmother. They have been more or less separated, since they had poor wee Amy; she's a sad wee soul. Thing is I think all his relationships failed for the same reason, he was still in love with your mother. Can we try to get them together?"

Dan Black grimaced he took a sip of his drink and looked around the table. "I suppose we really shouldn't interfere, but, if we don't, then their track record could mean they wait another twenty years before speaking again. We should ask ourselves though, is it worth it? It sounds as though they are both pretty feisty when they fight. Mum's like that with everyone, she takes so much then she just blows and takes no prisoners when she does. It's why we never got why she stayed with Kenny, and put up with his shit." Dan shook his head and looked at his siblings. "What should we do? Leave well alone, or engineer a meeting? Mum might go mad if we interfere. How would Tony react Anjya?"

Anjya smiled, "Dad's pretty even tempered it takes a lot to get a raise out of him, but, I suppose when pushed, he digs his heels in and can be stubborn. He loves her though; he's never stopped loving her."

"Where are, you staying Anjya?"

"The Dorchester, why Dan?"

"Let's get them together there? I think they actually need some help sort this all out." Dan grinned and looked around the table, "a few home truths, wouldn't go amiss here."

"Oh, Dan you might be wrong you could start world war 3 here." David said shaking his head. "You know what she's like, even when she's wrong, she's right!"

"They were fighting over telling Daimhim and Anjya about each other Davie. They know now, so it's out. Surely that will help?"

"Are you for real? Sometimes Dan, I think you're living in some sort of parallel universe. She's going to go nuts at Tony, for telling Anjya! Then us, for getting involved. It's okay for you two, you can fuck off back to Scotland. I have to live and work with her."

"My brother is a shitbag Anjya!" Daimhim said laughing. "You're scared of everything, aren't you Davie?"

David nodded he looked at his sister and smiled. "I'm cautious and there is nothing wrong with that."

"But it would be worth it to see her smile again, Davie! She has been so sad looking since it ended." Dan said, putting his arm around his younger brother. "Better go see if Harry knows where there's a flak jacket though."

"Ok!" David said quietly, "but one of you two is setting it up not me, because if it backfires, then I can claim that you did it."

"You are such a fucking woose Davie," Daimhim said. "You must get that from the Black side, and I'm grounded for the summer. So, I'll be the sitting duck this time not you!"

Caoimhe, picked up her mobile, Daimhim's name flashed up. "Mum, can you meet me and the boys in town for an early dinner? We've booked a table at the Dorchester?

"Not tonight darling, I have some work to do. I need to get it finished."

"Mum please!" Daimhim pleaded. "We haven't done anything since I've been here and it won't be a late one. Dan has his flight to catch. Come on, we never ask you for anything."

Caoimhe sighed; she had not been in the Dorchester since before Christmas when Tony had stayed there, it was the last place she wanted to be today. "Daimhim, please don't try to make me feel guilty? With Ed and Alex out of the country I can't just drop everything. Did you say David is with you? I've been looking for him."

"Oh, you can Mum, please? I promise I'll work for you this week, for free, David is here."

"I've been trying to reach him Daimhim. Tell him to put his mobile on."

"Tell him yourself, at dinner, come on Mum? You've got to eat, haven't you?"

"Oh, okay, but I mean it Daimhim, I need to be back here for nine o'clock."

Daimhim put the phone down. "Okay you'd better make sure they're in some private place when they meet up. She's not in a good mood. This isn't one for a public dining room, guys. Maybe we should think about where they can meet?"

David shook his head. "Anjya reckons they should meet in Tony's suite, we just have to work out how we get her in there.

They haven't spoken for three weeks now, so it could get heated. Have we done the right thing?" David said, looking around him.

"Who knows? But, at least we are trying to do something." Dan sighed. "Anjya It's pretty amazing you want them to be together! After what happened to your mother."

"Anjya smiled, "it's a bit like you three, I love my Dad and I hate to see him so unhappy. I do know he loves Caoimhe, and from what you say she loves him too."

CHAPTER
TWENTY-TWO

"What are you lot trying to do?" Caoimhe cried as Dan pushed her into the room where Tony stood with Anjya. She looked at Tony then at her children, she turned to Harry. **"Did you know?"** She barked.

Harry shook his head. "No, and I don't want to know now! I've established you're safe, scanned the room, my work is done. I'm going to find Annie and sit with her!" He smiled, shook his head and left the room.

"Mum this is Anjya, Daimhim's sister!" Dan said. "Look we all know what happened all those years ago, so there is nothing left for you to hide." Dan looked at his siblings and Anjya, then turned to look at his mother and Tony. "You two have left so many casualties in your wake! It's a disgrace, the way you're carrying on. If you are meant to be together, get on with it and sort it out."

Daimhim walked over to Tony, he immediately wrapped his arms around her. "We've a lot of catching up to do!" She said, her voice hoarse with emotion. "You need to sort things out with my mother first though, then we can talk ... Dad!"

Tony nodded, unable to speak, he looked at Caoimhe who was standing in the middle of the room her poker face giving nothing away. Daimhim glanced at her and shook her head as

222

she passed her. "I can't believe that you didn't tell me mother. I can understand you not saying anything when Kenny told me." She looked over at Tony, who was wiping away a tear from his face. "I would have gone looking for him, but to be with him for months, and not tell me is shocking Mum, I'm deeply wounded, and hurt." Daimhim motioned with her head, to her siblings, "come on, there must be a drink somewhere in this place?"

"Well?" Tony said as the door closed behind their children.

"What do you want me to say Tony?"

"Well you could start with sorry."

"I'm not sorry Tony, I can't believe they're all right with it all, how much do they know? I don't know what to say now. I was going to tell her at the weekend we were going to go to my country residence in Buckinghamshire and I planned to tell her." Caoimhe sat down on the sofa and looked at him. "Did you tell them?"

Tony shrugged, "I told Anjya everything a couple of weeks ago, Caoimhe. It turned out she and Daimhim already knew each other. What has happened since then I don't know? I can only assume that Anjya told them." He sat down beside her. "Caoimhe I love you so much, but I needed her to know Daimhim is her sister. I also wanted Daimhim to know I didn't abandon her."

"Tony, I was scared about how she would react; Daimhim I mean; she is so like me. I've missed you dreadfully Tony. I wanted to call you but I felt so fucking stupid about the way I carried on. I kept trying to tell Daimhim, but I just couldn't find the words to say, I lied, I do know who your father is." Caoimhe smiled through tears. "I sat today and wrote it all down. I was going to take her to Dorneywood and give it to her to read. Tony, I also can't believe Anjya is alright with it all, she knows what we did to her mother and she is standing there smiling at me? What did you tell her?"

Tony sighed and took Caoimhe's hand. "I didn't mean to tell Anjya, she found me crying, watching question time and asked what was going on. She guessed about you from red hair in the plughole of my shower. It just all came out when she said she and Daimhim knew each other."

They heard a noise and Caoimhe slipped off her shoes, got up and walked on tiptoe to the door. She pulled it open and David and Daimhim fell in the door. "For fuck sake! What age are you two? Give us some privacy please?"

David looked sheepish, but Daimhim stood up and faced her. "Mum, I don't think you're in a position to call us childish, after the juvenile way you two have behaved." She looked at Tony and smirked, "and you owe me twenty years of pocket money!" She turned to her mother, "I am so not finished with you yet Mum. You have so much explaining to do."

"Well I'm not doing it tonight Daimhim, and I'm certainly not doing it here." Caoimhe said as she slammed the door shut. "What are you laughing at?" She asked Tony, "this is not funny, and our children have just been devious."

"I am just thinking how like you she is sweetheart! That is exactly what you do when you are in the wrong, you go on the attack."

"I know, it scares the shit out of me, she's even more bolshie than I am Tony. I really do have great kids, how Kenny and I managed it is beyond me, but, they are all different. Dan is really laid back, but caring and thoughtful. David, is such a bloody worrier, intelligent, intense, sometimes. Daimhim, well, as you just witnessed, she just goes where angels fear to tread. Sound like you did a pretty good job with Anjya too. Hopefully some of her calmness will rub off on her sister."

"Maybe? But Anjya tends to be too sensible, she maybe could learn from Daimhim about taking risks. Do you know she didn't even want a party for her twenty first? She lives like a middle-aged spinster." Tony turned to Caoimhe his face becoming serious. "Daimhim's right though, Caoimhe, we have behaved like children. All the fighting and stuff, we need to grow up and stop it." He stood up and walked towards her putting his arms around her and pulling her to him. "I love you Caoimhe Black, with every bone in my body. You're a fucking lunatic at times, but, I love eccentricity you have. You're going to marry me and stop all this messing about!" He let her go and walked over to the door pulled it open and looked out. "They've gone!" He shut the door and locked it. "Come here?" He said smiling, "let me touch you." She moved towards the bed, but he grabbed her arm pulling her back, taking a chair from the dining table he sat on it. "This is the memory I've carried with me for 21 years Caoimhe. The last night we were together before my accident. I need to recreate that scene."

Caoimhe smiled and removing her underwear and hitching up her skirt, she straddled him. kissing his mouth, she looked into his eyes.

"You remember?" He whispered.

"Of, course I do!" "It was my masturbation thought, it was pretty erotic, wasn't it? I'm not twenty-four anymore Tony."

In response, he unbuttoned her shirt pushed her bra up and buried his face in her breasts. His hands came around and held them, as his mouth moved to her nipple. He took it between his teeth and gently nibbled as she reached down and unzipped his trousers, pushing them down over his knees. She guided his penis inside her and pushed herself down onto his lap. Tony looked into her eyes. "God Caoimhe I love you so much darling!" he whispered, "just fuck me babe, I need to feel you." Within minutes, they were both moving towards climax. He cried out, seconds after she shuddered and gasped as their orgasms overtook any other thoughts. Afterwards he held her on his knee kissing her face, which like his was wet with tears.

"Tony, I love you so much, I'm such a cow though. I can't help it, I just say things! I don't mean a lot of it, it's like a red mist sometimes especially when I drink too much. I can't believe you still want to marry me after the fucking stunts I have pulled."

He smiled. "I love you darling, I told you before I always have, always will, but you are a fucking nutter Caoimhe."

"Tony, there is one thing though."

"What?"

"I really do not want to have the talk we need to have with the kids tonight. Could we just sneak back to Downing Street and not tell them? I really do have work to do, I need to get home, do you want to come with me? In fact, maybe we should all just go to Dorneywood at the weekend and tell them the whole story." She smiled, "leaving out the sexual chemistry of course, no young person wants to hear their parents have more sex than they do." Caoimhe looked at Tony and kissed him. "We're only around the corner from the underground at Hyde Park Corner. If we can get out of here without the kids seeing us. We can just make our own way home. Harry will be with them, if I call him, I'll alert them to me going. Technically I shouldn't do it, but I am so sick of not being able to move around freely, Jed told us yesterday Ravi is in Turkey. So, the alert thing is just a precaution. If I call for a car, we'll have to wait around."

CHAPTER
TWENTY-THREE

Sitting in Anjya Carters hotel room, with his siblings and a drink in his hand. David Black switched on his mobile phone and immediately a message flashed up, he read it and gasped. "Fuck sake, Dan, go interrupt them, we need to get Mum out of here."

"What?" Dan asked seeing the fear in his brother's face, "what's happened?"

"Just go get her and Tony, I need to find out some stuff. I'll tell you when Mum's here." David dialled a number. "What do you want us to do? Jed, tell me what to do?"

Daimhim and Anjya looked on. "What is it Davie you're scaring me!" Daimhim said grabbing his arm.

David shook his sister away and continued talking angrily. "Don't you dare blame Harry, or Mum for this? How could you not tell her Jed? She's the fucking chancellor. Did you tell Alex or Ed? Does Harry know?" David, began to shout into the phone. "No I guessed as much. If anything happens to my fucking mother Jed, I'm coming for you. Do you understand?" David looked over at his sister, "Daimhim where's Annie, Harry, is with her."

"They're both downstairs in the lounge."

" There must be a problem with the signal Jed. I'll try it from here."

"Davie what's going on, is Mum in danger?"

David ignored his sister and continued to speak into the phone.

He told Jed where the two bodyguards were. "Okay its room 102! right okay, Jed, just make sure you do, hold on a second."

Dan ran back in to the room, his face concerned. "Guys they have gone! Obviously, they've sneaked out due to you two spying on them Daimhim."

David turned white, he spoke into his mobile. "Jed she's not there. She must have left the hotel! Didn't your guys see her and Tony? **What!** You are fucking joking? Your fucking head will roll for this and whoever was in charge at MI5. You'd better fucking find her, and do it quickly." David threw his phone across the room. "Oh Fuck!" He cried, "We have to find them Dan. Ravi has been following her! Jed didn't want to alert her, until they got a fix on him. They were hoping he would lead them to others. Apparently, MI5 didn't want anyone else alerted. He was outside this hotel an hour ago!"

"If they are watching, then they must have seen where Dad and Caoimhe went then, David?" Anjya looked scared.

David shook his head. "They went for coffee, would you believe, because they thought that we were having dinner. I can't believe that these fuckers look after the security of our country. Ravi went into a cafe, so they nipped into Costa-Coffee. When they came out, he was gone. They found an empty bag in the toilet of the café, which they think had explosives in it."

***

Giggling, Tony and Caoimhe made their way around to the station, both so wrapped up in themselves, they didn't realise they were being followed. They caught the tail end of rush hour. The station was busy with workers on their way home and with tourists leaving the closing, London, tourist attractions. "God I just want to get you home and into bed! The fuck on the chair has left me wanting more. Christ, Caoimhe, I can get hard just thinking about that." Tony whispered, in her ear, as they entered the underground station. "After I make love to you in your bed with me on top. We're going to have to have a serious talk, Caoimhe and lay down some ground rules. The kids are right we can't keep falling out. You need to start doing as you're told."

In response Caoimhe turned and kissed him on the mouth. Much to the amusement of a young couple entwined in each other's arms beside them. "What is it about you?" Caoimhe whispered. "I plan all the things I am going to say to you, then you look at me, I melt and just give in. It's just as well you didn't go into politics Tony, if you were in the opposition party, I would achieve nothing."

"I feel a bit guilty about the kids Caoimhe! We've just taken off and left them sitting in the Dorchester."

"My lot will live with it, they'll look after Anjya too; Harry and Annie are both there. I should be annoyed at them interfering, but I'm actually relieved, I didn't know how to say it Tony." She smiled up into his eyes. "I'm not good at saying that sentence."

"What sentence?"

"That one I don't like."

"Oh, would that be the one that starts with I am as stubborn as a mule and can't say sorry!" Tony said, his eyes twinkling.

Their train roared into the station and holding hands they stepped in to the busy carriage. Caoimhe nodded, "something like that. Thing is Tony, where you are concerned I'm not. I'm like a fucking pussycat, I just give in, don't I?" She shook her head and moved closer looking into Tony's eyes. "For twenty years, I planned what I was going to say and do to you." She put her mouth to his ear and whispered, "never at any-time did it involve sexual pleasure." Arms around his neck she kissed him, "I told you years ago, I was nuts Tony."

"Indeed, you did, but I was too far gone Caoimhe, you do my head in sometimes, but I have always been willing to put up with that for what we have. I think it's the fact that you are so predictably unpredictable I love. Don't ever change darling, just stop taking it all out on me. **JESUS!**" He let go of Caoimhe.

"What?" She said, looking at him. Caoimhe followed his gaze, Ravi was walking towards them. He was dressed in a heavy jacket and hat. Sweat poured down his face. A train roared out of the station on the opposite platform. Caoimhe couldn't hear what Ravi, was saying, but knew he was agitated.

CHAPTER
TWENTY-FOUR

"**Ravi where have you been?**" Caoimhe cried out. "We have been trying to find you. Are you alright?" "You need to get some help. **Ravi?** Caoimhe looked at the young man, who she'd known since he was born, and immediately realised that he wasn't hearing her. It appeared he was in some kind of trance. He was talking to himself, quoting some sort of language she didn't recognise. Suddenly he turned and pointed at Caoimhe, and his voice rose, when he spoke his voice resonated across the carriage.

"I am the vessel of the lord Allah; I will hence forth say his name in the garden as I sit by his feet. Blessed are those who are willing to pass by the sword to sit by the foot of Allah. Allah will be avenged on this day; the world will know the evil Caoimhe Black, is no more."

People around them began to move away, get off the train, someone pulled the chain above the door and an alarm went off. The doors of the train jammed open as people realised what was happening and evacuated. Ravi stood in front of them now muttering in a language that neither Tony nor Caoimhe could understand. Tony moved towards him.

"You have to listen Ravi!" He said pushing Caoimhe back towards the door. "Ravi stop this; remember Caoimhe is your friend? She has looked after you since you were a child. Ravi somewhere in your head, you know this. Ravi please stop this, before anyone gets hurt."

Ravi in response opened his heavy jacket and immediately Tony saw the strapping around his body, crisscrossing his chest and around his waist.

"Christ, Caoimhe, he has explosives, everyone, run!" Tony shouted.

People began to scream and run towards the exit. Caoimhe still holding onto Tony walked backwards towards the train door. Caoimhe saw David, Daimhim and Harry running along the platform towards the train. David reached her first; he stopped and looked at Ravi, who was standing in the door of the train. "Ravi what have you done? Ravi, it's me David, your friend, please Ravi, don't do this, you're going to hurt innocent people. This is not you Ravi, you know it's not. Please Ravi? Don't do what Achmad asks you. Remember what you thought of him at uni? Ravi look at me, please? Remember how close we are? You're our friend! You don't want to hurt me and Veenie."

Daimhim moved beside her brother. "Ravi!" She cried. "Listen to David; you don't want to hurt anyone. Ravi, you are the gentlest person I know. You're our friend. Please Ravi don't do it."

Tony, let go of Caoimhe and walked slowly towards Ravi, holding his hands in the air. "Ravi please listen to them! Your sister, Samira, is devastated at you disappearing. These people are your friends they care about you."

Jed Livingston appeared from behind a pillar approached Caoimhe and took her arm. "Start walking away Caoimhe please?"

"Fuck off!" She hissed. "My kids are over there; I'm going nowhere."

Caoimhe looked at Ravi. "Please Ravi? Listen to David and Daimhim, they're your friends please Ravi don't do this." She saw Ravi look from one to the other, for a second he hesitated, tears began to run down his face. He looked around and then begin to mutter again. His hands reached down and suddenly Tony broke away and sprinted towards Daimhim and David pushing them both out of the way. There was a terrible explosion. Caoimhe felt herself flying through the air, then there was darkness.

When Caoimhe came to, she tried to see, but there was smoke and rubble all around her. The first thing she saw when the dust cleared was Jed Livingstone. His eyes staring at her from his lifeless body, then she saw Ravi, his body blown apart. Caoimhe immediately realised when the explosion had taken place she'd been blown against a pillar where Jed having been directly behind her, had come between her and the stone. All around people lay groaning and crying and Caoimhe began to organise those who could walk to help those who could not. She looked for Tony and her family but could not see them. She helped tend the wounded, several people had lost limbs and she could see bodies lying still.

Her heart heavy with fear for her loved ones, she continued to help the wounded, telling them they would be rescued soon. Comforting crying badly injured people, whilst her mind raced wondering where Tony and her children were. A young man came forward, he and Caoimhe began to pull rubble away from the stairway, with their bare hands. Caoimhe realised he was the male from the young couple she had stood beside no more than 15 minutes earlier. "Is your girlfriend alright?" She asked. He nodded and pointed over to the side where the young woman was helping an elderly man to sit up and giving him a drink from a water bottle.

"Your friend shouting the warning meant we were farther away from the bomber than we would have been." They continued to clear the bricks from the stairs for what seemed like an eternity, suddenly they heard voices and saw light beyond it.

"Stand back!" A man shouted from behind the rubble, "we are almost with you." Caoimhe hugged the young man. "What's your name?" She asked.

"Kevin!" He said, "Kevin Walker, Mrs Black I just want you to know I think you're wonderful. I know you could have got away. I heard that big guy telling you to get out of the way, I heard you tell him to fuck off too."

"You're pretty amazing yourself Kevin." "Now I need to try to find my family?" "Oh, God, I'm so scared Kevin my children, my bodyguard and the man I love are somewhere under all that rubble. They were very close to the blast.

"You and I survived Mrs Black, they could have too. I'll help you." Kevin said following her.

"Please call me Caoimhe, Kevin, that's my name."

"Not Keevy, Mrs Black? That's how the people on the telly say your name."

"The media never get things like that, right, especially Gaelic names."

Suddenly Caoimhe saw Harry coming towards her through the dust. He appeared to be unhurt apart from a cut on his cheek.

"Where are the others?" She cried.

"I don't know Caoimhe I rolled over and over I don't know why, but I seemed to go in the opposite direction."

"I've covered Jed up, I never liked him Caoimhe, but I wouldn't have wished him dead. At least it was quick though." He shook his head sadly, "doesn't actually surprise me he was behind you though, he usually was. I don't want to speak ill of the dead and all that, but, he was a bullying coward who had more ego and ambition, than knowledge. Sorry Caoimhe that's unprofessional of me, he's gone. We need to find your family. They must be here; they were only feet away from me. My army training, must have been instinctive. I rolled and rolled."

Taking Caoimhe's hand, Harry led her quickly over the rubble and they walked towards where she had last seen Tony and her children. "Stop Harry!" Caoimhe cried out, she noticed a small child lying face down in the rubble and lifted him, realising immediately there was nothing she could do. She choked on a sob and covered him with her own cardigan. Tears ran down her face as she realised she had been the target. Ravi had meant to harm her, and she herself, was mostly unhurt.

Caoimhe and Harry with help from Kevin, searched all over the platform. They dug through bricks and rubble with only their hands as tools, but there was no sign of anyone. They moved over to the opposite track and looked down, there were piles of grey rubble and suddenly Caoimhe saw a foot sticking out from the pile of bricks and dust. The foot was wearing her shoe. **"Daimhim!"** Caoimhe screamed jumping down onto the track. She and Kevin began to pull the rocks from the pile and quickly uncovered her daughter. Her heart pounding in her chest Caoimhe put her ear to her face and realised Daimhim was breathing. She pulled her daughter towards her. Harry lifted Daimhim on to the platform. A paramedic in a green jumpsuit took over, as she as Kevin continued to search.

They began to dig again and a few seconds later she came across her son. "David!" She whispered tears blinding her when she realised he wasn't breathing. **"No David, please God, no!"** She cried out. "Not like this please David!" She pulled him into her arms; Kevin reached down and touched him.

"Mrs Black, I mean Caoimhe, he's still warm, he has no pulse we need to try to revive him." She and Harry began to try to resuscitate David. Caoimhe tilted his head and blew into his mouth as Harry thumped on his chest. Nothing happened, it seemed like an eternity.

The paramedic who had now put Daimhim on a stretcher jumped down on to the track carrying a defibrillator case and oxygen. **"Stop!** He's breathing, give me oxygen?" She cried. David coughed and opened his eyes. Caoimhe kissed his face gently. "I need to find Tony, darling.

David spoke to her, his voice merely a whisper. "Mum, Tony was over there. He was speaking to me and then you pulled me out and everything went black. Where's Daimhim Mum?"

"She's unconscious, but breathing. Just relax, David and let this man here look after you, I need to find Tony." She shouted without looking back. "Harry stay with them, I have to look for Tony." Suddenly there was a flurry of activity as rescue workers began to descend on them, Caoimhe began to dig again in the rubble, her hands bleeding and covered in dirt. A police man grabbed her and held her back from the rescuers. He sat her down beside David. Who was now fully conscious, talking to the Harry and the medics.

Caoimhe watched in terror as they brought Tony out, he was conscious, but, she could see he was in a great deal of pain. Blood dripped from a wound on his head as they lifted him out on to the platform. Caoimhe dropped to her knees, as the paramedics worked with him there was lot of blood on his face and body. She sobbed. "Tony talk to me."

"You're okay? The others? Daimhim? David?" Tony whispered.

"David is conscious and speaking to us, his legs look as though they're broken. Daimhim was unconscious but she's come around and seems to be okay, she has a head injury. Harry is like me unhurt, we'll be a bit bruised but that's all."

"Caoimhe, I can't feel my legs!" Tony cried out, grabbing her arm, he pulled her down and whispered in her ear. "I can feel my arm is broken and pain from my head to my stomach, but, nothing after that."

"Tony, we need to wait until the doctors have seen you. Please rest, I'll come to the hospital with you."

He shook his head, "Caoimhe your kids need you more than I do just now. Can you make sure that Anjya is alright? She is going to be devastated and worried about me? For years, it was just her and I ... I need you to look after her for me. I love you babe, if I die please look after my girls."

Caoimhe bent and kissed his forehead, "I love you Tony Carter, you're not going to die on me. No way! I won't let you, no matter what happens I'll be your wife. "When I was digging for you and the kids. I realised what is important in life Tony. Just you and them, the fucking country can go fuck itself, for all I care now."

CHAPTER
TWENTY-FIVE

Caoimhe insisted on walking from the ambulance which she shared with Kevin and his girlfriend Bridget. They were all very shocked. As she walked into the accident and emergency department, a figure broke away from the people standing waiting and ran towards her. Dan Black wrapped his arms around his mother. "Thank God you're alright," he sobbed. "We were not sure how you would go home, so we split up to look. Anjya and I went to Green Park station with Annie. I was hoping you'd got a taxi but the doorman heard you saying you were going to use the underground when you couldn't get a cab."

"Mum, it wasn't just Ravi! There was a string of explosions all over the capital. All suicide and car bombs and there are a lot of casualties. David Summerville's house was targeted; he and his family weren't there. Alex's London home was bombed, his house-keeper was badly hurt. Thankfully Jill and the children were on the Isle of Wight." Dan put his hand on his mother's arm. "The worst though Mum, was Iain and Lucy Milton-Daws. I'm really sorry to have to tell you this, but they were killed by a suicide bomber who threw himself across their car in central London"

Caoimhe gasped. "I'll need to get to Downing Street Dan. There will be no one able to deal with this. Ed and Alex are both away."

"Not now Mum, Alex is on his way back by chopper. You

should get checked out. For starters, you're going to need stitches on that cut Mum."

"What cut?"

"The one on your head Mum, you're dripping blood through the dressing. Mum! Christ, someone help!" he shouted, catching Caoimhe as she fainted.

Caoimhe groaned as they lifted her onto the bed. "I'm so sorry!" she whispered. "I can't believe I fainted. There are people who have lost limbs out there and they are making less fuss."

The young doctor smiled. "You have some fairly serious injuries Mrs Black! You've been running on adrenalin since it happened, so you haven't noticed. Nurse, can you get her into a gown please?" he said, motioning for Dan to sit down on the other side of the room and pulling a curtain around the bed where Caoimhe sat.

"That's okay, I'll do it," Caoimhe said. She moved to undo the buttons on her blouse and her hands wouldn't work. She looked at her fingers. They were raw and bleeding and one of them was twisted, facing the wrong way; her thumb hung useless and twisted.

"She is out again!" the doctor said, smiling and shaking his head. "Is she always like this, determined to keep going? I probably know the answer to that."

Dan smiled. "Pretty much. She's quite mad. Is she going to be alright?

The doctor nodded. "We are just waiting for x-ray to clear to get her down then it will be theatre. I'm afraid her arm is definitely broken, maybe in more than one place." The doctor looked at Dan and shook his head, "when we took off her boots, her ankle looked fractured."

"She walked in here on a broken ankle?" Dan gasped.

The nurse tending to Caoimhe smiled and pointed at her foot, the ankle was swollen and turning black.

The doctor shook his head, "I suspect there are several ribs gone. Her skull looks to me as though there is a small fracture under that cut, so she may have concussion. She'll need a scan too just as a precaution. All things considered, she's been really lucky though. Judging by the state of her hands, she's been digging with them. She is going to be in a lot of pain when the adrenalin rush wears off." He lifted her hands, "look, there's no skin left on them."

Caoimhe came around and tried to sit up, "Dan I need to know about David, Daimhim and Tony!"

"Mum, you need to lie back and let them look after you. Anjya is with Tony, David and Daimhim are going to be okay. They've taken David to theatre to set his legs and arm. Daimhim has a broken arm and a skull fracture but they're going to be okay. I don't know about Tony yet. I'll go and check on them, but you need to stay here Mum."

"Anjya, how is he?" Dan said, seeing Tony's daughter standing across corridor. Anjya's face crumbled and she held a tissue to her eyes. Dan held her as she sobbed on his shoulder. He waited, still holding her, until she composed herself and then led her over to the seating area.

"He's paralysed Dan; they don't know whether it's permanent or not, it's too early to say. They need to do more scans; he's being moved to a specialised spinal unit at Stoke Mandeville hospital so they can assess him."

"Oh, Christ, Anjya, I don't know what to say. Can I go see him?"

She nodded, "he's in there, but he is pretty much out of it on painkillers. What about David and Daimhim and your mum?"

"They're doing well. David and Daimhim have had surgery but they're going to be okay. Mum is fine. Would you believe she walked into the hospital on a broken ankle and didn't know? She's waiting to go for surgery. I'll wait till she comes around before I tell her about Tony. She'll literally need to be spoon fed for a while due to her hands being torn to shreds. She has a couple of broken fingers and her wrist has a fracture. We think she dug them out with her bare hands Anjya."

"Dan, Dan, where is your mother?" Hearing his name, Dan turned around still holding Anjya, Alex Stanley was rushing through the doors. Dan pointed to the room and watched as Alex went inside.

Harry came up and put his arms around Dan and hugged him. "Where is she?"

"In there, but Alex just went in. I would leave them for a few minutes. I'm going to go see Tony, he is in a bad way, Harry."

Harry sighed. "I heard, fuck that's harsh."

"Harry, we didn't get time to introduce you properly earlier, but, this is Anjya Tony's daughter."

"We've met before Anjya! I don't expect you'll remember?"

Anjya smiled. "At Toria's wedding, you helped me when Caoimhe's husband got drunk and started making a nuisance of himself."

Harry nodded. "I'm really sorry about your dad, I hope it's not as bad as they think, miracles do happen. I was in Afghanistan when I was in the marines. I saw loads of recovery no one thought possible. Your dad's a great guy Anjya, I really like him. You just need to keep hoping and take one day at a time."

Anjya smiled, "thanks Harry, that means a lot. Do you want to come see him?" Anjya opened the door. "Dad you have visitors." Dan and Harry followed her in to the room. Tony was laying on the bed with a neck brace on. His face was swollen and bruising was already coming out and there was a large stitched cut on his forehead. His right arm was in a splinter and he stretched out his left arm taking Dan's hand.

"Your mum is alright?"

Dan nodded. "She has a broken ankle and wrist and some fingers are broken, she's going for surgery just now. She walked in here with a broken ankle Tony. She asked me to come and find out about you. What do you want me to tell her?"

Tony looked straight at Dan. "Nothing now Dan, she'll be worried enough about Daimhim and David. I can't believe what happened. How can someone who grew up with you all do that?

Poor Samira, she'll be distraught." Tony closed his eyes and Dan realised he was drifting off.

Dan shook his head, tears welling in his eyes. "Ravi was my best friend Tony. I just feel that I should have known he was ill enough to do this."

A porter entered the room, accompanied by a doctor and a nurse. "I'm sorry Mr Black!" The nurse addressed Dan. "We really need to move Mr Carter now, there's a helicopter ready to take him to Buckinghamshire and we need to go. Time is of the essence with a spinal injury I'm afraid."

"Anjya, what are you going to do? Can you wait and I'll drive you?" Dan asked. "Stoke Mandeville is quite near Dorneywood, so I'll arrange for you to stay there. Mum will probably go straight there too from the hospital. It's a really great place where she can chill, well as much as my mother is able to chill."

Anjya smiled. "That would be wonderful Dan, but you have a lot to do here. I'll get there under my own steam."

Dan looked at Harry. "Harry, could you do something for me? Could you take Anjya to Stoke Mandeville? They're taking Tony by chopper, so she'll have to make her own way there. I probably need to be here just now."

Harry nodded. "Of course, your mum is not going anywhere tonight. Annie is here anyway, she came in with me. Colin and Ronnie have been called in, they should be here soon."

Alex came out of Caoimhe's room; Harry told him his plans. Alex agreed Harry should take Anjya and stay with her until there was some news. A porter and a paramedic pushed Tony, now strapped to a medical trolley, out into the corridor. Alex looked at Harry. "Can you take her to Dorneywood afterwards Harry, stay with her? I think Caoimhe was actually planning to go there this weekend anyway so they should be prepared for guests."

Dan turned to Tony's daughter. "Anjya, Harry will take you in Mum's car. You can go via the Dorchester and get yours and your dad's things." Dan smiled at Anjya. "He's alright, a really great guy, he's been with Mum for five years now. He'll stay with you until there is some news." Dan hugged her and kissed her cheek, "it'll all work out Anjya. Tony, I'll be rooting for you. I really hope things go well for you. I'll no doubt see you soon, cos my mother will need a chauffeur to visit you." He took Tony's hand again and squeezed, "good luck mate."

Tony, obviously fighting the sedatives, gripped Dan's hand. His voice almost a whisper, he gasped, "Dan I don't need to say this to you, but please look after your mum. You know as well as I do, that her way is to show determination and brashness, to hide how scared and worried she is."

Dan nodded. "I will, I promise, as soon as she is on her feet I will bring her to see you." Tony sighed and closed his eyes. They watched as he was wheeled down the corridor. Dan put his arm around Anjya. Together the three of them walked out to the car. Dan shook hands with his mother's bodyguard. "Thanks for this Harry, I'll keep you posted."

"The press is starting to gather Dan; you'd best stay inside the hospital after this."

"Oh, I think there will be enough to keep me going for now Harry, I'm going up to see David and Daimhim, they should be coming around. Hopefully Mum will be out for a few hours. She is fucking murder when she is ill, she will not do as she is told."

Harry smiled. "You don't say." He looked at Anjya and smiled, "I think I got the best deal today. Dan, let them all know I'm thinking of them."

"Will do Harry and we will probably be at Dorneywood as soon as she is treated."

"Dan! Harry!" A familiar voice behind him called, Dan looked around, Samira stood behind him.

Harry ran over and grabbed her. "Sami what are you doing here? You should have stayed in No 11, I'm so sorry about Ravi darling."

Samira shook her head, her eyes were red and sore looking, "I was so worried about you all I had to come. I can't just sit doing nothing folks. I have to be useful." Suddenly there was a bright flash.

Dan shielded Samira, "look we need to get inside. Harry, I'll

242

call you later. Samira, this is Anjya, Tony's daughter, he's got a spinal injury and is going to Stoke Mandeville. Harry is taking Anjya there."

Samira nodded. "I'm Samira, Caoimhe's private parliamentary secretary and her friend." She looked at the ground, "and the sister of the man who did this to your father."

"Samira no, you don't apologise for this, we all knew Ravi as he was before, he was ill. Someone exploited him." Dan gasped.

"Dan, you need to take Samira inside now." Harry said, get her away from the press. Then get someone to take her back to Downing Street. Sami is Karen home yet?" Samira shook her head, "she's on her way, she was in Boston."

"Perhaps I should make my own way to Stoke Mandeville Dan and let Harry take Samira home." Anjya said quietly.

"No!" Samira sighed. "I'll be fine I need to see Caoimhe and the others. Anjya I'm really sorry that your dad is hurt I've known him for years, he's a good man."

Anjya took her hand and then hugged her. "I'm so sorry this has happened to you Samira."

"Thank you."

Harry, helped Anjya into Caoimhe's car and then got into the driving seat. Cameras flashed as he drove out of the hospital car park. Dan put his arm around Samira and together they walked back into the hospital. They hurriedly went up to the private wing of the hospital where the family had been taken for privacy and security. The doctor, who had been working with Caoimhe, came out to meet them.

"Please sit down Mr Black I have some bad news!"

"What's happened? Is it my sister or brother?

"Your Mother is in surgery Mr Black; I am afraid it was more complicated than we thought. We gave her a scan as a precaution as I said we would." He shook his head, "The fainting was due to a blood clot; we've had to open her skull. She's in the best hands there are, I need you to sign some paperwork though. It was an emergency, so we had to go ahead."

"She won't die, will she?" Samira gasped, looking around at them. "She can't die Dan, she can't, I can't lose her too."

The doctor looked serious, "it's a difficult one, but hopefully because it happened in here she'll have a fighting chance. It's fairly common, with head injuries folks and something I should have realised right away. She didn't have any other signs, which is probably good because, it might mean that we caught it before any damage is done."

Dan smiled through tears, "fuck I hope so," he looked at Alex who had appeared at his side. "She is fucking mad enough, without brain damage too."

Alex shook his head his eyes filled with tears. "Dan it's pretty awful, I hope she's alright." He pulled Dan aside and spoke quietly to him. Listen! I don't want to add to your problems, but, your fucking Father has been talking to the press. You need to try to silence him, unfortunately asking MI5 to take him out isn't an option, they're rather busy. He's given an interview about her and Tony being together. The fucker is playing the wronged husband card."

Dan shook his head. "I'll fucking swing for him, I swear! This is all we need. I'll go and call him now. Can I use my phone up here?" he asked the doctor."

"Go into your brother's room, he is awake and asking questions."

Dan entered the room, David was lying back on the pillows his face ashen, but he was alert. "Thank God you are okay Davie; did they tell you about Mum?"

David nodded. "Alex came in and told me. Dan, she can't die bro, she just can't."

Dan looked him in the eye, "she won't Davie; they won't let her die. These people operate on head injuries every day. I'm going to have to phone our fucking father though, he's squealing to everyone around him, playing the wronged husband."

"I fucking knew he would do that Dan. He's always the same, it's all her fault not his. Fuck, why couldn't Tony have been my dad and yours?"

"You okay with me calling him?"

"Yes, you're always a lot calmer than me anyway."

"Not this time Davie! I'm so angry I could cheerfully fucking murder him."

Kenny Black was obviously drunk when Dan called him. "Daniel!" he slurred. "I was wondering when I would hear from you; my firstborn, fruit of my loins. Or are you another of Carter's bastards? I always knew your sister reminded me of someone, and as soon as I heard the news I knew."

"You know what Dad, I wish Tony Carter was my father because he's more a man than you'll ever be! I'm fucking ashamed that I have any part of you. I know it all Dad everything you did to her and I've tried to understand, but I will never forgive you for what you have done today. My mother is in surgery, fighting for her life and not able to defend herself. You are talking shite to the press, how fucking low can you go Kenny."

"I'm your fucking father Daniel, just you see you show me some respect; she was fucking him when she was married to me. She is nothing but a whore, you show me some fucking respect, boy."

"Respect you, alky bastard you ruined my childhood you ruined Davie's and you treated Daimhim like a fucking pariah her entire life. I don't know why Mum stayed with you. I don't know why she put up with your abuse of her, but so help me Kenny, I'll go to the fucking press and tell everything there is to tell about you. You are a wife beater, a liar and a fucking parasite, a total fucking waste of skin. if you say one more word against my mother I'll fucking swing for you. I'll give them all the pictures of Mum with bruises my grandparents have and I'll hang you fucking out to dry. Grow a fucking set Kenny, stop blaming her for all your shortcomings, you would have been dead years ago, if it wasn't for my mum! She was with Tony because you were fucking bad to her, and I'd rather have him than you as my father. Now fuck off, and never contact either me or her again."

When Dan put his phone in his pocket, David was watching

him. "Fuck me Bro, have you had a personality transplant?"

"He told the press about Mum and Tony. He has obviously put two and two together and worked out Tony's, Veenies father. Fuck, I wish you could divorce your parent."

"Hopefully you'll have shut him up. Will Mum be alright?

Dan sighed and wiped away a tear, "I feel really bad Davie. She kept passing out when she was in accident and emergency. We were laughing at her, the doctor treating her, and me, we thought it was exhaustion. I'm so fucking scared."

David pulled himself up on the bed his broken legs were raised on a pulley at the foot of the bed. "Dan, Mum will be fine. Can you imagine her in front of her maker, arguing with him? She won't die, she can't die. Have you told Veenie?"

Dan shook his head, "I came in here to phone Kenny."

"Well, you'd better go speak to her bro, she needs to know. What about Tony? Is he with Mum?"

"Davie, Tony isn't with Mum, he's paralysed they have taken him to Stoke Mandeville. I sent Harry with Anjya, they'll stay at Dorneywood. Alex is here and he okayed it, I didn't want her going herself. Samira has also turned up here Davie, she's outside."

"How is she?"

"Like you would expect bro, holding it together but fuck, Ravi? I just don't understand how he could have done this? I'm probably running on adrenalin, it's going to hit, he was our oldest friend, as much my brother as you really."

David sighed, tears pricking at his eyes. "It was like a stranger Dan. We went up to him, Veenie and I. We tried to make him remember, but he just looked right through us, as though we weren't there. Then there was this flicker of recognition. I thought he was going to respond, instead he started saying all this stuff in a different language. He would have killed us, if Tony hadn't dived at us."

"What?" Dan gasped, he looked at his brother who was nodding at him.

"Tony, must have realised he was going to pull the wire and he ran at Veenie and me. Jumped on top of us. There was a bang and then the place came down around us." David reached for a tissue and blew his nose. "He saved both of us! That's probably why he has the spinal injury bro, he shielded us with his body."

The door was tapped and Alex came into the room pushing Daimhim in a chair, he smiled. "This young lady was pestering the staff to let her get up." Alex said, standing beside David's bed and looking around. "I hear we have a family of hero's here. You two trying to talk to a mentally ill crazed suicide bomber. Your mother, rescuing and calming countless people when she must have been worried sick about you lot. Then digging for the rescue squad as well as digging you out with her bare hands."

David looked up. "Tony too, he pushed Veenie and I out of the way and shielded us from the blast." "Really, he did, he was beside Mum he pushed her over then ran at us. He must have seen Ravi go to detonate the bomb. How could this have happened Alex with all the security around you, Mum and the others?"

Alex sat down on the chair at the side of the bed and looked around at Caoimhe's children. "Jed Livingstone died in the blast David, but to be honest and I can't believe I'm about to say this! He would be facing disciplinary action. He knew that Ravi was following Caoimhe, because MI5 told him. He'd known for a couple of weeks he was back in the country. They were more interested in getting to the centre of the cell he was involved with. They were hoping Ravi, would lead them to others. I think Jed was thinking of his promotion chances within MI5. He told no one until they realised they'd lost sight of him, put your mum in danger. However, whoever exploited Ravi, knew Ravi was being watched. That meant that the focus was off others, including me and Iain. So, Ravi, in theory was the decoy, so that they could get to others."

"Neither Ed nor I, were informed about Ravi being in the country and being under surveillance folks. Your mother certainly wasn't told about it. Headstrong as Caoimhe is, she would have never put you lot in danger if she had known. She would definitely not have gone into a station at rush hour. We all knew Ravi was ill and that it was likely that someone had exploited him. He was to be treated as a sick man and arrested on sight! Yet they let it get to this. There will be an enquiry, no one is going to come out of this in a favourable light. Ed is on his way back, he should be here in the morning. What a fucking year, we've had!"

"How many dead, Alex?" Daimhim whispered.

"Six in the station, including Ravi and Jed, really bad though, there's a two-year-old and his mother. The mother was deaf. She wouldn't have heard the warnings being shouted. It's bad enough, but certainly not as bad as it could have been. There are three people who have lost limbs and seven seriously injured. Then you three and Tony." Alex shook his head, "it was rush hour it could have been so much worse. Apparently, you lot talking him down, alerted people around you and that bought some time, for them to escape. You know about Iain and Lucy?"

David nodded, "I saw it on the news, that's awful, isn't it? We're so lucky to be here. They've targeted prominent people, this time. Rather than the public though, that's different."

"There are a few casualties in the other blasts, but on the whole, it was a miracle that so few were hurt." Alex shook his head, "it's still awful though, isn't it? People think by maiming and killing they can make us all live in fear. I think the objective of this attack was to show us they can do it!"

The door opened and a man dressed in blue scrubs entered the room. They all looked at him expectantly. "She's in recovery." He said smiling. "We'll keep her heavily sedated for a few days. It sounds as though if we don't, she'll be up and running the hospital for us."

"Can we see her?" Daimhim asked.

"For a few minutes, they should bring her up in about an hour." The doctor said shaking hands with Alex.

Daimhim looked at her brothers and smiled. "After that, I'm going to Dorneywood. I need to go see my dad and Sister."

"You know then?" Alex asked.

"Did she tell everyone, except me?" Daimhim snapped.

"No calm down young lady, you're so like her Daimhim. You just go in fighting. It wasn't like that, she told Ed and I, because, she was afraid that it might get out if someone else noticed the resemblance. She was working up to telling you Daimhim. You know, as gene pools go darling, you got some pretty amazing ones."

David smiled. "As opposed to us with Kenny's genes Cuckoo; I think you won a watch with Mum and Tony."

Alex looked from David to his brother, "oh I don't think there is much of Kenny Black in you two either. You are actually, more like your Granddad Bert. Speaking of which, are you going to pick him and your gran up at the airport? Or do you want me to send a car? Your aunt and uncle are there too, I got them into the City Airport as soon as the airspace conditions were lifted."

"Oh, I'll go." Dan said quickly, "You better phone Dorneywood, Davie and let them know it will be a full house. Mum has a lot of explaining to do and Christ knows how Bert and Morag will react, with their Catholic views on fidelity and such."

Daimhim looked thoughtful, "Well that's where the press does the hard stuff for us I suppose. With Kenny telling all and sundry about my parentage and Auntie Ciara already knowing. The shock will be over, by the time they get here. I mean they know the truth about Kenny probably more than we do. They were there when he was knocking her about. They also made her marry him, in the first place. So, we always have that card to pull out, if all else fails."

CHAPTER

TWENTY-SIX

"Mrs Black if you do not get some rest I'll knock you out again!" The doctor shook his head at Caoimhe. He turned to the room full of people. "Right all of you who are not patients, out, including you Prime Minister! Sorry Mr Wilson, you might be in charge of the country, but I'm in charge of this hospital. Those of you who are patients, get back into bed."

Caoimhe raised her heavily bandaged hands. She was finding it difficult to be looked after and was generally driving the nursing staff mad with her reluctance to be nursed. She was, despite the brave face she was putting on, desperately worried about Tony. She looked at the surgeon, a stern expression on her bruised face. "I might be stuck here and out of my face on painkillers Mr Jones, but there is still a country to be run. I need to speak to the Prime Minister and the DPM about matters of state, so if you could all leave."

The surgeon shook his head. "Right now Mrs Black, you're my patient and not a servant of the country, and you'll be discussing no matters of state."

David wheeled himself over and kissed his mother. "You're about to have the phone call to a certain Mr Carter you've been requesting."

The doctor shook his head. "They're having problems with the conference link, so you'll just have to content yourself. If you continue to make progress, we will discharge you tomorrow, along with David here. The nurses have been sent ahead to your country residence to prepare it for you. David, could I speak to you outside please about the arrangements?"

Ed bent and kissed Caoimhe's forehead. "I'll come back in this evening to see you. There are some things that we need to discuss."

Morag Magill hugged her daughter, tears in her eyes. "Darling we've been so worried about you," she whispered. "Dan thinks we should all come to the country with you, but your dad, Ciara, and I, are going to head back to Scotland now you're on the mend. Phil has, of course, gone to see Tony. I think we need to talk once you've recovered and made some plans." Morag kissed her daughter's cheek and wiped away a tear. "It's nothing that can't be sorted sweetheart." Morag smiled at Caoimhe, "Dan is taking us out to dinner tonight in London, some posh restaurant. So, we won't come back in if Edward is going to be here. I'll come see you tomorrow. You need to do as they tell you Caoimhe. Just for once in your life, let yourself be looked after." Morag turned to the others in the room. "She was always the same, even as a small child she had to fight. It didn't matter what the challenge was, Caoimhe did it her way. When she was born, Bert's Mother named her Caoimhe, it means magnificent. But also, gentle, beautiful and precious," she said proudly.

Caoimhe looked up at the people in the room. Alex and Ed were smirking and David and Dan, also trying not to laugh, had turned their backs. "Okay!" Alex laughed. "We'll give you beautiful and precious but gentle? She's like a bull in a china shop Mrs Magill. We have all been torn to shreds by her gentleness at some point."

"Well it's very hard to judge character with a day-old baby!" Bert Magill laughed. "But, we really should have known. She came early, screamed the place down. That red hair was the giveaway. Ciara had been such a quiet, sleepy baby and well, maybe

251

me old Ma thought Caoimhe would grow into the name?"

"What about Auntie Ciara? What does her name mean?" Dan asked.

Bert smiled and put his arm around his eldest daughter. "Dark haired beauty!" he said, smiling. "She was the first baby born to our family who was dark haired, she got Morag's colouring. Now can we go back to the house to get changed?" Bert kissed his younger daughter. "You, just for once Kee, please do as you're told."

They stepped outside into the corridor and Ed motioned for them to go into the private relatives room. Bert sat down as Dan pushed David's wheelchair into the room. "We need to tell her folks and very soon. She'll suss that there is something, we can't keep newspapers and television away from her much longer, and, there's Tony, what is he playing at?"

"He's refusing to speak to her, there's nothing wrong with the conference link. He apparently said he didn't want it. I think it's because of what my dad has done, David sighed.

Morag stamped her foot. She was a tall, delicate looking woman but like her younger daughter she could be forceful and determined. "When I think of all the beatings Kenneth gave her, how dare he do this to her now. Imagine telling everyone that my daughter was a loose woman. I don't agree with what she and Tony did, it was wrong, but if he hadn't been making her life a misery, maybe she wouldn't have found comfort with another man. I'm sorry boys, I know he's your father, but he is a nasty, vindictive bully."

David shrugged. "Don't worry Gran we've no illusions about what he is. I want to go and shake him. Mum doesn't deserve this."

Ed looked thoughtful. "To be honest I think your mum has a lot of support. There will be people who will believe what they want to believe. Haters gonna hate, and all that. My honest opinion is we release all the coverage of what she did that day. Admit MI5 and our own security head kept us in the dark and hope for the best. David, can you link with your team and do a sensitive piece with them. Carly is coming in to help you." He smiled, "We hear that you and her work well together!"

Dan nudged his brother, "for God sake Davie, just make sure you ask her out this time!"

Ed sighed and looked from David to Dan. "If you don't mind boys, I would rather be the one to tell her what Kenny has done?"

Dan shrugged. "Be my guest, but you do know that Mum quite often shoots the messenger, don't you?"

"Oh yes!" Alex said smiling. "We've been on the receiving end, many times."

"Well good luck with that!" Bert said. "Now come on and let's get out of here. We'll want to be on the other side of town when they speak to her. She's going to get out that bed soon you know?" He looked around the room, at the bemused faces. "You're a very brave man. No wonder they made you Prime Minister!" Bert said, shaking Ed's hand."

"Oh, I'm scared of her too; she does have a particular way of putting her view across." Ed smiled, "but there's a gentler side of her too, as you all know. She is a real enigma, isn't she?"

Bert nodded. "None of us ever got why she stayed with Kenny. I suppose Morag and I feel guilty. We made her marry him in the first place. She was 16 years old, just a child herself. I've wanted to kick his head in so many times over the last thirty years." Bert shook his head and his eyes filled with tears, which he quickly wiped away with the back of his hand.

"I remember that day so clearly when she came and told us she was pregnant. I knew she didn't want to marry him," Morag said sadly, "I saw it; she was looking at us, pleading with her eyes but saying nothing."

Bert sighed. "I said to that bastard ... "

"Bert, language!"

"Sorry dear!" He looked at the assembled group. "I said to that animal. 'If you don't want to marry her son, you can walk away and we'll look after her and the baby.' I thought she had tried to trap him. I don't know why I didn't see it, she wasn't scared of us. Caoimhe has never been scared of anyone. She just stood there and said nothing." He looked around him, and his voice broke.

"I was just thinking about what everyone would think. The first person we told was the priest, and he just said," Bert shook his head, *"get them married off as soon as she turns sixteen. She's not the first and won't be the last.* I've regretted that conversation so many times over the years."

Morag looked at the assembled group. "Then, I made her get married in a cream dress. You know, more humiliation! Show everyone you're not pure." Morag began to sob and Bert put his arm around his wife.

"It was the way it was hen. You did what anyone then, would have done."

Dan stepped forward. "Gran, Mum has never blamed you for it. In fact, I think she wanted to be like you and Gramps."

"Ciara got married a couple of years later. I remember we made a big thing about her being able to get married in white." Morag sighed. "Caoimhe never said a thing, she just accepted it. That's how it was in those days. She was a child and we sent her to live with that that Madra."

"Here we go!" David whispered to Alex. "She starts swearing in Gaelic!" She thinks it's not as bad to do that. Madra means very bad man."

We should have said, "Focal Leat."

"Fuck off!" David whispered.

"Teigh trasna ort Fein! Cnapan Asal!"

"Go fuck yourself. You cock of a donkey."

"David stop translating please, there is nothing wrong with my hearing. Your father, boys, Ragallach Mac Tuilidhe."

"Yes, Gran he is a worthless bastard and we all know it," Dan said quietly.

"Daniel, wash your mouth out with soap."

"Why does everyone have Gaelic names except you two? Did Kenny not let her?" Alex asked.

David smiled. "No, the spellings on our birth certificates are D-o-m-h-n-a-l-l for Dan and D-a-i-b-h-i-d-h for me. She deliberately chose names which are pronounced the same. Aunt

Ciara, did the same with her daughter, B-h-i-o-c-t-o-r-i-a, its pronounced Victoria. It's because so many people pronounce Mum's name wrong. There are many Gaelic names which do sound the same in English. Daimhim, we've worked out, is because of the Deerhunter which was Tony's first hotel, and where she was probably conceived. The name means little deer."

CHAPTER
TWENTY-SEVEN

"Tony, you can't be serious?" Phil looked at his friend. "You've been in love with her for over twenty years and now you're just going to walk away."

"Phil, I don't need to explain myself to anyone, but I need you to tell her I cannot be with her. I don't want to be with her. I can't walk away which is why I won't be with her."

"You're a fucking liar Tony, what is it? Because, unless you speak to me mate, and tell me why you're doing this to her, you can tell her yourself."

"I can't do that. I can't speak to her or see her because if I do, then I'll not be strong enough to do this. You knew that all those years ago, Phil. That's why you made sure I didn't see her or hear from her."

"But you're both fucking divorced now Tony! I don't get it?" Tony turned his face to the wall. "It's over Phil," he said quietly. "You need to tell her I can't see her anymore. Phil you're my mate and you love Caoimhe, it needs to be you."

"No, I'm not doing this Tony; you're going to need her in the months to come. For fuck sake! You are as fucking mental as her. You've been happier in the last six months than you've been in twenty years Tony and you're going to throw it all away. Do you blame her for this?"

"No, of course I don't, but I can't go on with it. You've seen the papers, haven't you? They believe Kenny's shite, and that can't be good for her. If she stays with me, she will most likely need to resign by the looks of it. I couldn't make her happy twenty years ago. I certainly won't be able to make her happy now."

"You're supposed to be calling her in an hour, Tony, she'll be waiting for the call."

"I can't, call me a coward, but I can't. If I speak to her, I'll want to be with her."

Phil shook his head. "I don't believe you Tony, there has to be more to this. Fuck sake, you and her, you are supposed to be together. It's not right, when you really need her you're going to push her away. What about Daimhim and Anjya?"

"I don't know, Daimhim is great, really lovely girl, I'm going to try to make her and Anjya go back to Scotland. They need to get back to university. I'll make them go, then make decisions. I need more surgery anyway. This is the best place to have the first lot of it, it's scheduled for tomorrow. Tony put out his hand, Phil took it and the two men embraced. Tony looked his lifelong friend in the eye and gripped his hand, "I'm going to a place in Arizona for further surgery and rehabilitation. But you are to tell no one where I am Phil. Not even Ciara, she'll tell Caoimhe."

"America! Fuck sake mate, you're going to run away from everyone who cares about you? Know what? You and Caoimhe, you're well fucking matched. You're so fucking blinkered and self-centred." Phil pulled his hand away from Tony and glared at him, "you look after your own selfish needs first and hard luck if someone else gets hurt."

"I need to do it alone Phil, it's the only way I can cope with the enormity of what changes I have to make. As you put it when I'm feeling sorry for myself I'm selfish anyway." He smiled for the first time. "There are worse places to feel sorry for myself. At least it'll be sunny and warm."

"No fucking way Tony, you're not going through this on your own, at least tell me the truth."

"I've told you, I face years of surgery and I want to do it my way. I don't want her looking at me and asking herself 'why am

257

I still with him?' The way she did with Kenny. I don't want her giving up her career, then hating me."

"What happened at the meeting with the doctors Tony? Anjya told me you were seeing them yesterday."

Tony shrugged. "Just the same thing mate; no prognosis. My spinal cord is damaged and they can't tell how long it will take to heal, but the damage is significant, and I won't walk properly again. They'll make sure I'm not in pain with the treatment in Arizona, and teach me how to live with my disability. Be the best I can be. I'm a fucking cripple Phil, and will be till I shuffle off this mortal earth."

"That's what this is about? You fucking fool! You don't want to be a burden to her? She'll work that out Tony. She won't abandon you mate, you'll not get rid of her that easy. This is Caoimhe Black we are talking about here. She won't accept any of that. Her own fucking father is scared of her."

"If I refuse to see her, there's nothing she can do about it. You all need to support her. I'm not going to speak to her today Phil, I can't do it. If I hear her voice I'll crumble, and I won't do that to her. I will not be a fucking burden to her Phil. Without me, she'll ride this storm with Kenny and fight. If she stays with me, she'll give in. Caoimhe needs to be angry to succeed in anything. I'm doing this for her Phil."

"No Tony, you're being a fucking wimp and feeling sorry for yourself. You know mate, I've told Caoimhe loads of times she treated you badly, way back all those years ago, before the accident. I told her that she was a selfish fucking cow for what she did. Then when I found out she was pregnant I called her every name under the sun. I didn't fucking speak to her for over two years because of what I thought she had done to you." Phil looked sadly at Tony, "I never told you about you and her when you came out of the coma because I thought you'd be better off without her. If I'm honest, I was also thinking about how I was going to explain it all to my wife. I knew then how much she meant to you, and I stopped you and her coming into contact loads of times. I felt like a real bastard, but I thought I was doing the right thing for you both. You are worse than her with what you are doing to her now! She fucking loves you; she tried to dig you out with her fucking bare hands Tony. She broke her fingers and faces months of surgery to sort out her hands; they're in shreds."

"Phil, I can't make her happy, please just leave it. Tell her I'm not the fucking man she thinks I am and then support her. If she gets angry she'll function. She can't be angry at Ravi. She won't be able to be like that, she needs to be angry at someone."

"Tony, what the fuck am I missing here? This is not you, she won't care you can't walk. She won't care, she loves you. Did you get a bump on the head Tony? Don't do this, you can't do this? You're leaving me to pick the fucking pieces up, again."

"Phil, I can't have her stay with me because of pity. She would too, and then I would look at her and know. I want you to go, I'm really tired mate and I don't want to fall out with you either." He pressed the buzzer and a nurse appeared in the door way. "Caroline, can you show Phil out and see that I'm not disturbed. No visitors!" He glanced at Phil. "No phone calls either. Phil, please look after her for me."

Phil shook his head and looked at his friend. "I never thought I would ever be sad and ashamed to be your mate, Tony."

The nurse showed Phil out of the room. Tony turned his face to the wall and began to sob quietly to himself. "Please God let me have the strength to do this."

Wearily, Phil made his way back to the hired car. He phoned Ciara and told her what Tony had said. "Ciara, go home and I'll get a flight tomorrow. I need to see Caoimhe and tell her."

"Phil, perhaps I should stay and be with her."

"Ciara, she won't want you there, you know what she's going to do. Let me speak to Dan please?"

***

Dan walked into the room; Caoimhe was sitting looking out of the window. "Dan I'm not in the mood to have a conversation.

I don't understand why he won't talk to me. I thought, at first, it was just because of the phone lines being bad."

"Mum, Uncle Phil is here, he's seen Tony."

Phil entered the room and asked Dan to leave. Caoimhe looked at him, her eyes filled with pain that had nothing to do with her physical health. "Caoimhe, I have spent the last few days with Tony, he doesn't want to see you sweetheart. He thinks it's best if you end your relationship now."

"Did he say why?" Her voice was calmer than she felt. Caoimhe was a proud person, too proud normally to admit she was dying inside. The last few days, however, had taught her she needed to stop hiding her feelings.

Phil nodded. "Caoimhe, it's because of his injuries he says he will not be a burden to you. He reckons he'll ruin your career if he remains with you. Mainly it's about the stuff Kenny has said. He thinks that he wasn't able to be enough for you twenty years ago and can't be now."

"I'm going to Stoke Mandeville!"

Phil shook his head. "He won't see you Caoimhe, he has made that clear. He's sent the girls away too; he reckons he has to do the next bit alone. "

Caoimhe began to cry. "Phil, for the first time in my life, I know what and who I want, and I can't have it. My career means nothing to me now without him. I'm going to resign anyway."

"Caoimhe don't do that, you are going to need something to keep yourself busy." Phil sat down on the bed, wrapped his arms around her and kissed the top of her red curls. "You're good at your job and this country needs you. You've been through a traumatic experience. This is not the time to make life changing decisions."

"Oh, it is so the right time Phil! I don't want to go on without him; I can't go on without him. Phil, I love him so much. I can't think of how I'm going to get through life without Tony."

Phil smiled through his own tears. "Of course you will darling, you did it for twenty years. At least people who love you can support you this time. I'll be there for you too Caoimhe. I let you down twenty years ago. I'll be there for you this time. I don't know why he has done this Caoimhe. I've stuck by all his decisions and helped him. I kept you two apart because I thought it was for the best. But this time I don't understand. I tried to get him to speak to you, so did Anjya and Daimhim, but he will not budge on this. I'm hoping it's just the shock of what happened and him having to get used to how he's been left. The place he is going to go to will help him to make the best of his situation and rehabilitate him. You're going to just have to sit tight, keep busy and get on with it. He's not going to see anyone. He doesn't want any of us to know where he is."

CHAPTER

TWENTY-EIGHT

The House of Commons was crowded as Ed Wilson stood up and addressed the house. The Speaker called for order. Ed, flanked by Alex, stood up. "It is with the deepest regret that we announce the resignation of Mrs Caoimhe Black as Chancellor of the Exchequer. Given recent events, she and her family feel she cannot carry on in office. We wish her a speedy recovery and every success in the future. There will be a statement from Mrs Black in due course." Ed left the House, followed by Alex, and they made their way wearily back to Number 10.

Alex sat down and took the glass from his boss. He looked at Ed. "We should have stopped her."

"How exactly were we supposed to do that Alex? Wild horses couldn't stop Caoimhe Black when she is in that mood. You heard her; she left us no option but to announce it."

"Couldn't we say she has a head injury and is temporary insane? It's only been eight weeks after all."

Ed smiled sadly. "She has always been fucking insane Alex, that's part of her appeal. I tried; she would not talk to me. I can't believe that we could have been wrong about Tony Carter!"

Alex shook his head. "I don't think we are wrong about him Ed. There is more to this than him just walking away from her, I'm sure of it. At least if we can talk her into staying an MP, she can be promoted later when she's in a better frame of mind. She's going to have to listen to someone Ed. You know I never really got

Caoimhe until I came to this job. She's something else, isn't she? She's resigning because she thinks she will do you damage if she stays; it's because of fucking Kenny's stuff."

Ed sighed and took a long drink from his glass and made a face at the bitterness of the whisky. "You and her are a good team Alex. I see the qualities in both of you that are needed to lead Britain and the Party. The galling thing is; I don't think that Kenny's revelations will do the damage she thinks."

Alex smiled. "It's no secret Ed, I'm ambitious. I wanted to step into your shoes. When you retired, not before," he quickly added. "Now I think that Caoimhe has all the skills and the integrity to be the next Prime Minister, she also has more balls than I'll ever have. Yes, she's headstrong, but she'll always do what's right for the country, even if it hurts her personally."

Ed looked thoughtful. "I actually have an idea Alex that might work, if you help me. Do you think you could make the switch to Chancellor?"

Alex smiled. "Yes, what are you going to do with my job?"

"Nothing as yet, I need some time. Andy Pierce retires this year and I'll make him temporary depute after he has given me his resignation."

"Why? He's a pillock."

"He won't stay on too long, that's why. He has a much younger wife and a villa in the South of France waiting."

***

"Mum, you really need to get out of your pyjamas and go out for a while. You've been in the house for nearly three weeks." David put a mug of coffee in front of Caoimhe as he spoke. He glanced at Samira, who stood up and picked up the remote control for the television.

"David, for God sake, please stop nagging. Leave me alone son! I don't want to go out; I can't go out. No Sami, don't switch the television on, I don't want to know what's going on in the world."

"Mum, it's out, the way Dad treated you! The press has done it themselves, found out about the beatings and the injuries." He looked sadly at her. "Tony gave them the story about Daimhim's conception and the relationship you had twenty years ago."

"He did that, but he won't talk to me. I don't understand why, I can't work out what I did. He's trying to restore my career, but I don't want a career now. For twenty years, I put everything and everyone before him, then when I try to put him first, he doesn't want me."

Samira looked at her and smiled sadly. "Kee, this wallowing in self-pity has to stop, David is right. You look fucking awful by the way. Now go and have a shower, get dressed, we can go out for lunch. If I can show my face in public, then you can too. You need to just do what you did twenty years ago, and get on with your life. At least he didn't leave you pregnant this time."

Caoimhe looked at her friend and, for the first time in weeks, she laughed. David shook his head. "Mum there's a public outcry; they want you back in office. There are all sorts of campaigns going on." He threw a newspaper at her, "look at what's happening. The British public are blaming Ed for you going! You're going to bring down the fucking government if you sit there in your own pish, letting this happen."

***

The phone rang loudly and Ed picked it up. Alex watched as the Prime Minister shook his head and smiled. "I thought that could happen; I kind of hoped for it if I'm honest. Good, good, have you prepared the statement I gave you David?" Ed tossed the TV remote control to Alex and motioned to him to switch it on. "Okay David, thanks for coming in, you're a star. I know David but you didn't need to. If this had gone wrong there would have still been a job for you in my press office."

"It worked then?" Alex asked, smiling.

Ed nodded, "I realised that she would always do the right thing. If she thought the government was compromised she might just come to the rescue." Ed took a sip of his drink, then he and Alex clinked their glasses together as they watched the BBC news make the announcement. Caoimhe Black reinstated in Cabinet, as Deputy Prime Minister, to be phased into post over the next three months. Meanwhile, Andy Pierce MP would hold the post along with Mrs Black.

CHAPTER

TWENTY-NINE

Caoimhe sat in her son and daughter-in-law's beautifully decorated living room. It was Christmas Eve, the space under the Christmas tree was laden with presents and those closest to her were around. The family had gathered in Scotland to celebrate, all of them thankful for the fact that they were still together. Caoimhe looked sadly at her hands, the only physical reminder of the tragedy she had lived through. Her doctors had advised her she would be scarred for life and there would be pain for a long time to come. She had 70% of the use of them back now. She wore special neoprene gloves to protect them most of the time, only taking them off to eat and bathe. Her other injuries had healed.

She smiled at Anjya, sitting with Harry on the sofa. That had been a shock, the calm, handsome but tough ex-marine bodyguard and Tony's daughter falling for each other. They'd become close in the days following the bombing when they'd been staying at Dorneywood. However, now, when she saw them together, Caoimhe realised they were perfect for each other. Harry was not much older than her sons. Caoimhe tended to forget this, as he had been with her since being invalided out of the marines. His promotion, to fill the post left open by Jed Livingstone's death, meant he was no longer Caoimhe's security but he had been replaced by the enigmatic Annie, which suited Caoimhe. The only person missing from the scene was Tony.

Daimhim looked at her mother. "I keep telling you, we honestly don't know where he is Mum. We both get emails from him, he just keeps telling Anjya and I that we have each other and that's all we need for now. Mum, you have to get on with your life."

Anjya nodded in agreement. "I don't know what's going on with him Caoimhe. He just blanks me every time I try. Daimhim and I thought about getting a private investigator, but what's the point? It's been six months now and still nothing."

"So, you're going back to work full time after Christmas then?" Caoimhe's father Bert asked.

Caoimhe nodded. "I might as well, I'm getting bored sitting around doing nothing most of the time." She smiled, "when I go into the office, I have to keep sorting out other folks' messes. In any case I felt I kind of owed it to Ed and Alex, they have been so good to me. It makes sense for me to be deputing I suppose. Ed is fit and healthy and with Caroline here and in remission, he doesn't have the same stress. I hated going into the post gradually. I can't believe the public thought they had ousted me because of my injuries." Caoimhe smiled. "Roll on the new year, new start. Anjya, what are your plans?

Anjya looked up at Harry, who tightened his arm around her and kissed her cheek. "I'm transferring to university in London. My grades were excellent, so it was not too much hassle to move. I told Dad and he's pleased for me and Harry."

"Did you speak to him?"

Anjya shook her head sadly. "No, the usual, by email. He did say he would call me and Daimhim tomorrow with it being Christmas."

"Is it alright if we bring Amy over for Christmas night Mum? She's really upset about her dad not being there," Daimhim sighed.

"At least he telephones her every week. She is a poor wee thing, but the calls help." Anjya's eyes filled with tears. "I can't believe what he has done to us all Caoimhe; this is so not like him."

Phil looked up from his drink. "He's in Arizona!"

"What!" Caoimhe said quickly, staring at her brother-in-law, then at her sister.

"You fucking knew where he was?" Ciara cried, "and you never said! What is it with you and him?" She glared at her husband. "You've been to see him! That's what all those American trips were for." She looked at her sister. "I thought he was having a fucking affair. He's been to see Toria four times since August, and then he goes AWOL for a few days." She slapped Phil hard on the side of his head. "I should have known it was your fucking bromance again."

"Ciara, I couldn't tell you, there were reasons, and before you start Daimhim, there was stuff he just couldn't tell his daughters."

Caoimhe stood up and looked sternly at her brother-in-law. "Phil, the dining room please? I think you'd better start explaining! Girls, please stay here just now. It sounds as though there are bits of this that your dad won't want you to know!" Phil stood up and led the way out of the living room into the small dining room which was set up for the next day's Christmas meal. Caoimhe slammed the door then looked at her brother-in-law. "How long have you known?"

"Since the start; I went over with him to get him settled. He is living in a rehab centre which specialises in spinal injuries. It's not good Caoimhe; he lost everything from the waist down." Phil looked sadly at her. "Someone had to be there for him, he wouldn't have seen you anyway Caoimhe. He knows if he does, then all his resolve will go out the window." Phil looked Caoimhe in the eye. "At first I bought his story of not wanting to be a burden to you and feeling that he would prevent you from resuming your career. Then two weeks ago, when I was over, he told me the truth. He's had a lot of surgery. As you know the spinal cord wasn't severed, but there was severe damage to it and this has got better, but six months ago there was no guarantee that it would. He has been having treatment for it."

"Will he walk again Phil?" Caoimhe asked quietly, looking directly into Phil's eyes. "Not that it matters to me."

Phil shrugged. "Hard to say, they think with more treatment he will be able to regain some movement. He doesn't always tell me what's going on, and he won't allow me to speak to his doctors."

"Why didn't he want me there Phil? Why did he think that I wouldn't want him? It's his legs that are damaged. We could have had a life, but he never even gave me the chance." She began to sob. Phil immediately put his arms around her and held her.

"Caoimhe, I think it's because he loves you and his daughters so much, that he went away."

"Phil, my heart is broken, I miss him so much. We wasted so much time messing around and not speaking. I'm only going back to work because I have nothing else to do. I would have given it all up and looked after him."

"I rather think that's what he was afraid of Caoimhe, you giving it all up to look after him." Phil smiled through tears and kissed the top of her red curls. "Caoimhe you and I both know that you need to be busy. Tony knows it would not have fulfilled you being a carer."

Tears ran down her cheeks and Phil handed her a tissue from a box on the sideboard. "How could he have thought I wouldn't do that willingly?"

Phil smiled, "because you were so driven, he thought he would hold you back Caoimhe. That you would never be happy if you didn't have your career."

"That's not it all, is it?"

Phil shook his head sadly. "No!"

"What is it then?"

"Caoimhe, because he has had no feeling below the waist he can't function as a man. He couldn't make love to you!"

"What?"

"Caoimhe, Tony told me what sex was like for you two, the connection, the electricity. He felt that because your relationship

269

had been so sexual, so mutually satisfying, he couldn't bear for you to stay with him through pity. He didn't want to be like Kenny, a parasite and a burden to you. He didn't tell me about the sexual thing until recently, he told me it was about your career. I should have guessed though."

"Phil thanks for telling me. I know that you and Tony keep each other's secrets and this must have been hard for you to do."

Phil shook his head. "Not really Caoimhe. You've got your career back on track, that's what he told me it was about. He wanted you to have your career; he thought it meant more to you than him."

"I can understand why he thought that Phil! I've always put some thing or other before him. First Kenny, then my degree, the kids, my career, my ego. Fuck I'm such a fucking selfish cow aren't I?"

Phil smiled and looked sheepish. "You're driven Caoimhe and that makes you passionate about things. Sometimes when that happens you forget about those around you, take them for granted. Other times, when people don't agree, you tend to just break them down until you get your own way. Caoimhe, Tony and I, well we're like brothers. I promised him I wouldn't tell you where he was. I've always been loyal to him, and he is to me, but in the past I have always done it blindly even when I thought it was wrong. I thought, for a long time, you and him were bad for each other, but neither of you can be happy apart. This time, I know he needs you and I think you need him. What are you going to do?"

Caoimhe looked at him and dabbed her eyes. "I'm going to go out there and apologise to my family."

"What for?"

"For leaving them at Christmas!"

"You can't be serious Caoimhe, it's Christmas. You'll end up spending it in transit."

Caoimhe picked up the telephone. "Oh, no I won't, I'm just about to abuse my power as a cabinet minister."

CHAPTER
THIRTY

Caoimhe gathered her belongings and smiled. The steward who had looked after her during the flight handed her the telephone. "It's the President again!" he whispered.

"Caoimhe, I just wanted to say good luck today, and Merry Christmas darling," Hank Butterfield drawled.

Caoimhe smiled. "Thank you for sharing your transport with me Hank. I would never have made it but for your help. Hope you don't get into too much trouble for allowing it. Merry Christmas Mr Butterfield, hope it's a good one."

Hank Butterfield laughed loudly. "Madam Deputy Prime Minister, it has been the honour of the American people to assist you in following the path of true love. But Caoimhe, if it doesn't work out and you need somewhere to stay, I live at 1600 Pennsylvania Avenue, Washington DC. You can't miss it; it's the big white building with the dome on top. Good luck pretty woman!"

***

The Christmas lunch was in full swing; Tony sat at the table staring at the food in front of him. He was emotional as he had spoken to his three daughters via Skype just before lunch. He had thought he could handle seeing them, but he couldn't, and had cut off the connection and cried. He realised how much he missed them. He wanted to ask Daimhim how Caoimhe was but he hadn't dared. He missed her so much and knew that if he spoke about her his resolve could waiver and that wasn't a good thing. Daimhim was also so like Caoimhe that the longing had been worse. He had to stay strong he told himself. He felt well physically and in one way was pleased with his progress. His recovery had been more than he could have hoped for six months ago, but he still felt like half a man. Wearily he wheeled himself away from the party along the corridor and back to his own room.

***

"Mrs Black!" a large man wearing a Santa suit and sweating profusely said, "I'm Albert Blackstock, Tony's surgeon. Please come into my office." He peeled off the beard and opened the suit jacket, underneath he wore a sweat stained t-shirt. He looked at Caoimhe. "I've had a personal call from the President about you. Apparently, you're a very important person Mrs Black, and we are to show you every hospitality. Just as well I'm a democrat isn't it, little lady?"

"How is he Dr Blackstock?" Caoimhe asked, looking at the man in front of her.

"Miserable, unhappy, quiet, emotional. Seeing his daughters on Skype earlier washed him out. He's a great man Mrs Black, a brave man and a very stubborn one. From what I hear, you and he are well matched in that area. Physically he is doing superbly; he has some feeling back and can stand up for periods of time. He is going to be moving soon to our facility in DC. He's had all the surgery we can do for the time being. It's all recovery and hard work now. Would you like a drink?"

Caoimhe nodded. "Vodka, soda and lime thanks."

"Ice?"

"Yes thanks." Caoimhe looked at the doctor and took the tumbler from him, the ice rattled against the glass as she took a drink. "What's his prognosis doctor? I need to know it all, the very worst of it and the best."

272

Albert Blackstock sighed. "That depends what you mean by prognosis? He'll never play professional football."

"He didn't before!"

"Exactly!"

"He will perhaps need crutches and rest. He'll need to walk with a stick probably, but I think over time he will function again."

"Fully?"

"You mean sexually?"

"Look Dr Blackstock, I actually don't care, but Tony will. He and I had a fulfilling sex life; there was a connection that never went away. It means more to him than me."

"He won't try Mrs Black." The big doctor smiled and cleared his throat.

"What?"

"We've asked him to try to masturbate but he won't. He's afraid."

"You're joking?"

The doctor shook his head. "No, he won't. Know what I think Mrs Black? Now that I have met you, I think I understand. He's afraid that he'll be able to function and he ended his relationship with you for no reason. You know that's why he refused to see you?"

Caoimhe nodded. "I'm really angry doctor ... that he could think I was so shallow. The fact he couldn't have sex wouldn't bother me. Our relationship was so much more than that. I love him," Caoimhe admitted. "Right now, I want to beat him to a pulp, but I'm sure that will pass."

The doctor smiled. "I shouldn't be telling you this Mrs Black. I could get struck off, but I like Tony. I think you're a very beautiful, desirable woman and I want to help you both. He says he can't get an erection, but I think it's psychological Mrs Black. He has a lot of his feeling back now after the last surgery. He's been standing in the frame for longer and longer periods and he can walk with help. He will, in my opinion, keep progressing which is why we're transferring him."

"Can I see him?"

Albert Blackstock sighed. "Technically we should ask him if he'll see you. Morally, we should ask him if he'll see you. Ethically, we should ask him if he'll see you."

Caoimhe raised her eyebrow. "If you ask him he'll refuse."

"What would you suggest them Mrs Black?" Albert asked, smiling slyly.

"I would suggest that you give me his room number and ask me to leave the premises." She grinned at the doctor and finished her drink. "Either that or you turn a blind eye when I break in during the night. So, it might be easier if you just show me to his room."

"All I can say Mrs Black is that would not be possible. I mean, if you went to room 106 accidently, Mr Carter would be extremely upset. If you were to look at the floor plan on the back of this door whilst I go to find security, then this would be disappointing."

Caoimhe made her way down the corridor. She approached room 106 and saw a young male nurse come out. The nurse smiled, pretending not to notice Caoimhe as she made her way into the room. Inside, Tony sat looking out the window, his kindle lying on his lap. He was in a wheelchair. Caoimhe watched him for a few seconds before he noticed her reflection in the window as she moved closer. He swung around and stared at her. "Are you real?" he asked, "or am I hallucinating?"

"Oh, I'm real Tony!"

"How did you find me?"

"Phil told me where you were."

"Why?"

"Because he thinks you are being a selfish prick Tony, and I agree with him. Look at you, sitting there feeling sorry for yourself, wallowing in self-pity."

"Caoimhe, I want you to leave!"

"Really? Well tough shit Tony, I'm staying here."

"I'll have you removed!" he said bitterly. "There's nothing

here for you Caoimhe, I can offer you nothing. I'm not a complete man."

"Oh, fuck off Tony and grow up. You ran away from me this time. If I leave this hospital tonight, then it will be me getting carried out, because I'm going nowhere without force. If you want me to leave, then you'll have to get them to carry me out."

"Caoimhe you would have no life with me! You would grow to hate me or worse, pity me, and I could not bear that."

"I don't pity you Tony, other than for being a fucking big girl's blouse." She moved towards him. "I love you Tony, I have loved you most of my adult life. You're not leaving me. I'll resign my post and I'll come to America, live here, until you're ready to come home."

Tony shook his head, tears running unchecked down his cheeks. "Don't you understand Caoimhe? I can't fucking make love to you," he sobbed, looking straight into her eyes.

"I don't care Tony, makes no difference to how I feel."

"Don't you hear me? I'm not a fucking man anymore! **I CANNOT FUCKING DO IT!**"

"I don't care Tony!" Caoimhe repeated, shaking her head, "I've a collection of vibrators for that, if I need it. There are other ways anyway for mutual stimulation. I'm actually really angry Tony. You didn't give me an opportunity to show you how little I care whether we ever have intercourse again." She grinned at him. "Besides I seem to remember you being pretty skilled with your hands and mouth too." She walked towards him and stood in front of him. "Tony, it doesn't matter. We'll find a way through this. I want to slap you hard actually, for what you have done to me and to your daughters. I get why you thought you couldn't be with me, but the girls, what difference would you being able to fuck have made to them?"

"I won't be a burden to my children Caoimhe, I can't be."

"You don't need to be Tony, you can have a life! Okay it might be a bit different to what we thought it would be, but it can be fulfilling and special, and you do have a lot to give. You can be a father, a husband … oh yes, you will marry me now … and probably, before too much longer, a grandfather … or … you can stay here and feel sorry for yourself for another six months."

She reached over and put her hands on his shoulders, moving in to kiss his lips. "Tony, please hold me. I need you so much; I need to be in your arms. I've spent the last six months just getting through one day at a time. Tony please? Don't send me away!" She began to sob. "Tony the sex was good, we will always have the memory if nothing else, but it doesn't matter, it was just a small part of who we are."

"I feel I've nothing to offer you Caoimhe," Tony sobbed, tears running down his face. "I've nothing to give you. If I touch you, I'll not be strong enough to send you away. I won't ruin your life too."

"You are really starting to get on my tits, Tony. Don't you hear what I'm telling you? If I don't have you in my life, I have no fucking life. I've realised what's important and it's you and our kids. I love Anjya and Amy; in the last six months I've spent time with them and they are part of my world. They need you, Anjya, Amy, and Daimhim needs to get to know you, not just by email. Tony, I'm going to stick around here and learn how to look after you. Can I sit on your knee without hurting you?" He nodded, gulping back tears. She sat down and wrapped her arms around his neck, then kissed him on the mouth.

He groaned and began to return her kisses. "I love you so much Caoimhe!" he breathed. "Every day has been agony without you!" He began to sob. "Caoimhe I'm so sorry, I thought I was doing the right thing for everyone. The doctors gave me the worst possible scenario, and I just thought I was going to be a burden on everyone I loved until I died. I didn't want to hope that there would be anything else for me, because I couldn't get into wishing. I mean our sex life was amazing, and suddenly I had this feeling I'd never be able to make love to you again. I still don't know if I'll be able to satisfy you!"

"Oh, you'll be able to satisfy me Tony, but even if you couldn't, it wouldn't matter. I'm quite hurt that you thought that sex was all we had. Tony, you are warm, loving, intelligent and funny! Yes, I'll miss intercourse if we can't do it, but I want you more than I want sex. Can I stay with you tonight Tony? Sleep with you?" Dr Blackstock said I could, if you agreed, just because it's Christmas apparently. I want to wake up beside you; I've missed you so much. I felt as though I had lost my arm or something."

He looked into her eyes. "How did you actually get here Caoimhe? It's Christmas Day yet you managed to travel."

"Well actually, I abused my power, and I could be sacked for it if I don't resign first."

"What have you done Caoimhe?"

"I telephoned Hank Butterfield and he lent me Airforce One for the morning."

"You asked the president of the United States for a loan of his plane?"

Caoimhe smiled and nodded. "It gets worse. I got a flight via the RAF to Washington last night. Hank was going to Nevada. I remembered him telling me that's where he was spending Christmas. So, I tagged along and then stayed on the flight; they refuelled in Arizona so I got off there."

"You're unbelievable. You could end up on the front page of the newspapers for that. Does Ed know?"

"Yes, he thought it was one of my better instant ideas. He said he is fed up with my moods and sad cow face. But, he did say that if I got caught then I would probably need to resign, so I did it anyway."

"Phoned the President?"

"No, resigned."

"What? Caoimhe you cannot be serious?"

"I have Tony! Ed says he won't accept it, but I'll do it if I have to."

"But being Prime Minister someday is your dream."

"No Tony, being with you is my dream now." They both jumped as the door was tapped loudly.

277

"Are you decent?"

Caoimhe moved away from Tony and sat down on the chair opposite him, as the door opened and Albert Blackstock and a male nurse entered the room. Well, Anthony? Do I have security throw her out in the street?" Albert said, grinning.

"No, she can stay," Tony replied, smiling at Caoimhe.

She laughed. "Just as well Tony, because I have nowhere else to go tonight! I never thought beyond getting here."

"Would you like to join us for dinner, Mrs Black?"

"Please call me Caoimhe. I'm hoping I won't be Mrs Black for much longer." She looked at Tony.

"No, Caoimhe, I'll only propose again when I can walk down the aisle with you."

"Whatever! You'd better get a move on then Tony, because I don't like waiting."

Albert smiled at them. "You are going to have your work cut out for you with her Tony. Now Caoimhe, let's go down to dinner. Some of the other residents have gone home for Christmas but Tony couldn't because it was too far."

The meal was light-hearted and relaxed. Caoimhe forgot about Tony's injury as they laughed and enjoyed the company of the other residents, Dr Blackstock and the nursing staff. Later Caoimhe watched as Billy, Tony's nurse, helped him in and out the shower and into bed. He smiled at Caoimhe and nudged Tony. "You're a lucky man Tony!" he whispered. "She sure is something else, isn't she? Mrs Black, we'll put a 'Do Not Disturb' notice on the door so you two can be alone. If you need us at all, which I doubt, just ring the buzzer." Billy walked over to the window and closed the blinds behind Caoimhe. He looked at Tony. "Good luck buddy!" he mouthed.

Tony smiled and nodded. "Goodnight Billy. Thanks."

Alone in the room with her man, Caoimhe suddenly felt nervous. She knew that she wanted to be with Tony but was afraid of how she felt about him. She stood up and began to undress. "Tony, I need to have a shower. I've been travelling since yesterday and I feel grubby and a bit stressed."

Tony pointed over at the ensuite door. "Be my guest!" he said, smiling. Caoimhe stood under the hot shower and wondered if she had done the right thing insisting she was allowed to stay with Tony. She was terrified she had put him under pressure, yet she needed to be close to him. She brushed her teeth and then, wrapping the large towel around herself, she went back out into the room. Tony put down his kindle and patted the bed. "Well, come on then! Let the dog see the rabbit."

Caoimhe dropped the towel and got into the bed beside him. "How come you have a double bed?"

"This is a rehabilitation unit, not a hospital Caoimhe. The idea is to make it as near to real living as possible. Some of the more badly disabled people need to be in hospital beds but they try to create normality." Tony wrapped his arms around her and pulled her closer. "You're so beautiful, Caoimhe!" he whispered in her ear. His mouth sought out hers and they kissed. He began to kiss down her neck and shoulders and his lips closed around her nipple. Caoimhe moaned softly and kissed the top of his head. Her body tingled and she felt him slide his hand between her legs and begin to rub her intimately.

Months of pent up sexual tension exploded her senses and she pushed her groin against his hand, moaning as her orgasm began. "Tony!" she gasped, "I love you." Her body shook as she climaxed, her back arched and she shuddered and held him. Tony wrapped his arms around her. Caoimhe looked up at him, her body still quivering from his touch.

"Caoimhe, I think I have an erection," he whispered.

Caoimhe reached down and put her hand on his penis. "Oh yes!" she said, looking him in the eye. She moved her fingers around his penis and felt him pull away from her.

"Caoimhe please don't!" he whispered. "I'm so scared I won't feel it." His eyes were pleading with her and she kissed his forehead.

"If that's what you want but wouldn't you rather know? Apparently, there are things that they can do to help."

He nodded. "Maybe, someday. Right now, I'm just glad that

I got you there. As long as I have this!" he said, holding up his hand, "and this!" he poked his tongue out between his lips, "I can make you quiver every bit as much as I could before. That's really important to me. I love you so much babe and I am glad you didn't give up on me. We have to work through a lot of stuff though Kee, you know that don't you?"

"We don't have to do it tonight though do we?" Caoimhe whispered, as Tony wrapped his arms around her. She felt herself drifting off to sleep, the sensation of his breath on her neck making her more contented than she had felt in months.

When she wakened in the morning he was watching her. She smiled up at him. "Good morning my love," she whispered. "I've slept better than I have since you have been gone."

"I've been thinking Caoimhe. I couldn't sleep!"

"That's not good for you Tony!"

"Caoimhe, I realise I was wrong to treat you the way I did. I want to be with you, but there is a condition."

"What condition?" Caoimhe asked, turning around and resting her head on his chest.

"Okay, my only condition is that you need to go back to work Caoimhe; I will not be a burden."

"No Tony, not negotiable, I don't want to work anymore." She smiled at him and kissed his mouth. "Takes up time I should be with you. You'll need to be in Scotland because of Amy, and I don't want to be in Westminster if you're up North. Besides you told me you're rich enough to keep me in the style I'm accustomed to."

"I'm not keeping you Caoimhe, you'll drive me fucking mad. Hell, you'll drive yourself mad. You need to work; I need you to work. I also need to go back to work Caoimhe. Once I'm finished in rehab I'll move to London, but you'll go back to work Caoimhe. I'll come to some arrangement with Angelina, probably give her more money as that usually works with her."

He looked at her hands, and then he took them in his own, to look closer. She pulled away and put them under the bed covers.

"Are they painful?"

"Sometimes, it's not as bad here as it was in Scotland; the cold made them hurt a bit. They're so ugly now, I used to have beautiful hands but look at them, all twisted and scarred."

"They're beautiful, like the rest of you darling. What about your other injuries?" He kissed her fingers one by one, looking into her eyes.

"They all healed. Well, my ankle gives me a bit of pain, but it's not too bad. The damage to my hands was the worst, and the blood clot I suppose. Everyone else was more worried than me. I was just out of it and not aware there was anything wrong."

"You had a head injury?"

"Didn't you know?"

"No! No one told me."

"I had a fractured skull and a blood clot. I had brain surgery Tony! I can't believe they didn't tell you. Maybe it was because you were so badly hurt yourself?"

"You could have died or had brain damage."

"My kids think I already had brain damage before anyway, so did you!"

"You could have died!" he repeated.

"Well I didn't Tony, we're supposed to live and be together. Marry me Tony?"

"Okay! When?"

"As soon as we can arrange it, let's just go to Vegas and do it. I'll phone Hank."

"No, you bloody won't. There will be no living with you if you get sacked."

"I'll phone him; he'll know how to do it quickly. We need to phone the children and tell them."

CHAPTER
THIRTY-ONE

The computer buzzed and Caoimhe's face appeared on the screen. It was New Year's Eve. Her children and Anjya gathered around the computer monitor in Dan's lounge. "What time is it? Where are the kids? I thought Amy was there?

"She is, but we've been out all day, and she's loving being with the other kids. She's a lovely wee thing isn't she? Great with our kids, they are loving her being here too. Its 10 p.m. Mum, they're all in bed. Why? What time is it there?" Dan asked.

"2 p.m. but it's a very special time. There is something we need to share in about an hour with you." Caoimhe turned the camera around to show Tony.

He waved. "Hi kids. Okay, here's the deal. We're about to do something really crazy and we want you to know," Tony said, smiling.

"What?" Dan asked, wincing. "With you two it could be sky-diving or parachuting."

"I'm about to marry your mother Dan. We just wanted you all to share it."

"Wow that's insane. Where are you?" Anjya gasped.

"We're in Vegas folks. We're booked to do it at 2.30 and we are going to do it on Skype so you can share it."

"Couldn't you have waited till we were there?" Daimhim asked.

"No, she wouldn't wait."

Caoimhe came back into view. "Sorry kids, we'll have a party when we get back, but this is just something we had to do. I need to marry him whilst we're talking cos you never know when we could fall out again. He's become awfully assertive and I need to re-train him, could be messy.

"Mum, Tony, we're really pleased for you and hope that you'll be happy," David said, smiling. "I'm even happier that you are coming back to work too. Do you want me to announce it?"

"What, that I'm coming back to work?"

"No. The marriage."

"Yes, I want the whole world to know. Although they probably will know because Hank Butterfield is my witness and his dad is Tony's best man. Well we don't know anyone else here."

"Mum, fuck sake! First you get him to give you a lift on Airforce One then you have him as your bridesmaid. You're so pushing Anglo-American relations to the limit!"

"David stop worrying about me and enjoy New Year, you'll give yourself an ulcer darling! Is that Carly I can see in the background?"

***

They came out of the chapel where the crowd of photographers gathered outside began to snap and shout to them. Tony had managed to stand throughout the service and now sat in his wheelchair holding Caoimhe's hand. Hank Butterfield smiled and waved. "It was a nice service!" he said to the assembled press. "Caoimhe is a beautiful bride, isn't she?" He nudged Tony, "you're a very lucky man Mr Carter."

Tony shook hands with Hank. "Thank you for doing this Hank, it means a lot to us."

"The pleasure's all mine Tony. I'm honoured to be the witness to your union. I hope you like my present to you. I've booked you into the honeymoon suite of the best hotel in town for a week, so you make sure that you see this pretty woman alright. Now let's

283

go eat, you'll need to keep your stamina up. I think the new Mrs Carter is one hell of a woman, but you've got your work cut out for you my friend.

***

"Tony look at this place!" Caoimhe squealed, as she looked around the honeymoon suite. "It's amazing."

Tony wheeled himself out on to the terrace. He looked at Caoimhe and smiled nervously. "It sure is. Come here."

"What?" She sat on his knee as he kissed her gently. "I can't believe we are finally married Tony."

"Mrs Carter."

"Hm, Mrs Caoimhe Carter, it has a nice ring to it." She looked down at her finger where the platinum wedding ring studded with diamonds sat. "It's beautiful Tony, I love it. Yours is so plain compared to it." She kissed him on the mouth. "Tony I've switched on the hot tub so we can just sit in it with a drink. Is that alright?"

Tony smiled. "Yes, that would be nice Mrs Carter; I think I'd like that. Can you help me in and out though?" First though, come through and see the bedroom? It's so cheesy and tacky, it's actually nice. Does that make sense?" Caoimhe followed her new husband into the bedroom. He wheeled his chair to the huge heart shaped rose petal covered bed and then stood up. Holding on to the chair he sat on the edge, and patted the space next to him. Caoimhe smiled and sat beside him. They lay down their heads on the pillows. Tony wrapped his arms around her and they began to kiss. Caoimhe sighed as his mouth moved to her nipple. She put her hand down to his penis which stood erect.

"Well Mr Carter, can I?

"Yeah but you might have to do the work."

Caoimhe put her finger to her lips. She loosened his shirt and trousers and helped him remove them. Then, standing up, she left him on the bed and walked through to the dining room table. She returned a few minutes later, stripped to her underwear, with

284

a chair and then helped him from the bed. He sat in the chair and smiled nervously up at her.

"It has to be this way Tony, I need to do it." She removed her robe and straddled him; he moved his head down and began to kiss her breasts. Caoimhe shivered and pulled his face up till it was level with hers. Her hands moved down and she put them around his penis. "Look at me Tony!" she ordered. She began to move her hand and she watched as he closed his eyes. She kissed his face, his neck and then wrapped her arms around him.

He groaned. "Caoimhe don't. I can't. I'm afraid."

"I'm not Tony. If it doesn't work this time it might the next time, but Dr Albert reckons that you can do this. Tony, can you feel it? It's hard. In fact it is really hard." Caoimhe pushed him back. "I'm going to make you do it to me Tony." She began to kiss him and after a few moments he responded and returned her kisses. She gingerly moved her hand down and sitting back a little she guided his penis inside her. "Oh God Tony, that feels so good, you inside me again, it's like we've come home."

She rocked and pushed down, kissing him. His hands moved and began to touch her breasts. He pulled her down and his mouth closed around her left nipple again, his other hand tightened around her back. Caoimhe felt her groin begin to tingle and as she moved towards climax she began to move faster. Suddenly Tony gasped and his body shook. "Caoimhe!" he cried. "I can feel it; I can feel something!" he shouted, the excitement in his voice unmistakable. "Fuck sake, Caoimhe, I'm coming, it's there, I can feel it. Oh my God babe! Argh! Caoimhe, I'm coming, I'm fucking coming. Do you hear me?"

"Tony the whole of Las Vegas can hear you," Caoimhe gasped, as her own climax began. She pushed down and then moved away slightly as he pushed towards her, his mouth now on hers as his hands pulled her closer to him. Caoimhe climaxed quickly, holding on to him.

He began to cry. He gasped as he reached the edge of his orgasm and passed over it. Afterwards she helped him back to the bed. She lay in his arms, both of them gasping for breath. "Fuck Caoimhe, I never thought that would happen again. I was so fucking scared!" he sobbed, holding her tightly. Her tears mingled with his as they clung to each other. She looked down at him and smiled through tear-filled eyes.

"Albert was right, it was psychological Tony," Caoimhe whispered. "I love you and the way you make me feel Tony, but it wouldn't have mattered to me." Tony closed his eyes as Caoimhe lay down beside him. She smiled, noticing how content he was, and kissed his forehead.

He moaned softly. "I'm sorry Caoimhe, I'm so fucking tired but so very, very happy. I love you my darling, I love you so much." In that instant, Caoimhe knew that their lives would be normal again and that they'd be together. This was how it was meant to be, she realised. "We can do this Tony!" she whispered.

"Hmm as long as you never do as you're told," Tony mumbled, smiling, his eyes tightly shut. "Now shut up and let me sleep.

Printed in Great Britain
by Amazon